When I turned twenty-one, he disappeared.
Just disappeared without a word.

Over a decade later,

and now he's back and more ruthless than ever.

BOOKS BY

C . M . STUNICH

ROMANCE NOVELS

HARD ROCK ROOTS SERIES

Real Ugly
Get Bent
Tough Luck
Bad Day
Born Wrong
Hard Rock Roots Box Set (1-5)
Dead Serious
Doll Face
Heart Broke
Get Hitched
Screw Up

TASTING NEVER SERIES

Tasting Never
Finding Never
Keeping Never
Tasting, Finding, Keeping
Never Can Tell
Never Let Go
Never Did Say
Never Could Stop

ROCK-HARD BEAUTIFUL

Groupie
Roadie
Moxie

THE BAD NANNY TRILOGY

Bad Nanny
Good Boyfriend
Great Husband

TRIPLE M SERIES

Losing Me, Finding You
Loving Me, Trusting You
Needing Me, Wanting You
Craving Me, Desiring You

A DUET

Paint Me Beautiful
Color Me Pretty

FIVE FORGOTTEN SOULS

Beautiful Survivors
Alluring Outcasts

MAFIA QUEEN

Lure
Lavish
Luxe

DEATH BY DAYBREAK MC

I Was Born Ruined
I Am Dressed in Sin

STAND-ALONES & BOX SETS

Baby Girl
All for 1
Blizzards and Bastards
Fuck Valentine's Day
Broken Pasts
Crushing Summer
Taboo Unchained
Taming Her Boss
Kicked
Football Dick
Stepbrother Inked
Alpha Wolves Motorcycle Club:The Complete Collection
Glacier

HERS TO KEEP TRILOGY

Biker Rockstar Billionaire CEO Alpha
Biker Rockstar Billionaire CEO Dom
Biker Rockstar Billionaire CEO Boss

BAD BOYS OF BURBERRY PREP

Filthy Rich Boys
Bad, Bad BlueBloods
The Envy of Idols
In the Arms of the Elite

BOOKS BY

C. M. STUNICH

FANTASY NOVELS

THE SEVEN MATES OF ZARA WOLF
Pack Ebon Red
Pack Violet Shadow
Pack Obsidian Gold
Pack Ivory Emerald
Pack Amber Ash
Pack Azure Frost
Pack Crimson Dusk

ACADEMY OF SPIRITS AND SHADOWS
Spirited
Haunted
Shadowed

TEN CATS PARANORMAL SOCIETY
Possessed

TRUST NO EVIL
See No Devils
Hear No Demons
Speak No Curses

THE SEVEN WICKED SERIES
Seven Wicked Creatures
Six Wicked Beasts
Five Wicked Monsters
Four Wicked Fiends

THE WICKED WIZARDS OF OZ
Very Bad Wizards

HOWLING HOLIDAYS
Werewolf Kisses

OTHER FANTASY NOVELS
Gray and Graves
Indigo & Iris
She Lies Twisted

Hell Inc.
DeadBorn
Chryer's Crest
Stiltz

SIRENS OF A SINFUL SEA TRILOGY
Under the Wild Waves

CO-WRITTEN
(With Tate James)

HIJINKS HAREM
Elements of Mischief
Elements of Ruin
Elements of Desire

THE WILD HUNT MOTORCYCLE CLUB
Dark Glitter
Cruel Glamour

FOXFIRE BURNING
The Nine
Tail Game

OTHER
And Today I Die

UNDERCOVER SINNERS
Altered By Fire
Altered By Lead

BECOM

Ag

ING US

air

this book is dedicated to Rhea French.

you believed in this story when nobody else did.

time to start planning our next trip to Paris.

AUTHOR'S
Note

Thank you for picking up Regina and Gilleon's love story. This book is one of my absolute favorites, and it's the one my best friend re-reads every few months; she likes to bring her tattered, wrinkled paperback copy on book signing trips which always makes me smile!

Becoming Us Again is a 124,000 word second chance romance with a hint of suspense. It's got a touch of Paris, a few secrets, and a lot of steam. It was originally published under my pen name Violet Blaze; nothing has changed from the original version. All the story needed was a fresh cover, a new title, and a second chance at life. Just like the characters in the book.

I hope you love it as much as I do.

Love, C.M. Stunich

BECOMING US
Again

C.M. STUNICH
USA TODAY BESTSELLING AUTHOR

CHAPTER
One

Diamonds.

They're supposed to be a girl's best friend, aren't they? So why, right now, do they look like the enemy, staring back at me from a tumbled heap inside the black duffel bag parked between my bare feet?

Sweat pours down the sides of my face, sticks my orange dress shirt to the skin on my lower back. I can't stop panting, my ragged breathing tearing from my chest as I wiggle my toes and try to convince myself that I did the right thing, that everything will work out in the end. If I believed that though, really and truly believed that, I don't think my heart would be pounding quite so hard.

"Ten minutes," Gill whispers hoarsely, his own breath even, his hands loose on the steering wheel. "Ten minutes and we'll be in the air." I sit up, forcing my stiff fingers to drop the edges of the bag and glance over at him. Something about my ex's expression, the set of his shoulders, the lack of sweat on his forehead, it bothers me.

Relaxed.

That's what he is. Relaxed. My life as I once knew it is *over,* everything changed in an instant, snatched up and twisted in the tornado that is Gill Marchal, and there he sits like he's on the way to the airport for a goddamned tropical vacation, some pleasure cruise that'll end in sand and surf and a ticket back home waiting for afterwards. This? This is nothing like that.

I have to say goodbye to Paris, for now, maybe forever.

Gone.

A split second decision made by a stuttering heart and it's all *gone.*

I sneer at him. It's a nasty expression, one that Gill's father used to call *mon visage laid,* my ugly face, but in this moment, it's beyond my control. Emotions are running too high, adrenaline is pumping too fast. Most days, I try to be pleasant. Today, it's not an option.

"Can you at least *look* like you give a crap?" I ask, but Gill isn't listening. His blue eyes are focused on the road ahead, his brow furrowed just so, just enough that I can tell he's buried deep in thought. Knowing him, he's probably going over the plan for the thousandth time in that thick skull of his, running through each possible scenario until he's picked it apart and prepared for virtually anything. It's one of the reasons I agreed to be a part of this, to take a chance on something that could easily end with me locked up in prison for life—or dead. It's also one of the reasons I fell in love with him—and then out of love with him.

Jesus, Regi, snap out of it! Reminiscing about the past never got me anywhere, not after Dad died, not after Mom died, not after Gill left ... Can't help it though. Memories are my coping mechanism, my way of slogging through the humdrum dull of everyday life. Anything a steaming espresso or a warm baguette can't cure, a good daydream can. But right now, when I'm running from a serious case of larceny, not a good time.

"Gill." I say his name slowly, calmly, firmly. *Look at me, damn it.* Thankfully he does, turning enough so that the soft light of morning limns his profile in gold. For the tiniest, briefest moment, he looks like a god.

"Don't worry, Regina," he tells me, his voice steady and smooth but still somehow rough, like those few years he spent on the street as a kid left a permanent mark on his soul. Or maybe it's everything that happened after. How the hell should I know? The man's a virtual stranger to me now. "I told you I'd get you through this, and I will. Relax, take a deep breath, and leave everything else to me."

I bite my lower lip and lean my head back against the black leather seat. I have some serious trust issues, most of which were caused by the asshole sitting next to me, so forgive me if I have trouble handing over the reigns, so to speak.

"Eight minutes," Gill says as I close my eyes and struggle to slow my breathing. "Eight more minutes." I open them back up and glance in the rearview mirror, looking for any sign of the police, any sign of flashing blue lights and the end of freedom as I know it. A dark chuckle cuts through the silence, drawing my attention back to Gill, to his strong jaw, the rough edge of stubble that grazes his chin. Even ten years apart couldn't dampen my desire for him. *Shit.* Well, at least I know there's no second chance for us, no way to rekindle the relationship we once had. This right here is a professional exchange and that is it. Period. End of sentence. "By this time tomorrow, you'll be lounging by the pool at the hotel."

"In *Seattle?*" I ask, raising an eyebrow. A scrap of blonde hair escapes my bun and I tuck it back. "In October? I find that highly doubtful."

"Maybe," Gill begins, his voice that edgy purr that always set my nerves on edge, "it'll be an indoor pool? And heated? Or maybe you'll be immersed in the warm, warm waters of a jacuzzi?" The way my ex says *warm* makes me question my own sanity. Shouldn't be legal to make a simple syllable sound so ... dirty. "Wherever you find yourself," he continues as the car slows and we make a left turn towards the airstrip, "I can promise you, it won't be behind bars. You have my word on it."

X X X

"I've never flown on a private plane before," I tell Gill after our flight, the two of us comfortably seated in a dull gray rental car, some sedan named after a horse or a deer

4

or ... a bull, maybe? Yeah, I think it's a Taurus or something. "And I don't ever want to repeat the experience."

Gill smiles at me, but he doesn't laugh. Once again, he's too absorbed in the execution of his brilliant beyond brilliant plan to pay me much attention. Honestly, it's all sort of starting to get to me: his sudden reappearance, his lack of emotion, his too tempting offer. *All I need is a key, a code, and a clue, Regi,* that's what Gill told me when he came waltzing into his father's apartment in the trendy Parisian *arrondissement* known as Le Marais.

The area reminds me in the best of ways of New York's SoHo neighborhood: trendy boutiques, haute cuisine, and lots of high-end vintage shopping. Also, like SoHo, it's way above my pay grade as a jewelry store sales associate. So, every morning before work, I'd diligently walk my ass over to my stepdad's place and enjoy the views of the courtyard and the bustling Rue Amelot.

That particular morning, Cliff and I were sitting at his kitchen table, cups of coffee clutched in our hands, reminiscing about the States, my mom, life in general. We were laughing so hard about our first few weeks in France all those years ago, about being whiny expats, about Cliff's still admittedly terrible French, that we didn't hear the front door open. Like an ethereal memory, Gilleon was suddenly just there, drifting across the polished wood floors like a ghost. Cliff's adopted daughter, Solène, shouted some horrible French curse words that even *I* didn't know and snatched my pepper spray out of my purse before I could remind her that the dark haired, blue-eyed bad ass standing in the doorway was her ... brother. Well, as much her brother as he was mine, really.

I felt all kinds of things in that moment—fear, hope, anger, the dying embers of a once requited love—but Gill? Shit. From the look on his face, from the dull, familial hug he shrugged over my shoulders, he didn't feel anything for me. I mean, not that I cared. I've long since moved on, to be honest with you. As Solène is proving to me, preteens might well be capable of holding onto some serious grudges and unrequited passions, but as an adult, I just can't do it. Takes too much energy, gives too much pain, and offers absolutely zilch when it comes to the future. Still ... I'll just be glad when this is all over, I have my payout, and Cliff, Solène and I are cozied up in some sweet Seattle digs. Gill'll leave again and things can go back to normal.

"I'm gonna call home," I say, not even bothering to think about the massive international phone charges I'll be racking up. From this point on, I am officially rich. Yup. That's right. *Loaded.* Regina Corbair is now capable of buying a house in Mount Baker, a vintage car like the one in *Supernatural*—holy crap, Sam and Dean are *hot*—and adopting some ugly mixed breed dog of questionable parentage. A friend of mine once picked up a short-legged, half-hairless beast more akin to a rat than an actual pooch from a Native American reservation in California. She paid eight dollars for the creature and loves it like the kids she doesn't have. Considering the amount of green that Gill promises I'll be swimming in, maybe I'll fly down to Cali—first class, of course—search out the sister I haven't seen in years and camp out at her place on the reservation until I find the right canine companion. Hell, I don't even have to work anymore, so why not?

I smile and search around inside my purse. The expression only lasts so long as it takes me to realize that my phone is missing.

"Gill."

"You didn't really think you'd get to keep the phone, did you?" he asks, again letting that low, deep rumble of a laugh seep into his words. This time, I'm ready; my shields are up and the sound doesn't so much as scrape across that barrier I erected so long ago.

"Guess I'll call them when I get to the hotel then," I say, sitting back with a sigh, letting the patter of Seattle rain soothe my nerves. As much as I fell in love with Paris, I missed the hell out of the Pac Northwest. I can't explain why but something about it says home to me. Must be the dreary weather, cheers me up somehow. It's like, how can I be upset when the sky's already weeping for me?

"Unfortunately, you'll have to wait until they land to see them. Right now, phone calls are too risky." I give Gill another show of my 'ugly face' and stifle the urge to say something mean. It's not his fault, really, just nerves. No matter what happens from this point on, I have to take responsibility for my own actions. Gill might've made the proposal, but I'm the one that went along with it.

"So ... how exactly does this all work?" I ask, wishing I was the kind of person that was okay with comfortable silence. To me, though, all silence is awkward, punishing. I have some sort of strange compulsion to fill it. "I mean, you deliver the diamonds to your client and poof, he hands over some cash?" Gill's full lips twitch, but he doesn't respond right away, probably mulling over what he can and can't say to me, what might break some rule of thievery that I'm not in the privilege of knowing. "Sorry," I say, before he tries to placate me with some bullshit that I'm not likely to believe. I hold up both hands, palms out. "I don't even want to know."

"I'll answer your question if you answer mine," Gill says, a bit of wry humor sneaking into his words. I stare down at my bare toes, at my purple painted nails, and I try to remember when, exactly, it was that I lost my high heels. The day's a complete blur, a twisted snarl of shock and adrenaline, a fuzzy, blurry memory that I know won't come into full focus until I'm completely relaxed and at ease. Stressful situations are like that, you know? In the heat of the moment, they're just smears across your consciousness, a series of actions you take from muscle memory and reflex. Afterwards, when you're lying in the dark and the full force of your decisions comes crashing down, that's when things get high def.

"What's your question?" I ask, my stomach tightening with anticipation. I have no clue why. I mean, I trust Gill as a business partner, as a master of his trade, but otherwise, he means nothing to me. So why is my body trying to act otherwise? "If you tell me, I'll give it some serious consideration and then perhaps I'll take you up on the offer." I turn and lift my chin, giving him my haughtiest facial expression; it only makes Gill laugh.

"Why didn't you tell me you had a boyfriend?"

Gill's question catches me completely off guard, and my cheeks go up in flames; my jaw clenches. *Shit.* Yes, Mathis caught me by surprise this morning, showing up at the jewelry store with brioche in one hand, coffee in the other. He practically ruined the entire gig with his romantic notions. Still ... the gesture was kind, and I'm already starting to wonder if I'm going to miss him.

"Didn't seem relevant to the situation," I say, knowing that's complete crap. I let my gaze fall on the window, on the water droplets clinging to the glass and then spinning away like leaves in a storm. Absently, I smooth my hands over my white pencil skirt, straightening out the wrinkles. As of now, this is the only outfit I have. For Gill's plan to go off without a hitch, I had to leave it all behind, everything I owned. Well, all except for my mother's things. I'd rather die than let go of those. I lean against the car door and let the comforting pressure of my purse dig into my side, just to make sure it's still there. "I'm sorry he tried to tackle you, but you did have a gun to my back."

"He's a handsome guy," Gill says, and I swear to God, it sounds like he's gritting his teeth.

"Gill, don't," I say, glancing over and finding his usual calm expression sitting pretty on that rugged face. *Son of a bitch.* "We're not friends anymore."

"We could be," he says, his voice even, no hint of

what he's really trying to say with those words.

"Oh?" I ask, more than a dollop of sarcasm creeping into my tone. "You planning to settle down in Seattle? Getting to know your sister, maybe?" My words have such a double meaning, one that I hope Gill doesn't notice, that I end up being the one clenching my teeth. Old anger rides over and through me, but I ignore it, letting it seep away into the sudden silence. Gill's lack of an answer is all I need to know that he's never going to change, never going to stop doing what he does best: stealing shit. He might call himself a thief, might be able to pull off jobs that nobody else can, but so what? In all reality, he's just a common criminal and that's it. Nothing —and I mean *nothing*—is more important than family. But Gilleon apparently thinks so, so screw him. "If you want to tell me how I almost screwed everything up and got you arrested, go ahead, I deserve it."

I slump back in my seat and run my hands over my face. Makeup smears across my skin as I drag my fingertips over my eyelids and down my cheeks, dropping my fists into my lap. I would've liked to tell Mathis goodbye, gauge his expression when I told him I was leaving and never coming back. This time though, it was my turn to run off and disappear without a word. Right now, shock's got a cold, white hold on my heart, and I can't seem to feel much of anything. I wonder if it'll hit me later, some sort of overwhelming grief. I mean, Mathis and I weren't head over heels in love or anything, but he made me smile. That's gotta count for something, doesn't it?

"I'm not angry with you, Regi," Gill says, taking a waterlogged exit out of the flow of traffic, our tires splashing mud and leaves against the guardrails on either side. "And I'm sorry I dragged you into this, truly I am, but—"

"But the payoff was colossal, I get it." I raise my hands up, copper bracelets jingling. The smell of my perfume drifts in the air between us, the scent of peonies suddenly cloying. I roll the window down a crack and let cool droplets of water splatter against my face. "Besides, my position at the store made it an easy gig and all that. Stop apologizing, Gill. It's not like you forced me into this, remember? I made my own choice."

I don't let myself wonder *why* I made the choice to begin with. All that matters now is that I've got a chance at a fresh start, an easy life, an opportunity to sit back and figure out exactly what it is that I want from this spinning hunk of dirt. I want to prove to myself that I'm more than stardust, some cataclysmic chain reaction that started with the Big Bang and ended up with little ol' me. I want to feel again, really feel something like I did when I was a teenager, before everyone significant in my life died or left and drew open this gaping hole in my heart.

I grind my teeth again and roll the window down a little further, closing my eyes against the spray of cool autumn rain.

"We're here," Gill says, not bothering to acknowledge my statements. Why should he? After today, we might see each other one, maybe two, more times. Me and him, we're just strangers now. "Reservation's under the name

Mia Logan, credit card's in your bag."

"I got it, Gill," I tell him as he pulls the car up in front of the lobby, "I know the plan."

I shut the door and step back, pausing to say something, anything to him before he leaves, but the window's being rolled up, and the gray Taurus is disappearing into the grainy gray of the storm.

CHAPTER

Two

By the time I hit the hotel room, exhaustion is already sinking its ugly claws into me, drawing me onto the bed without even bothering to climb under the covers. As soon as my head hits that pillow, I'm done for, lulled into a solid sleep that even my anxiety can't find a way to penetrate. Everything else fades away—Mathis, the heist, the day long plane ride, the hotel employees raising their eyebrows at my bare feet—even thoughts of Cliff and Solène whisper away and leave me with ... memories.

x x x

Sixteen is a rough age.

What a crock.

I roll my eyes and flip through the songs on my iPhone, looking for something cheery and upbeat.

Outside, the sky breaks into pieces and sheds the tears that won't fall from my eyes. I can't cry anymore; I refuse to.

"Dad is dead," I whisper, but the words don't drop me to my knees like they used to. Three years now and I can say that without having a panic attack. Still, what my mom's doing seems like a slap in the face—both to me and my sister. To Dad. "I hope that wherever you are," I say, brushing my fingers across a picture of Dad and me at the St. Patrick's Day Parade, "you can't see what she's doing. It's not right."

I start a playlist titled 'CHEER UP, BITCH' and shake out my shoulders. I can't believe my mom's trying to chalk up my attitude to my age. It's not the decade and a half that I've lived, or the many years I'm lacking on her, it's the fact that my dad is dead and gone and nobody can replace him.

Cancer.

I fucking hate cancer, especially the kind that sneaks up on you and bites you in the ass. Dad was healthy; nobody in our family ever died from cancer except my Great Aunt Blythe and she smoked. Dad just ... he ran a lot and he didn't wear shirts. Or sunscreen. The poison, it got into his skin, and now here I am, pushing aside my curtains and looking out the window, at the car that's pulling up outside.

My sister, Anika, already bailed to live with our grandma, left me here to face this crap alone. But that's because she's selfish, always has been, nothing like an older sister is supposed to be. Mom needs us, not in spite of the bad decision I think she's making but especially because of it.

The doors to the car open and I back away. I don't want to see Cliff, the man my mom's going to marry, even if I like him. And I especially don't want to see his seventeen year old son either.

I hold my arms out to either side and fall back on my bed, the music drilling its way into my skull as I mouth the words and wish I was somewhere else, anywhere else, but here.

After a dozen or so songs, I realize that nobody's going to come looking for me. Either ... they're trying to respect my privacy or ... they don't care. Truthfully, I'm not sure which one's worse right now.

Curling onto my side, I close my eyes and let sleep take me. When I open them, I'm face to face with a boy, a boy with dark hair and gently parted lips, a pair of earbuds stuck in his ears, and the prettiest blue eyes I've ever seen, like two icebergs ringed in sapphire. Ethereal.

I startle, shoving back from him and slam into my headboard, tearing out my earbuds with my left hand.

He, he just smiles at me, sits up slowly, lazily, like a cat waking from a nap.

"Hi, Regi," he says, extending a hand, "I'm Gill."

✗ ✗ ✗

I snap to, sitting up as suddenly as the teenage self in my dream, heart pounding in my chest like it did on that long ago day in my bedroom. This time though, everything's different. I'm thirty-one and single, stripped bare of that youthful crush I developed in an instant, lost in the too

15

blue of my lover's eyes.

"Oh, hell no," I murmur, shaking my hair out and combing my fingers through the honey gold strands. What started off as a perfect bun early this morning is now a rat's nest of epic proportions and here I sit with no hairbrush, no toothpaste, not even a clean pair of panties to call my own. "There's no way in freaking Hades that I'm going to start dreaming about Gilleon Marchal." I stand up and yank the orange sherbet colored blouse the rest of the way out of my skirt. I actually despise the color, but Cliff talked me into it and he was right—it brings out the gold in my eyes.

I glance up into the mirror, at the lacy white Ella Moss tank I layered under my blouse. I should've probably left it behind with all my other clothes, but I figured nobody would notice one extra missing shirt. I finger the crocheted hem and let myself remember my mom, the effortless modern bohemian look she could pull off like nobody else. This top reminds me of her, so it had to come. It just had to. Besides, it's perfect for wearing down to the bar to grab a drink—and I could *really* use a drink right about now.

I call down to the front desk and manage to wrangle up a pair of shoes—flip-flops, actually, cheap plastic ones meant for use in the indoor pool/spa area that Gill promised me. My feet twitch at just the *idea* of wearing of them, but my Louboutin stilettos are long gone and I'll have to wait for Gill's promised cash flow to come in before I can grab more.

"*Merci beaucoup*," I gush, clutching the shoes to my

16

chest and passing over the single and only US dollar that I have to the sour faced hipster hotel attendant. She's wearing a PBR pin on her uniform, right next to one with a unicorn on it. I suddenly feel a whole lot less guilty about giving her a shitty tip.

"Uh, sure, *de nada*," she says and shrugs before shoving the bill in her pocket. I cringe and hope to crap she doesn't really think I'm speaking Spanish.

"What the hell's wrong with kids these days?" I murmur as I lean against the doorjamb and shove the flip-flops on my battered feet. I stepped on broken glass yesterday morning, ran across cobblestone streets, all of it sans shoes. "I spoke French and German *and* Spanish when I was her age." True, I'm probably only a decade older than that brat, but I was motivated. I wanted to do things, see things, *be* something. And then Mom died ... and Gill left ...

My heart catches in my throat and I steer my mind back to the present.

Fresh start. Forcefully dug out of my rut. New life.

All I have to do is maintain a positive attitude, something that I'm remarkably good at.

"I am a wonderful and beautiful person who deserves to be happy," I say, using some seriously peppy self-talk to make myself feel better about what I did yesterday. Guess I'm not going to be able to pull the whole *Gill's a thief* routine when I'm trying really hard to make myself hate the memories of him. I'm a thief now, too. We both are. "I am a strong woman who can do anything she puts her mind to."

I check to make sure the keycard's in the front pocket of my skirt and let the hotel room door slam shut behind me. As I walk, I hold up a hand and start ticking off fingers. Five positive self-talk statements per day, that's what my mom always did and she was successful and happy, even after she lost my father and to a degree, my sister.

"I am going to be superfluously successful in life." I smile at the strange looks passersby are tossing my way. "I am not going to let the negative opinion's of others affect me." *Even if I'm wandering the halls of a Best Western talking to myself.* "I am not going to let Gilleon Marchal's beautiful blue eyes get to me."

"My what?"

I jump and my heart slams into my throat, choking me.

I stumble in my plastic flip-flops and barely manage to catch myself on the wall.

"Gill," I breathe, clutching a hand to my chest and turning to glare at my ex. That motherfucker is standing in a decorative alcove, leaning against the wall and blocking my view of the ugly hotel oil painting behind him. "You scared the crap out of me," I whisper, my heart still hammering away in my chest. I straighten up and toss my hair over my shoulder. So he heard me compliment his eyes? So what? It's no secret that I've always liked them. "Why the hell would you do that?" I ask as he chuckles and focuses that laser vision of his on me, giving me a head to toe once-over that draws goose bumps up on my arms. "Sneak up on me like that?"

Gill stands up straight and moves toward me, close,

too close for my liking, but I'm not about to back down. He's at least got on a normal outfit today—plain black tee, jeans, run of the mill brown boots. Yesterday, he was all geared up like he was getting ready to star in a big budget action flick. He looks a lot less intimidating this way.

I glance up into his face, brushing some stray strands of hair from my forehead. I'm tall—five foot eleven to be exact—but Gill is absolutely massive, and I'm not just talking about what's under his jeans.

"God, have you gotten *taller*?" I ask, taking a step back to examine his six foot four frame, the corded muscles in his arms, the lean but muscular body I've always admired. Gilleon has this quiet strength about him, this power that seems to come from somewhere deep down, some place that he's never let anyone else see—not even me. At least, that was the case when he left. By now, he could be married with kids for all I know. Of course, he does keep in touch with his dad and Cliff's never said anything to me but ... maybe my stepdad was just trying to spare my feelings?

I surreptitiously snag a look at his ring finger, but he catches me in the act and lifts his left hand.

"Not married," he says, wiggling his fingers and smirking at me. "Not that I'd be wearing a ring if I were —job hazard."

"Uh huh," I say, turning away and putting my hand on the railing of the stairs. The hotel has an elevator, of course, but after living in Paris for so many years, especially in an older area like Le Marais, elevators are either nonexistent or they're broken. Anyway, the idea of crowding onto an elevator with Gill is terrifying in its own right. "Aren't you supposed to be off doing ... whatever it is that you do?"

Gill jogs down the first few steps and then keeps pace with me, tucking his fingers in the front pockets of his jeans all casual like. What a front. I've seen the man move like a jungle cat, muscles sliding underneath his skin, as he broke a man's arm with his bare hands. Gill is anything but casual, calm, normal.

He's a monster.

I swallow hard and curl my fingers tighter around the railing, letting my palm slide along the polished wood.

"I wanted to make sure you were alright." His voice is smooth and low, pleasant enough to bring back memories of warm afternoons snuggled up together in his bed, spent from lovemaking, sweaty and content and happy.

I clench my jaw and force myself to sound as pleasant as he does. *Soon this'll all be over and I'll probably never see him again.* I hate that that thought does nothing to calm me down.

"Is there a reason I wouldn't be?" I ask and he shrugs, just like that. If something's gone wrong, is *going* wrong, he won't tell me about it. And since I'm not a master thief, a career criminal, all I can do is sit here and wait and hope that he comes through on his word. He's never broken a promise to me before—only my heart. And that, he left shattered in so many pieces that I'm only just now finishing up the repair. *I am a strong, powerful woman and I don't need Gill, don't need any man to make me happy.* Some more cheesy positive self-talk makes me feel better and I relax, taking a deep breath as we hit the first floor landing.

"Most people wouldn't be quite as comfortable in this situation as you seem to be," he murmurs, scanning the lobby with a practiced eye. I sweep past him, letting him do his thing, and saunter over to the hostess station for the hotel's restaurant, pretending I'm dressed in my best Parisian couture. *I can work these fucking flip-flops.*

"One, please," I say and the hostess grabs a menu.

"Two," Gill interjects, appearing out of nowhere behind my right shoulder. Immediately, the woman's eyes catch on his face, her throat working against the surge of hormones that must be rocketing through that petite little body of hers. Small blessing, he doesn't even glance her way. I'm no idiot; I'm sure in the ten plus years that Gill's been gone that he's slept with people, dated them, maybe even loved them. But I don't want to see it.

"You joining me for a drink?" I ask, tossing the words over my shoulder at Gill. His dark hair gleams under the dim orange and red pendant lights that line the restaurant, but his face betrays nothing.

"For old time's sake?" he asks, and the words cut straight through me. Old. That's what our love is—old and feeble and frail. No, no, it's even worse than that: our love is dead and there's nothing that can be done about it. Death is the end; death is final. Life's taught me that lesson more than once.

"As long as you give me an update about Cliff and

Solène, I suppose I can tolerate your presence for a little while." I slide into the booth and immediately kick off the flip-flops under the table. *"Dieu merci,"* I breathe. *Thank God.*

Gill scoots in the other side, his long legs bumping mine for a moment before he adjusts himself. That small touch is enough to heat my blood and force me to take a deep breath to calm down.

"They should be landing in ..." Gilleon checks his phone and his lips twitch in amusement. I wonder what it is that he's looking at and then forcefully remind myself that it's none of my damn business. "About an hour or so. My partner will pick them up at the airport and bring them here. I'll make sure they have your room number."

"Partner?" I ask, just before our waiter stops by and asks us for our drink orders. Gill gives me a feral grin and lets me sweat out the question while he pauses to order.

"Johnnie Walker, Double Black if you've got it." He leans his elbows on the table while the waiter glances over at me.

"Dirty martini, *s'il vous plaît,*" I say and get a sexy smile from the man. I smile back and tuck some hair behind my ear, watching as his gaze lingers on my lips as he walks away. When I glance back at Gill, he's still grinning at me.

"I can see your charm is as powerful as it ever was," he tells me and I shake my head, sliding one of the two water glasses our waiter dropped off over to me.

"You're one to talk," I tell him, letting the surrealism

of the moment wash over me. *I robbed a jewelry store yesterday, flew on a private plane to the States, and now I'm sitting here with my ex, a man I loved and lost, a man who's dangerous as hell and twice as sexy.* "Did you *see* the look our hostess was giving you? Like she wanted to chop you up and eat you for breakfast."

I take a sip of my water and lean back, draping my left arm along the back of the booth. Across from me, Gill sits all loose and languid, his blue eyes half-lidded and his mouth set in a bemused imitation of a smile. Even though I know it's all for show, even though I've been duped before, I almost fall for it, almost let myself relax around him.

Almost.

"So you were saying ... partner?" I ask, not bothering to hide my curiosity. What I do hide however is my jealously. I have a tremendous amount of pride and a serious wallop of dignity that I'd like to keep, thank you very much.

Gill takes his time, snagging a sip of his water and then mirroring my position by crossing his legs and throwing his tattooed right arm over the back of the booth. Nothing he does—*nothing*—is ever unintentional, but I can't figure out what it means, so I tuck the thought away.

"My business partner," he breathes, taking a big breath and then running his tongue across his full lower lip. I won't let my eyes follow the motion. "My ... partner in crime, so to speak. But that wasn't really your question, was it?"

"Says who?" I ask, realizing we're both asking a lot more questions than we're answering. Our drinks arrive, and I make sure to order another, letting my fingers linger on the back of our waiter's hand before I turn back to Gill and study his freshly shaved face. Yesterday's stubble is nowhere to be seen. I'm not sure which look I like better. Apparently, Gilleon Marchal looks good in everything.

"Why are you really here right now? It's not to check on me, so don't lie about that."

"I thought you were forever the optimist, *ma belle petite fleur?*"

I purse my lips. *My beautiful little flower.* Really? Did he just say that? I pretend not to notice.

"I'm an optimist who dabbles in realism. So." I take a breath and lift my martini to my lips. When the glass comes away clean, I frown. I miss my Ruby Woo lipstick already, that bright red smudge that somehow says *I'm here* to the whole world. "Answer my question and I'll forgive you for knocking my boyfriend out cold."

"He came at me first," Gill says, tossing back his Scotch. His demeanor's changed since yesterday, some of that careful intensity dialed back a bit. I study the gentle slope of his jaw, the rounded squareness of his chin, the perfect proportion of his shoulders, his chest. Most men with Gill's strength are like walking mountains of meat, upside down triangles made of fucking ham or something. Ech. But Gilleon ... he's got a leanness to him, a look that my dorky childhood friend, Leilani, used to call 'a ranger's body'. You know how in some video games, there's the big guy in the shiny armor? All wide ass

24

shoulders and overblown chest? See, that's the meaty kind of guy I'm talking about. Gill is like the ranger, the archer, the one in the green tunic with the bow. Strong, but not overdone.

Damn him for it.

"He came at you, but you still punched him in the face and dropped him like a sack of potatoes. He was only trying to protect me," I add, letting that guilt over Mathis bubble up in my belly. I won't let the words *what have I done* run through my mind, but really ... *what have I fucking done?!* I take another breath and give a coquettish wink to our waiter when he drops off my next martini.

I lock gazes with Gill, hook my caramel brown eyes on his feral blue ones. Once, when I was little, my grandmother's Siamese cat had a litter of kittens with a feral tom. One of them was jet black with the sharpest blue eyes I'd ever seen, a sleek predator draped in contrast. Gill's always reminded me of that cat with his eyes, his hair. I have no idea what nationalities are in Gilleon's background because Cliff can't—or maybe just won't—talk about his past, not about Gill's mother, or his own parents.

Gilleon's skin is as naturally pale as my own, but right now he's got this breath of color on his face, the gentlest caramel kiss on his skin that keeps him from being my same shade of alabaster. It takes the dark ink of his tattoos, all of those blacks and grays, and blends them, turning the hard, sculpted muscles of his right arm into an artist's canvas. Gill's already good-looking enough on his own, but add in the tattoos and he's just gone from handsome to tragic, like a broken god with those calloused hands and that rugged wildness. It seeps from his pores, giving him all the marks of a beautiful but deadly beast, one with claws and teeth and the most disarming of smiles.

His hooded eyes look me over and I know he knows I'm analyzing him, studying him; he's doing the same to me. I feel suddenly naked and my breath leaves me in a rush, stolen away in a split second memory of his hands on me, his teeth grazing my skin, his body sliding between my thighs.

I blink it all away in an instant.

"You might not believe me," Gill says, sliding his whisky glass towards the center of the table, "but it's good to see you, Regina." He slides out of the booth, turns to me and smiles. The expression on his face makes the fine hairs on the back of my neck stand up straight. Not sure if that's a good or a bad thing. "I had a rare moment of downtime, so I came here to check on you. I couldn't imagine a more worthy cause."

And then he winks at me, turns, and walks away.

I'm left behind with a whole host of memories and nobody to reminisce with.

CHAPTER
Three

I'm lying in bed the night before the heist, sweat pouring down my forehead and dripping onto the pillows beneath me. I've been over this a million times with Gill, know the plan like the back of my hand, but I can't stop running through every possible scenario.

Just like him.

I know that's what he's doing right now, holed up in some hotel or safe house or hell, maybe he's down in the catacombs beneath the city. I might not know where Gill is, but I know what he's doing. He's a professional, a perfectionist, and there's nothing in his life he's ever loved half as much as a good challenge.

Not even me.

I sit up in bed and swipe a hand across my forehead,

drawing moist fingers away to curl in the pale cream, peach and pink of my comforter. Knowing this is the last night I'll ever sleep in this bed, in my apartment with the blue and white tile and the rustic beams, the pain is sudden and intense, taking over me and curling my body into a tight ball. It's an effort to force myself to breathe.

I made this choice, made it by telling myself that I was stuck in a rut, that I needed to move on and let the ghosts of the past be just that, but deep down, I know it's all a lie.

I made my choice for a love lost, for Gill.

The look on his face when he sat down with Cliff and me, started to tell us why he was suddenly there in our kitchen, like a zombie risen from the dead, it told me all I needed to know.

Gill is in trouble.

He'll never admit it, never tell Cliff or especially me why, but I can see it, sense it, feel it.

This heist, it's more than just a job, more than about the money.

And he was going to do it with or without me, that much I know. So I had to help him, even if he betrayed me, left me, walked away without telling me why.

I know doing this job won't heal my wounds, won't bring him back to me (even if I'd want him back, which I don't), but I'm going to do it anyway.

"You're such an idiot, Regina," I moan, leaning back again, nesting my head in the feather pillows and listening to the soft buzz of the TV I left on in the living room.

After awhile, the mindless sound lulls me to sleep.

When I wake, it's to the sound of a gun being cocked.

I open my eyes slowly, carefully, knowing what I'm going to see but scared nonetheless, my heart pounding and my body quivering as I let my gaze rest on Gill and the impassive blankness of his facial expression.

"Get up," he says, his voice a monotone, his simple words laced with threat. For this whole scenario to work out the way he wants, the way that'll make my life easiest, we have to play our parts from start to finish.

"Gill," I whisper, hating how my voice shakes and my throat goes dry. The barrel of the gun is inches from my skull, a gleaming stretch of deadly black that could end my life with a single twitch of his finger. Even though this is all pretend, just an act, I don't doubt that his gun is loaded. "What are you doing here? Why do you have a gun?"

Something flashes in his eyes, a twist of dark shadow that covers the bright blue of his irises for a split second. Before I can even begin to decipher the expression, he's reaching down and yanking the covers back, letting the warm air of my apartment caress my bare legs.

I remember a time when he'd run his long, strong fingers up the inside of my leg, past the sensitive spot behind my knee, up my inner thigh. Now, whether for show or not, he doesn't even bother to glance down.

"Stand up, get dressed for work. I'm not back in town for a family reunion."

I swallow hard and do as he says, just as we planned, just as I knew I was going to do. When I drop my

29

nightgown to the floor, I steal a quick look at his face, but there's nothing for me to read in his expression.

I put on the white tank, the orange blouse, the pencil skirt with the pockets, and then I let Gill lead me out the front door, down the stairs and over to the jewelry store where I work.

And then we rob it.

X X X

I order dinner in the restaurant and eat alone—something that I'm unfortunately quite used to. I mean, it's not like I don't always have an open invitation to dine with Cliff and Solène, but sometimes that's even worse. I sit there with them and I think about my mom, wonder how she and Cliff might've been as a couple if they'd been married for the past fifteen years instead of the single one they had.

When the waiter stops by with a complimentary martini for me, I carry on a little harmless flirting with him until the restaurant closes and I leave feeling just a little bit better than before. A few drinks, a kind smile just for me. So much better than Gill and his unreadable expressions.

"Fucker." I toss back a quick drink of the water my friendly waiter friend sent me out with, something to clear my head he'd said. Of course, he also sent me out with an invitation to bring some chocolate cake up to my room for me. Another time, I might've said yes, but the idea that Gill could show up at any moment, virtually anywhere—no thanks. I'll wait to pick up gentleman callers until after this is all over and Gill has moved onto

30

another job, another city.

When I get back to the room, I check the time again. Shouldn't be too much longer before Cliff and Solène arrive. Even though it's barely been two days since I last saw them, the thought of seeing my stepfather and the little girl who's more than just a sister to me, well, it helps clear up the strange feeling of detachment that's creeping up my spine and taking hold of me.

In the span of an instant, my life's taken a drastic turn that I can't undo, will never be able to undo.

And I did it all for Gill.

I grit my teeth and shake out my hands.

No, no, no. I can't let that thought enter my head, not now, not ever again. I'm not normally a big fan of lying to oneself, but shit. This time, I'll make an exception.

"Going to buy a house in Mount Baker," I snap, slamming my water glass down on the dresser and hitting the bathroom to turn on the shower. Too bad the hotel doesn't have a boutique, some place I could use to grab a new outfit—or at the very least some new underwear. Then I could charge it all to the room, like I did with dinner. Oh well. At least there's one of those fluffy white hotel robes hanging on the back of the bathroom door. There's a card sticking out of the pocket, something about the price if I want to take it home. I toss it in the trash and lay the robe out across the counter before getting undressed and climbing into the hot water.

As soon as the droplets caress my skin, I'm hit with more memories, flooded with them. See, that's the issue of using them to get by. It's like an addiction, like having a drink when you're stressed or puffing on a cigarette, only memories can come and go as they please, feeding the need even when I try to fight it.

I close my eyes against the spray and hold my breath, drowning myself in the hot water. Doesn't help though, just plasters images of Gilleon's naked body across the backs of my eyelids. He's ... matured so much since he left, and in the best ways possible, too. Gill is the epitome of masculinity, but he doesn't have that churlish chauvinism in him that makes my teeth hurt, not even after all this time in what has to be a testosterone driven business. Then again, what do I really know about career criminals? That's right—squat.

I wash up with the hotel toiletries and climb out, wrapping my towel around my hair and slipping into the robe. By the time I open the door to the bedroom, Cliff and Solène are already waiting for me.

"Regina!" Solène shouts, throwing herself off the bed and into my arms. "*Dieu merci!*" She glances over her shoulder as I smile and ruffle her dark curls with my fingers. "*Cette femme,*" she growls in her best know-it-all preteen voice, drawing my attention to a woman standing in the corner by the window, "*est extrêmement grossière et inculte. Elle ne parle même pas anglais correctement—ne parlons même pas de son français.*"

This woman is extremely rude and uncultured. She doesn't even speak English correctly, let alone French.

"Listen up, Princess," the redhead says, shoving a cigarette between her full lips, "I have no fucking clue what you just said, and I don't give two shits about it.

I'm here for Gill's benefit, not yours."

I glance over at my stepdad, but he simply shrugs in response, his dark hair, once so like Gill's is thinning and gray, making him look much older than he is, especially in this light. I hope the stress of all this doesn't royally screw up his retirement. With a growing sense of horror, I clutch my sister to my chest and grit my teeth.

His partner in crime, huh? That son of a bitch.

The redhead standing across the room from me lights up, cracking the balcony door like that'll make all the difference in the smell. I guess a two hundred dollar cleaning fee isn't a big deal anymore. Besides, all this is going on Gill's tab anyway. Still …

"Essentially," Solène says before I get a chance to speak up, "I said that you're an idiot."

"Solène," I warn, trying to figure out why there's some curvy babe in ripped jeans and a loose black T-shirt standing in my hotel room. I know it sounds a little sexist, but I was kind of expecting Gill's partner to be a guy. Or hell, maybe it was just wishful thinking. Should've known.

"*Écoute, il faut appeler un chat un chat,*" Solène sniffs. *Listen, I'm just calling a spade, a spade.*

"Sorry," I say to the woman, squinching up my face a little, "she's only nine, but she thinks she's thirty, talks like it, too. I blame Cliff." I point at my stepdad and a smile slips across my face unbidden. Ever since Mom passed away, Cliff's been my support system, my parent, my confidante. I'm beyond glad to have him here. "Anyway, I'm Regi. And you?"

33

Badass Redhead Thief Chick clears her throat and moves forward, holding out a hand for me to shake. Her palms are as calloused as Gill's, her arms corded with muscle, but still feminine, like all of that strength and power in her body is cloaked with a soft layer of padding. Tough as nails, but all woman, all curves and perfect lips and gleaming red hair. I'm not self-conscious or anything —I'm a pretty good looking chick—but wow.

"Aveline," she says, nodding her chin at me as we shake hands. "Thanks for your help in all this," she begins and my throat tightens. I feel something more beyond her words, something more motivating than diamonds and greed. *I knew it; this isn't about the fucking jewelry at all, is it?* Rather than explain any further, Aveline waves her hand around dismissively and steps back. "Anyway, Gill's all booked up at the moment, but I'll be in the hotel tonight if you need anything. Think of me like a bodyguard on call or something." She smiles at me, but her face is tight, hiding that same secret that Gill's carrying around. I wish I could dig beneath the surface and find out what it is. "I've got the room next door." She hooks her thumb at the wall to her right. "Your Dad and sister are on the other side. If something happens, don't try to be PC about it. Scream bloody freaking murder."

"What kind of something?" I ask, getting a little chill that has nothing to do with the air conditioning that's inexplicably blasting cool air into the room. It's raining cats and dogs and it's like fifty four degrees outside. "Are we expecting company?" I glance over at Solène, hoping to hell that I didn't get my family into a hole we can't climb out of.

"No, no, not at all," Aveline says, taking another drag on her cigarette, "I just like to present what-if scenarios. Just ask Gill." She winks at me, but I'm not sure how to interpret the motion, watching as she moves to the door and grabs the handle. "Sleep tight."

Her red-lipped grin haunts me well into my dreams that night.

CHAPTER
Four

When I wake up the next morning, I find Gilleon asleep in a chair by the window. He's sitting up still, but his face is resting on his fist, his eyes closed tight against the world. The very fact that he got in here without my knowing is terrifying.

"Hey," I say, sitting up and making damn sure the robe is covering up my breasts.

Gill opens his eyes, but he doesn't startle, smiling at me in that infuriating way of his, like his expression means nothing and everything all at once.

"Why the hell are you in my room?"

"Needed a place to sleep for a few," he says, and I know without asking that he means *minutes* and not hours. I don't know how the man functions on so little sleep. Gill's wearing the same outfit he wore yesterday, but it doesn't look any worse for wear. I try to take that as a good sign, like maybe we're in the clear, no trouble on the horizon.

His gaze is sharp and penetrating, and it's too damn early for me to deal with that, so I drag my eyes away and focus on the skull tattoo that decorates his bicep, the raven standing atop it so realistic that I feel as if I could brush my fingers over its feathers. *Thieves of the animal world. They see something shiny, they pick it up. And if it's a challenge to get? Even better.* Gill told me that once, his words dancing in my skull like they're being said even now.

"We need to move hotels today," he tells me, and I nod. I don't ask why or demand an explanation—Gill won't tell me any of that unless he wants to. I don't really care either way, so long as we're not going to get arrested or murdered by some rival jewelry thieves or something.

I am going to have a beautiful day today, I tell myself, letting my eyes trail down my ex's arm, over the black and gray tattoos that wrap his muscles. Might as well start off with a good heaping of positive self-talk. Otherwise, I won't make it past breakfast with this man. *I am going to learn something new today, something useful. I'm going to do this because I'm a smart person and I make good choices.*

"You're still doing that?" Gill asks, and I narrow my eyes at him, adjusting my legs and rustling the white comforter on the bed. He looks so ridiculous stuck in this hotel room with its navy blue walls and tasteful but boring accent pieces. Gill is ... he's too big to be contained, too explosive, too unpredictable. He's a lion that can't be kept in a cage. *I want him to go away, want this to be over with.* Can't start a new life with cobwebs clinging to my face. That's what Gill is—cobwebs complete with spider. Complete with *poisonous* spider.

"Doing what?" I ask, shoving back the covers and standing up. I run my fingers through my hair and bump into a snarl. A second later, there's a comb landing on the mattress next to me. It's just a small, cheap plastic thing, but ... I look back at Gilleon.

"Picked it up at the front desk. Thought you might need it."

"Thanks?" I say. It's almost a question.

"You're still doing the self-talk thing?" he asks, turning the conversation back to its original course. "Has it worked well for you?"

"I don't know," I tell him, rising to my feet and moving into the bathroom. I flick on the lights and stare at myself in the mirror, at my eyes, the color of a good café au lait. Coffee. Oh *God,* coffee. I need a cup and I need it now. I glance over at Gill. "You tell me. Here I am." I lift my arms out to either side and the robe slips down my bare shoulder.

Gill's breath catches, but he composes himself so quickly that by the time I blink, it's like nothing at all has happened. He's sitting there staring at me with such a blank expression in those bright blue eyes of his that I wonder if I might've imagined his reaction in the first place. Huh. I fix my robe and turn back to the mirror to brush my hair.

"Do you think Aveline has any eyeliner that I could borrow?" I ask, tossing the question out there as casually as I can. Of course, nothing gets past Gill, but I might as well make a show of it. Without answering, he rises to his feet and moves around the bed, coming to stand a scant few inches from the bathroom door.

Trapped.

I try not to think of it like that, but I can't help it. I don't know how he feels, but to me, being around Gill is still surreal, like standing on a platform that isn't quite straight. The world tilts and shifts around me while I struggle to right myself, but every correction I make feels like an overcorrection. It's infuriating.

"I can ask her, if you want," he says, checking his watch. "We have a few minutes to spare if you want to do your makeup." I glance over at Gill and find him smiling at me again, always with that damn smiling. When he was a teenager, it was charming, a light to blot out some of the darkness that I always knew was crouching deep down inside of his soul. Now ... it's a little scary. "Oh," he says, like he's just remembered something. I know that's not true though—Gill can't remember anything because he never, ever forgets. "Aveline sent me a very bizarre series of texts this morning, something about how getting out of a clean shower into dirty panties was the worst feeling in the world. Here." My blood goes hot and the words I was going to say sear into my throat like burns as Gill digs into his front pocket and pulls out a pair of white lacy panties, complete with tags, tossing them at me without changing a single thing about his facial expression. "I figured you still wear the same size, so I hope they fit alright."

I catch the underwear in one hand, fingers curling around the scrap of white fabric.

I don't know how long Gill plans on sticking around, but I hope it isn't long.

I don't think I can survive it.

X X X

"There's a new guy in my biology class," Leilani says, biting her lower lip and practically bouncing up and down. "He's got hair like ... like the night sky, only without any stars."

"And cornflower blue eyes," I ooze, batting my lashes and then rolling my eyes. "I know. You'd have known it, too, if you ever checked your text messages." Leilani makes a face at me. She's always so busy with her video games that she forgets to charge her phone; it's pretty much eternally dead. "Remember how I told you that Cliff had a kid?"

"You're saying that's him?!" she asks before I can even finish the story. Her cheeks turn a spectacular shade of red when she blushes. "That guy's like ... like your brother now or something?"

"Our parents aren't married yet," I murmur, knowing it's only a matter of time. Well, two weeks to be exact. Two weeks until our family doubles in size, until I can't stop denying that the bedroom across the hallway is no longer my grandma's occasional guest room. "Anyway,

his mom's gone completely crazy, says Jesus is always yelling at her or something and that she can't hear anyone but him. It got to the point where she was forgetting to buy food and stuff." I tuck some hair behind my ear and try not to think about the boy who barged into my bedroom yesterday and laid on my bed like he owned the place.

I touch my fingers to my throat and feel my racing pulse.

"You okay?" Leilani asks, pausing in the middle of the busy hallway, her book bag slung over one shoulder, her dark hair swinging in her face. "You just got sweaty all of a sudden."

"I'm fine," I snarl, giving her my best ugly face. I don't know why, but I feel so protective of this new feeling, this strange emotion, that's brewing inside of me. "Sorry," I add because I know I'm being kind of a bitch to her.

Leilani raises her eyebrows, but doesn't say anything. Guess she knows me well enough not to.

"So his mom wasn't feeding him or something?" she asks, prompting me to pick up the conversation where I left off.

"Yeah," I say, pausing next to my locker, turning the dial to my combination and swinging the door open. "And she wouldn't let him go to school, said all his teachers were demons. When she found out he was sneaking out and going anyway, she beat him with a baseball bat." My stomach turns as I think of the bruises on Gill's arms. He wasn't shy about them, explained

41

them immediately when he caught me looking.

"She's my mom," he'd said, eyes downcast, fingers spread wide, two of them sporting little splints. "When she came at me, I was so surprised, I didn't know what to do. And I knew ... I know she's sick, so I just couldn't seem to fight back."

"Cliff didn't know about any of this?" Leilani asks as I stuff books inside my locker.

"Not until child protective services called him," a voice says from behind us. I jump, spinning around to find my new stepbrother in a black hoodie and jeans, a pair of black and white Converse on his feet.

"I ..." I try to figure out what to say, try to decide if I should apologize to him for telling his story behind his back. But he doesn't look mad. In fact, his blue eyes are sparkling and his mouth is twisted to the side in a smile. I find my eyes drawn to his mouth. I love his lips. I don't know why. Never before in my life have I even thought to look at someone's lips, let alone trace them with my eyes, imagine what they might feel like pressed against mine ...

I take a sudden step back and slam into the bank of lockers.

"I wanted to stay with my mom, even though I knew she was sick," Gill says, coming closer, pausing next to Leilani. I watch her watching him, sizing him up, checking him out, but he doesn't seem to be looking at anyone but me. "I wanted to take care of her, do anything I could to help her get better, so I told my dad exactly what I knew he'd want to hear." Gill wets his lips and takes a deep breath. I can't stop staring at the sheen *on his full lower lip. "But the neighbors called the police and they took her away." His breath catches like he's in pain and he turns his face away to stare at the floor. "Family is everything though, you know." His fists clench tight. "Everything." Another long pause. "I'm glad you're going to be a part of mine."*

When Gill swings his bright blue gaze up to mine, my heart skips a beat and I know then that I'm in trouble.

✕ ✕ ✕

I grab another quick look in the mirror before stepping into the hallway to find Aveline waiting for me in a dusty colored tank and some faded jeans. Her makeup is thick but flawless—sexy cat eye, bright lips, perfectly sculpted cheekbones. I managed to get Gill to snag a black eye pencil from her, scribbled across my lids like a preschooler's art project, and then mussed up the color with some lip balm. Just one of the many tricks I learned in Paris—effortlessly dewy eyes.

"Don't you look fab," she drawls, looking me over, sizing me up. I stare right back, enjoying her brazen, outgoing attitude. Gotta love Americans, right? "All chic and shit." She lifts up her hands, palms out, and then drops them against her thighs.

"Thanks," I venture, hoping that was a genuine comment and not a hidden slight. I have a feeling that if Aveline wanted to insult me, she'd say something outright. "Gill's not driving me to the next hotel?"

Aveline shrugs.

"He calls me *partner,* but in all reality, he's the boss. I just do what I'm told," she says with a tight smile.

43

Somehow, I find that very hard to believe. I watch as she slips her fingers into her front pockets and eyes the hotel room door where my stepfather and sister are staying. I wonder if Gill's in there with them? Wouldn't surprise me. Gilleon might've abandoned me, but he's always stayed in touch with his Dad. "What do you say we get out of here? I'll even treat you to a pumpkin spiced whatever-the-hell-it-is that I'm sure you probably drink."

"Actually, I don't think I've ever had a pumpkin spiced anything. I'll take an espresso though." Aveline raises her eyebrows at me and shrugs again. I don't know what she sees when she looks at me, but I can tell her initial impression isn't a good one. It makes sense, especially if she and Gill really are an item. I can only imagine what he's told her about me.

"Truck's parked out front," Aveline tells me as I follow behind her in my shitty flip-flops. I think I've already got a blister by the time I get to the parking lot, but oh well. If an espresso's really in my future, then I can grin and bear it. "Climb on in."

Aveline pauses in front of a champagne colored truck and unlocks the doors with a lump of keys and mangled keychains. I pause for a moment to take it all in—the mud splattered across the sides, the bumper stickers with offensive phrases like *Trucks are for Bitches, You Dick.*

Huh.

"So you live around here?" I ask, trying to put together the pieces of the puzzle. If I don't, nobody'll do it for me; Gill thinks all information—even the most menial of facts—is on a need to know basis. I'd expected

Aveline to be driving some generic rental like Gill, but this ... this is clearly nobody else's vehicle but hers. It just seems to suit her somehow.

"Yup. Moved to Washington from Nevada when I was seventeen." I grab the door handle and let myself into a virtual smorgasbord of old fast food bags, wrappers, a scattered assortment of dirty tools. Interesting. With Gill as obsessive compulsive as he is about everything, I find it hard to believe that he'd pick a partner—either romantically or otherwise—that's as out of control as Aveline seems to be. "I've been working with Gill for a few years now, helping coordinate things Stateside."

I buckle up and have to clench the sides of the seat as Aveline peels out of the parking space like a madwoman. As we zoom by the lobby, I catch a small glimpse of Gill out the window, standing with his hands clenched by his sides, his mouth tight. Without even really thinking about what I'm doing, I toss him a little wave and a kiss.

I have just enough time to catch the surprise on his face before we're out of the parking lot and on our way down the street.

CHAPTER
Five

"*Seriously,*" *I laugh, my feet dangling over the edge of the fountain, toes trailing the cool water and drawing the tiniest ripples. The moon catches on the copper and silver change at the bottom as I curl my fingers around the brick edge of the wall and glance over at Gill. "I haven't. I'm not even kidding.*"

"*I don't believe it, not even for a second.*" *I stare at him, at the white-blue halo of moonlight on his dark hair. I have to fight against the urge to bite my lip as butterflies take flight in my belly. I thought getting a stepbrother would suck, but ... I actually like Gill. A lot. Like, in a different way than I like anybody else I've ever met. "Don't worry. I'm sure you'll have a bunch of French guys banging down the door. Hell, I bet as soon as they see us move in, they'll be outside on the street trying to serenade you."*

I snort.

"You seem awfully calm about this whole moving fiasco that my mom's sprung on us. I mean, I have like, a year of French under my belt. How am I supposed to talk to anybody?"

Gill smiles and I can't seem to keep my eyes from following the movement of his mouth.

"You can talk to me."

I blush and turn away, fully aware that I just admitted to never having been kissed. I'd hoped ... well, hell, I don't know what I'd hoped. Is it weird to want your stepbrother to kiss you? I think about my friends at school, what they might say if they knew about the crush I have on Gilleon. Nobody but Leilani knows, and I'm not sure that I want to tell anyone else. I'm not ashamed or anything, but this feeling inside of me is so ... it's so ...

"I want to kiss you, Regi," Gill says, his voice a whisper in the wind.

My gaze snaps up to Gill's, to those eyes that mimic the beautiful blue-white of the moon above our heads.

Suddenly, I find it hard to breathe, find my hands trembling as I pull them into my lap and try to figure out what it is that I'm supposed to do. Down below, I feel a pulsing, a dark heat blossoming that makes all my feeble attempts at masturbation feel like matches paling in the warmth of a bonfire.

"Regina?" For once, Gill's wry humor is gone, leaving him sounding vulnerable and unsure and oh-so

seventeen. I open my mouth to speak, to tell him that the whole reason I brought him out here in the first place was so that we could be alone, so that maybe something like this might happen. But my mouth goes dry and my heart starts to thump so fast that I get a little dizzy. The world shifts and tilts around me and before I even know what I'm doing, I'm leaning in and smashing my lips against Gill's.

Our teeth bump together at first, and I think I taste the metallic hint of blood, but as soon as my mouth touches his, something breaks inside me, something special, something different.

His hands come up and encircle my waist as we lean in together and find a position that works, that lets us open to each other, tangle our tongues. Gill tastes like lemon sherbet, sharp and bright, snapping my senses to full attention. His scent invades me, a spicy sweetness that I can't place but suddenly feel like I could never live without.

When he pulls back, his breath sliding across my moist lips, a strange groan slips out of me and I jerk back, clamping my hand over my mouth.

His bemused smile turns my cheeks a brilliant red.

"Are you sure that was your first kiss?" Gill asks, his hands still on my waist. I can feel each and every one of his fingers through my baggy sweatshirt, like little brands searing themselves into my skin. "Because your tongue did things I didn't even know were possible."

I pull away from his grip and reach down, cupping a handful of water to throw at him.

"You ass," I say, splashing him and then throwing my legs out of the fountain and standing up. No way I'm letting him get me back. Gill just laughs at me. "You go to hell," I tell him and shriek when he lunges after me, chasing me across the courtyard and into the shadows of a tree. When I turn, my back hits the bark and then we're suddenly kissing again, grabbing at one another like we can't get enough, might never get enough.

✕ ✕ ✕

Being in Seattle, coffee is, of course, courtesy of Starbucks. Company, courtesy of the rashest, filthiest mouthed person I've ever met in my life. I decide then and there that whether she's fucking Gilleon or not, I'm kind of in love with the woman.

"So I told the motherfucker to grow some ovaries and stop being such a whiny, little bitch. Guess he liked me well enough, so he introduced me to this guy who introduced me to another guy who introduced me to Gill." Aveline shrugs and sips her coffee, pulling into the hotel parking lot and squeezing her Silverado into a compact space near the front door.

As I'm artfully trying to compose some sort of fishing question, some bait that'll bring the truth of her and Gill's relationship swimming to my lure, my ex appears outside the window, face tight and jaw clenched.

I open my door slowly, carefully. I don't think it's me he's mad at me, but it never hurts to be cautious.

"Coffee was not on the agenda," he tells Aveline, their gazes locking, a line of tension stretching between the two of them. I sit back, trying to figure out if I could climb from the truck and squeeze past Gill without touching him. I decide it's not worth the risk.

"You never said *not* to get coffee," she replies coolly, shrugging and climbing out before slamming the door behind her. I look at Gill and find him staring back at me.

"Take a walk with me?" he asks, and I feel my fingers unconsciously curl against the paper cup in my hand. It crunches in my grip and hot coffee oozes out the opening, burning my skin with fingers of liquid magma.

"*Merde!*" Out of reflex, I drop the cup and Gill catches it in midair, taking a step back and gritting his teeth against the slosh of hot coffee that hits his hand. "Oh God, Gill, *je suis désolée.*" *I'm sorry.* I clamp a hand over my mouth and watch as his grimace turns into a half-smile.

"I take it you're not interested in going for a walk with me?"

"In these flip-flops?" I ask, reaching down into Aveline's pile of fast food wrappers for a stack of unused napkins. I dry my hand off as best I can and pass the rest over to Gill. "And you're wondering why I freaked out?" I try to make a joke of it, keep the situation as light as I can. When I got into this, my assumption was that I'd be spending little to no time with Gilleon. Why he keeps pushing for an audience is beyond me.

"I'm glad you're still you," he says, handing back my coffee. Try as I might to keep our fingers from brushing, the inevitable happens and my fingertips graze his calloused palm. I watch as his entire body goes rock solid, the muscles in his arms standing out against the black and gray wash of his tattoos.

"And that means what?" I ask, pretending I don't notice Gill's reaction to me. What am I supposed to do with it anyway? Knowing he still ... feels something for me—whether it's just lust or nostalgia I'm not sure—won't do me any good, won't do either of us any good.

"I mean," Gill starts and then takes a step back, letting me climb out of the truck in my bare feet, flip-flops clutched in one hand and coffee in the other. He closes the passenger side door behind me. When I look around for Aveline, she's nowhere to be seen. "You're so ..." Gill's mouth twitches. "Grown-up. Sophisticated." He gestures at me, his blue eyes searching my face. "Fashionable." I raise a brow and glance down at my wrinkled blouse. "It's nice to know there's still some Regi there in all that Regina."

"Hah," I say, moving over to a strip of green that lines the parking lot. My toes sink into the moist grass and suddenly, I feel a whole hell of a lot better about everything. "You're saying it's nice to know I'm still the clumsy young adult you left behind?" The words are supposed to be a joke, but as soon as they slip into the air, I can feel a change happen between us. Gill turns away, his dark hair fingered by the electric breeze in the air; another storm is coming.

"Regina," he says, but I can't take the tone in his voice. I don't want an explanation. I don't want it because it doesn't matter, because it'll never change the raw truth of the situation: Gill left me. He abandoned me. He took my heart and ripped it in two. Truthfully, I don't *care* why he left. No reason is good enough, none.

"I'll walk barefoot. Tell me the plan," I say, hoping to hell that's why he asked me to walk with him in the first place. *I'm a tree with roots that stretch deep; no wind can topple me.* I'm going to need loads and loads of positive self-talk to get through the rest of this unscathed.

Gill closes his eyes for a moment and I turn away, giving him time to get his emotions in check. Luckily, he's a master at it, and it only takes a second.

"I wanted to talk to you about the short-term."

"Short-term?" I ask, looking up at the hotel. It's a local place this time, somewhere I've never heard of, but it looks nice. "You mean here?"

Gill takes a deep breath and walks along beside me, his boots squishing into the earth, leaving marks that my bare feet don't. He keeps his gaze straight ahead, but the muscles in his neck are tight, like it's an effort not to look over at me.

"I mean a safe house, some place you and Dad and Solène can stay while we wait for things to settle down. We talked about this before, remember?" I search my mind, but I come up with a dozen plus conversations about this and that and the other thing. Honestly, when Gilleon first showed back up, I was so stunned that I didn't know what to do. Our initial conversations are all blurred generalizations in my brain at this point.

"Uh, I guess?" I brush some hair back from my face, but the wind grabs it again and twists it into a mess of honey blonde strands. "Why can't we just stay at the hotel?"

"Because there are credit cards involved and no matter how good Aveline is at what she does, at some point, someone could find you here. I won't risk that." He snarls that last bit out, passion lacing his words and drawing goose bumps up on my arms. Interesting. I raise my face to the sky, to the gray clouds and the small shafts of sunshine that manage to sneak past them.

"Okay, so can I go out and buy a place or something?" I look over at Gill and try to smile. "You promised me big money, brother." His lips twitch, but he doesn't let the expression take over his mouth.

"I did, yes, but a house purchase is big, traceable, *especially* one that happens in cash." Gill runs his tongue across his lower lip. Uh oh. I'm not going to like what he's going to say. Great. "For a few weeks, maybe a few months, I need you to stay in a safe house."

"Gill," I start, trying to keep my calm, trying not to let the freak-out that I can feel looming beneath my skin come loose. "I left my apartment in Paris. I left my job. I left my boyfriend." *Breathe, Regi, breathe.* "Please tell me I'm not going to regret all of that." *I did it for you.* I don't want to think like that, can't think like that. I won't hold Gill responsible for my decisions, not even if he had an influence on them. And I won't start pitying myself either. I can, however, let myself get pissed at deviations in the plan. "I thought this was all set in stone, Gilleon."

"It was," he says, his voice low and dark. I have a feeling most people would shit a brick at the sound of it. But even if he's a stranger, I know him well enough to know that this is Gilleon going into defensive mode. "But some things have come up that I'd hoped wouldn't happen. It doesn't mean the plan isn't going as it should, only that we're on a slightly curvier path than before. The safe house I'd planned for you isn't good enough. I need you closer to me."

The fine hairs on my neck stand up straight and I suck in an involuntary breath.

"All of you—Dad, Solène." Gill stops and turns to me, his eyes so intense that I have to look away. Ouch. All of that ice in there, that pain, when does it stop? Why does he have to keep directing it at me? "You'll stay at my place until things blow over."

My heart stops.

"Your place?" I ask, imagining some small, featureless apartment that Gill probably uses once a year or less. He travels all over the world, that much at least I do know. When I'm having a good day and Cliff doesn't think it'll upset me, he'll toss a tidbit or two about Gill out there, just some general *he's in Germany right now, Bavaria actually* or something like that. I didn't even know that he had a place in Seattle.

"I know what you're thinking," he tells me, but I don't really think that he does. "But it won't be like that. You'll have your own room, bathroom, and it'll be nowhere near mine."

"And now why do you think that'd be a concern of mine?" I ask, even though I feel suddenly light on my feet, like the wind could blow me away at any moment. *Live* with Gill? I can barely stand to be in the same room as him. Tack onto that Cliff and Solène ... *What the hell have I gotten myself into?*

"Regina," Gill begins, reaching out a hand, sliding his fingers down the silk arm of my blouse. He's looking right at me, something hovering beneath the surface that he wants to say.

"I guess you won't be around much anyway?" I ask, stepping back, lifting my coffee to my lips just so that my hands have something to do besides shake. I thought watching him ignore me was hard; this is worse.

Overhead, the sky breaks and tiny droplets of rain begin to fall.

"I should get you back inside," Gill says, turning away towards the parking lot. Whatever thought was drifting behind his eyes, I hope it's gone now—and I really hope it doesn't come back.

x x x

Cliff reaches across the table in the restaurant—some trendy little bistro that sits adjacent to the lobby of the hotel—and squeezes my hand. From the corner of my eye, I can see Aveline watching us from her bar stool, an astute and patient bodyguard. I invited her to sit with us, but she said *no go, girl* and retreated into the background with nothing but a basket of fries and a soda. I guess alcohol's off the menu when you're on duty with Gill.

"How are you holding up?" Cliff asks as Solène peruses the menu with a deep set frown and several well-placed sighs.

"I'm fine," I say, waving my free hand dismissively. Cliff is like his son; he's way too perceptive for his own good.

"All of this nonsense about staying with Gill and you don't have a single thing to say about it?"

I purse my lips and stare Cliff down, right into those blue eyes of his. They're lighter than Gill's, less saturated, but I can see why my mom found him so handsome back in the day.

"It's been ten years, Cliff," I grind out, hating that he knows me so well—loving it, too. There's nobody in the world that understands me as well as my stepfather; he's the only person that's privy to all my secrets, to all the pain I felt when Gill left me with an engagement ring on my finger and ... so much hurt inside my heart. "After a decade, it doesn't seem to matter so much anymore, does it?"

"Bullshit," Cliff says, giving my hand one last squeeze and then letting go. Behind her menu, Solène snickers. "I'll be the first to admit, my son is an asshole. For all his skill in navigating the world, he still has a bit of trouble understanding the true human experience."

I roll my eyes.

"Thanks, Papa. I appreciate the concern, but I'm fine. I figured there'd be some snags in the plan." I sigh and flip open my own menu. "I might've expected issues of a different variety though," I mumble, my fingers tightening on the plastic. *And I might actually have preferred the feds or the CIA or whoever the hell takes on international jewelry thieves. Prison ... or living with Gill. I'm not sure which is worse.*

"Don't be silly," Solène says, tossing a big grin across

the table at me. Her dark hair is straight, not curled like usual, and she's wearing the same outfit as yesterday. For a moment I just sit there and stare at her, letting the full force of my decisions wash over me. I can't very well complain about any of this when I've dragged her into it. Solène didn't have any choice in the matter; I did. "I know Gill *looks* kind of scary, but he's nice. And strong. I feel safe when he's around, don't you?"

"Sure do, *mon petit chou,*" Cliff says with a warm chuckle. I smile, but it doesn't quite reach my eyes. Solène doesn't know about my past with Gill—our romantic past that is. As far as she's concerned, Gill's our distant 'brother' and that's that. At least he remembers to send Solène presents on her ... birthday.

"So whatever he did to you, you'll just have to forgive and forget," she tells me with the confidence of a nine year old and the wisdom of someone much, much older. *If only things were that simple ...* "Anyway, holding grudges is bad for the skin." Solène pats her pale, pink cheeks and gives me such a serious look that I can't help but laugh.

"I don't think I've ever heard that one before. Where'd you learn that?"

"*Vogue Paris,*" she states with a flourish of her hand. Nine years old and she's already into fashion magazines. I think Cliff and I might be in trouble.

"And who said you could read that?" my stepfather asks, giving Solène a look of mock seriousness. I feel my lips curling into a smile. Life might be uncertain right now, and Gill might be an asshole, but it's not all bad.

Even in darkness, there is light. *I am a happy person and I deserve that happiness.*

"Let's just say," Solène says, giving me a theatrical wink. "That somebody slipped it in under my bedroom door." I wink back at her and we both end up laughing. "Now, I'd dare say, all you need is a new pair of shoes and we can be on our way. Those flip-flops are absolutely not *en vogue.*"

CHAPTER

Six

"Thanks for taking me out," I tell Aveline as she opens the door to a shop in Belltown, Seattle's most densely populated neighborhood and home to some seriously chic shopping. It's no Paris, but then again, I just left the fashion capital of the world for ... rain, coffee, and hipsters. I smile anyway because hey, I happen to like rain, coffee, and hipsters. Well, okay, I happen to like rain and coffee at least. "I know it doesn't seem like much, but having something else to wear besides this," I gesture at myself, at my plastic flip-flops and the blister between my toes where the strap won't seem to stop rubbing, "will make me feel more like a person again."

Aveline shrugs as she lets me in behind her and watches as I close my eyes and take a deep breath of the lilac scented air in the shop. A few well-placed candles spread the sweet smell around the shop, letting it mix with the crisp bite of cotton and denim. *God, I really am going to miss my closet back home.* I wouldn't call myself a fashionista or anything, but I do like to keep up with trends. Besides, what girl doesn't like to dress up? It's like Barbies for grown ups.

"I'm not really into fashion," Aveline says, a navy hoodie tossed on over her tank top. I think she's got a gun hidden away in there somewhere, but I'm not about to ask. "I'm just psyched we snagged that parking space." She jerks her thumb out the window and then glances around at the tables of perfectly folded clothes. "Take your time, pick out whatever you want. It's all on your brother, so I don't care how much you spend. He said he didn't either."

I smile tightly, but I don't say anything, instead trying to distract myself with a rack of designer tops.

It doesn't work.

I glance back at Aveline, at her perfect makeup and her casual clothes, her sharp eyes taking in the entire store with a single sweep. She might have a messy truck, but she's a lot more similar to Gill than I ever was. I have a habit of looking at the world through rose-colored glasses. Why not try to see the best in everything, in everyone? The world is already cruel enough; I'd rather look for beauty than trouble.

"You gonna try all of that on?" Aveline asks, trailing me as I start to load up my arms with clothes. Everything I had, everything I was, it all got left in Paris. If I have to start over, I'm at least going to do it in style. If a nine year old can call me out on my fashion faux pas, then I know I'm in serious trouble.

"Of course," I say, handing my growing stack over to an employee when she asks if I'd like her to get a dressing room ready for me. "Don't you try on clothes before you buy them?"

"Sugar, I buy my shit from *Le Target,*" Aveline laughs, pronouncing the superstore's name as *Tar-jay* and shaking her ruby red hair out around her shoulders. "I don't have time to shop for stuff like this. Besides," Aveline begins, lifting up a Herve Leger dress in a metallic rose gold color, "can you imagine me trying to do my job in this? I mean, I know I'm more on the 'paperwork' end of things, but I like to be ready." She puts the dress back on the rack and watches as I run my fingers across sleeves, hems, straps. I want to dress her up so bad it hurts. Aveline has a perfect figure, sharp green eyes, and hair the color of cherries. Anything I'd pick out would look great on her. We're strangers though, so I don't feel comfortable asking.

"Paperwork?" I ask, deciding to steer the conversation in a different direction. "I didn't know your and Gill's job required much, um, paperwork." I pause to pick up a pair of designer jeans and Aveline gets in close, putting her red lips close to my ear.

"How do you think you're going to live a normal life without a passport? A driver's license? Maybe you might want a birth certificate. That's my thing." Aveline leans back as I look over at her and realize for the first time that I'm actually about four inches taller. Wow. Attitude really is everything, isn't it? If asked, I would've said Aveline was about ten feet tall.

"Do you use the originals to ... you know ... uh ..." I look around and I'm not sure what to say. I know how picky Gill is about procedure and all that. What am I free to talk about here? "Procure new ones?"

"Don't need the originals," Aveline says as I start to wander towards the shoe section in the back. "I have my own methods of getting shit done. You don't worry a thing about it though. Really, you've done enough."

"I didn't really do much of anything," I murmur, my eyes scanning row after row of designer heels and boots. *Nothing much except let Gill pretend to abduct me, force me to let him into the store, show him where the safe in the back was.*

"You have no idea how important you were to all this," Aveline says, her voice softening a little. She picks up a metallic fringed sandal and frowns. "Don't let that asshole brother of yours tell you otherwise."

"He's not really my brother, you know," I say, expecting her to respond with something like *oh, I know, but stepbrother's the same thing, isn't it?* Instead, Aveline lifts her face up to mine, her eyes wide and her sensual mouth parted just so. *How could Gill* not *be in love with this chick? Mon Dieu.* Aveline really is gorgeous.

"He's ... Cliff isn't your dad?" Aveline says as I blink back at her in confusion. "I heard you call him Papa—more than once."

"Yeah, well, my mother married Cliff when I was sixteen." I take a deep breath and feel that familiar pain yawning open inside my heart. "She died when I was seventeen, not long after we moved to France. Cliff took care of me, got me through it all. He ..." I can't tell the rest of the story, not now, not here, not to some woman I just met. "Gill's technically my stepbrother," I say and recognition flickers in Aveline's green eyes. "He didn't bother to tell you that?"

"He doesn't tell me shit about shit, not unless it pertains to the job." *Sounds like a typical Gilleon reaction to me.* "Who, exactly, you, Cliff and Solène were wasn't important, not really. It took a whole lot of pressing on my end to even get him to admit that you guys were family at all. The rest, I was just guessing." Aveline pauses as I pick up an open-toe bootie and ask the sales associate if they've got a women's ten in the back. I'm kind of done with the subject, but I can see Aveline's not ready to move on. "So is Solène your sister then? Or Gill's?"

"Cliff adopted her after my mother passed away," I say and then attempt to change the subject. "Do you like this?" I ask, turning to hand the bootie over to Aveline. "I think you'd look amazing in it. *Très chic.*"

"Not really my thing," she replies, her eyes narrowing slightly, cogs and wheels spinning in her gaze as she puts the information I've given her together. I'm absolutely dying to call up Leilani and have a mindless conversation about which episode of *Supernatural* is our favorite—it changes on every re-watch and during every new season.

Leilani won't twist my words back at me, read between the lines, try to analyze everything to within an inch of its life. But I can't call her, not yet, not until Gill says it's safe. Technically, I'm supposed to be dead.

I put the display shoe back and accept the box from the sales associate, sitting down and draping the clothes I'm carrying over the bench next to me.

"So ... what about you? You said you met Gill through a series of business associates, but is that all there is to it?" I put on my best conspiratorial girlfriend voice, the one I use with all my friends when I'm fishing for gossip. I didn't plan on asking Aveline about Gilleon outright, but fuck it. "Are you guys a couple?"

"Holy hell, no," Aveline says with a curling of her lip. "I'd sooner date a brick wall. Gill's hot, I get it. I mean, I've seen the man naked once or twice, but we've never gone there with it. Dating him would test the patience of a saint." I decide not to ask Aveline when and where and how she managed to see Gill naked because, honestly, that would imply that I cared. And I don't. I don't give two shits about it.

I slip my foot into the bootie and slide the zipper up to the top, sighing at the feel of soft suede against my skin. When I get the other one on my foot and stand up, a rush of calm settles over me. It sounds stupid, I know, to let shopping have this big of an effect on me, but it's not about the shoe really, or the act of purchasing it. I just ... when I'm dressed up like this, I feel as if I'm put-together, like I'm in control of myself. I think of my clothes as a uniform for life, a weapon. If I look good and feel good, then nobody can wield that insecurity against me.

"What do you think?" I ask Aveline, but she's not looking at me, instead opting to do another quick scan of the store behind me.

"Those look great on you," the sales associate says, some young chick with perfect highlights and a silver nose ring. "I could box them up and have them waiting at the counter for you when you're done with your shopping?"

"*Oui, ça marche,*" I say and then realize I've switched back to French again. "Yeah, that works. Thanks." I sit back down and start taking the shoes off.

"Wonder why Gill gave me shopping duty today," Aveline muses, crossing her arms over her ample chest. "He keeps looking at you like he's got something to say. You two have a big blowup or something?" *And here it comes, the subject that never seems to go away.*

"Or something," I say, spotting the panties and bras across the store and deciding that they're far more important than shoes—though I'm not done with those yet either.

"Must be a pretty big something, the way he fucking stares at you like that." I squeeze the bundle of clothes in my arms a little too tight and end up stabbing myself with a wooden hanger. *I am a beautiful person who deserves nice things. The past doesn't have any bearing on my future, not unless I want it to. I can and will succeed in life.*

"A silly misunderstanding is all," I reply, even though

that's about as far from the truth as I could possibly get. Misunderstanding? What Gill did was no misunderstanding—the letter he left made his intentions, and his actions, pretty goddamn clear.

I'm so nervous, I can barely even stand up straight, using the wall in the hallway to keep myself upright. Gill's right by my side, biting his lower lip and locking his fingers together behind his neck. He's nervous, too, even if he won't admit it out loud.

"Come on, Regi," he says, dropping his arms by his sides and reaching out to take my hand. I stare into his blue eyes as he pulls me to him, tucks me against his chest with a sigh. I try to resist, too nervous to stay still for long, but as soon as I feel Gill's body heat, smell his scent, I relax.

I can't help it; I'm in love.

"We can do this, ma belle petite fleur.*" I roll my eyes, but a smile takes over my face anyway. Gill's fluent in French since he used to live in Toulouse with his parents as a kid. He spends half his day coming up with stupid pet names for me; he knows that one's my favorite. "Nobody's going to care."*

"So you think," I say, knowing my mom has a tendency to overreact sometimes. I know it's just because she loves me, but I've got to admit, coming to her to confess my sins is a little daunting.

"We'll never know unless we try," Gill whispers, pressing a kiss to the top of my head. My heart flutters in my chest and I have to force myself to breathe. Being

with Gill ... it's like his presence is all I need to stay alive, like food and water and air don't mean a thing. Somehow, over the past few months, I've fallen completely head over heels for him, for his dry humor, his wry smiles, all of that passion and dedication that rests inside his heart.

Gill kisses my head again, and I stand up straight, looking him over in his black hoodie. I keep feeling stupid for noticing, but ... Gill's getting muscles from all that working out he does. He's starting to look less like a teen and more like a man.

I swallow hard.

How stupid of a thought is that?

I take a deep breath and tuck my hands inside the front pocket of my dress. It's a cute little blue and white striped number that makes Gill's eyes widen when he sees me wearing it. I like looking nice for him. Hell, I just like looking nice. It feels good, you know? I don't want to be one of those vain bitches at my school or anything, but I want to feel like I can stand up to them, too.

"Let's go," I say.

Gill and I make our way down the stairs, navigating our new Parisian apartment with ease. Ten weeks in and the transition isn't as bad as I thought it would be, not with Gill by my side. I feel like I could do anything with him, move anywhere. I could pack up right now and scrape together a living in the Australian Outback, on the top of Mount Everest, in the middle of a Louisiana bayou, complete with alligators or crocodiles or whatever it is that lives there.

All I need is him, his love.

My mom and Cliff are sitting at the dining table in the massive open room that makes up our main living area. There are no walls here, just perfectly placed furniture and accessories to designate the spaces. Mom's pretty damn stylish.

"Hey there," she says, closing the top on her computer and smiling a big, bright wide smile at me and Gill. "I was just about to come looking for you two. Cliff and I thought you guys might be interested in going out to eat?" She raises her blonde brows at me and gestures for us to take a seat at the table. My stepdad's squinting at the screen on his phone, no doubt trolling the internet for the next best place to eat. Both my mom and Gill's dad are crazy obsessed foodies.

"Actually," I say, my voice warbling as I struggle to pull together the words that are so desperate to escape my chest, "Gill and I wanted to talk to you about something."

"Oh?" Mom asks, leaning back in her chair, her gold Valentino sandals glinting in the bright pendant lights that hang from the vaulted ceilings soaring above us. She fingers the necklace around her throat, the one Dad gave her the year I was born. A diamond pendant hangs off the end of the silver chain, winking at me. "What about?"

I look over at Gill and find him staring right at me, his face stripped bare and full of emotion. His long, dark lashes rest against his cheek as he closes his eyes for a moment and takes a deep breath. When he opens them back up, there's a spark in there that I know exists just for me. *This thing between us ... I know it's more than hopeless teenage affection. I can feel it.*

"Elena, Dad," Gill begins, but I cut him off, desperate to be a part of this. *I can't and won't leave Gilleon to fight for us alone.*

"Mom, Gill and I are in love."

The words break in the open air like fireworks and even though I should still be scared, worried about my mom's reaction, I feel a sudden rush of relief.

She blinks at us for a moment and then, like the sound of ringing church bells, a laugh escapes her slender throat.

"Oh, Regi," she says, and I clench my fists at my sides, thinking she's going to patronize me, belittle my feelings. "It took Cliff and me about two weeks to see you two were crushing on each other."

I blink back at her in surprise, the room and its tastefully exposed brick walls, white couches, perfectly placed bunches of flowers, all of it spinning around me. Gill reaches down and takes my hand, curling his long fingers around my own.

"You're not ... mad?" I ask, looking over at Cliff and his gentle smile, the dark goatee around his mouth that my mom finds so attractive. "But he's my stepbrother. That's weird, isn't it?"

"Hey," Gill murmurs, looking at me with a crooked smile taking over his lips, "don't argue a battle we already seem to have won."

"I suppose it's not entirely conventional, but you

won't find me fighting for convention even under the best of circumstances." My mom rises to her feet, reaching out and inviting me into a rose scented hug, her perfume blooming around me as she pulls me against her. *"I don't care who you date so long as they treat you right."* She gives Gill a look over my head. *"And I know Gilleon's a good man, aren't you Gilleon?"*

"I'd hope so," Cliff says from behind us. *"Considering the genetic blessing my genes gave him at birth."*

"You're hilarious, Dad," Gill says, rolling his eyes as I look back at him. Holy crap. *Is this all really going to work out so easily? I mean, isn't life supposed to suck? What's that phrase? Life's a bitch and then you die?*

"You two can date provided, of course, that the normal rules are followed. No sleeping in each other's rooms, no locking the door when you're in a room alone, and no sneaking out of the house. If you need something, please ask. I try to be reasonable."

I wipe a sudden rush of tears from my face. I have no idea where they're coming from, but there they are anyway.

"I thought you were going to freak," I laugh and my mom joins in as I pull away and reach down to take Gill's hand again. His skin is warm against mine, the feeling traveling straight through my veins to my heart. I feel like it's trying to beat in time with his.

My mom tucks some honey blonde hair behind an ear and smiles at me again.

"Freak-outs should be saved for drugs, crime, and

violence. *As long as you're safe and happy, that's all that matters to me."*

"*I love you, Mom,"* I say, the words falling out before I can stop them. I blush and look away as Gill grins at me. *"When you're being cool, I mean. Only then."*

"*Of course,"* she says, reaching out to pinch my cheek as I bat her away, *"only when I'm being cool."*

Six months later and she was dead.

X X X

I step out of the dressing room in some designer denim, the fabric kissing my skin like a pair of old lovers reunited. I run my fingers down my thighs and try to push the analogy away. A second chance romance is the *last* thing I want to be thinking about right now.

I move over to one of the benches that face the dressing room and sit down, a box of shoes at my feet and a new Milly tee on that says *I'm not bossy, I'm the boss.* It's all good and paid for, courtesy of Gilleon, and a prepaid debit card that Aveline produced from her back pocket. I convinced the girls behind the counter to cut off all the tags for me and let me use one of the dressing rooms to change my clothes. I've got on new panties (*thank God*), a new bra, and now I'm going to slip into some Louboutin red soled ankle boots in black.

"What's next?" I ask, standing up in my new boots and grabbing a quick look at myself in one of the decorative mirrors leaning against the shop's walls. I know how silly it is to be here, doing this, know that I should've just let Aveline go out and grab some clothes from Target for me, but ... I don't let myself think about Gill, about what my needing to dress up might have to do with him. Or why he let me go out to shop. Surely, there's some inherent risk in all of this? "I feel like I could take on the world." I smile back at Aveline and she raises her red brows at me.

"Next up, is a trip back to the hotel. One, maybe two more nights there if it's safe, and then onto the next for another night or two. After that, you can move in with Gill."

I wince and of course, Aveline notices.

"Oh, come on. I know your stepbrother's an asshole, but he's got a great place. Bought it a year or so ago, if I remember right. It's some 1912 remodel with like five bedrooms or something. I was wondering why a single guy needed a house that big, but it all makes sense now."

A chill travels up my spine and makes me clench my hands into fists at my sides.

Gill's been planning this for a year? The thought shouldn't surprise me, but it does anyway. I mean, I know he's thorough, researches the shit out everything, but ... that means for at least a year he's known he was going to come see me, ask me to give up my life, bring me here.

And that whole safe house bit? A bullshit lie. He knew from the start that we'd be living together for at least a little while.

"You alright?" Aveline asks, and I nod, forcing myself to recite some positive self-talk to keep my emotions in order. *You can handle this; you can handle anything. In the ocean that is life, this is but a drop. You'll get through this, Regi, and you'll do it looking fabulous.*

"Fine," I say, brushing hair behind my ear and nodding. "Just fine."

"Alright, let's head out then," Aveline says, leaving me to carry the two massive bags of clothing—something about keeping her gun arm free or something. I don't mind, lifting them up and following her out the front doors of the shop and down the sidewalk towards the truck.

I'm so lost in thought that when Aveline stops dead in her tracks, I run right into her.

"Are you—" I start to ask, but she's already turning, grabbing me by the arm and yanking me forward. I fall against the pavement with a grunt, the bags landing beside me as I scrape my palms across the cement, drawing blood.

"Stay still," Aveline growls, reaching under her hoodie and pulling out a gun. I'm too shocked by the sudden turn of events to do anything but lie there as she lifts the weapon up and fires twice. The mid-afternoon crowd around us erupts into screaming panic, feet pounding by as Aveline grabs my arm again. "In the truck," she snaps as I struggle to stand, leaving the shopping bags behind. As soon as I rise to my feet, I see the broken window in the back of the cab, right where I'd been standing.

I was *this* close to being ended with a well-placed bullet.

I don't stand around to check it out, scrambling for the passenger side of the truck and finding it unlocked. Aveline climbs in beside me—my bags in her hands—and tosses them into the back seat.

"Gotta be thorough," she says as she turns the ignition and pushes the truck into the street, careful to avoid the panicked crowd. My eyes feel like they're stuck open, and I can't stop staring at the scuffs on the toes of my new boots. *I almost died. I almost just died.* Bile rises in my throat and I wrap my fingers around my neck, turning to look at Aveline's pursed lips and her tight fingers wrapped around the wheel. The gun sits silent in her lap. "Can't leave any evidence behind."

For once, I don't care one bit about the designer clothes.

If I'd have died today, it wouldn't have mattered what I was wearing.

CHAPTER
Seven

Aveline calls Gill on our way back to the hotel, and he's waiting outside when I get there, standing strangely still in front of the entrance, his eyes like pools of rainwater resting undisturbed. *If only there were ripples.*

"Are you alright?" he asks me, little emotion lacing his words, like this is a formality and nothing more. His gaze catches on the bloodstains that my palms left on the jeans, resting there for a moment before lifting back to my face.

"I almost got shot in the head," I whisper, my voice hoarse. "What do you think?"

"Who was it?" Gill asks Aveline, his fists curled tight at his sides, apparently done with our conversation. *Stupid motherfucker,* I think at him, still trying to get my breathing under control. Nothing like that has ever happened to me, not once. I mean, I knew the risks getting into this, but what the fuck? That was no cop, come to arrest me. I was shot at in the middle of a crowd.

"One of Karl's guys, for sure," Aveline says, brushing some ruby strands from her forehead. "Just one. Like he wasn't really sure we'd be there at all. I think the guy got cocky and thought he'd go for the glory. I don't really think anyone was supposed to be shot today."

"Take the rental," Gill says, holding out a key fob. Aveline takes it from him with a nod. "Go switch it out for my car and meet me back here. I'll have you take everyone to my place. There's no point in playing games if Karl already knows we're here."

"Got it," Aveline says as she steps back and then gives my shoulder a squeeze for comfort. "Be right back."

I watch Aveline walk away, her booted footsteps loud against the moist pavement. As I stand there watching her, the clouds shift and the small slice of sunshine that was peeking through disappears. For a moment there, I consider asking Gill about the whole safe house thing, but I can't find it in me to care. I just want Cliff and Solène to be safe.

I turn back to Gilleon, focusing my gaze on his muscular chest instead of his face. That emptiness is back, that emotionless pit that he's become. I don't know why I almost let one weird moment get to me. *Regina.* His voice swirls around inside my head until I blink it away.

"Where's Solène?" I ask, wondering if he's noticed. *When* he'll notice.

"In the room with my dad. They're fine. Everything's going to be fine." The certainty with which Gill speaks scares me. I know that he'll do whatever he has to to make that statement come true. Tonight, this Karl guy or his men, some of them might die.

"Remember when we first moved to Paris and you let me sleep in your bed?" I ask him, thinking about warm nights cuddled against Gill's black hoodie, the both of us fully clothed under the blankets, some instinctual protection perhaps against the passion that burned so hot between us. "Cliff and Elena left us alone to hit that work function she had." I swallow hard. I can still remember the gray tulle gown my mother had worn that night, how beautiful she'd looked. "We were just starting to fall asleep when you heard a noise. We went downstairs and found that some guy had forced his way into the apartment and was rifling through stuff. You didn't even blink, didn't stop to think about what you were doing. Gill, you walked right up to him and broke his arm when he tried to take off. That night, you scared me a little bit, even though I knew you were trying to protect me." The thief had run off after that, and neither Gill nor I had ever told anyone else about it.

I make myself look up at my ex's face, still impassive, still no sign of his feelings—if he even has any.

"Right now, I feel the same way. I believe that you'll take care of everything, but I'm afraid of how you're going to do it."

I walk past him, careful to keep my arm from touching his, and head towards the stairs.

Gill follows behind me, his footsteps heavy and solid. But he doesn't say anything, not one damn thing.

✗ ✗ ✗

"*This* is where you live?" Solène asks, pressing her hands against the car window and gazing up at Gill's four thousand square foot Colonial. She's spent her entire life living in apartments, and I feel a small smile hit my lips when I imagine her actually having a yard of her own to play in. Hey, as much as I love the city, suburbia definitely has its upsides. "It's positively enormous." She sits back and brushes some hair behind her ear. "*J'adore ça, c'est tellement joli.*" *I love it; it's so pretty.*

I stare at the back of Gill's head, trying to keep my cool. The more time I spend around him, the harder it seems to get. I clench the leather seat beneath me in tight fingers.

"What do you think, Regi?" Solène asks, reaching over and poking me in the bloodied jeans. We didn't tell her anything about what happened today—after all she doesn't even know about the heist. All I said was that I fell and left it at that. I wrap my fingers around hers and give them a quick squeeze.

"It's nice," I admit begrudgingly, but I can't bring myself to feel anything when I look at the house. "A little large for a single guy though," I add, unable to keep from picking at Gilleon. He *knew* we were going to be staying with him, even planned for it by buying some suburban wonderland in Mount freaking Baker. I feel a childish urge to kick the back of his seat come over me but push it back. *Fuck him. Yeah, that's right. Fuck you, Gill.*

"Is there anyone else living here?" Cliff asks, his face scrunching up as Gill pulls into the driveway and turns off the ignition.

"No." One word, crisp and curt. Gill hasn't spoken since we left the hotel, leaving the three of us to talk around him, his presence like a dark cloud shadowing our conversation.

"Well, it's beautiful anyway, son. You've done well for yourself." Cliff reaches over and grips his son's shoulder. I see Gill stiffen, but I can't watch anymore of this, so I climb out and look around the neighborhood, at the mature trees with their red and gold leaves, the perfect lawns and the well-trimmed hedges. Hopefully nobody will try to shoot at me here.

"Come inside," Gill says from behind me, his breath warm on the back of my neck. When I spin around to glare at him, his face is still a blank mask, his muscles tight with tension. "I don't expect any trouble here, but it never hurts to be safe."

"Yeah, okay." I step around him and move towards the front door when I feel his fingers curl around my upper arm. That simple touch is enough to make my knees weak, my head spin. "Let go," I say, my voice strong, words clear.

"I'm sorry about what happened today. If I'd have thought there was any chance—"

"So you do make mistakes?" I ask, glancing back at

him and raising an eyebrow. "Gilleon Marchal isn't as perfect as he pretends to be?"

"I'm not perfect," Gill growls, his jaw clenching and his fingers tightening on my arm. "And I make mistakes, Regina. You should know that better than anyone." I wrench myself from Gill's grip and try to still the rapid thumping of my heart. Rage consumes me like a flame, and it takes some considerable effort on my part not to respond to that. There are so many things I want to say, words that I've kept locked up inside for over ten years.

"Don't push me, Gill," I tell him as I climb up the cement steps to the front door, the wind picking at my hair and sending it flying around my face like a veil. "I'm trying to stay positive here, but I'm losing patience and I'm losing it *quick.*"

"What can I do to make this easier on you?" he asks, coming up right beside me, using those long, strong legs of his to make up the difference in distance. "Tell me and it's done."

"Gill," I say, turning to look at him, hating how badly my heart aches when I look into his face. He's a man now, strong and beautiful—and he should've been mine. I should've been able to watch the transformation, to be a part of it, to shape him the same way he should've shaped me. We could've been partners, lovers, best friends. This house right here, it could've been ours. It could have been *ours.* "What I want is for you to stay away from me. I want you to figure out what the *fuck* is up with this Karl guy and I want you to do your best to make sure that Cliff and Solène don't get shot and killed over a bag of stupid shiny rocks!" My voice raises in pitch until I think I'm yelling and have to force myself to close my eyes and calm down.

I don't want to be mad at Gill, to hold onto this anger. It isn't healthy and it isn't helping, but I can't be around him. I just can't do it. I'm not sure what hurts worse: the expressionless mask he wears or the cracks I keep seeing in it.

"Get it done, Gill," I say, opening my eyes back up and locking gazes with him. "Get it done, get us our money, and get the hell out of our lives."

I move into the house and—despite the fact that it belongs to Gill—I slam the front door and lock it behind me.

X X X

My bedroom has a balcony and a view of Lake Washington, not to mention original hardwood floors, a small sitting room, and a fireplace. *Holy crap.* If I had to take a guess, I'd say this house was worth a clean million—maybe a million and a half. But then, I guess that's chump change when you're an international jewelry thief?

"This is clearly the master," I tell Cliff again when I lean into the hallway and smile at Solène as she races around the second floor, exploring each and every nook and cranny in the house. "Are you sure you're okay with me taking it?"

"Take it," Cliff says, smiling at me through the gray stubble on his chin. "You deserve it." I know Cliff loves me, know that he's one of the best friends I've ever had or

81

will have, but sometimes I feel like he does things for me to try to make up for Gill. I hate it when he does that.

"Thanks," I say tentatively, wondering why Gill himself hasn't taken up residence in the master. There's a king-sized bed in here, a nightstand, a dresser, and two chairs in the sitting room with a coffee table between them. Otherwise, it's empty. I mean *completely* empty. No pictures, no vases, no lamps, nothing but two white pillows and a white duvet on the bed.

Gilleon's room, on the other hand, has a mussed up bed, a closet full of clothes, a rug, some pictures of his dad, of Solène ... of me. I almost took that one back, confiscated it and shoved it to the bottom of my shopping bags so I didn't have to look at it. For whatever reason, Gill has a family portrait sitting on his dresser—a shot of my mom, Cliff, me, and him at our parents' wedding.

I'm so confused right now.

"I'm gonna lie down and take a quick nap," I tell Cliff and retreat back into my room, closing the door behind me. A quick glance out the curtain-free windows shows me Gilleon standing on the lawn, his cell pressed to his ear as he paces back and forth and talks to God only knows who. I wonder what the neighbors here think of him, this big, burly guy with his steel toed boots and his mean face.

Like he can sense me looking his way, Gill turns and glances up at my window, forcing me to take a step back. Shivers break across my skin.

I shake out my hands and take a deep breath, sitting down on the edge of the bed and pulling off my new boots. Even though I thoroughly washed my hands and picked out the bits of grit and rocks that had stuck in my open wounds, every little movement of my fingers hurts. I grit my teeth and toss the shoes to the floor, slipping out of my new jeans and double-checking to make sure I locked the door before I slip out of my bra and decide on just the tee and panties. In my desperation to build up a new wardrobe, I forgot about pajamas entirely. Oh well.

I pause on my way to the bathroom, my eyes catching on my purse. The sight of my mother in her chic white wedding dress, her eyes sparkling with happiness ... I find myself drawn to the bag, taking it back to the bed and dumping it out on the white comforter. Every picture I have of her is with me, every piece of jewelry, a few pieces of paper with her handwriting on them. The big things, the ones I knew I couldn't take with me, like my mother's vintage nightstand with the hand-carved roses, I finally gave in and sold them to some friends of mine in Paris. I bought new chairs, just to keep up the illusion that everything was fine, everything was normal.

I shift through the photos with a sad smile on my face, trying really, really hard not to miss my dad or my sister or ... Gill. I shove the pictures away and pick up the diamond pendant necklace, lacing it around my throat and struggling with the clasp for a moment before I finally get it in place. I wasn't sure if I'd have the stomach to wear diamonds after the heist—it just felt distasteful— but this piece ... it holds too many good memories to be tainted.

"What would you have to say about all this, Mom?" I

ask the necklace, fingering the diamond between my injured fingers. "About Gill leaving? About the heist? About ..." I can't even make my lips form the words that I want to say. Instead, I let the subject drop and curl into a ball on the bed. Outside, the rain starts up again and batters the windows, lulling me into a deep but fitful sleep.

X/ X/ X/

I open the door to my apartment, hands trembling. Behind me, Gill says nothing, acting as if this is all for real, every single second of it.

"Take yourself there, Regina, and let yourself believe it. If you do, then so will they."

That's what he'd said last week when we'd gone over the plan again. And again. And again.

So. Gill is going to abduct me at gunpoint, walk me to the store where I'm suppose to open for the morning, and use me to find the safe. The security guards who're supposed to be on duty, and the ones who are supposed to switch shifts with them, have already been dealt with.

Dealt with.

When Gill had first said those words to me, I'd trembled in my seat. I know it seems silly to be afraid of someone that I was once so close with but ... there's something different about Gill's face now, some emptiness that I feel could swallow him whole and leave him a barren black nothing.

I don't say anything though, don't let my memories overwhelm me, and glance over my shoulder. Sure enough, Gill's gun is hidden in the folds of his coat and I

84

can't see a thing. We'll make it to the store without anyone realizing what's going on.

"Why vintage jewelry?" I'd asked Gill when he'd come to me and started to explain his plan. He and his crew would rob my store, whether I was involved or not, but if I helped, if I made things just that much easier for them, he'd give me a cut, give me a new life in the States where I'd never have to worry about money again.

That wasn't what motivated me; money doesn't motivate me at all.

But Gill does.

I know this job, whatever it is under the surface, has more to it than jewelry and a big payout.

Gill is in trouble.

I'm scared for him.

In typical Paris fashion, the sky shifts from sun to rain, dropping wet splatters on my face and hair. I lift up my umbrella to shield myself from the clouds, taking a path I know full well. I've worked at this same shop for seven years, seven long years of wondering what else there was for me, what else I should be doing. I've made so many mistakes over the years ... too many to count. And then there's the biggest one of all, the one that Gill still doesn't know about. How he missed it is beyond me. Maybe he doesn't want to see.

We turn the corner and the weather shifts again, sunshine streaming down, draping the buildings in golden light. I barely notice any of it, tucking my umbrella away and focusing solely on keeping my breathing steady.

Two blocks left. Just two short, little blocks until my life changes forever.

I think then about putting all of this on hold, turning to Gill and begging him to reconsider, but honestly, I'm not sure what would happen if I did. Would he take my words into consideration? Or would he really hold me at gunpoint then, go through with the robbery anyway? The fact that I don't know the answer to that question scares the shit out of me.

"Regina!"

My heart drops to my stomach.

Up ahead, standing on the sidewalk with a white bag in one hand and a coffee in the other is my boyfriend, Mathis Vidal. Shit.

I can feel *Gill tensing behind me and my mouth goes completely dry. Will he shoot him?*

"Bonjour, mon étoile," he says with a sly smile, turning my insides to ice. Mon étoile, *my star. It's a pet name that he came up with a few months into our relationship. I hated it at first because it reminded me of Gill.*

Gill.

Who's standing behind me with a gun in his jacket.

"Bonjour," I say, pausing a few steps away from him. When I don't come in for a kiss, Mathis frowns and glances at my silent companion. His brown eyes immediately narrow and the smile slides off his lips. He's been out of town for several weeks now, must've just gotten back. I've been avoiding his calls, not because I don't like the guy but because I do. He doesn't need to

get caught up in all this, and I don't love him enough to stay out of it.

"Gilleon Marchal," Gill says, putting a cold smile on his face.   When I look over at him, I know he'll do anything to see this plan through – anything.   "And you are?" he asks, not even bothering to switch to French. His voice is hard as steel, wrapping around my neck and stealing the breath from me.

"Is everything okay?" Mathis asks, his English heavily accented and lilting.   "I was hoping we might have some breakfast together?"

"Can't," I say, my lips tight, my throat aching. "Désolée, je suis occupée."   Sorry, I'm busy.   My hands are shaking like crazy as I unlock the metal grating on the front of the shop and lift it up, moving to the door before Mathis can see the erratic quivering.

I don't like blowing him off like this, but I don't know what else to do, how else to act.

"Maybe some other time," I hear Gill say as he moves into the store behind me and locks the door, the glass cases winking in the sunshine that breaks through the windows.   I step over to the alarm next and feel a sudden pressure in my spine—the gun.

"Don't even think about alerting the police," he whispers, his warm breath grazing my ear.   I hate how tight my muscles get when I feel him so close behind me.

Instead, I just swallow and nod, putting in the code and stepping back.   A quick glance over my shoulder and I see that Mathis is still standing outside looking dumbfounded.   After a moment, he turns as if to walk *away and then changes his mind, heading straight for the front door and knocking on it with his fist.*

"Shit," Gill growls under his breath. "What a persistent little fuck."

"What do I do?" I ask, panic lacing its way between my words. "Please don't kill him," I add for good measure, knowing that the cameras are watching, always watching. Even that's part of the plan.

"Answer the door and ask him to leave," Gill grinds out, and I'm pretty damn sure his frustration is genuine. I do as he asks, opening the door and then stumbling back when Mathis shoves his way in, pushing me aside in a valiant act of heroism.

"Run!" he screams in English, tackling Gill and dropping the coffee and the bag of brioche to the floor. A golden brown roll tumbles out and hits me in the toes of my Louboutin heels as I scream a very genuine scream of terror. I know what Gill is capable of; Mathis has no idea.

Gilleon avoids Mathis with ease, gliding back on feet as sure and nimble as a cat's, watching as my boyfriend stumbles into a case of jewelry and grunts.

Meanwhile, I stand there like a complete idiot, knowing I can't very well run away from all this.

Fuck.

Mathis makes another growling sound in his throat and spins—right into Gill's fist. My ex doesn't break a sweat when he reaches out and slams his knuckles into Mathis's face. The man drops like a sack, just crumples to the floor with a bloody nose and a groan.

I scream again, another real sound, and kneel down to roll Mathis over, checking to make sure he's still alive. Sounds silly, I know, but Gill is strong, crazy strong.

"Get up."

Gill has the gun on me again, his voice just as hard and cruel as it was before. Only ... this time there's a little bit of heat in all that ice. I watch as he grits his teeth, the muscles in his jaw working furiously as he tries to process what just happened.

I do the same, staring up at him for a moment before I realize what that strain is that I hear in Gilleon's voice.

It's jealousy.

CHAPTER

Eight

I wake up early the next morning, my heart pounding in my chest, sweat beading on my forehead. It's just starting to get light outside, dawn cresting the horizon and casting its golden fingers across the surface of the lake.

I stand up and open the doors to the balcony, not caring that I'm still in my underwear, and lean over the edge of the white railing, closing my eyes against the sharp bite of autumn air. I *need* to stop dreaming about Gilleon, but I don't know how to quit. Even unconscious I'm addicted to memories; I can still see the clench of Gill's jaw, hear that small spike of heat in his voice.

But I can't dwell on it.

"Shit." I cross my arms on the railing and lean my forehead against them.

"You look like you could use a cup of coffee."

I jerk my head up at the sound of Gill's voice and peer over the edge of the railing at him.

For whatever inexplicable reason, he's standing on the driveway near his car, dressed in a pale blue shirt, jeans, and work boots. His dark hair is wet, like he just showered, and his face is freshly shaved again.

I stare down at him from the second floor, hoping the angle at which I'm standing and the railing are enough to keep him from seeing the emerald green panties I'm sporting. I mean, it's not as if he hasn't seen all of this before, but ... it's not his to look at anymore.

I purse my lips.

"What part of *I want you to stay away from me* do you not understand?" I ask, looking down at him, my legs crossed beneath and behind me as I lean forward over the railing, gold hair draping down on either side of my face.

Gill stares up at me, a wry smile building on his lips.

"To be fair, I am *away* from you right now. Two full stories down." He pauses, smirks a little, the expression reminding me so much of better times that my chest gets tight. "And still in view of your underwear."

I stand up straight, proving that I don't give two shits, and lean sideways against the railing, knowing the curvy pale line of my hip is showing. If Gill's grown into a man since he's left, then I've become a woman. I suppose if he's already looking, I might as well show him what he's missing. *Must be all the stress and the anxiety getting to me,* I think. *Because I feel like I should have more of a reaction to being an accessory in a high stakes*

91

international jewelry heist. Or maybe I really am just crazy?

"Okay," I say, crossing my arms over my chest, fully aware that my breasts are perky, nipples erect in the cool morning air. "I'll come down for coffee, but only so we can discuss ... *this.*" I gesture between us and move back into the bedroom, yanking off my T-shirt and dropping my panties to the floor. A quick shower later and I'm pulling on a square-neck sheath dress in white, belting it at the waist with a strip of thin, black leather, and thanking the Parisian designer Roland Mouret for creating something that I can feel confident enough in to face Gilleon.

I don't have time to get my hair right, so I give it a quick blowout with the blowdryer I stole from the hotel, and line my eyes with the dark pencil that Aveline gave me. My mother's necklace swings enticingly as I sit in one of the two chairs in the sitting room and slip on some red platform pumps that are way too fabulous for this early in the morning.

"I am beautiful just the way I am," I tell myself as I stand up and check myself in the mirror on the back of the bathroom door. "I wear the clothes; the clothes do not wear me." I take a massive breath and let myself out into the hallway, moving slowly and praying that I don't wake either Cliff or Solène.

I take the back staircase, the one that leads directly into the kitchen, and find Gill already waiting for me at the bottom, pouring a cup of steaming hot coffee into a navy blue mug. He turns at the sound of my heels, and I know, *know,* for a fucking fact that his jaw clenches and his breath hitches at the sight of me. He even manages to spill some of the steaming coffee on the table.

"Shit," he grumbles, returning the pot to the coffeemaker and grabbing a roll of paper towels from the counter. When he turns back to face me, all traces of the slipup have been wiped from his face.

"Good morning," I say, running my hands down the front of the dress, fully aware of how I look in it. "I take it no one tried to assassinate us while we slept?" Gill grunts, like he's halfway between a laugh and a scoff. Not sure what that means, but I'll take it. Anything to prove to me that he's still human. When we were teens, he used to wake me up with pancakes and bacon, plated in silly faces, and he'd deliver them with the biggest grins I'd ever seen. *What happened to you? What happened to pull that darkness out and let it take over, Gill? We were going to have a good life, a great life.* "Milk and sugar, please," I say before he can ask.

Gill sets a small silver pitcher of milk and a matching sugar dish in front of me. Fancy. Since he doesn't strike me as the kind of guy who'd give a shit about things like that, I have to wonder ... did a girlfriend ever live here with him? Maybe I'm reading too much into this whole house thing? Maybe, just maybe, this house *wasn't* meant for me and Cliff and Solène, but for a future wife, a future family, that he was supposed to have.

I decide there's no other way to know than to ask.

"Did you buy this house for us?" I ask, my voice steady. I scoot my coffee mug closer and pour in some milk. "I mean, specifically to use as a safe house for this job? I'm just asking because it seems awfully nice, and awfully large, so ..."

"Where am I hiding my wife, two kids, and golden retriever?" Gill asks, leaning back in his chair with a creak, a cup of black coffee cupped in his strong hands. My own tremble a little as I spoon sugar into the mug and try to ignore the aching throb of the scabs on my palm. "They're in the backyard, stuffed in the shed next to the minivan."

"Please don't deflect my honest questions with humor," I tell him, lifting my chin up and giving him my most haughty glare. I refuse to smile at his joke, flat out refuse. My lips struggle to betray me anyway. "Gilleon, I want an answer. I feel like I deserve one after what happened yesterday." The memory of the gunshots makes my head hurt, so I push it back, refusing to acknowledge how close I actually came to dying.

"I bought this house in preparation for the job, yes." Gill leans forward, the front legs of his chair hitting the floor with a crack. Some of that gorgeous dark hair falls into his blue eyes as he stares at me, my own gaze dropping to his chest, to the tightness of that T-shirt and the smooth slide of muscles beneath it. Every move that Gill makes is done with feline grace, a slick sureness that whatever the prey is, however fast or strong or cunning, he'll be the one to take it down. "And no. No, there is no one, Regina. I don't have a wife or a girlfriend or kids."

My throat works hard to swallow past the sudden lump that forms and I choke on my coffee, turning away and closing my eyes for a brief moment.

"What's wrong?" he asks me, but I just shake my head, hating him for being so damn perceptive. *This is going to get old fast, isn't it?* "Regina."

"Gilleon," I say, turning back to face him, finding his eyes on my body, roving over the smooth square of chest and cleavage above the neckline on my dress. He lifts his gaze back to mine as I reach down and pick up my coffee. "I don't care about any of that. That's not what this is about."

"Bullshit," Gill growls, tightening the muscles in my lower belly. He bares his teeth at me in a small scowl. "Why can't we just be honest about what's going on here? You've been cold and distant since the moment I set foot in Dad's kitchen."

"Me?!" I ask, and I can't seem to keep the shriek from my voice. I point at myself, right at the diamond pendant hanging down on my chest. "*I'm* the distant one? I'm not the one that puts on expressionless masks, that goes all cold and dark and deep, retreats so far into his fucking self that even though he sees everything, sees it all, he's blinded by it and misses the most important things of all."

"What, Regi? What is it that I'm missing?" His blue eyes are vacant, focused on the tabletop as the fingers on his right hand curl against the polished wood. I don't miss the bunching of muscle in his arms, the tension in his jaw. When he flicks that gaze up to me, all of the emptiness breaks and I have to really struggle to catch my breath.

"If it seems like I've been cold and distant," I say, already regretting the massive hint I just dropped on him, "it's because I've been trying to be cordial and pleasant. Because, after all these years, I see you appear like a ghost from the grave. Because the first time in a decade that you decide to talk to me, it's about a robbery. Because ten years ago, you left me with an engagement ring on my finger ..." I suck in a deep breath, fighting against the prick of tears behind my eyes. This is why I *hate* reliving this shit. Not seeing him all that time, it was really a blessing in disguise. Love can't be killed. Once it's there, it sits in your heart forever. Sometimes, it morphs or changes. Sometimes, it grows. And sometimes, it lies dormant, like a seed in dry dirt. I don't want this particular seed watered because I don't want it to grow thorns. I've bled enough already.

"Listen," I say as slowly and calmly as I'm able, "we both know what you did to me, how you left." I lift up a hand when he starts to speak. "I don't care why. *Why* isn't important to me, Gilleon. But you and me, we had something ..." My voice gets rough and low, but I don't care. Maybe that's why fate brought us together again, just so I could say this. "We had something special, Gill. Some," I curl the fingers of my free hand against my chest, "some rare and wonderful spark. When it was snuffed out, I thought I would die of heartbreak. But I didn't. I knew I'd lost something one of a kind that day, but I got through it, worked past it."

I stand up from the table, still not looking at him. He's looking at me though. I know that because I can feel it, can feel his gaze burning through my dress and straight to the red bra and panties that I've got on underneath. A strange, distant part of me wants him to bend me over this table and fuck me, but I know I'll feel even worse if we do that, even more empty inside.

"I'm sorry if I'm being aloof, if I don't seem like I want to make friends. To be honest, Gill, I don't. I just ... want to keep things professional, okay? Please don't bring the subject up again."

I shove away from the table and storm out of the kitchen, my heels loud on the wood floors as I head towards the living room and the main staircase. I'm barely out of sight before I hear a growl and a crash, like the sound of glass shattering.

I pause for a moment and then turn around, moving slowly back towards the kitchen. When I peer inside, I find Gill bent over the table with his elbow on the wooden surface, his head in his hand. On the floor next to me are the remnants of a navy blue mug and a sea of rapidly cooling coffee.

I sneak away before he sees me and retreat back to my bedroom.

To my credit, I don't shed a single tear.

※ ※ ※

Memories poke and prod at my subconscious, but I brush them away, shoving at them with angry fingers. *Not right now,* I snarl, my mental voice taking on the same violent, wild pitch that had burst from Gill before he'd thrown the coffee cup.

What the hell is going on here?

"*Je pense que je perds la tête,*" I murmur. *I think I'm losing my mind.* I put my fingers against my forehead and close my eyes, slowing my breathing down to a manageable level.

But no. No. That's not how I operate.

I open my eyes back up.

"I will handle this situation with grace and dignity," I say, reverting back to some positive self-talk. "No matter what comes my way, I can handle it." *Except for outlaws with guns,* my cynical self tries to add. I shove that thought back, too, and start pacing, the click of my heels on the floor a comforting sound, a familiar sound, one that says that I'm in control. Me. I decide where I walk, how quickly I go; I steer my own destiny.

If I had a cell phone—or any phone at all for that matter—I'd call up Leilani right now, even though I'm not supposed to. It'd be nice to have someone to talk to about all of this. My usual go-to, Cliff, isn't looking like a great option right now. Normally, when we talk about Gill, it's like we're talking about some distant, fictional character, some figment of my imagination that only haunts me in dreams. Right now? When I see Cliff and Gill together, I get a sick feeling in the pit of my stomach. The stepdad that's become like a true father figure to me, he's *really* the dad of the man that shattered my heart and stepped on it. And he loves his kid, like any good dad should, for all his faults and shortcomings. So how can I possibly talk to him about this?

The sound of a car pulling into the driveway draws me to the window and I pause, looking down to find Aveline stepping out of some generic black rental sedan.

My fingers twitch on the windowsill.

I might've just met the woman, but I could really use a friend right now. Plus, she knows Gill. Plus, she's a badass capable of saving me from armed gunmen.

Yes.

It's her that I want to talk to, hang out with.

I fix my dress and head back out into the hallway, pausing at the top of the stairs as Gill moves toward the front door. When he looks up at me, the mask is back in place, fixed firmly across those full lips, those beautiful blue eyes.

I can't resist ...

"Is my coffee still on the table?" I ask, moving down the stairs, my hand sliding over the banister. "I could still use that pick-me-up."

"I'll get it," he tells me, opening the front door before Aveline can even knock. I wonder if he's cleaned up the mess yet. "Can I get you some coffee, Ave?" he asks, moving back down the hall and trusting his partner to lock the door behind her.

"Black," she says, giving me a once-over and a raised red brow. "Wow, fancy. You got plans today?" I'm sure the question's rhetorical, but I answer anyway, watching as Aveline shrugs out of her navy blue coat, revealing a brown shoulder holster and the black pistol that's tucked away inside of it.

"Only if you don't," I say, flashing my best smile. Aveline narrows her eyes at me, the dark black makeup emphasizing the bright green of her gaze.

"I'm on guard duty today," she says, moving down the hallway towards the kitchen. *Perfect.* I smile and follow after her, both of us pausing when we find Gill on his knees cleaning up the mess of broken glass and splattered coffee. He doesn't even bother to look up at us. "How on earth did you manage this one?" Aveline asks, running her fingers over a splatter of coffee on the wall near her head.

Gill doesn't respond, pulling the trash can closer with his tattooed hand and slamming a wet paper towel full of glass into it with a crunch.

"Never mind," Aveline whispers, holding up her hands and moving to the cabinets to grab a mug for herself. "I don't want to know."

"Regina," Gill tells me, standing up straight and spraying the wall with cleaner before wiping it clean, "I'll be in and out today, but Ave will be here if you need anything. I don't expect anymore trouble, but try to stay in the house for now."

"When do I get a phone?" I ask as Aveline starts rifling through Gill's cabinets like she's been here before. She emerges with a granola bar and peels the plastic back, shoving it between her teeth before throwing her black duffel bag down on a kitchen chair and unzipping it. "When can I call Leilani? Or my sister?"

"It depends on the information that I get today," he tells me, setting the cleaner down on the table and running his fingers through his hair. The dark perfection of it, the way it glistens in the sunshine from outside, it's ... difficult to look at. I swallow hard. "Hopefully by next week you can start living normally. By next month, you should be able to get your own place."

"Next month?" I try not to choke on the words, but I can't help it. Gill's attention snaps right to my face and he steps close to me, his boots touching the toes of my red heels. We're two polar opposites—a soft, strong feminine and a damaged, brutal masculine. The contrast hurts too good to breathe.

"Think you can suffer my company that long?" he asks, and I get this really weird feeling that he wants to kiss me. But no. Gill turns away and heads over to the sink, grabbing his coffee and downing it, the corded muscles in his tattooed arm tensing with the motion, far too much strength in them for such a simple task. "I'll be back in a few hours. Aveline?"

"Yeah, yeah, I know what to do if the shit hits the fan. Have some faith in me, will you? I saved your sister a bullet wound to the head yesterday."

Gill grits his teeth, but he doesn't say anything, stalking from the kitchen with those sleek, strong predatory movements that put me on edge. I know, just *know,* that at any moment, he could quite literally reach over and snap my neck. I don't think he'd ever do anything like that, but just knowing that he's capable is kind of scary.

"Whoa," Aveline says, tossing a pile of papers onto the kitchen table and whistling, "he is *pissed.* What happened this morning?" I get myself another cup of coffee and sit down at the table next to Aveline.

"Nothing," I lie, sipping carefully and watching as she

101

shuffles through the green folders, finally passing one over to me. I open it up and find a series of documents— a passport, driver's license, birth certificate, social security card, a book of blank checks, a few credit cards —and all the ones with pictures ... feature yours truly. Only ... I look a little distorted. Still me, but different. "Fia?" I ask, staring at the foreign name printed beneath my picture. "My name is Fia now?"

My head spins and I have to sit my coffee cup down before I drop it.

"Fia Marie Levine," Aveline says, crunching down on her granola bar as I sit there and gape at the papers. Somehow, I can't imagine being anyone but Regi Corbair. I mean ... I knew this was coming, but it's still difficult.

"Why does my face look different?" I ask, touching a fingertip to my driver's license picture.

"I wiped your records, but you never know who might have a photo of you. Facial recognition technology is too good now. It's a little scary." Aveline taps her red painted fingernail against the card. "I altered this just enough that you should still pass if anyone looks at it, but different enough that you shouldn't be found either. Gill begged me to find someone with the middle name Regina, but there weren't any good candidates. Sorry."

"Find someone?" I ask, not sure I really even want to know. "Fia is a real person?"

"Was," Aveline says and my stomach drops. "And the reason she's past tense isn't any of our doing. I don't kill innocent people, just look for ones that are already dead."

I reach over and grab another file, finding Cliff's

papers—sorry, *Ivan's*—and Solène's. Her new name is *Giselle,* apparently. Fitting, but ... "Her last name is the same as mine," I say, flipping between Cliff's documents and my own. His new last name is Bernard.

"Yeah, about that." Aveline sits down and pushes the papers towards me, dunking her granola bar in her coffee. "With the age difference between him and her, it was hard for me to find a suitable match. It was much easier to call you her mom and be done with it."

My throat closes up.

"You know, the strangest thing came up when I was working last night," Aveline begins and I feel my head start to spin. "I was going through your old docs, wiping them from the system, when I happened upon something."

"*Bonjour.*" Cliff's cheerful voice breaks through the tension and pulls me up for air, drawing my attention to the archway into the kitchen. "How are you lovely ladies faring this morning?" I smile at my stepfather and curl my fingers around the files. How is he going to react when he sees this?

"Fine," I say, even though I feel anything *but* fine. "Did you sleep well?"

"Regina Elaine Corbair," Cliff says, putting his hands on his hips and looking me over. "You look anything *but* fine." I narrow my eyes at him and glance over at Aveline. She doesn't say anything, just leans back in her chair and shoves the last of the granola bar into her mouth.

"Got our new names today," I tell him, standing up and passing the files over. I get myself yet another cup

103

of coffee and drink it down like it's a shot of vodka. When I'm done, I slam the cup on the counter and gaze out the window at the trees separating Gill's house from the neighbors. After a minute, Cliff comes up behind me and puts his hand on my shoulder, squeezing tight, just like he always did for Gill, a comforting gesture.

"It'll be okay, Regi," he tells me as I stare dry eyed out the window and wish for a moment that I was anywhere but here. "Maybe ... it's about time all of this came up?" I take a shuddering breath.

"No," I tell him, and I know he'll respect my wishes on this. "It isn't time until Gill opens his eyes and looks." I turn around and face Cliff. "All he has to do is *look*."

CHAPTER

Nine

True to his word, Gill pops in and out of the house during the day, but I don't talk to him, hardly even glance his way as he trudges in, tracking the floor with mud from his boots. Dressed in my T-shirt from yesterday and a pair of designer leggings, I lounge on the couch and scroll through movies on Netflix, looking for the most horrific, gruesome one I can find. The worse the movie is, the better I feel about my own life. A coping mechanism, I know, but my past is catching up to me, trailing behind and breathing hot against my neck; I could use a distraction.

"You can call me Ave, if that'll make you feel better," Aveline tells me, appearing in the darkened living room. I closed all of the curtains, blocking out the beautiful golden sunshine and the view of the lake. It's not a pity thing, just a practical one. Who watches horror movies in bright, glaring sunlight?

"And how will that work?" I ask, wondering if Solène and Cliff are still upstairs reading. They're both literature buffs, spending countless hours in silence together, rehashing old classics and brand new bestsellers both. Cliff is a good dad, a perfect one, really. I know he doubts himself because of what happened with Gill and his mom, but his son *chose* to live with her, and he was trying to be respectful. It was a mistake, yes, but a forgivable one; he had no clue she'd drop off the deep end like that.

"If you call me Ave, you can pretend we're friends and then sharing secrets together will be no big deal." A smile twitches at the edge of my lips as she sits down next to me and passes over a glass of red wine. "It's not some fancy French *boudoir* or whatever, but it'll do the trick."

"I think you mean *Bordeaux?*" I ask, but Aveline waves my words away, nodding her chin at the TV. I notice she doesn't have a glass of wine in her own hand. She must take this whole no drinking on the job thing very seriously.

"What are you watching?" she asks, her eyes scanning the curtains, her arms stretched out alongside her, draped over the back of the couch. Even now, when she's trying to look relaxed, Aveline looks tense to me. "Been hearing a lot of screams in here."

"Horror," I tell her, twisting the remote around in my

hand. "Makes me feel better."

"About what?" Aveline asks, and I feel my walls cracking, my shield breaking. I *want* to talk to someone about all of this, tell them *everything*. Right now, she's all I've got. That, and I kind of ... like her. Besides, Gill trusts her with our lives, so why can't I spill some of my secrets?

"About Gill. About ... Solène." I glance at the staircase through the archway behind us, but nobody's there, no creaking of floorboards or snicking of doors.

"Ah," Aveline says, running her long fingers through that ruby red hair of hers. It's half up in a messy bun and half hanging down around her ears. "That."

"Yeah, that," I say, picking at the design on my leggings, the black and gray triangles that make up the pattern. "I knew working with Gill would be hard, but I didn't know it'd be this bad."

"You still love him?" she asks me, and I feel something shatter deep inside, shards of glass cutting at the edges of my soul. My breath hitches and it's the only answer she needs. Aveline's a smart woman. "Have you talked about that with him?" she asks tentatively, her voice holding onto something that I feel like I should be able to decipher.

"I can't," I tell her. "No, no, that's not right. I can do anything I set my mind to." Self-talk, always helps. "But I *won't*."

"Why not?" she asks me as I look up and meet the spring green of her gaze. "Listen, I don't know what happened between the two of you, but Gill's never shacked up with anyone as long as I've known him and I've known him for *years*."

I hate how much that thought heats my blood.

"Have you ever slept with him?" I blurt, needing to know for sure. It's not that I'd hold it against her—or even Gill for that matter—but I want to know before I tell her anything else. Aveline recoils a little, like the thought's an anathema to her.

"Like I said, he's hot, but—and no offense to you or anything—he's a little prickly for my tastes. What I mean is, he's kind of a dick." Laughter bursts from my throat and I clamp a hand over my mouth. Aveline smiles softly at me.

"But you said you'd seen him naked?" I ask and understanding dawns on her pale features.

"Gill and me, we've been through some shit together. I've happened to catch a glimpse of him nude, but it was nothing like that." I breathe a sigh of relief, grateful that the only friend I have to talk to isn't one of my stepbrother's lovers. "So I'm a safe bet. Tell me whatever you want to tell me, and it won't leave this living room." *So perceptive.* It's a little unnerving to talk to someone like that, but I'm used to it.

"Gill and me … we … were in love once."

※ ※ ※

I wet my lips and pause outside Gilleon's bedroom door, listening to the silence of the apartment and the gentle ticking of the clock in the living room. Outside, the rest of Paris goes about their business, not knowing or caring that this moment, for me, is a historic one.

I reach down for the knob and turn it slowly, finding my stepbrother sitting on the edge of his bed with a book in one hand. He looks up at me as I walk in, smiling softly. I wonder if he can tell from my facial expression what I've got planned.

"Hey there," he says, closing the book and tossing it onto his nightstand. "I was wondering when you were going to come out of that room of yours. Don't you know that Dad and Elena are gone for the night?" Gill grins big and brushes some dark hair from his forehead. "I was thinking we could make out."

"I was hoping to do more than make out," I tell him, reaching down and hooking my fingers under my T-shirt. My heart hammers in my chest and I take that brief moment when the fabric is covering my face to snatch a deep breath. I toss the shirt onto the floor, feeling so exposed, so naked in my lacy blue bra. It's the fanciest one I own, purchased at one of the boutiques in Le Marais with my savings.

Purchased just for this.

"Regi," Gill says, standing up suddenly, the warm glow of his bedside lamp illuminating the straight sturdy perfection of his nose, the slope of his jaw, the dark brows framing his brilliant eyes. I bite my lower lip hard enough to hurt, but I don't wake up from this dream, this spell that I find myself under every day that I wake up and see Gill for the first time. "Are you sure about this?" he asks, taking a long, slow, deep breath.

I've never been more sure of anything in my life. But I don't tell him this. The words sound too sappy, too cliché, even if they're true.

Instead, I answer him by reaching down and popping the top button on my jeans.

Gill's hands curl into fists by his sides and then relax as I move towards him, pausing at the end of the bed, my eyes hooded and my pulse pounding.

"Regi," Gill says again, more softly this time, his bare feet quiet on the wood floor as he steps over to me, his hands hovering above my hips like he's not sure this is even really happening. Gill and I have gotten close to taking things all the way, but we never dropped over the edge, never let our hearts take us where our bodies so desperately wanted to go.

When Gilleon finally lays his fingers against the bare skin of my hips, I have to bite back a gasp, little thrills of pleasure arching up my spine and making my head spin.

"I love you, Regi," he tells me, and I know he's not just saying it to get into my pants. I'm glad he's going to be my first. I can't even imagine doing this with anyone else.

Gill leans in and our lips meet softly at first, tentative strokes of tongue as our bodies come together, the cups of my bra pressing against the hardness of his chest. One of his hands roams up my back along my spine, drawing goose bumps up on my skin. When he cups the back of my head, tangling his fingers in my hair, I groan hard and the passion that we've kept such a careful eye on breaks loose.

I laugh as Gill swings me onto the bed, climbing on top of me and pinning my head with his hands. His eyes sparkle as he wets his lips and looks down at me, studying my face, absorbing it into his memory.

"You make me feel so lucky, Regi," he says, closing the distance between our mouths and crashing our lips together. Down below, I can feel the hardness of his body through his jeans, that tight bulge that tells me for certain that he wants me as much as I want him.

I reach between us, searching for the button on his jeans and snapping it open, moving straight to his zipper. Gill stops me by pulling back and grinning, hooking his fingers on the waistband of my pants and pulling them down, dragging them right off and over my bare feet, before he tosses them to the floor.

I curl my knees up, suddenly embarrassed by the ruffled panties with the tiny blue bows.

Gill doesn't look embarrassed though; he looks thrilled.

"Are these for me?" he asks, eyes sparkling.

"No, I bought 'em for my last boyfriend." Gill just laughs and I toss a pillow at him. Before I can think up another insult, he leans over me and runs a finger down the seam of my panties.

"There's a wet spot here, Regi," Gill says, and I blush, heat rushing to fill my cheeks. "I'm pretty sure that *isn't for your last boyfriend.*"

"Screw you," I tell him, reaching up and wrapping my hands around the back of his neck. "I'm nervous and scared and you're not making this any better."

"You? Nervous and scared? I don't think so," he breathes, kissing me again. I taste his mouth, inhale his scent, like bergamot oil, a spicy sweetness that makes my head feel light. Gill takes advantage of the moment to slip his fingers under my panties and inside me, drawing a gasp that gets swallowed up by his hot mouth.

As embarrassing as it is, I can't keep my hips from bucking against his hand as he teases me, slides his fingertips into my warm body. I keep my arms locked around his neck as he draws the sensation into a throbbing ache and then just ... stops.

A moan of disappointment escapes my lips as Gill sits up and strips off his black T-shirt. The disappointment dies right there, right when I see the hard planes of his chest, the swell of muscles that mark Gill as a man, and not a teenager. Not anymore.

I can't even believe he's mine.

"I love you, too, Gilleon," I tell him, his answering smile enough to warm my heart to the point of bursting. I bite my lip again and run my fingers up his abs, over his chest, curling them over his shoulders and pulling him back down to me. I take a small break to reach down and unhook the front clasp of my bra, getting a pair of raised brows and a surprised facial expression from Gill.

"I didn't even know they made these," he whispers, and I laugh, the sound turning into a moan as he pushes the cups back and takes my breasts in his hands.   I bought it special for you, *I want to say, but the words won't come, replaced by animalistic groans that bring more heat to my face.*

I can't seem to help it though. With Gill's hands on my breasts, his body between my legs, it's hard to *remember to even breathe.*

"*One second,*" *I whisper, rolling partially onto my side and snagging my jeans off the floor. I came prepared.* "*Got it,*" *I say as I pull a few condoms out and flop back onto my back, looking up at Gill and his bemused facial expression.* "*Here. Put this on.*"

"*Wow, you really did think this whole thing out, didn't you?*" *he says, his voice warm and his eyes gentle. Gill's strong, no doubt about that, but he knows when to show a different side. I can see it right here, right now, and it's the most beautiful sight I've ever seen. I don't tell him that out loud though—he'd probably tease me if I did.*

"*Just put it on,*" *I whisper, a fire burning down below that I can't wait to quench. If his fingers feel that good then ...*

"*Oui, mademoiselle,*" *he whispers back, leaning down and kissing me softly, our lips barely brushing as he breathes against my mouth,* "*I aim to please.*"

I bite my lower lip as he scoots back and slides off the end of the bed, dropping his pants to the floor and giving me a wry look over his shoulder.

"*What do you think? I've been told I have a nice ass.*"

"*Screw you,*" *I whisper, but my voice sounds too breathy to really be mine. I sit up, shrugging off my bra and tossing it to the floor. The panties follow after, smacking Gill right in the chest—totally by accident, of course.*

The warm air in the bedroom seems suddenly chill as I pull my legs up to my chest and wrap my arms around them, watching as Gilleon stands there buck naked and peruses the writing on the condom package.

"I know we're both virgins, but it's not that hard to figure out," I say with a slight smile. Butterflies are taking over my stomach and making it hard to think straight. Mostly I just want him to stop looking at it and put the damn thing on.

"Feels like nothing at all," Gill reads and then smiles, looking up at me. "Did you pick these out special?"

"I ordered them off the Internet—after reading lots of reviews." I turn away because it's hard to have a conversation with someone who's so buff and beautiful and ... excited. His laughter makes me purse my lips as he climbs back onto the bed and curls his fingers around my knees, slowly opening my legs up.

I turn back and we lock gazes, blue to brown. Gill's lips are gently parted as he looks down at me, watches me lean back onto the bed, my honey blonde hair spread out across the stark white of his pillowcase.

When he leans down over me, our bare skin brushing with an electric thrill, heat rushes through me and I find myself opening wider, reaching up and resting my fingers on the back of Gill's neck.

The talking is over, the joking put on hold.

I feel him at my opening, hard and ready, as desperate for me as I am for him.

"Regi," he whispers as he pushes inside, sliding deep and drawing a sharp gasp from me. It doesn't hurt, not really, but I feel tight, stretched, full. Knowing that that's Gill, the boy with the sharp wit and the fierce love,

114

the loyalty that never quits, makes my head spin in the best way possible.

I groan, the hardness of my nipples brushing against the muscles of his chest as he starts to move, slowly at first but picking up speed, abs contracting as his hips move to a rhythm that we both somehow know instinctually.

I close my eyes, lashes fluttering against my cheeks, as pleasure slides through me, like ripples in a pond, starting down below and taking over until I can feel Gill everywhere—in my fingertips, my toes, my lips. He leans down and kisses me fiercely but lovingly, like I belong to him and he belongs to me. Together. Forever. I really believe that, really and truly believe that. Gill and me, we're made for each other.

My eyes open and I stare up into Gill's as his breath comes faster, as mine picks up speed to match, our bodies slipping and sliding together in an erotic dance. I raise my hips to meet his, hook one leg tightly around him and encourage him to go deeper, move faster, hit harder.

When the orgasm hits me, suddenly and unexpectedly, my body soars while my heart falls. Far. And hard. I fall so hard for Gilleon Marchal then that I know it'll be impossible to ever climb out.

X X X

"We met when I was sixteen and he was seventeen," I tell Aveline, memories sweeping over me and threatening to smother me in the avalanche of emotions that comes with them. *The past doesn't control me; I control my future.* I take a deep breath and lean back, relaxing into the white and blue throw pillows and tugging the white afghan over my legs. Aveline listens intently, even as I know she's keeping an eye and an ear out for trouble. "That was the day he moved in for good, two weeks before our parents' wedding. I'd known Cliff for a while before that, and I liked him alright, but I was really upset about my mother getting remarried."

I tap my fingers on the back of the couch, forcing myself through a condensed version of the story. If I have someone to talk to for this next week of forced isolation, I'll feel a whole lot better. It's almost become a desperate need for Aveline to know everything. "My dad died of melanoma a few years earlier and I still wasn't over it." I swirl the red wine around in my glass and then take a tentative sip, letting the alcohol crash into my empty belly. "Gill helped me through that. He was ... nice and he was funny and he was the only person I'd ever met who valued family as much as I did. He *understood* me, and when he looked at me, I felt like he saw me." I take another sip of wine. "Really and truly *saw* me. When we moved to France, he kept me going, helped me when I stumbled through the language, when I missed my friends, when I thought about flying back to live with my grandma in California. He kept me there, taught me to be happy, to appreciate my new circumstances." My eyes mist as I get to the next part of the story. I won't cry about Gill, spent way too many years crying over him. But my mom? Ouch. That still hurts, and I'm not ashamed of it. "When my mother passed away in an accident, he was there for me. In fact, to this day I feel like he's the only reason I survived that."

I check the stairs again, check to make sure we're really and truly alone. I know Cliff knows this story, but Solène ... she doesn't need to hear it.

"We stayed together until I was twenty-one," I say, my eyes glazing over as I remember the ring Gill gave me, tucked it right in my hand while we were taking a walk. He didn't even say anything, just looked at me with that love in his eyes and ... I was his. Of course it was a yes. It was always going to be a yes. "But then one day ... one day he just left." I fight back the pain, kick at it and shove it until it falls away and leaves the emptiness. I don't like that either, but it seems to fade more quickly, so I'll take it. "He left a letter telling me how much he loved me, but how we wouldn't work. Said he was going and that he wouldn't be back, that he'd asked Cliff not to give me his number or his address, that maybe one day we could talk but it wouldn't be anytime soon."

I feel my jaw clench, that old anger rising up to bite me in the ass.

I want to stand up right now and throw my wineglass at the wall, scream and shout and curse his name like I did that day. But I don't. I won't allow myself to get that caught up in a memory.

"I ... had something to tell him, but ... when I tried to contact him ..."

My stomach twists when I think about how I begged and pleaded Cliff, how I browbeat him into giving me Gill's temporary address at that hotel, how I went there, how Gill refused to answer the door. I knew he was in there though, so I rented the room next door and went onto the balcony. That's when I saw him, sitting in one of the chairs outside, staring into the night sky with tears on either side of his face. I knew then that he wasn't going to talk to me, that no matter what I said, it wouldn't change things. "I got Cliff to tell me where he was anyway, went and banged on the door to his hotel room." I sigh at the sad, miserable person I was then. I feel for her even now, but I promised myself that I will never, ever let myself become her again. "He didn't answer, even though he was inside."

"The thing you went to tell him about ..." Aveline begins and I nod. She's perceptive enough, smart enough, that I don't even have to say anything aloud.

"The day I found that letter, the day he left, I spent the morning walking around the city with some girlfriends of mine, shopping for the future we'd never have. I remember feeling so much love for him that I thought my heart would burst from my chest." My fingers tighten around the stem of the wineglass. "That letter was the last thing I ever expected to find, and it nearly killed me." I swirl my wine around and take another drink. "My love for Gill very nearly killed me."

Before Aveline can respond, there's a knock at the front door and she gets up to answer it, sliding off the chains and flicking the deadbolt before Gill steps inside. When he looks over at me, blue eyes sparking, I feel a little thrill of fear inside my chest and can only wonder how much of my story he managed to overhear.

CHAPTER

Ten

"Ooh!" Solène exclaims as I turn the page in the magazine and her fingers trail across the sea of colorful dresses. *"Je les aime tous." I love them all.*

I shake my head.

"Nope," I say, leaning my head against hers. "You know the rule. You have to pick one." I sit up and laugh as she pouts her lips and shakes her dark curls out. We're almost a full week into this mess, but at least we've got the basics back—underwear, pajamas, toothbrushes, a curling iron for Solène. I can't believe she's nine and already curling her hair, but I roll with it. I suppose I really don't have any room to talk. I snuck red lipstick to school when I was her age and got in trouble from the teacher. My mom, though, she didn't mind. No, I don't think she wanted her nine year old wearing grenadine red lip color, but she smiled softly and showed me how to put it on properly, and then she explained that I was still a kid and that I should enjoy being one while I could.

I miss her so bad it hurts and find my fingers unconsciously drawn to the diamond pendant hanging around my neck.

"This one. Don't you think it would bring out my eyes?" Solène blinks her long dark lashes at me, showing off those pretty cornflower blue eyes of hers. "Papa, don't you think I'd look pretty in this?" She lifts up the magazine and shows it to Cliff. He immediately takes his eyes off the TV and gives Solène his full attention, reaching out to grab the magazine between his fingers.

"Oh, that one is beautiful," he tells her, examining the page with true interest. "The skirt's a little short though."

"Papa!" Solène whines, laying her head back against the couch. I take that moment to glance surreptitiously towards the formal dining room where Gill sits, watching us. Our eyes meet, but he doesn't look away, challenging me with that sharp gaze of his. For the past week, he's been avoiding me, and when I track him down to ask questions, he gives me vagaries that make my teeth hurt. I'd think something was wrong if I wasn't so sure that he just didn't want to talk to me anymore. *How much of that conversation between Aveline and me did he hear?* I feel like it must've been more than just a word or two.

I stare back at him as Solène presents a brilliant feminist argument in favor of the dress that far exceeds her years, and challenge him with the look. *Why are you staring, you prick? Do you wish you had a family? Do you regret abandoning us all those years ago? Well, fuck you.*

More and more lately, I notice Gilleon watching, cataloguing, surveying. He keeps examining Solène, examining me. I said all he had to do was open his eyes and look; I'm terrified that he's looking now.

X X X

The next day, Gill interrupts me in the middle of a horror movie, coming into the living room and sitting on the coffee table. He's wearing a red T-shirt, black jeans, and a black shoulder holster. I look at the gun tucked away in it and then back at his face, pressing pause on my movie.

"When's Solène's birthday?" he asks me, looking right into my face. My hand clenches on the remote and my breath comes in shallow bursts. I know Gill notices, know it with every fiber of my being, and suddenly I'm scared. Terrified. Sweat beads on my forehead and my mouth goes dry.

"Why?" I ask him, brushing some honey gold hair from my face and glancing at the white linen curtains across the room from me. "Is that important somehow?"

"I want to make sure all of my records are straight. I don't have access to her real information anymore since Aveline got to it." Gill reaches into his back pocket and produces a small piece of paper with a date scribbled on it. "Is that right?"

September seventeenth.

"That's right," I say, staring at the false birthday I had Cliff give Gilleon when he told him he was adopting a baby girl. If that birthday were true though, it would make Solène a nice round nine years old instead of the nine and a half she really is.

"Hmm." Gill stands up and moves away, back into the dining room, sitting down at his computer with a clenched jaw. *April seventeenth.* That's Solène's real birthday. Six months after Gilleon left.

I stare at the TV, but I can barely get my shaking hands to press the play button on the remote. I don't care about my movie anymore, don't care about anything but keeping my secret.

I'm scared.

I'm really and truly scared.

I don't want Gill to know about my daughter.

My daughter. No. That's not right. *Our* daughter.

Ours.

Mine and Gill's.

✗ ✗ ✗

My heart is light, like a butterfly, resting softly inside my chest. Yes, it's tinged with a bit of sadness, with memories of my mother and her gentle smile, the way she wore her hair in a loose chignon and sung to herself when she was making coffee in the mornings. She'd have loved to be here today, shopping for the baby, sitting across from me at lunch, picking out odds and ends for my surprise plan for Gill.

But she isn't here and that's okay. I'm young, in love, in Paris, and I have a whole gaggle of girlfriends around me, primed with inappropriate commentary that sounds even more vulgar when it's in the language of love.

"Tu me fais bander," my friend, Katriane, says, doing

122

a very poor imitation of Gilleon's voice. *"Let me take you over the dresser and I'll show you how hard I really am."*

"You think Gill's going to tell me about how hard he is and then fuck me? That *is your best guess on how he's going to respond to finding baby clothes and stuffed animals on our bed?"* She shrugs and pouts her pale pink lips at me, her lightly accented English a beautiful lilt against the murmur of the city streets.

"It's how I'd respond, were I male. Fortunately for us all, I am not." I roll my eyes and allow her to open the door to the next shop, ushering me inside ahead of everyone else.

"He bought you that beautiful ring," Jacqueline says, keeping the conversation in English for my benefit. I've been living here for four years now, and my French is pretty damn good, but I still prefer to speak in my native language. I mean, who doesn't? Normally, I speak French with the girls, but today's been declared a national holiday by the four of them—the day that I announced I was pregnant.

It took me a while to figure it out, longer than it should've, but things with Gill are always a whirlwind of love and sex and witty repartee, that I hadn't realized what might be happening until a few weeks ago. The news has been sitting on the tip of my tongue since then, on the verge of breaking out at any moment, but Gilleon's been so preoccupied with work that I didn't want to waste it. I want to savor the moment, like I've savored all the other wonderful milestones in our lives: the day I first met him, when we first kissed, when we got our own apartment.

I surreptitiously run my thumb over my engagement ring, a gorgeous vintage piece with an infinity twist on either side of the center diamond. The whole front half looks like it's paved in jewels, frosted in gems that sparkle when I move. It's more than I ever could've hoped for—especially because of the expression on Gill's face when he gave it to me. I could see the excitement there, the love, the promise of a good life.

"Stop daydreaming and let's shop," Jacqueline says, grabbing my arm and tugging me away to browse rack after rack of clothes, row after row of furniture, and a whole host of accessories that I don't even begin to know what to do with. Oh well. Gill and I can worry about the practical stuff later. Right now, this mission is just for fun, for me to grab whatever catches my fancy. When I get home, I'm going to lay it all out on our bed and wait for Gill to come home.

As soon as he sees it, he'll know.

I smile to myself and let loose, emerging from the store with a brown shopping bag full of assorted clothes and toys. My friends walk me home, kiss my cheeks and bid me au revoir.

I head upstairs, a bounce in my step, a smile locked onto my face that I just can't seem to get rid of. And who'd want to anyway?

I smooth my hands down the front of my black sheath dress, just in case Gill's already home.

"Gilleon?" I ask, setting my bag down on the floor

near the front door. *"Are you home?"* When he doesn't answer, a little thrill of excitement shoots through me. *Good.* I can set up my surprise and be waiting with a glass of wine and a sexy set of lingerie on before he gets here. Maybe Katriane is right—well, sort of. I don't think Gill will launch into a five minute description of his rigid cock before he takes me in his arms, but I can definitely see us both shoving the baby stuff to the floor for a quickie.

I move into the bedroom and reach back to unzip my dress when I see the note. I don't think anything is up at first—Gill's always leaving little love letters around the apartment. So I take my dress off, hang it back up in the closet—this little black number is designer wear, a gift from Cliff, and is definitely dry clean only.

I slip my heels off next and tuck them away before sitting down on the end of the bed and grabbing the note. I expect something like 'Love ya, See you tonight', but end up staring down at a full page of writing.

It doesn't start off well.

Regi,

Please forgive me for what I'm about to do.

Before you read this, I want you to take a deep breath and think of all the wonderful times we've had together. I have loved—and still love—you with a passion that's difficult to express in words. Still, I'm going to try because this could be the last time I ever get to tell you.

You're strong, strong enough to get through this. I

know it won't be easy because it isn't easy for me either, but you'll survive and be even better for the experience. I know that because it's one of the things I love about you; your ability to survive, to thrive through the most difficult of times is unmatched. If I could, I'd stay by your side forever.

But it won't work; we won't work.

I can't tell you why now, but I hope you can believe that I have no other choice.

I won't forget for even a single second how good it feels to talk to you, to hold you, to lay next to you at night and wake up to you in the morning. Just know that I'm thinking of you always.

I'm leaving Paris today, and I won't be back anytime soon—maybe not ever. One day, I hope we can reconnect, look back on this moment as a dark splotch in an otherwise bright history together. Just so you know I'm safe and well, I've given Cliff my new number and address, but I've asked him not to give either to you. It's better this way. If I see you, talk to you, after all of this, I might not have the strength to do what needs to be done.

If I do that, I'll be condemning us both and I love you too much for that.

Stay safe, be happy, and don't let this ruin the beautiful future I see for you, Regi.

I love you, and I always will.

Gilleon.

My heart refuses to comprehend the words that are

etched into the paper in my hand.

I curl my fingers tighter until the paper crumples, the ink blurring into jagged lines as I squeeze and don't stop until the page is contained in my shaking fist.

"Gilleon?" I ask, like he can hear me, wherever he is. I reach up suddenly, finding tears on my cheeks that weren't there before. I stare at the droplets on my fingertips, sitting there alone on the end of that bed in my bra and panties, a baby in my belly and a ring on my finger. Two blessings that suddenly feel like curses in light of the letter. "This can't be happening."

I shake my head and put my hand up to my forehead, my thoughts spinning dizzily. No. I don't believe any of this. There's no way that Gill, my Gill, would do something like this. Five years we've been together— since I was sixteen years old. I don't know anything else, don't need to know anything else. I love Gill and he loves me. That's all there is to it, right?

I open the letter back up and read it again. And again. And again.

When I hear a knock at the front door, my heart soars and I wipe the tears away with my arm.

Gilleon.

That has to be him there, waiting for me outside, ready to apologize for the cruel prank he's pulling.

I stand up and snatch my robe from the bathroom, throwing it on and hurrying to the front door as I belt it closed.

"Gill?" I don't even bother to check and see who's outside, throwing open the door and finding Cliff

127

standing there, his face broken and just as confused as my own.

"Regina," he says, holding up a letter of his own. I lift up my own hand, realizing suddenly that I'm still holding the damn thing. Cliff nods once and steps inside, closing the door behind him.

"Papa?" I ask, not understanding, needing to, falling into a million jagged pieces that I'm afraid I'll never be able to put back together again.

I take a step back, clamping my hand across my mouth to hold back a scream. I'm not sure if it's sadness or rage or both that wants to come crashing out. Cliff takes a step forward and bumps into the shopping bag, knocking it over and spilling a dozen useless items across the floor. He pauses to pick up a stuffed green cat and a tiny yellow and white striped one-piece.

"Oh, Regi," he breathes, dropping them both to the floor and putting his arms around me. "We're going to be okay, you and me," he whispers, "I promise."

I want to believe him. I do. I want to, but I don't.

The love of my life, the beat of my heart, the other half to my soul, he's gone.

Nothing will ever be okay again.

✕ ✕ ✕

Gill's waiting for me outside my room the next morning, leaning against the door in his usual wear—T-shirt, jeans, gun—his eyes hooded and thoughtful. When he turns to look at me, I feel his gaze scorching through me, burning away the navy jumpsuit I slipped into this morning, his attention lingering on my cleavage, on the curve of my waist, on the cutout detail that exposes my bare back as I turn and close the door softly behind me.

I'd been hoping to get up early enough to catch Aveline before she left this morning, taking last night's shift from Gill so he could finally get some sleep. So far, whoever this Karl guy is, he hasn't sent any more of his people after us. I'm hoping at this point that it was just a random fluke. A fluke that almost ended with me getting a bullet to the head, but hey, if it doesn't happen again, I'm willing to overlook that.

"*Bonjour,*" I say, smiling tightly as I cross my arms over my midsection and wait for Gill to say something, explain what he's doing here. When he doesn't respond, I decide to ask. "*Qu'est ce que tu veux?*"

"I wanted to talk to you about something," he says, his voice tight and laced with an emotion that I can't quite place. It's not jealousy this time, although I'm still trying to figure out what that was all about. It sounds a little bit like ... anger. I reach up and adjust my messy bun, noticing that Gill can't take his eyes off my face, my lips. I guess the haul of MAC makeup that I had Aveline bring over for me is worth its weight in gold.

I went simple but dramatic today—a little bit of liner, a dust of blush, and red, red lips. Pretty sure that's what's really getting Gill's attention.

"Is this about a cell phone?" I tell him, raising my brows. "Because Fia Levine could really use one to call her sister." Gill waves his hand dismissively, like he doesn't give two shits about my desperate need to talk to Anika or Leilani. I stare at him, at the preoccupied

129

expression that's taken over his strong face. "Not about a cell phone then."

"I thought you might be open to going to breakfast with me. Aveline'll be here with Dad and Solène." I purse my lips and tuck my hands into the stylish side pockets on the jumpsuit. On my feet, a pair of nude Jimmy Choo pumps stares up at me.

"Gill, every time you ask me to do something with you —take a walk, have a cup of coffee—things seem to go south pretty quick. What'll be different about today?"

"I want to talk about Solène."

Ice travels up my spine, curling at the base of my neck and giving me an instant headache.

I stand completely still, refusing to let my body language give anything away. *You son of a bitch.* For years, *years,* I wanted Gill to look at our daughter and see *us* in her face, her eyes, her hair, her intelligence, her bravery. I wanted him to know without my having to tell him. I know it might seem selfish, foolish even, but knowing Gill the way I do, it shouldn't have been hard for him to figure out. He didn't *want* to see it.

The question is: does he see it now? Does he see *her* now?

"What do you want to talk about? Did something happen?" I ask, knowing full well that's not what this is about. Gill stands up straight, a veritable badass with muscles and a gun, a cold stare and a ruthless heart. I know it's ruthless because I've seen the edge of that cutting blade hit me right in the neck.

"I don't want to have this conversation here," he says,

his voice little more than a rough whisper. I study his clenched fists, the rise and fall of his chest as he takes several deep breaths. If he's finally figured out that Solène's his daughter, he sure is having a strange reaction to the news. Gilleon's on edge, obviously, but there's something else there, that weird anger I keep picking up on. "And anyway, I'd love to take you to breakfast."

Love to.

What do I make of that?

I reach up and touch the diamond pendant for reassurance. I wish I were half the mother that my mom was. Even if Anika might disagree with me, I know Elena always did what she thought was best. Letting my sister move in with her grandma, that almost killed her. But she did it because she didn't want Anika to hurt anymore, didn't want the sting of losing our father to snap back and blind her a second time. My sister didn't want a stepfather; I don't know how I'd live without him.

"I'm not sure what you mean by that," I begin, trying to gauge Gill's facial expression. He holds my gaze, but gives me nothing to go off of. I lift my hands up in surrender and let them fall to my sides. "But I'm up, I'm hungry, and I'm willing to hear what you have to say."

I can be an adult about this, can handle it like the thirty-one year old capable adult that I am.

"Thank you, Regina," Gill says, his voice rough, sliding across my skin and diving deep until I can almost feel the words reverberating in my bones. He tries on a smile, but it doesn't reach his eyes, giving me a sad, sad glimpse of the teenage boy that he used to be. "I'll try

131

not to be an asshole today, okay?"

"Okay," I say with a false smile of my own. Deep down though, a tiny thread of hope stirs inside of me. If he has made the connection about Solène, maybe he'll handle it like an adult, too. Maybe, just maybe, we can conquer this once and for all.

It'd be a good start for my new life—a great start.

XX XX XX

The car ride to the restaurant is a bust, a void of sound and conversation that makes my ears ring. *Talk to me, damn it,* I think, wishing Gill would just bring up the subject and get it out there for us to discuss. I want to know what he's thinking, if this is all really about what I think it is. There's no way I'm bringing it up first.

I glance over at Gilleon, at the tightness in his jaw, at his hands wrapped so firmly around the steering wheel. There's that anger again, showing in his face as it bubbles up inside of him again. It seems like the more he thinks about this, the worse he starts to feel. That's what happens when you internalize feelings like that.

I am going to handle this situation with grace and poise. I'm calm and I'm ready for this.

I touch the diamond pendant again.

"That was your mom's, right?" Gill says finally, snapping the bubble of silence wide open. Sounds rush in around me—the whir of cars outside the window, the splatter of rain on the roof, the gentle buzz of the radio in the background.

"It was," I say, leaning back against the seat and closing my eyes against Gill's scent. Even after all this

132

time, he still smells like bergamot oil, like a really good cup of earl gray tea. Strong, masculine, but with this undertone of sweetness that makes my mouth water. Shit. "Why do you ask?"

"I remember her wearing it is all."

And then he stops talking again, bringing up our past like it's nothing, and dropping it just as quick.

It's a relief when we finally get to the restaurant, and I scramble out of the car before Gill can come over and try to open my door. He did it when we got in and it just made things that much more awkward. I don't want to see any shallow examples of chivalry from him.

"Two please," he tells the waitress when we step inside the café. She nods and takes us to a table in the back, right up against a bank of windows overlooking the street. Plants hang from the steel beams overhead and crowd the boxes in the corners, filling the room with a sweet, floral scent. The floors are cement, the tabletops made of reclaimed wood. Yep. We're definitely in the corner of eco-friendly and industrial chic. *Welcome to Seattle.*

I order an espresso and then lean back in my chair, letting my eyes trail over the restaurant. Gill is definitely getting some looks, but so am I. I wonder if we make an interesting couple? I always thought we complemented each other well.

"The omelets are damn good," Gill says as he copies my pose, leaning back and acting like it's no big deal that he's got a gun tucked under his black jacket. He knows exactly how to sit so that the front of the coat gapes open, but the weapon stays invisible. He even pushed the sleeves up to his elbows, making it seem like the jacket's a fashion statement instead of a necessity.

We stare at each other again, something we seem to be doing a lot of lately. It's hard to explain, but seeing someone you used to know so well after so long, after they've become a stranger, it's a weird feeling. I imagine it'd be easier to start a brand new relationship than repair one that's deteriorated to this level.

"It's been good having you around," Gill says and my lips purse. "Even if you hate me," he adds which just irritates me. I know he's trying to make light of his first comment, but it isn't working.

"I don't hate you, Gill. I just don't understand you, don't understand what it is that you want from me. You keep sending mixed signals. One moment, you couldn't care less, and the next, you're just staring at me."

"Is Solène your daughter?" he asks suddenly, and I feel lightheaded, like the restaurant is spinning in circles around me and I'm the one sitting still. Gill stares hard at me, his blue eyes open and locked onto their target. "I've been watching you with her, and I can't get past the resemblance."

"I ..." It takes me a moment to figure out the expression on his face, understand the anger resting there, realize what his exact words were. *Your daughter.* He doesn't think she's his. Whether it's because of the false birthday or because he's so unwilling to face the truth of his life, I don't know.

I feel sick.

I stand up and the room shifts around me.

"Please don't walk way," Gill says just before the waitress sets my espresso and his orange juice down on the table. She gives me a look and then scurries away like she'd rather not get involved. I decide to sit down, but not because Gill asked me to, because I have nowhere else to go. I don't have a car, don't have the money he promised me yet, don't have a phone.

"What are you asking exactly?" I ask, my voice breathy.

"Is Solène your biological daughter?"

"Yes." That one single word burns across my tongue as I say it, and I find that I can't look at Gill, can only look down at the place setting in front of me, the cup and plate with the word *espresso* stamped all over them in cursive writing.

When I glance up, I see Gill nodding, the muscles in his shoulders tight and stiff, his teeth clenched.

"I thought so," he says and my stomach drops. I pick up my coffee with shaking fingers and take a scalding sip, not caring that it sears over my tongue. "I'm sorry to call you out like that, but I'm ... I'm not usually this caught off guard by things." *How's this for catching you off guard—she's your daughter, too, you asshole.* "Maybe this wasn't the right way to go about it, but I needed to hear it from you."

"Damn straight it wasn't the right way," I whisper fiercely, my temper flaring as I clench my own teeth and squeeze the espresso mug in my hand. "You brought me here to interrogate me about it, not to talk."

"I'm not interrogating you, Regi. I'm just surprised is all."

"Surprised?" I blurt, feeling a rush of white hot pain as I switch my gaze to his tattoos instead of his face. I can't look at him anymore without feeling sick. "How are you surprised? You've been gone for ten years, Gill. You don't know anything about me. I could have a half dozen kids for all you'd know."

"I ..." Gill sounds like he's about to say something and then changes his mind. "I just didn't expect you to go out and meet someone three months after I left."

I stare at him across the table, completely aghast at his statement and his reasoning.

Gill is mad. He's upset. He's jealous. And all because he thinks I went out and fucked some guy a few months after *he* abandoned me.

"You really have changed, haven't you?" I say, standing up again. I have to fight the urge to throw my espresso in his face. But I, I am a fucking grown-up, and I will handle this like one. "The Gilleon Marchal I used to know was kind and sensitive and strong, not some stone hearted asshole who was quick to judge and even quicker to condemn." I spread my fingers and stare at my palm for a moment before turning and walking away, right out the front doors of the restaurant and into the rain.

Droplets splatter against my hair, against my bare arms and the exposed skin on my back, but I don't care. I step out of my heels, grab them, and start walking down the street, right through the puddles and the scattered yellow leaves.

I know the second he starts after me, can feel his presence like a whirlwind chasing along the sidewalk.

"Regi, wait," he says, catching up to me and slinging his jacket over my shoulders. "Please don't walk away. I'm sorry I said that. I ..." His jaw clenches again and the next words come out in a low growl. "I'm just jealous."

"Jealous?" I ask as I stop and turn to look at him, at the dark strands of hair plastered across his forehead from the rain. "Why would you be jealous? You left me, Gilleon. You walked away from what we had and never looked back."

"Oh, I looked back plenty," he snarls, and I can't tell if it's me he's angry with—or himself. I watch as droplets of water cling to his muscles, sliding across the black and gray of his tattoos, leaving them shining and stark in the clear morning air. "I've been watching you for years, Regi."

"And that's not creepy at all," I say, taking a step back and giving him a look that I hope showcases how bizarre I find that last statement. "What the hell does that even mean?"

"It means," he says, taking a step towards me, water running down that perfectly straight nose of his, catching on his lips, "that no matter how far I run or how fast I go, what country I'm in, or what the job is, there's always been one constant in my life."

I can't look at Gill's face right now, can't take the cracks that are showing in that cold, professional facade

C. M. Stunich

of his. In this moment, I can hear the echo of the old Gilleon, the one I fell in love with. The sound's almost too painful for me to bear.

"What are you trying to say?" I ask him, my voice catching. My body's painfully aware of his nearness, of the sharp contrast between the cold of the rain and the warmth of his skin. The water sticks Gill's shirt to his chest, highlighting that perfect body of his.

"You're my constant, Regi," he growls, clutching at the fabric over his heart. His strong fingers twist the material, turning his knuckles white, emphasizing the straight, sharp lines of his tattoos. I watch him breathing hard, drawing in rain drenched breaths, but I can't make myself take a single gulp of air. My chest is still, my heartbeat slowing. "I never forgot you for one single moment, never spent a single day without wishing I was with you, without missing you so bad it hurt."

Before I can even move, Gill is stepping towards me, cradling the back of my head in his strong hand, pulling my face up to his. My lashes flutter and my body betrays me as I open my mouth and feel his hot and insistent against me, his tongue sliding between my lips. Gill's other arm encircles my waist and pulls me towards him, drawing me up onto my bare toes.

My high heels fall to the sidewalk as my fingers go slack and my mind goes blank, completely and utterly blank. I can't think beyond Gill's kiss, against the heat of his hands, or the quietly restrained strength in his arms.

Memories reach up and grab me, sending me to a hundred other moments, a thousand other seconds, reminding me how good it feels to be with the person you love—even if they've done you wrong, even if you know it can't work out, even if you know it'll all end in heartbreak.

Gill tastes exactly like I remember him, our bodies molding together like we were made for each other, like all the days that've passed between then and now don't mean a thing. I exist in spans and segments, pockets of time where Gilleon and I are together. The rest just seems to fade away until it doesn't matter anymore.

Water sluices between our lips, sliding down my bare chest and underneath my jumpsuit. Each drop is intense, painfully so, dragging itself down my heated skin until I'm panting and shaking, until my knees feel weak and my fingers slide up and curl in Gill's soggy T-shirt of their own accord.

A soft growl escapes Gill as he pulls me tighter against him, and I moan, not caring that I'm standing right there in the middle of the sidewalk, rain plastering bits of hair to my face, sticking my clothes to my body. They feel stifling, suffocating, and I can't wait to tear them off.

Tear them off?

A small part of me—a *very* small part—snaps to and sends a blurry haze of memories crashing against my psyche. *Coming home and finding our apartment empty, my fingers clutching the letter so tightly it crumpled, setting up a crib in Cliff's spare bedroom, naming my baby alone and leaving her with her grandfather because I'd let myself feel weak and small.*

I don't feel weak and small anymore.

I break the kiss and push back, almost stumbling when Gill releases his grip on me. My knees are still like jelly and my brain is only working at half capacity, but I know beyond a shadow of a doubt that this right here, this can't happen. It won't be good for anybody, least of all me.

"Some mistakes are too big to be erased with the shadow of a promising kiss."

I wipe my mouth on my arm, like that'll somehow make me forget the heat and the passion in Gill's lips, his face, the shockingly bare emotions flashing in his gaze. I look up into those eyes, like the surface of a lake on a clear day, right before the clouds roll in and ruin everything.

I turn away.

Besides, didn't he just accuse me of running off and having a kid with some guy right after he left? Even if I had, it would've been completely in my right, completely understandable, and absolutely none of his business.

The worst part of it all? The fact that it is entirely and completely part of his business.

Merde. Shit.

"Can you take me home, please?" I ask, turning away and bending down to pick up my heels. I don't acknowledge his words—*I'm jealous*—or his confession—*you're my constant*—because I can't. I can't do this right now, can't do this ever.

He left.

And he didn't come back for *over ten years*.

That's a long time to make someone wait.

140

CHAPTER
Eleven

"I think Gill's trying to get back together with me," I blurt as I stare across the breakfast table at Cliff. Aveline's in the dining room working furiously at her computer while Solène naps on the couch. I have no idea where Gilleon is. Since yesterday's ... fiasco, I'm going to call it, I haven't seen him much except when he passes in and out of the house on business.

Until this morning, I didn't have the courage to tell my stepfather the story. Now that I have, I can see why I waited. The look on his face is hard to interpret. I watch in tense anticipation as he rubs at the gray stubble on his chin.

"He ... he really had the nerve to take you out, ask you that, and then respond the way he did? I'm ... that boy

..." Cliff runs his hands down his face. His eyes, so like Gill's, tell me a thousand times over how sorry he is. But I asked a long time ago that my stepfather stop apologizing for his son. "I oughta take him over my knee and give him the belt the way I never did when he was a kid. Maybe that's what's wrong with him?"

I laugh and cover my mouth with a hand.

"Papa, as much as I'd love to see that, I have a feeling he could bench press both of us at the same time. Not sure you'd be able to subdue him."

"Ah, but you'd be surprised how a father's wrath can transform a man. Parents have been known to lift cars when their children are trapped underneath. When a child's in trouble—no matter how old they are—a dad can find the strength if he needs it to do anything for them."

"But Gill's not in trouble," I say, wagging a finger at him.

"No, but you are," he says, reaching over the table and taking my hand. My heart warms and a smile spreads over my lips.

"I'm not in trouble though, Papa. Really."

"If you kissed him back, then I'd say you are. You're not truly thinking of taking him back?"

"No!" I say, setting my coffee down with a thump. It sloshes over the edge and onto the table, some beautiful gray and blue and green striped thing made out of reclaimed wood and polyed until it shines. "Of course not. And I mean, I'm not even sure if that's what he was really saying."

"It's what he was saying," Aveline says from behind

me, making me jump as she steps into the kitchen, her red hair braided down her back, looking fierce in a black tank and jeans. She reminds me of Lara Croft or something, some badass video game chick. I stare at her back as she pours coffee and then turns around to look at me. "For that emotionless robot to say *anything* like what you described is a miracle. I've known Gill for about, uh, I don't know, six years now, and I've never seen him act like he gives two shits about anything at all."

"Thanks for eavesdropping," I say, picking up a croissant from the center of the table and biting into it. Aveline shrugs and pauses as the front door opens and the sound of Gill's footsteps move towards the kitchen.

Even though I can't see him, I can feel him pausing in the archway behind me.

"Good morning," he says, his words firm but also, somehow, tentative, like he knows he's the current subject of conversation. I give Cliff a look across the table that says *please don't say anything,* and he nods at me, almost imperceptibly. I'm sure Gill notices though. He can pick up on stuff like that but somehow can't seem to see that the little girl with dark hair and blue eyes is his daughter. Go figure.

"Good morning," Aveline says when neither Cliff nor I respond.

"*Bonjour,*" Solène says, surprising me. I turn around and smile at her as she steps into the kitchen and around Gilleon, moving to the table to steal a croissant. "It's always polite to greet someone when they're making an effort," she scolds, giving me and Cliff looks.

"You're very right," Cliff tells her, looking up at his son as he enters the room. "*Bonjour, mon fils. Comment ça va?*" Gill pauses next to the sink and stares at his dad for a long moment before flashing me a look. It only lasts a split second, but I have a feeling he knows I've confessed everything to his father. It's no secret that Cliff and I are close.

"Fine, thanks," he says, his voice thick with suspicion as he approaches the fridge and opens it, reaching in and grabbing some kind of smoothie drink in a bottle. "I'm still looking into the shooting on Regina, but there's something about it that doesn't make any sense. I know you're all *anxious* to get on with your lives," Gill stresses the word anxious enough that I can tell he's tense, "but you'll have to bear with me a little longer."

"It's not a problem," Cliff says, smiling tightly and then refocusing his attention on Solène. "You like living here, don't you?" he asks, reaching out and tugging down the black and white striped sweater dress that she's thrown on over red leggings. That girl has a fashion sense that's all her own, always one step ahead of the crowd. "You told me last night that this house has a positive vibe."

"She said that?" I ask, my lips quirking up in a smile.

"*Oui,*" Solène says, finishing her croissant and then reaching for another. "I can feel the history here." She pauses and cups a hand around her ear. "Listen, the walls talk. Can you hear what they're saying?"

"Enlighten us," I say, parking my chin on my hand and raising a brow in question.

"*Il n'y a pas plus sourd que celui qui ne veut pas entendre,*" Solène responds proudly, winking and saluting us before disappearing back into the living room. Cliff and I get a chuckle out of that, and I can't seem to resist glancing over to gauge Gill's reaction. A small smile teases his lips before he turns away and opens a cabinet next to the sink, searching around inside for something.

"And that means ..." Aveline asks, gesturing at me for an explanation.

Gill shuts the cabinet and turns, a granola bar in one hand, answering before I get the chance to.

"It more or less translates to: *no one is as deaf as the man who will not listen.*"

I can almost swear he's talking about himself when he says it.

✗ ✗ ✗

The next night, I'm parked in my now usual spot on the couch when Gill comes in and tosses something at me. I catch it out of reflex and feel a surge of joy when I see that it's a new cell phone.

"Thank God," I groan, swiping my finger across the lock screen and feeling my stomach drop when I see that the background has already been changed from the default. *I'm Sorry, Can You Ever Forgive Me?* is printed in a speech bubble next to a little girl in a large floppy hat. She's bending down, a flower clutched in hand, and offering it to a sad faced basset hound. The whole thing is in black and white and reeks of old school Gilleon. He used to grab those sappy old fashioned cards from the store and scribble silly things in them before slipping

145

them under my bedroom door.

My chest tightens, but when I turn to look at him, his face is pinched and unhappy. *What's going on now?* I wonder as I wait for him to explain. He's still standing by the front door, eyes tight and mouth set in a thin line.

"You can call whoever you want," Gill tells me and then turns, giving me his full attention. His expression shifts from angry to ... sad. That can't be good, can it? "Do you mind if I sit down a moment?" I nod, wary of what's to come, and gesture to the overstuffed armchair that Cliff's claimed as his own. Right now, though, he's upstairs sleeping and I don't think I can handle having his son any closer than three feet away.

"Everything alright?" Aveline asks as she walks in and pauses, arms crossed over her ample chest. As soon as she sees Gill's face, she nods once, and turns back to head into the kitchen. The hell is going on here?

"Gill, you're scaring me," I tell him, but he swallows once and lifts a hand, palm up.

"I have everything under control," he tells me, but those words only serve to further freak me out.

"What is there to have under control?" I start thinking about the authorities, about them zoning in on this place, surrounding us with SWAT team members or something. I mean, how serious is an international jewelry heist anyway? Ugh. I sit up straight and tuck some blonde hair behind my ear. "Tell me, Gilleon. I have a right to know."

"You do," he says, and I breathe a small sigh of relief that I won't have to wrestle with his stubbornness today.

He's wearing his gun again, right out in the open in a shoulder holster. Seems to be a normal part of the uniform as of late. Aveline tells me that the neighbors all think Gill's a detective who does a lot of undercover work. Go figure. "But I have good and bad news. Which one do you want first?"

"Always the good," I say, because the good can always temper the bad. I don't want my happy news tainted and tossed in as an afterthought. I clutch my cell in my lap and meet his eyes, relieved that he's decided to treat me like an adult for once. I know how stingy Gill can be with information.

"You can call your family, give them the story we originally agreed on." I nod, trying to remember all the details. Knowing Gill, he's got some dossier somewhere that outlines it all. "You can even call your friends in Paris if you want." He takes a deep breath and closes his eyes for a moment. When he opens them, I can almost swear they've darkened a shade or two. "But you might want to wait a while longer. I'll let you make that decision when you hear the rest of the story." I nod and wet my suddenly dry lips. On the positive side, Gill's being respectful enough to include me in the current goings-on. On the other hand … if that's his positive news, then what's the bad? "As far as the authorities," he continues without changing his wary expression, "you can leave that concern at the door. We're in the clear."

"Oh my God." I put a hand to my chest, feeling a huge weight lift off my shoulders. No authorities? How? How does someone just get away with a haul worth over a hundred million dollars? "Are you serious, Gill?" I swing my feet to the floor and lean forward, a thrill of excitement shooting through me. Guess all of the sacrifices were worth it—leaving everything behind, vanishing without a word, letting Aveline wipe us from the system.

Gill smiles softly at me, but his fingers are curled around the arms of the chair, the tattoos on his index and middle finger blue-black in the glow from the table lamp. I'd been reading when he came in, some terribly depressing literary fiction that Cliff had recommended. Spoiler: everyone dies at the end. I'm not even entirely certain how that happens since the whole thing is about a group of ladies who own a yarn shop ...

"There can't be any bad news with all of that good," I tell him, still smiling broadly. "Now I can stop waking up to the neighbor's shouting. When she really gets going, I start having dreams about the CIA breaking into my room and finding me in my underwear."

Gill laughs and runs his fingers through his hair, watching me carefully, studying my face.

"Do you accept my apology?" he asks, changing the subject. I pause for a moment and look down at the phone again. It's a sappy, stupid apology, but it feels sincere. Anyway, I'm not one for holding grudges.

"While I still feel what you did was inappropriate," I decide to clarify here because, honestly, that kiss was half me, "taking me out and questioning me like that, making the accusation that you did, I do forgive you, Gill. Let's just forget it, okay?" I set the phone on the coffee table and lean back into the pillows.

Maybe I should tell him about Solène? Maybe that's what a truly mature person would do, someone who's completely and utterly moved on?

But I can't.

I know Gill, how perceptive he is, how smart. And I know he knows me, even if it's been a while since we last saw each other. He should be able to figure it out. I just want to see him put the effort in.

Why?

My subconscious asks a question that my conscious can't seem to answer.

"Thank you, Regi. Really. I didn't mean for things to go the way they did yesterday." He pauses for a moment, thoughts flickering over an unusually expressive face. When his jaw sets firm, I have to brace myself for what's going to come next. "But I did mean what I said about ... about being jealous. And about you being my constant."

I take a breath to stop him before he really gets going, but he leans forward, boots squeaking against the hardwood floor, muscles sliding beneath his skin, tattoos dark and mesmerizing.

"And I meant that kiss."

"Gilleon."

"I want to talk about what happened."

"We can talk about the kiss later."

"It's not the kiss I want to talk about," he says with an intensity in his gaze that makes me shiver. "I want to talk about the day I left."

My heart turns to ice in my chest, and I can't seem to

hold his eyes, so I look away, at the rug on the floor beneath the coffee table.

"But right now, I have to tell you the bad news first."

"What could be worse than talking about that day?" I try to make it a joke, but it just sounds sad to me. I smile anyway.

Gill takes a breath, shoulders rising and falling as he sits back and looks at the ceiling for a moment.

"The robbery was never reported to the authorities."

"Never ..." I start and then wrinkle up my brow. "How is that even possible? How does a hundred million in jewels go missing and nobody talks about it?" Gill's good at his job, but not *that* good.

"The reason I hit that store was the same reason you got hired to work at it," he tells me, his voice grave and full of a thousand and one regrets that hang heavy in the air around us. If only the tang of regret could make up for a decade lost. "The man who owns that shop ... he's owned me for the last ten years of my life."

Gill stands up suddenly and buries his fingers in his hair, closing his eyes against a grimace of pain. The expression crosses his face suddenly and without warning, fading away just as quickly. It could be that whatever he's trying to tell me is taking its emotional toll on him, but ...

"Let me see your shoulder," I tell him, standing up and tossing my blanket back on the couch. Gill takes a step back from me, almost like he's afraid of what I'm going to do to him. Silly that, though, because I don't think Gilleon's afraid of anything at all. "Did something

150

happen today?"

"Nothing that I couldn't handle," he says, but he doesn't pull away when I close the distance between us, reaching my hands up and sliding my fingers under the short sleeve of his shirt. It's tighter on this shoulder than the other, something I should've noticed when he first walked in. Underneath the dark blue fabric, a square of white is taped to Gill's skin, just the faintest hint of red peeking through. Obviously the wound's been doctored, probably by someone far more adept at this sort of thing than I am, but I feel my heart start to pick up speed.

"Did you ..."

"I got shot," Gill says, matter-of-factly, in a voice I might use if I was telling a girlfriend about a cat scratch. "Well, more like I was grazed by a bullet. It's not a big deal."

He reaches up and takes my hand with such gentleness that my breath hitches. With all of the power in his body, he could snap my fingers with a squeeze of his fist. But he doesn't. And he won't. Not to me anyway. At least, I want to believe that, that some of the old Gill is still in there keeping this new badass persona of his in check.

"It's a big deal, Gilleon," I tell him, wondering if the person who tried to shoot him was the same one that tried to shoot me. "What's going on? Please, I know you like to keep things to yourself, but I have a right to know if there's a serious threat to my family."

"Am I still included in that?" he whispers, his voice far too husky, too intimate for the close space we're currently occupying.

151

I make myself take a step back.

"That's one of those questions that sounds so simple, but in actuality, it's the most complicated thing there is. I don't have an answer for you right now, Gill. I'm sorry."

When I look up at his face, I can see the walls crashing back into place, hiding his emotions away behind a safety blanket of steel.

"I guess it's time for the bad news then?" I ask, trying to smile, to lighten the mood. I feel like my muscles are made of molasses, slow and heavy, refusing to obey my command. Gill stares right back at me, his eyes darkening like the sea before a storm.

"Karl. You've heard the name before. That's the man whose employee took a shot at you. He's got a grudge against me, a hundred million in missing diamonds, and the means to get them back."

CHAPTER
Twelve

"I know you don't want to betray Gill's confidence, but I need to know if I made a mistake in coming here. I ..." I glance back at the hallway door, leaning against the wall in Gilleon's office while I watch Aveline do whatever it is that she does on the computer. "I need to know if dragging my aging stepfather and my daughter to the States is going to get them *killed*." I hiss the last word and then run my hands down my face.

I tried to sleep last night, but couldn't get my eyes to close without a conscious effort. Even then, my brain swam with what-ifs and whys, trying to convince me that this'll all be worth it in the end. Whether that'll be the case or not, I don't know, but what I do need to know is this: why did Gill need my help in the first place. I know why I gave it, but why did he want it? After his cryptic declaration last night, Aveline came into the living room and the two of them started talking security concerns, leaving me to puzzle out his words alone.

So. All I know is this: the man who tried to have me shot has a grudge against Gilleon, a grudge that goes beyond the missing jewelry if my intuition is dead-on. And it usually is.

Aveline pauses, shuts her laptop and then swivels to face me, leaning back and letting her red hair trail across the desk behind her.

"Gill and I, we won't let anything happen to you guys. Besides, Seattle is our home base. We've got more than just me and him on this one. You'll be safe here, even if it is getting a little old, sitting inside all goddamn day." I wonder if she's talking as much about herself with that one as she is me. "Truthfully, I don't exactly know the whole story, only that this job, this heist, it was what Gill needed to break ties with Karl."

I blink in surprise at that one.

"Gill was working with Karl?" I ask, trying to figure out what could've happened for Gilleon to turn on the guy, to decide that involving his family was worth the risk. Or maybe he doesn't think of us as family? Me, I'm just the stepsister/ex-fiancée while Solène ... and Gill barely even keeps in contact with his own father.

If that's the case, what was up with that question last night?

"Yeah, I mean ... I can't tell you any details, but he was working with Karl *and* with us for years. Didn't

154

want to be though. I have no idea what that man held over his head, but it must've been bad for Gill to keep putting up with it."

"So he was like, a double agent or something?"

"Something like that," Gill says, appearing in the doorway like a ghost, a slight smile drifting on his lips. "I see you two are getting along?"

"Well, we both hate you, so it makes it easy for us chicks to chat," Aveline says, smacking her gum and standing up out of the chair. "I'm gonna go do a quick perimeter check, maybe flash my boobs at that nosy neighbor of yours. Every time I walk the property line, she lifts her blinds up and glares at me through the window until I'm done."

Aveline rolls her eyes as I smile and watch her walk out of the office and disappear down the stairs.

"If you have questions," Gill begins, but I shake my head, uncrossing my arms from my chest and letting them fall to my sides. I notice Gilleon's gaze follow the movement, his eyes tracing the line of my body beneath the emerald green sheath dress. His look doesn't stop at the hem, dropping down to the bare curves of my calves and pausing at the sexy black pumps on my feet before he raises his face to meet my gaze.

The attention doesn't go unnoticed by either of us, my body warming and my thighs clenching unconsciously. Old habits are hard to break, and Gill is a gorgeous specimen of humanity. Besides that, his smell is overpowering, simple and spicy and sweet. I want nothing more than to get up on my toes, press my breasts into his chest, and kiss the side of his strong neck, breathe in his smell.

"You can ask me anything," he says and I raise a brow.

"I can ask, but that doesn't mean you'll answer," I say, brushing some of my hair back and watching him take in my makeup—the dewy eyes, the highlights on my cheekbones, the nude lip. Almost impulsively, I suck in a deep breath.

Sex.

That's what it is that's getting between us, twisting things, making it hard to figure out which end is up.

"I'll try," he offers with a slight shrug and a gritting of his teeth when the movement pulls at his injury. "I know I'm more close-lipped than I should be." He forces a more pleasant expression to his face and raises his brows. "Job hazard?" he offers.

"Apparently," I say as he holds out a hand and I almost, almost, *almost* decide to take it.

"I know you're probably dying to get out of the house."

"Are you offering to take me?" I ask as he smiles sadly and drops his hand to his side. We both move towards the door and I watch as he pauses and gestures for me to go first.

"Maybe we could all go out to dinner somewhere tonight? I'll call in some favors and get someone else to watch the house while we're gone. Although we might have to take Aveline." He grimaces and then pauses as Solène comes skidding around the corner and slams right into him.

"*Excusez-moi,*" she breathes as Gill reaches down and steadies her with a hand on either shoulder. "So sorry, Gilleon, please excuse me."

The moment is so innocent, so normal, so unremarkable that I almost don't see it happening.

Gill looks down at Solène and smiles—at first. She gazes right back up at him, completely and utterly unaware that anything significant is happening. Her blue eyes, so like his, sparkle, and her mouth quirks at the corners as she contemplates whatever it is that she's up to today. Dark hair escapes her ponytail and falls across her brow, across the paleness of her skin that's a seemingly perfect mixture of mine and Gill's.

When his eyes widen and his mouth falls at the corners, I know.

He's looking.

"Gilleon," I say, but it's too late.

"When's your birthday, honey?" he asks, trying to keep his voice calm. The muscles in Gill's arms tighten, the tattoos on his skin stark against the taut flesh. Still, he keeps his grip on our daughter gentle. *The truth was only a simple question away.*

"*C'est le dix-septième avril,*" Solène says proudly. "April seventeenth. I'll be ten in only half a year." With one last grin, she excuses herself and takes off towards her bedroom, leaving me a sweaty, shaking mess in the hallway.

"Gilleon," I begin again, but he's just standing there, staring at the floor, a tornado of emotion swirling across his face. I'm not going to apologize, no, or make excuses, but I do feel like I need a chance to explain.

"April ..." he says, his voice a strangled blur as he takes a step back and leans heavily against the railing. I'm almost afraid he's going to topple backwards and fall right down the stairs. When he does lift his eyes to look at me, there's a panic there, the wild fear of a realization come too late.

I'm standing there shaking and having a small panic attack myself, but I don't let it show on my face.

"Solène ..." he says her name like a whisper on the wind, his eyes flickering as he mentally pushes the puzzle pieces into place. We don't break eye contact when he says it. "She's my daughter."

I nod my chin, almost imperceptibly, but that's okay— I'm sure Gill is *really* looking now.

"When you left me, I was pregnant. Actually, funny story, the exact *day* that you left, I was going to tell you. I'd come home from shopping with a whole bag full of fun baby stuff. Was going to leave it on the bed for you to find. Only ... I found a note there instead." I try to keep the bitterness out of my voice, but some creeps in anyway. "And then at the hotel ..." I trail off because he knows. Gill knows exactly what I'm talking about.

A door opens behind me, but I don't turn to look.

"Oh? Something happening out here?" Cliff asks cheerfully. He must know that that something is bad, based on his son's body language, but he comes up to stand next to me, planting a loving kiss on my cheek anyway. "You're white as a ghost."

"You knew about all of this?" Gill asks his father, his

158

voice dropping, the heat of anger creeping into his words. Cliff turns his attention back to Gilleon and raises a graying eyebrow. "My ... you've been raising my daughter all this time and you didn't think to fucking tell me?"

"Whoa there, son," Cliff says, raising his hands palms out. "You need to keep your voice down. Solène doesn't need to hear a bunch of foolish adults hash out their problems, especially when those problems have nothing to do with her."

"Nothing to ... are you fucking losing it, old man?" Gill snarls, his face a wild and unpredictable storm. Holy shit. His gaze flicks back to me, making me take a step back. The strength of feeling in him right now is a dreadfully beautiful sight to behold. I don't know whether I should be glad that he cares so much, or terrified about what he's going to do with this knowledge.

"Our choices weren't her choices," I tell him, crossing my arms over my chest. "Can we go somewhere else and talk?"

Gill runs his hand over his face.

"I can't even fucking goddamn believe this shit," he snarls, shaking his head like that'll clear some of the sharp, violent anger from his expression. Without answering me, he turns and starts down the stairs at a jog, taking two at a time in his rage.

"Don't let him intimidate you," Cliff tells me, reaching down and taking my hand. "He has no right to judge, especially not given the decisions he's made in his life."

I nod and take a deep breath, steeling myself for a

159

conversation I've been waiting over a decade to have.

"I won't."

"Do you want me to come with you?" he asks and I shake my head.

"He'll just yell at you if you do. He wants to take his anger out on someone, but for whatever reason, he seems unwilling to send any my way. I'll talk to him." I give Cliff's hand a squeeze and head down the stairs, past a baffled Aveline and out the back door into the chilly afternoon air. The sun was out earlier, but it seems to have retreated behind some clouds.

Gilleon's on the deck, bent over at the waist, his hands on his knees as he struggles to find his breath.

I watch him cycle through the emotions and thank God that he's not being apathetic about this. If he'd shrugged, acted like it was no big deal, like he didn't give two shits about it, that would hurt. Hell, that might leave a wound that would never stop bleeding.

"Gill, I know I maybe should've had Cliff tell you one of the times you called him or hell, even when we first started talking about doing this job. But I ... At first, I couldn't forgive you for leaving and then later, it just never seemed like the right time. I was such a mess that I couldn't give Solène the life she deserved. Cliff ... he really stepped in and made things good for her." I wait for a response from him, but he's still bent over, his dark hair fluttering in the breeze, orange and yellow and red leaves spinning around the deck at his feet. "It seemed so obvious to me. I felt like ... all you had to do was look, Gill, just like you look at everything else in your life. I wanted you to figure it out, and you did."

More silence.

I shift on my feet, the cold gusts of wind slicing through the thin material of my dress. I'm about to turn around, head back inside, when I hear him speak.

The words are not at all what I expected.

"I'm sorry, Regina," Gill says, standing up, looking me straight in the face. "I am so fucking sorry."

He moves across the deck towards me, booted feet loud against the wood, as I stumble back and bump into the wall.

Gill's face is a broken, shattered maze of glass, jagged pieces of his soul lying everywhere. The skin on his forehead is tense, his eyes wide, like he's fighting against the urge to drop to his knees and weep. I wouldn't believe it if I'd never seen it before, seen it that night on the hotel balcony. Gill is a man, and he's strong, and he's a motherfucking badass, but he knows when it's okay to cry.

He doesn't now, but he does reach out and rub his thumb along the line of my jaw.

"If you'd have known," I start, but my throat catches on the words and they get stuck behind my tongue. I close my eyes and take a deep breath, wetting my lips and trying again. "Would you have come back?"

"No," he whispers, but the answer doesn't make me feel worse—it makes me feel better. I didn't *want* Gill to come back out of a sense of obligation, didn't even want him to come back for our daughter. The only reason I ever wanted Gilleon to come back was for me. I know it sounds selfish, but I think it's okay to think like that. Yes, I love my daughter, but one day, she's going to grow up and fall in love with somebody, start her own family. A partner's supposed to stand there at your side and watch it all unfold, love you more than anything and anyone, give your kid a platform to stand on and a safety net to fall into. "But I would've ... made an effort to see her." His voice is soft, stuffed with secrets. I think he's getting ready to tell me them.

I'm almost scared to hear. What will they change? What will they do to me, as a person? To us. To *us*. If you could really even say there is an *us*.

"If I were a better man, I'd walk away right now, find my head, calm down. Then I'd come back and we'd have a rational, adult conversation." Gill licks his lips. "But I'm not a good man, Regi. I'm a terrible man who's done terrible things. I'm also a man that's still in love with you."

When Gill leans down and captures my lips with his, I could pull away. I could easily push him back, tell him not to touch me ever again, and be done with this whole thing. But I can't. I can't do anything but kiss him back, let his strong, warm arms encircle me and pull me against him.

I curl the fingers of my left hand in his dark hair while my right slides up the firm muscles of his chest, bumping into the shoulder holster and the gun that's tucked away inside it. It should turn me off, remind me of the issues at hand, the reality of the situation, but it doesn't. Instead, it turns me *on*.

There's no waffling on the issue, no panicked thoughts about what might happen after this is over. I don't know about Gilleon, but right now, I'm not in my right mind—my body's in complete control.

When he reaches down and starts unbuckling his belt, I don't stop him, nipping at his bottom lip and tightening my grip on his hair. This isn't about foreplay or fun or even pleasure, this is all about connection.

"Regina," Gill growls against my mouth, the sound curling my spine as I slide my hips forward and grind against him, against the hard bulge in his jeans. He groans in response, shoving up the lacy fabric of my dress until it's bunched up around my hips, leaving the black satin panties underneath exposed to the chilly autumn air. Even that's not enough to wake me up inside, remind me that this is a *really* bad idea, that Gill has too much focus, too much passion, to be dissuaded once he's got something in mind. If that something is getting me back then ... I shouldn't even put myself in the position to deal with that.

But I can't stop.

Gill finishes undoing his pants and lifts me up, slamming my back into the side of the house. With the strength in those arms, that back, his chest, he has absolutely zero problem holding me there while I wrap my legs around him and we tangle tongues, his hard cock pressed tight against the front of my suddenly wet panties.

I run my fingers over his tattoos, over the swirls of black that stand out sharply in the gray gold air of

163

morning. He tenses wherever I touch him, goose bumps rising on his skin, his nipples hard against the tightness of his T-shirt, physical proof of the effect I'm having on him, the same effect that he seems to be having on me.

I reach between us, push my panties aside and guide him to my opening. As soon as I do, Gill's thrusting forward, slamming me into the wall with a growl and a groan that I can't help but echo, biting down on his lower lip to keep my voice down. In the very back of my mind, I'm aware that my daughter, my dad—*our* dad, as creepy as that sounds—and Aveline are inside the house. Not to mention that pesky neighbor across the fence.

Fuck her, I think as Gill's body fills mine, both familiar and foreign all at once. I lock my ankles together behind his back, thanking the heavens above that I was blessed with long legs, and let my head fall back. Gilleon's lips find my throat, kissing and biting as he thrusts deep, his balls pressing tight against me as we grind together in a moment of senseless passion.

It shouldn't be happening, but it is.

I am so going to regret this later. My brain gets that one last jab in before I'm a mess of hormones, a sighing, sweating, tangled mess of heartstrings and sighs, of throaty moans and hitched breathing.

Gill ... he's like an animal, his eyes dark and his body hard beneath my hands, hot and sweaty and wet where we slide together, our bodies joining in a wild frenzy that I haven't felt in years. I've had other lovers since Gilleon, yes, but they were nothing like this, droplets to his storm, a pond to his ocean. I feel like I've spent a decade being eternally thirsty and now I'm drowning, drowning in him and his smell and the way his mouth always tastes bright and fresh like citrus.

My body begins to pulse, my muscles holding tight to Gill, to the long, firm length of him, while his hands cup my ass in a bruising grip that's still only a fraction of his real strength. He holds me up as easily as if I weigh nothing and yet he's still holding back, keeping himself in check.

I can feel the pleasure curling in the base of my spine, crouching there with the same feline grace that I see in Gilleon's every move. It creeps up on me quick, drawing another gasp from my throat as Gill snarls and lifts one hand up, slamming his palm into the wall while he comes, his entire body stiffening even further as I do the exact opposite and relax, letting the pleasure hit me in waves.

The sensation's so intense that I feel dizzy, my vision blurring as I come down from the burst of adrenaline and hormones that are surging through my body, making it difficult to stand when Gill pulls out and sets me gently on the wet surface of the deck.

I fix my panties, pull my dress back into place, and smooth a hand over my hair while Gill turns away, panting and straightening out his own clothing.

When I head over to the back door and move inside, he doesn't follow.

X X X

I take a long, hot bath, my knees up to my chest, arms curled around them as I close my eyes and force my racing thoughts to a crawl. If I let them run wild like that, I'll never get myself together. What just happened between Gill and me, that was good. It was necessary. We were so caught up in all the hormonal bullshit brewing between us that we weren't thinking clearly. Maybe now that we've both gotten some of that weird hate/makeup sex crap out of the way, we can realize the truth of the situation: me and Gill back together, never going to happen. I can only hope that he understands that and stops saying and doing weird shit.

"*Merde,*" I curse, putting my forehead against my knees. Knowing that Gilleon knows about Solène is a weird sensation, one that I'm not even sure I can put a name to. I can't tell if I'm relieved or freaked out. I'd love to talk to someone about this, but I don't know if Aveline's a great option at the moment. The look she threw me when I walked into the kitchen was nothing short of lascivious. Let's just say, avoiding her company has now shot right up to the top of my priority list.

Then again, Gill did say I could call Leilani or Anika. But then he also said I should use caution, that there's a possibility—however small—that Karl might decide it's worth the effort to use them against me, against him, as leverage for the diamonds.

I decide that no matter how conflicted I am, I can't risk them.

"Fuck this," I growl, the sound reminding me of Gill and the wild look on his face while he screwed me against the wall of his 1912 fucking Mount Baker goddamn Colonial. Ehh. The conversation we're going to have when I leave this room, it's not going to be fun, is

166

it? And I can only imagine how Cliff will react when he finds out. Even if I don't intend to tell him, he'll know. He's just like that.

I stand up and grab a towel from the stand under the window, drying off with the plush pink perfection as I try to decide what to wear. Obviously this morning's dress is not an option. I don't know if I'll be able to wear that in front of him ever again, or at least not for a while. And that's assuming it's even clean—I know my panties have certainly seen better days.

I swipe the towel across the mirror and lean in, staring at myself, at the blurry dampness of my reflection, my skin flushed and pink, my lips swollen and my pupils dilated. I'm not even going to give half the credit for that to my bubble bath. Sex with Gill is ... well, it's always been the best. Mathis, and the dozen or so men before him, none of them could hold a candle to my first love, to the stepbrother I never wanted and then grew to never want to live without.

But I learned to. It was one of the hardest things I've ever done, learning to adapt to the absence of his smile, to the coldness of my bed at night, to the quiet in the mornings.

Young love is so manipulative to the heart, promising that if you lose it, if that person leaves, that you will quite literally shrivel up and die. At least, that's what it told me, but I survived, and I'm a better person for it.

However, none of that will stop me from dressing up again, putting on that uniform for life and marching out there looking my best.

I wrap the towel around my body and move into the bedroom, slipping my mother's diamond pendant around my neck and then pausing in front of my closet. I decide to go with another jumpsuit—still sexy, but something with less ... accessibility might be nice. If it takes more effort to get it off, then I'll have more time to talk myself out of it. *Not that I'm going to need it,* I tell myself as I pull the black V-neck off the hanger. In the few minutes it takes me to get dressed, dry my hair, and apply some minimal makeup, I really and truly believe that.

As soon as I step into the hallway, my Oxford blue peep-toe pumps hitting the floor with a clack, I see Gilleon and the entire argument goes completely out the window.

Oh shit, I think as I feel flames tickling my belly, my muscles tightening in anticipation of ... of *nothing* because nothing else is going to happen between us.

"Regina," he says, shirtless and beautiful, droplets of warm water clinging to his chest, just as fresh from the shower as I am. His tattoos end right at the shoulder in a swirl of darkness that begs for me to run my fingertips across the lines, trace each and every one to their source, to the raven, the fox, the sleek, svelte little feline that curls around his bicep. But there's nothing nice about this kitty cat, with its dark eyes and narrow pupils.

I force my gaze over to his left shoulder, to the angry red of the bullet wound—nothing sexy about that, right? Doesn't help. *Damn it.* I glance back at Gill's face.

"Gilleon," I say, glad that my voice comes out the way I want it, strong and clear and lacking in any sort of emotion whatsoever. I refuse to play my cards first with this man.

"About earlier," he says and my chest tightens, "when I said I wanted to go to dinner. I still do. Only ... I think maybe you and I should go alone, so we can talk."

"We do need to talk," I say, my heartbeat picking up speed as I stand there and pretend that nothing is happening to me, nothing is changing inside. I'm afraid that everything is.

Gill smiles, his perfect mouth sliding to the side in an imitation of the wry grins he used to give me as a teen. His blue eyes are locked onto mine, searching me, trying to decide how I feel about all of this without a single word leaving my mouth.

I glance away as Solène opens her door and appears in the hallway, giving Gill's shirtless body a raised eyebrow before she looks over at me.

"I want to show you something, Regina. Quick, come look." She retreats back into her room before I get a chance to respond, throwing a look Gill's way to judge his reaction. The sadness etched into his features makes my heart hurt. How different things would be if he'd never left. I remind myself that that was his choice to make.

I move down the hallway, past his door, hating the nearness of his half-naked body as my heels click across the wood.

"She's beautiful," he whispers as I pass by, "just as beautiful as you."

My skin ripples, his words brushing across them and

drawing goose bumps, before I breeze past and slip into my daughter's room with a sigh. She glances back at me from her seat at the white writing desk in the corner, blue eyes wide and questioning.

"You certainly do fancy him, don't you?" she asks as I raise an eyebrow and come to stand next to her shoulder, surreptitiously leaning forward, pushing back the curtain, and glancing out the window to make sure she didn't have a clear view of Gill and me. I hate that I'm only thinking of this after the fact, but down there on that deck, I wasn't entirely in my right mind.

Thank God. The porch that wraps this side of the house blocks that portion of the deck. Solène would only have been able to see if she'd gone outside, and from the look of the locked French doors, the gray dreary weather out there, it's highly doubtful.

"Now why would you go and say that?" I ask as Solène shuffles some magazines around, pushing them away from the black drawing book that's sitting directly in front of her. I drop the curtain and shift back, tucking my hands in the front pockets of the jumpsuit and smiling innocently.

"Because you're always gazing at him," she tells me matter-of-factly. "Oh, and sucking in deep breaths like this." Solène gasps and then puts her hand to her chest, glancing at me and batting her eyelashes like I'm sure I never do. Unlike her and her dad, I don't have long curled lashes *to* bat. It'd take some serious mascara work —maybe even a fake set—to get mine to do that. "Just like all the women in the movies do when they're in

170

love," she continues, drawing a faint blush to my cheeks. I'm getting told by a nine year old. Isn't that great?

"I'm not in love with Gill," I tell her, trying to take the polished, knowledgeable adult route. I reach down and ruffle her dark hair, tucked up in a loose messy bun. "Children shouldn't speak of such matters, you know?" I say, giving her a look that she returns without a hint of shame.

"I simply won't take no for an answer, Regina. You are in love and that is a fact."

"Who taught you to talk like that?" I ask, knowing full well that it was Cliff. The two of them have been known to curl up in the living room on a Saturday night, sharing a pint of ice cream and watching black and white romance movies like old girlfriends. Believe it or not, they're both gossips, too.

"Papa says I should watch out for you, that you could use a clear head and a bright smile on your side." Solène opens her drawing book to a black and white sketch, complete with measurements and tiny scribbled notes in French. Since she could pick up a pencil, my daughter's been obsessed with designing outfits. If she had a sewing machine here, I have no doubt that she'd be begging fabric off of Gill or Aveline and spending half her day on that end of the design spectrum. I have a feeling that we've got a future designer in our midst. "Aren't you lucky that you have me as a sister?" she says, and my heart drops a little. I wish I could tell her. I've thought about it a million times, but for some reason, I can't. Perhaps it's cowardice?

"So lucky," I say as I kneel down and she proceeds to show me her newest designs.

Eventually, I'll tell Solène everything, but I think this family's had just about enough revelations for one day.

I know I have.

CHAPTER

Thirteen

This time, when Gill comes out of his room, I'm the one standing there waiting for him.

He doesn't look surprised to see me, dressed in a suit and and a white button-down, the first few buttons undone enough that I can see a bit of the hard perfection of his chest. I imagine that he's dressed up not for me, but so that he can have some plausible way to hide his gun while we're in the restaurant. I have to admit though, Gilleon does clean up nice. The suit jacket and matching black slacks are tailored perfectly, highlighting the strength of his shoulders, the length of his legs, like all good clothing should.

Me, I'm still rocking the V-neck black jumpsuit. We might be going out to dinner, but this is by no means a date.

"Where are we going?" I ask, trying to keep the conversation neutral, pleasant, unassuming. *I don't give two shits about what happened between us today,* my voice lies. I hate that my nipples get hard at just the sight of him. Good thing I slipped on a strapless bra with this baby. Most of my friends forgo undergarments when they wear strappy or low cut tops, but I don't have that luxury. I wouldn't call myself big in the chest, but I've got a nice pair of solid C cups that *really* hate gravity.

"An Italian place on Post Alley," Gill says with a slight smile. "I thought we could take a walk afterwards and look at the Gum Wall."

"Hah," I say, leaning back and crossing my arms over my chest. "An entire wall covered in used chewing gum. Now *that* is an attraction worth leaving Paris for. How could Mom have ever thought to steal us away from such a city." I lift up a hand and smile jokingly, only … mentioning my mom and our shared past doesn't seem all that funny to me. Not to Gill either, I guess, because his face shifts with emotion and he glances away, at Solène's bedroom door. "Though I don't suppose a walk would kill me," I add, trying to lighten the mood. Gill looks back at me and then steps forward, holding out an arm for me to take.

I decide against it and uncross my arms, tucking my clutch by my side like a shield before moving down the stairs ahead of Gilleon.

"Don't you make such a handsome couple," Aveline coos from her perch on the back of the living room couch. Her sharp green eyes sparkle as she takes us in. "Mr. Tall Dark and Handsome with Blonde Beautiful and Buxom."

I ignore her, breezing towards the front door while Gill pauses and narrows his eyes menacingly.

"Aveline," he begins, but she cuts him off with a wave of her hand.

"I glanced out the back door to make sure you two weren't going to kill each other when I find you balls deep, Gill. I think I have the right to make a couple of well-placed quips."

"Just don't let it go to your head. You have a job to do tonight," Gill growls, the sound making me dizzy with desire. *Damn it.* I glance over my shoulder and find him staring at me again.

"A job that I've been doing perfectly well for weeks. Don't forget, I saved your girlfriend's life once."

"I'm not his girlfriend," I say, if only because I feel like somebody has to say it and Gill doesn't seem even remotely interested in balking the falsely descriptive noun.

"Right." Aveline snaps her fingers together, standing up and tugging up her baggy gray sweatpants. "You're his *sister,* aren't you? Definitely looked like a sibling bonding moment out there earlier. You two are just lucky the neighbor didn't see. That bitch would happily host a sniper for Karl, take both of you assholes out."

"Goodnight, Aveline," Gill snarls, moving away and pausing by the front door while I grab my coat. If I'd have given him the chance, he would've gotten it for me and tried to help me into it. Can't deal with any niceties or favors from him right now.

"Where are you two off to?" Cliff asks from behind us. I turn as I slip my arms into the black and white wool coat, the one with the houndstooth pattern that I've been dying to wear since I bought it. Tonight's the first real opportunity I've had to get out of the house since that ill-fated breakfast with Gilleon. A double-breasted princess coat fits the occasion perfectly.

"Dinner," I say before Gill can interject. "To talk," I add, knowing Cliff will sympathize.

"Well, don't stay out too late," he says, coming over to me with a coffee mug in hand, and kissing both my cheeks. *He doesn't know yet.* Thank God Aveline was the only person in the house to actually see the deed go down. "And stay safe." He gives Gilleon a pointed look and turns away, heading back towards the kitchen and whatever novel's caught his fancy today. Gill, surprisingly, has a very large collection of classics and brand new bestsellers both. Go figure. Must run in the family.

"See you later, Papa," I say, giving Gill the opportunity to open the front door and do a quick sweep of the yard and the car before I go out. I watch from the window as he greets a friend of his, some off duty cop who's sitting in his cruiser across the street. A police officer helping protect a jewelry thief from the guy he stole from. Interesting.

"And don't let him get to you," Papa warns before he disappears around the corner and I hear a chair scrape

"Definitely don't do that," Aveline purrs, winking at me and turning away join to Cliff.

"I won't," I call back at them and then wonder if I already have. *Am I letting Gilleon get to me with his big, blue eyes and his full lips? He says all the right things, does all the right things, but I can't trust him, not like that. Not ever again.*

"All clear," Gill tells me, gesturing for me to join him on the front porch. I step outside and close my eyes for a moment, listening to the quiet silence of the evening, breathing in the smell of wet leaves and autumn. There's a cold snap in the air that promises that winter is on its way. "I'm sorry about Aveline," he says as we descend the front steps and ... he pauses to open my door for me. *Damn it, Gill.* I know it doesn't seem like a big deal, but the more I let him in in little ways, the more he'll get to me in a big way. That's Gilleon. Love letters, black and white cards with silly sentiments, breakfasts in bed, quirky smiles, impromptu dance parties in the living room. It's what he does, and he does it well. Too well.

"Don't apologize for your friend," I tell him as we climb into yet another vehicle—an SUV this time. Gill's car's now parked in the garage, and new rentals keep appearing. I don't know how that really helps if this Karl guy knows where Gilleon lives. Maybe it just makes it harder for the guy to find him when he goes out? "She's right anyway."

"Right?" Gill asks, raising a dark brow and turning to look at me. The close confines of the vehicle are hard to deal with, especially after what just happened between us. *Start the damn car,* I think at him, but he just sits there staring at me. "Right about what?"

"What we did was stupid," I say, and I refuse to let my stomach fill with butterflies when I think about it. A quickie was all it was, just a stupid, meaningless quickie. "Solène could've seen us." I pause and purse my lips, looking out the window and not at his face. "Or Cliff."

"You're right," he says, and my stomach drops a little. I don't know why. I *want* him to agree with me, move past this so we can talk business. "We should've been more discreet with so many people around." He leans over with a creak of the leather seat and presses his hot lips to the side of my neck before I can stop him, sending a wildfire burning through my body that I don't even begin to know how to stop.

I breathe out with an involuntary sigh, and my breath fogs the passenger side window.

"Gill," I snap, turning towards him and putting a hand on his chest. He's already pulling away, lips twisting into a devilish smirk. "That wasn't the only thing that was wrong with what happened today. You know that?"

"We didn't discuss protection first?" he asks, finally starting the ignition and pulling out of the driveway. "At least you can rest assured that I'm clean."

"Always use a condom with your girlfriends?" I ask and he shakes his head softly, giving me another smoldering look that makes me clench the seat with tight fingers. I really *am* letting him get to me, aren't I? A thirty-one year old woman acting like a teenager. Not

178

particularly flattering. I need to get a rope around these hormones.

"I haven't had many girlfriends," he admits with a small shrug. "None of them matched up to you."

I snort and put my forehead against the palm of my hand.

"Would you please stop? This dinner is supposed to be about our *daughter*," I say, glancing up in time to see him clench the wheel with tight fingers.

"It *is* about her. But it's also about us. I want us to be a family again, Regina."

"Go fuck yourself," I tell him, the words slipping out before I can stop them. Not very mature, I know, but wow. Really? The nerve of this asshole. A family? He *had* a family and he tossed it away like it didn't mean shit.

"Speaking of families," he begins again, clearing his throat a little. "No condom?"

"I have an IUD," I snap, rubbing my temples in little circles. "I don't plan on having another child, especially not by accident."

"Not ever?" Gill asks innocently, and I swear, I'm about to reach over and break some of the fingers on his right hand. I'm not usually prone to violence, but really?

"Gilleon, I don't know what's happening here, but it isn't going to go the way you want it."

"And how's that?" he asks me, his voice dropping a little, into a deeper, more primal sound. "How do you think I want it, Regina?"

"I think you want me back," I say, and feel my heart

start to pound. I look over at him, refusing to be intimidated, and find his eyes half-lidded and focused entirely on the road in front of us. He doesn't even glance my way. The blue lights from the dashboard cast shadows on his face, highlighting those strong cheekbones, that perfectly straight nose, the round fullness of his lower lip. The shading gives him this scary-pretty look, like the strength that's resting just beneath the surface of his skin could burst free at any moment and wreak some serious havoc.

"Aren't you going to say anything?" I ask, hating how nervous I am right now. Whatever he says, it doesn't matter, doesn't change anything about the past or the future. Gill and me, we don't have a future together anymore. We did, but that's all gone now, torn away by a split second decision and a handwritten letter.

"What does Solène know about ... me and you?" he asks finally, choosing to pretend my statement isn't sitting in the SUV with us, the proverbial elephant in the room. I decide that I'm just as happy to drop the subject and lean back in my seat, my heartbeat slowing to something much closer to normal.

"She thinks Cliff is her dad," I say, and I'm not ashamed to admit it. I'm sorry, but life worked out the way it did, and explanations were needed, and Cliff and I did what we thought was best. After all, it was just me and him there at the time and Solène is a smart girl. She looks like me, like Gill, like Cliff. Obviously, there's blood there. She just believes that it's my mother's and Cliff's blood. "She thinks Elena is her mom, that she died right after she was born." *Instead of the four years before that, shot to death right here in Seattle on a business trip away from Paris.* "When she says you're her brother, and I'm her sister, she really thinks it. I mean, she knows we're stepsiblings, but ..." I pause and trail off before I keep talking and find that I can't stop.

"Did you ever think about telling her?" he asks, and although I want to tell him to mind his own damn business, the natural curiosity in his voice makes me think twice. He *is* her dad and I *didn't* tell him about her. True, it wouldn't have changed anything, but I think it's okay, good even, that he's interested.

"Dozens of times. Hundreds, maybe." I shrug and then sigh, memories flooding my frontal lobe. There were opportunities, plenty of them, but I just couldn't do it. Maybe it was because telling her about me would mean I'd have to tell her about Gilleon, about how he abandoned us both. I didn't want her to feel like her dad didn't want her, and with Cliff right there and ready to help, I didn't have to risk that. "It feels like it's too late now. I'm afraid that if I tell her, it'll break her heart."

"I wish I'd known," Gill whispers, his voice laden with regret, heavy and wistful, like he can imagine a different future for us all. I could too, once upon a time. "Regina, I really am sorry. If I could've stayed, I would've."

"Gill, please don't go there. I don't want to talk about it."

"But I do. I want to explain things. I know you'll never be able to forgive me, but I feel like you should know what I was thinking and why."

"That our life was too boring? That I wasn't enough? That you were bored, maybe? I mean, we were each other's first loves, first times. I always just assumed you needed more. The challenge of a new life, the thrill of a new girl, the excitement of sex with a stranger."

"It was *none* of those things," he snaps, running a hand through his raven dark hair. "I love you with a fierceness that scares me sometimes." *Love.* Present tense. I suck in a deep breath. "It was never about the job or the sex or anything like that."

"You're telling me you haven't had your fair share of girls over the years?" I ask, raising a brow and knowing the fourteen lovers I've had since he left—most of them one-night stands when I was trying to forget—have to be nothing compared to his count.

Gill's mouth twitches and I know that he finds my interest amusing. The bastard.

"Hate to disappoint you, Regina, but I've had less one-night stands than I have fingers on my right hand."

"Fuck off," I tell him, completely disbelieving that statement. What's the rule with guys? I thought when they told you about the number of people they've slept with, you're supposed to divide by two and subtract one. With women, it's multiply two and add one, right? Shit, I don't know. Screw gender stereotypes anyway. "You're telling me in ten years that you've slept with four people?"

"That's what I'm saying."

I catch on to his word play and try to trick him into

telling the truth.

"One-night stands. Okay. How many people have you dated?"

"Zero."

"Bullshit," I snap, my heart pounding and my hands getting all sweaty. Why is this conversation so exciting to me? I'm not a jealous person, and even if I was, I don't care what Gill's been doing. It's his body, his choice. "Four people. You're saying you've slept with five people your entire life?"

"That is exactly what I'm saying, Regina," Gill tells me, his voice bubbling with amusement. "Why so shocked? Even if I had been looking, this job doesn't exactly allow for a lot of movement or mingling. I've spent weeks on the run, one step ahead of the authorities. I didn't have time for sex." He pauses and his breath hitches a little, some of the amusement leaking away. "Besides, I've never given up the idea of you. Those one-night stands, I didn't even mean for those to happen. It was only when I was feeling hopeless, when I was certain I'd never get what I really wanted, that it happened at all."

What I really wanted.

I swallow hard and tuck some hair back behind an ear, just so my shaking hands have something to do.

"Fourteen," I tell him, watching as his face twists, heats with some of that raw anger and jealousy that I keep catching glimpses of. "I've had fourteen lovers. Four of them actual boyfriends. The rest were ... they were nothing ..." I say, wondering why Gill's pulling over on the side of the road, slipping into an empty parking lot and guiding the SUV into a space beneath a cluster of red alders. "What are you doing?"

He turns the ignition off and then leans over until his forehead is touching the steering wheel, hands resting on either side. At first, I think he's having a fit of some sort, like maybe I've set him off and that jealousy of his has morphed into something raging and terrible. And then I realize that he's laughing.

"What's so damn funny?" I ask, feeling suddenly warm in the closed in space of the SUV. The windows are already starting to fog up as I turn to Gill and cock my head to the side, studying him with no small amount of confusion. "Seriously, talk to me."

"I have the strangest urge to track down and break the necks of each and every guy you've ever slept with."

"That's funny to you?" I ask as Gill leans back and wrinkles his brow at me, those perfect lips twisted to the side in a bemused smile. He looks just like the Gill I always knew and loved right now, like we're sharing a private joke that nobody else is in on. "I think that qualifies more as dangerous stalking behavior than a joke."

"Oh, like you wouldn't want to get your hands on the women I've slept with."

"That's assuming I give a shit about who you sleep with. Gill, we were lovers once. We aren't anymore."

"I think anyone presented with a recap of today's events might argue otherwise," he purrs, low and deep, the sound making my chest tight with desire. *Thank God*

I'm wearing the jumpsuit. Right here, right now, it'd be an incredible feat to get me out of it. Not that I want to. Because I don't. I don't.

"I ..." I look at Gilleon looking at me, his blue eyes hooded, sitting slumped in the corner of his seat like a lazy house cat getting ready to take a nap. It's all an illusion though—one twitch of those muscles and he'd be up and ready to fight. To kill even. Can't ever forget that. I look down at the center console, the gear shift, the only things separating the two of us. "I feel like you're warming up to something, like all of this hot and cold stuff you're doing is an attempt to hold back."

"Because I am holding back," Gill whispers, changing the entire feel of the air, charging all of those molecules with need that I can feel from over here. Unconsciously, I squeeze my thighs together, a pulse of pleasure ricocheting up my spine. "If I stripped bare and showed you everything I was feeling, you'd run from me. I know you too well, Regina."

"You don't know anything about me," I tell him, watching as his eyes trail down my face, my throat, to the deep V-neck of the jumpsuit and the smooth, rounded curves of my breasts. "You did once, but not anymore. I'm not the same person you left behind."

"No, I knew you wouldn't be. You're stronger than that. You've grown up, Regina, and I'm in awe of all of you."

Gill leans forward and takes one of my hands in his, the whirls of black ink that make up his tattoos stark against my bare skin. I trace the dark whorls of vines

185

that wrap his middle and ring finger, across the back of his hand and around his wrist, disappearing under the sleeve of his suit jacket.

When he pulls me toward him, his touch is light, unassuming, giving me the chance to say no. And I should say no. I made this mistake a scant few hours ago, and I shouldn't make it again.

But his hand where it touches mine, it feels electrifying. I want that sensation all over and inside— *everywhere.*

I unbuckle my seat belt at the same moment he does and then reach out my other hand, letting him pull me over with that unrivaled strength of his, until I'm half on my knees, half straddling his lap.

"I knew it was a good move to go for the SUV," he whispers, leaning down and pushing a button that slides the seat back, giving me just enough room between his chest and the steering wheel to breathe. I adjust myself enough to feel the hard bulge inside his slacks.

Leaning forward, I lay my fingers on either side of his face, tracing a path that was once familiar, that still is if I'm honest with myself.

Gill slides his hands up my arms to my shoulders, chasing a line of goose bumps up my flesh before he hooks his fingers on the black straps of the jumpsuit and slides them down enough that my bra is showing. Without breaking eye contact with me, he traces up my shoulders, my throat, and then back down again, running his fingertips across my collarbone and over the rim of my strapless bra.

I follow his lead, caressing my way along his jawline and then down to the firm, hard muscles in his neck. When he swallows hard and leans forward, I oblige, opening my mouth to him, tasting the sweet brightness of his lips as his own hands roam down my back, pushing the jumpsuit to my hips.

I can't seem to pull my lips away from Gill's, so I don't bother trying to get the suit jacket off, instead reaching down and sliding my fingers along his bare chest until I find the first button. It pops open, followed by the next, and the next. I don't even mind the two guns strapped on either side of his chest.

When I've got the shirt entirely undone, I reach up and grab the lapels, yanking them open with a rough fierceness that I didn't even know I had inside of me until this moment. Shit. Maybe I am jealous? I can't imagine another woman touching Gilleon, tracing their way down his abs the way I'm doing now.

I find the button and zipper on his slacks and rid him of those, too, sliding my hand in and freeing his cock with a groan and a sigh that I don't even bother to try to control.

Gill moans against my lips, his voice rough and deep, vibrating my bones with the sensual sound of it, tightening his fingers against my hips until they hurt. I already have slight purple bruises there from earlier, but I don't care. Having him hold me there, it feels too good. I feel like a queen with this powerful beast locked beneath me, rippling with strength but biting it all back just because I said so. It's heady, this feeling.

I pull back from Gilleon enough that we can make eye contact, my hand sliding along his rigid cock, gripping him tight at the base until he grunts and a growl escapes those handsome lips. His hooded blue eyes stare into mine, burning with a fierce desire that he suppresses, letting me stroke him until he starts thrusting against my hand, letting his head fall back with reckless abandon.

When I feel like he's close to coming, I let go and lean back, watching as he looks up at me with hunger shining brightly in his gaze.

"Get it off, Gill," I tell him, resting my back against the steering wheel, hoping the horn doesn't go off. If somebody interrupts me right now, well, it won't be pleasant for either of us. Gill leans forward, reaching around behind me to find my zipper and pulling it down enough that he can grab hold of the waist and pull, sliding the jumpsuit down as I stretch one leg out, using the space between the seats for extra room. It's no easy feet, scrunched up as I am, but we manage. When something burns this hot and heavy, there's no other choice than to feed the fire.

The wide leg of the jumpsuit slides right over my shoe as I pull up my knee and manage to free my left side completely. The right side, well, fuck it. What I need free is free.

I shove the fabric of my outfit to the side, the right leg still trapped inside it and scoot forward, raising up enough for Gill to pull my panties aside and angle himself at my opening. I relax downward, sliding onto him with a groan, my hips picking up a rapid rhythm that's wild and careless and completely unrestrained.

Gill and I moan together, the car rocking slightly beneath us as he drops his lips to my throat and scrapes his teeth across my skin, nipping and sucking, making me gasp. His hands roam my back again, trace up my spine until the fingers of his right hand wrap in my hair, curling around the ends and pulling gently, making my head fall back. I let him bite and kiss my exposed throat, grinding our pelvises together hard enough that I can feel the movement in my clit.

My body clenches tight and squeezes around Gill as I grab onto the seat beside his head for support, sliding his body in and out of mine with violent thrusts of my hips. Once again, I've let myself get caught in Gilleon's whirlwind ... and I love it. And I hate exactly how much I do.

"Regi," Gill whispers gruffly, his voice breaking against my skin, the words hot on my neck. "Regi." I grind harder, move faster, until he can't talk anymore, until pleasure is ripping through me and I'm collapsing against his chest, panting and shuddering as he finishes inside of me.

So much for resisting temptation.

※ ※ ※

It's an awkward couple of moments after, getting me back in my seat—and in my clothes. Honestly, even though we're in a fairly large sized SUV, there's not all that much room in the front. I don't even know how it all went down. I guess nature always finds a way? Unfortunately, she doesn't provide easy and ready to go cleanup options, too.

I brush some hair behind my ear and search around inside my clutch for a baby wipe or a napkin ... anything really. All I have is some MAC lipstick (ironically titled *Evening Rendezvous*), my new driver's license, and the cell phone Gilleon gave me.

"Can we go home?" I ask, trying to keep my voice normal and neutral, and my gaze trained on the inside of my purse.

"Are you upset?" he asks me as I try to read his expression from the corner of my eye. All I see is dark, mussy hair and a rumpled suit jacket. Too sexy. Ugh.

"I'm not going to dinner with wet panties, and I have to pee. Just take me home, so I can get my shit together, okay?" The words come out a lot angrier than I intended. *Deep breath. Self-talk. That's what I need, positive fucking self-talk.*

You are a strong and reliable human being.

"You're doing it again, aren't you?" Gill asks, starting the car with a smile lingering on his lips. "The self-talk thing?"

"Doesn't matter what I'm doing," I say, hating that he can so easily read me. "Take me home and I'll decide if I still want to go to dinner with you."

"I could help with that, you know."

"*Self*-talk, Gill. Self. A singular endeavor." He chuckles softly, his voice smoky and full of self-satisfied mirth that makes me want to strangle him. A cat that got the cream. That's what Gill reminds me of right now, if we're carrying on the feline references.

"If it helps, I think you're amazing. And beautiful. And strong. You've obviously done a great job with Solène."

"Thank Cliff for that one," I whisper, leaning back against the seat and trying to breathe. My whole body is tingling with the ghostly memories of Gill's hands, of his body sheathed inside of mine. I want to curl up in a bed with him, snuggle close and go to sleep. *How did I let this happen?* I have to remind myself that climbing onto someone's lap and doing crazy acrobatic maneuvers to remove one's jumpsuit doesn't exactly count as 'just happened'. There was intent there—on my part.

"Even if she doesn't know that you're her mother, Solène worships you. I can tell you guys must spend a lot of time together." He swallows hard and grips the wheel tight as we pull back onto the street. "Regina, I really am sorry. I should've noticed sooner. Now that I have, it seems so obvious."

"It *is* obvious," I snap, putting on *mon visage laid* and letting a little sneer crawl across my lips that I have to force back. Anger won't help here. The only real reason it's rearing its ugly head here is because I'm conflicted and confused. Masking those feelings with rage, it's just childish. I take a deep breath. "I'm just surprised it took you so long to figure it out—especially after you pieced together that she was *my* daughter. How could you think I'd have someone else's baby so soon after you left? I mean, I would've been *well* within my right to do so, but come on, Gill."

"That false birthday was really throwing me off. You,

Cliff, and Aveline were all giving me the same story. Besides, I thought you'd have told me or at least have had my dad tell me at some point." His voice drops, heating a little with some sort of repressed anger, probably towards me. I get it. Even if Gill says knowing about Solène wouldn't have changed things, I never even gave him a chance to get to know his daughter. "But you know what the real truth is, Regina? I didn't *want* to see it. It was right in front of my face and I couldn't be bothered to really look." Gill clenches his jaw and shakes his head like he's disgusted with himself, glancing over at me with that laser eyed gaze of his. I can feel his stare cutting into the side of my face, but I don't meet it, looking out the window at the rush of traffic and the wet blur of red brake lights.

"All of this ... none of it turned out the way we expected it to."

"No," he agrees, his voice softening enough that it gets under my skin and makes me want to sigh. I can remember that very same voice whispering sweet nothings in my ear, waking me from sleep with a smile and a hope, a hope that each day was going to be better than the last. Until they just weren't. That first morning, waking up without him, I felt like a hollow shell, like a soulless person with no direction and a shattered heart.

I decide to tell him this.

Fuck it.

It might be therapeutic to finally face the source of my inner demons. Okay, so there's no doubt that I have issues with my father's death, my mother's death, with my sister's abandonment of both me and my mom, but that's all stuff for another day.

"When you first left, I was so broken I didn't think I'd make it to Solène's delivery date, let alone anything beyond that. But then a week later, maybe two, I started to get hopeful again. I started to think that maybe this was just some ... I don't know ... like a phase or something? I'd wait around at the kitchen table, hoping that the next knock on that door would be yours, that the next phone call would start with your voice telling me how sorry you were."

"Regina—" Gill begins, but I cut him off.

"No, let me finish. You told me you wanted to talk about your leaving, so let's talk about it. Let's just get it all out there." I lift my hands, palms out and shrug my shoulders. "I'm tired of tiptoeing around this."

"So am I," Gill says, his voice tight and laced with violence. I snap my gaze over to him and find his eyes not on me, but on the rearview mirror. Shit. "But it'll have to wait until later. Regina, take your seat belt off and get on the floor."

CHAPTER

Fourteen

My heart leaps into my throat, but I do what Gill says, sliding down and curling my knees against my chest. It's a tight fit, but I manage. While I'm down there, I take off my pumps and half stuff them in my unzipped clutch. If I have to run, I'll go twice as fast in bare feet.

"What's going on?" I ask, praying that Cliff and Solène are safe right now. I have to believe they are and focus on the situation at hand otherwise I'll let my mind get away from me with worry. I glance up at Gilleon, at the strangely violent calm that's settled over his features. When he gets like that, he almost looks inhuman.

"We've got a tail, damn it," he growls and then, strangely out of place for the situation, a wicked grin curls his lips. "Shouldn't have stopped to fuck."

"Especially not now that I have to run for my life with

wet panties," I bemoan and he chuckles. Maybe it's not appropriate to joke in this sort of scenario, but what else do I have to do? "Anyway, if you've only had four lovers in the past ten years, I don't blame you."

"Are you trying to say that I'm backed up?" he purrs, using that eerie calm to pitch his voice in a way that makes me bite my lip.

"Yeah, actually, I am."

"You're probably right," he tells me, and I tense as I feel the SUV slowing down.

"What's going on?" I ask, getting ready to open the door and run if need be.

"There's a red light," Gilleon tells me, his voice tinged with the slightest whisper of amusement. "We might have a tail, but we're still in the middle of the city and we don't need cops looking our way. Besides, *I* know they're there, but I don't need to let on that I do."

"Ah." I take a deep breath, relieved that Gill's still got a sense of humor in him. If he goes dark and cold like he did the day of the heist, it'll make this a whole hell of a lot harder. "That makes sense." I put my chin on my knees and try to breathe—not an easy fit jammed as I am between the front seat and the glove compartment. "And am I down here because we're worried about stray bullets?"

"Well, not stray bullets," Gill says and a chill travels down my spine. "If they shoot at us, it'll be with a very specific purpose in mind." He looks over and something he sees on my face spurs him to add, "but don't worry, *ma belle petite fleur*. I won't let *anything* happen to you."

I almost comment on the *beautiful little flower* remark, but the growl in his voice, the ferocity with which he spoke, makes me decide to let it go. In this situation, Gilleon is the expert and I don't have any qualms with following orders—or letting him call me old pet names in French.

"Where are we going?" I ask, knowing he won't take us back to the house if we're being followed. *So much for clean panties.* My after sex glow is fading fast, replaced with the rapid thudding of a frightened heartbeat. I'm not about to have a panic attack or anything, but I won't lie about my fear. Running, hiding, from that particular emotion, never turns out well.

"You'll see," Gill says, and I know that if he could tell me, he would. I let him do his thing and close my eyes for a moment. *Please tell me I did this all for a good reason, Gill,* I think at him, knowing that our next heart-to-heart is going to have to touch on whatever secret it is that he thinks he's hiding from me. "Sit tight, Regi, and we'll get though this."

Ten minutes later, I feel the car slow to a stop for good this time, opening my eyes to find Gill shutting off the ignition. He waits for a moment, eyes trained on the rearview, and then looks down at me, pupils dilated like a cat's. I can almost swear that I see the light of a passing car reflect off the backs of his irises.

"You can sit up now," he tells me, "and put your shoes back on if you want." Gill gives me a small, tight smile and slides the car keys in his pocket, taking a moment to button up his gaping shirt. When I uncurl myself with a

196

groan, my muscles and joints protesting the tight quarters, I look out the window and find ... that we're at Pike Place Market. We're parked right in front, on the brick road of Pike Place itself, sitting pretty in front of a white and blue sign with a wheelchair emblazoned on it. Without skipping a beat, Gill leans over and opens the glove compartment, withdrawing a matching blue handicapped parking permit and hanging it over the rearview. Outside the window, tourists abound in a thick stream, some of them towing young kids, probably looking for the infamous 'Rachel the Pig', the golden pig statue that graces the market—a massive piggy bank who's rumored to grant good luck if you make a donation and rub her snout. *Oh, Seattle.*

"What are we doing here?" I ask Gill as I slip my shoes back on.

"Pull down your mirror and put some lipstick on," he orders, dropping his eyes to his wrists and adjusting his cuff links. Normally, I wouldn't much appreciate a statement like that—or have even the slightest desire to listen to it—but this is different. I know that by questioning anything Gilleon tells me, I'm putting my life at risk. His life. Maybe even Cliff's or Solène's or Aveline's. "Smile at me while you're doing it," he adds, looking over at me with an affectionate expression, one that I have to wonder at. Either Gilleon's an amazing actor or ...

"Gum Wall before or after dinner?" I ask, withdrawing the dark plum lipstick and sliding it across my mouth. I definitely don't miss the spark in Gill's eyes as he watches me trace my lips. I pucker them up and then slide my index finger into my mouth, withdrawing it more slowly than I probably should. It's just a trick to keep the color off my teeth, but it serves to draw Gill's breath from his chest and curl his fingers into tight fists.

I put the lipstick away, fighting back a smile and wishing I had some liner or gloss or something other than just color. Oh well. I didn't even reapply any makeup before this little not-date of ours—I hadn't expected to want or need anything like lip gloss. Or wet wipes. Or— little trick I learned when Gill and I first got together—a small tampon. Keeps all that exciting quickie cleanup to a minimum when there's no bathroom nearby.

"Oh, definitely after," he purrs, reaching over and touching the side of my face with his tattooed fingers, drawing my gaze over to his. I let him, telling myself I'm just playing along with this little charade for whoever happens to be watching us. "Dinner and then ... a wall covered in used chewing gum. The air is heady with the smell of romance."

"Isn't it?" I ask, raising my brows and hating the small surge of disappointment I feel when Gill drops his hand away from my face. "Sex in a parking lot, being tailed by some rival criminals, and a romantic Italian dinner."

"I'll let you in on a secret," he whispers, leaning across the car and whispering in my ear, "we won't be making it to dinner." Gill's hot breath makes my entire body light up. And the innuendo present in that statement? Damn it. I wanted after-sex to be awkward with him, horrible, guilt ridden. But it's just not. It's so

198

... right. Fuck. "Get your stuff and take this," he hands me a large black leather purse—a Saint Laurent, I think—that he grabs from the backseat. "Wait until I come over and open your door. Stick close to me and hold onto my arm—do *not* under any circumstances let go of me or let yourself be separated by the crowd. I don't care if you have to strong-arm a toddler out of the way."

Gill pulls away without waiting for me to acknowledge his words, climbing out and walking unhurriedly over to my side of the SUV. I take that moment to stuff my clutch inside the larger bag, right on top of some folded clothes. Hmm. When he opens the door, I take his hand and let him help me out.

I almost feel sorry for whoever's following us—the parking down here is just horrible. We got the last handicapped spot in a sea of tourists and there's absolutely no where to idle, to stop and watch. Obviously, Gill knows how to pick his battles well.

He guides me through the crowd, moving carefully but not quickly, picking his path with a precision that I don't even begin to try to understand. This, this is Gill's world and I'm just a guest in it. After this is all over, he'll keep doing what he does and Cliff, Solène, and I will move on with our lives. If he'll decide to have a relationship with his daughter is anybody's guess.

"You still know how to shoot, right?" he asks me, and I nod. Way back when, before we moved to France, Cliff used to take Gill and me to the outdoor shooting range to blow off some of that infamous teenage angst. It's been a while since I've handled a gun, but I never forgot.

199

"Good." That's all he says, not bothering to elaborate. *Great.* If this day comes to a close and I end up with blood on my hands ... No. I won't think about that, not right now. I have to trust that Gilleon will do whatever he has to to keep that from happening. On the other hand, if someone's threatening my life—or the lives of anyone in my family—I won't hesitate to pull that trigger.

People swirl around us in a mess of color and laughter, smiles flashing and eyes blinking past. I don't see anyone that looks suspicious, but then, that's the point, isn't it? Smells overwhelm me, making my mouth water and my belly clench tight. Damn it. Tonight was supposed to be about dinner and conversation, not running from bad guys. Or sex. It definitely wasn't supposed to be about sex.

"Tell me this is all for a good reason, Gill," I say suddenly, the words falling past my lips before I can stop them. I realize this isn't the time or place for a proper conversation, but I just want to hear him say ...

"It is." He pauses—only in speech, we keep walking—and then takes a deep breath. "A selfish reason, maybe, but a good one." Gill glances over at me, his eyes sharp and cutting, splitting me open with a single look. Shit. I don't like to make a habit of it, but I glance away first. "This way," Gill whispers suddenly, turning us around on a dime and blending back into the crowd that's flowing the opposite direction.

Within a few minutes, we're back where we started, rain pouring from the sky in sheets, the sudden downpour corralling everyone inside and away from the street. Gill keeps us dry, but walks us along the edge of the open air market like he's looking for someone or something. I half expected to see the SUV surrounded by a bunch of guys in leather jackets and sunglasses, but that's not the case. It sits there, glistening in the rain, completely and utterly unmolested as far as I can tell.

I pull my gaze away, knowing there's no way Gill would take us back to that particular vehicle, and wonder what he plans on doing. At least, I hope there's a plan in all this. I consider asking, but then again, this is Gilleon Marchal we're talking about—of *course* there's a contingency plan in place.

We walk for a little while down Pike Place and then circle back towards the Skybridge and the parking garage. Before taking me down that way however, Gill pauses near the restrooms and waits for a break in the crowd before dragging us *both* into the ladies' room.

Unfortunately, *break* in the crowd doesn't necessarily mean *nobody is in the bathroom.*

I smile an apology at the gray haired woman glaring daggers at us from the sinks.

"Gill," I begin, but he ignores me, ushering me into the largest stall at the end and ignoring the passive aggressive huffs of the angry lavatory patron. My guess? It'll be a matter of seconds before she's off to find an employee of some sort to complain to. "What are we doing in here?" I whisper as Gill slides his arm from mine, depriving me of that strong warmth that I hadn't realized I was enjoying until now. I purse my lips. Not at him, but at myself.

"Hand me the bag," he instructs, and I pass over the black leather purse—*definitely* a Saint Laurent and probably *very* expensive. I kind of want to keep it.

I watch quietly, not wanting to draw any extra undue attention to our stall, as Gill pulls out a long sleeved red T-shirt and a pair of jeans, passing them over to me. He withdraws a similar outfit for himself, only his tee's black, nice and plain. Mine has fish on it and the words *Seattle, Washington* scrawled in navy blue cursive. A tourist's shirt.

"You could've taken your clothes and changed in the men's room, you know," I say, an ulterior motive buried behind my words. Changing in this stall with Gill means stripping down next to Gill. I know we're on the run and all, but hormones will be hormones. My body already misses the tight pressure of him buried inside of me, the heat of his fingers roaming over my hypersensitive skin. I grit my teeth a little, but force myself to take a breath and calm down. Calm is the *only* thing that will keep me safe in this scenario; panic never helped anybody do anything.

Seems Gill can pretty much read my thoughts off my facial expressions alone.

"I won't look," he promises with a slight smile that I meet with raised brows.

"Like I give a shit about that," I lie, reaching back to unzip the jumpsuit, the movement sparking an immediate recall of what went down in the SUV. "But that lady's going to search her angry little heart out until she finds someone to complain to. We don't need that kind of attention right now."

Gill's mouth tightens a little and he turns away as I drop the straps on the jumpsuit. Huh. Not the reaction I expected from him. I thought he'd be appreciating the view.

"I would've loved working with you," he says quietly, his voice like satin over steel. Pretty to listen to, hard to come up against. Almost as hard as the strong, thick muscles in his back when he shrugs off the suit jacket, shoulder holster and button down. "I think you would've been good at it."

"At ..." I almost say *stealing jewelry,* but I'm not that stupid. I might not be a master thief, but I do have a lick of common sense. Guess I'll have to clarify with him later. *You could've asked me to come with you, Gill,* I think, wondering what his day to day life is really like when he's not playing bodyguard to the rest of us. I bet he's seen the world by now. Being a professional thief was never a dream of mine, but being with Gill was. If he had asked, I probably would've gone with him.

A melancholy sigh slides past my lips, but I shake off the feeling as I drop the designer jumpsuit to the floor, the wide legs falling right over my pumps like they did in the SUV. I kick them off anyway, so I can put the jeans on.

They're a perfect fit.

Hmm.

It's hard enough to find well-fitting jeans for myself, let alone some that were purchased for me without my knowledge. *Holy crap.* Gill's infamous perception skills apparently extend to my body—and knowing it intimately through a single glance. He had to have grabbed these before today, before we had sex. He just ... knew how they'd slide over my hips and cup my ass in perfect blue denim.

"I didn't want to leave you," Gill says and my heart skips several beats, thinking he's bringing up *that* day again. But he's not. Silly me. "If I went in the men's room and then came out to find that Karl's guys had already grabbed you ..." I watch as his fists curl with imagined rage. Even *thinking* about it is setting him off. I half expect a snarl to tear from his throat. Instead, Gill shakes his head and drops his slacks, giving me a perfect shot of his ass in the black briefs he's wearing.

I turn away and stare at the wall until I hear him rustling around in the bag again. He drops a pair of ... fucking flip-flops in front of me and dons a pair of his own, stuffing our other clothes and shoes into the massive purse and giving it back to me.

"Can you put your hair in a ponytail?" he asks, handing over a hair tie he must've gotten from the bag. "You'd be surprised at how much a different hairstyle can throw someone off."

"No wigs?" I ask, looking up into his blue eyes as I collect my shoulder length locks into a ponytail and snap the band over it all.

"Unless it's a good wig, a really good one, and it's cut just right for your head, it looks like a wig. And wigs draw attention. Best to stick with your real hair." He reaches over and brushes some of mine back before steeling his expression, like he's pushing away tender thoughts. I feel a chill creep up my spine. Gill turns away and grabs the shoulder holster he's flung across the toilet, slipping it back on, both guns still firmly locked in place, and then throws a black North Face jacket over it all. Praise the heavens for letting big, bulky purses be the norm in fashion right now. "Let's go."

Gill opens the door and saunters right past a woman and two little girls, both of them around Solène's age, without batting an eye.

"We're in Seattle," I tell them as I follow after, "gender is fluid."

The older woman snaps her mouth closed as I breeze out of the bathroom and stand next to Gill, who's smiling so widely and brightly that he doesn't even look like the same man from a few minutes ago.

"So, honey, where to now?" he asks, tucking his hands in his pockets and glancing over at me.

Take yourself there, Regina, and let yourself believe it. If you do, then so will they. That's what Gill told me when I asked why we had to start the heist off with a gun to my head. It's all about acting like you know who you are and what you're doing and convincing everybody else that that's the truth.

"Actually, I'm a little beat. You want to get out of here? I'd like to go back to the hotel and watch *Netflix* on my laptop." I give him an overwrought smile, letting it stretch across my face.

"I was hoping to have a beer at the Athenian," he says, checking his watch and then shrugging. "But I guess we can do that tomorrow? We have a whole two days left in Seattle."

"Don't forget about the Space Needle!" I say with false enthusiasm. Gill chuckles and wraps his arm around my waist, pulling me in close and tucking me against him. I fit there like I was made for it. And I hate that. And I love it. *Shit.* "Am I overdoing it?" I ask and he chuckles, the sound vibrating through me, straight to my cold, bare toes.

"A little, but that's what I like about you. Better to achieve more than less."

"In reality, I just hate tourists. When I pretend to be one, my inherent ire leaks out of my pores." Gill laughs again, the sound genuine and real, old school Gilleon. It makes my heart hurt.

"We're going to head into the parking garage. A bit risky, but there should still be plenty of people to provide some cover." I nod and let him lead me across the Skybridge with its teal metal walls and massive windows looking out over the street and the stream of silver rain cascading down to the pavement below.

"Where did we park again?" I ask, letting my brows wrinkle up and tapping a finger against my lips. Gill glances over at me with a smile and then freezes, like he's seen something he wishes he hadn't. Without a word, his hand flies out and grabs my wrist, yanking me against his chest. He cups the back of my head and kisses me, sliding his tongue deep.

I take the opportunity to enjoy being undercover. If I wasn't, I wouldn't be able to kiss him like this, taste him

206

and hold him and pretend for one easy fucking second that we really are a couple dressed in silly tourist duds, exploring a new city and worrying only about what restaurant we're going to eat at for breakfast in the morning. I wanted that with Gill, desperately.

I like being with him, even now. No. No. I love being with him.

The realization hits me like a shock wave, making me tighten my grip on his neck, press deeper into the kiss. It can't come true, can never be real again, because I won't let it. You don't get hurt as badly as I do and walk away without a limp. I can never forget what Gill did to me, to Solène. If I let myself really love him again, really and truly, I could never trust him. And what's love without trust? It's like a skyscraper with no foundation. Sure, it can touch the sky, but even a small gust of wind can knock it over.

Doesn't stop me from gnawing on his lower lip, inhaling hard each time our lips break and then touch again, leaning my body as close to his as I can get it.

"Regi," he whispers as his hands knead my hips through my jeans, his fingertips brushing a bare bit of skin between the cotton of the T-shirt and the blue denim. I slide my tongue across Gill's teeth, tasting him, absorbing him with my mouth. "Regi," he says again, a bite of wry amusement in his voice. "They're gone."

I pull back with a start, blinking away my emotions with a few bats of my eyelashes, praying that Gill won't realize what I was doing. *Please attribute what I just did to overacting,* I think at him, knowing full well that he's already picking up on my feelings. Even if he's not showing it at the moment, he knows. He always knows.

The barriers I've erected to keep myself safe seem to have holes in them.

I'll have to figure out a way to repair them—and fast. If Gill really is trying to get back together with me, then he'll pursue my heart with the intensity of a cat stalking its prey. And if he knows I miss him, that I still love him, then he'll never let me walk away.

I take a deep breath as Gill wraps his hand around mine, his eyes scanning the parking garage with that laser sharp gaze of his. He keeps an easy smile on his face while he does it, pretending to search for our car, but his eyes ... they stay cold and clinical as he pauses next to a white minivan and slides a key from his pocket.

I don't wait for instructions, moving over to the passenger side and grabbing the handle as soon as he unlocks it. Unhurriedly, Gill starts the engine, checks the rearview, and reverses out of the space.

I don't let out an easy breathe until we pull out of the parking garage.

CHAPTER

Fifteen

I won't say that I'm *happy* about sharing a hotel room with Gill, but it is what it is. We're here; we're not going back to the house; there are two beds. *Thank God.* In all the best romance movies, there's always that silly tussle when one of the two characters sharing a room realizes that there's only a single bed and hilarity ensues. And sometimes sex does, too. I don't intend for either of those things to be a part of my evening, but I do appreciate the fact that Gilleon didn't make any assumptions about us.

"You sure you're not worried?" Gill asks, tilting his head to the side and looking at me with unabashed curiosity. His blue eyes are lit from within, sparking with the flame of the hunt, the thrill of adrenaline, the grit of a

challenge; Gill likes challenges.   Loves them, maybe.
And that could be all I really am to him—a challenge.
One of few single women he couldn't get to look his way
if he wanted them to. Hmm. "The heist didn't seem to set
you off, the shooting, this." He gestures around at the
room and then sits down heavy on the bed next to me.
The mattress dips towards his large frame and our thighs
bump together, sending a thrill of energy through my
body.

How ridiculous.

I'm in my thirties. I don't need electric pulses and
fireworks and butterflies, definitely not quickies in the
front seats of SUVs. I don't need any man really, but if I
were going to look for one, I'd be aiming for one I could
trust. I can't trust Gill anymore—not with my heart. But
I can trust him with this.

"I'm not worried because I know you wouldn't leave
your dad to die at the hands of merciless criminals." I
force a tight smile to my face. "And I know you wouldn't
leave your daughter either." My voice gets really soft
when I say that, too soft. Gill looks at me and we stare
into each other's eyes for a long, long moment.

Daughter.

That's a weird word for me to say. I don't even usually
let myself think it. I feel like a failure as a mother, like I
should've stepped up and given Solène everything I could
give *and* everything that Gill should've given. But I
couldn't, and I didn't, and that's okay. I've made peace
with that. But this ...

"I can't believe I have a daughter," Gill says, and then

210

looks away. I glance down at his fingers, at the dark whorls of tattoos as he curls his fingertips into the white comforter. I'm not sure how to respond to that, so I don't. I keep on going with the previous conversation.

"If you say that Karl won't hit your house, I believe you. What I'd like to know is *why*."

Gill sighs and stands up, the mattress evening out as his weight lifts off it, giving me some very sudden and explicit memories of nights spent in bed with this man. I almost wish that was all he'd ever been to me—good sex. Great sex. The *best* sex. If that was it, I could walk away right now and forget he ever existed. But it's not. It's the soft half smile on his face when he turns to look at me, the way his eyes seem to shift to different shades of blue depending on his mood, the simple fact that he gives a shit about what I have to say. Gill never just let me talk; he listened.

"I have so much to say, and not all of it's good," he admits, shrugging off the North Face jacket and tossing it on his bed. Carefully, he slips off the shoulder holster and lays that down, too.

"Start with this," I say, gesturing at the hotel room, the guns. "Tell me who Karl is and why he hasn't reported a hundred million in stolen jewelry to the authorities."

Gill sucks in a breath and rakes his fingers through his hair.

"Do you want to take a swim first?" he asks, and I raise an eyebrow.

"A swim?"

Gill tosses a wry smile my way.

"In the indoor pool? I have a lot of ... energy that I want to blow off," he says, shaking out his hands, and neither of us misses the unspoken joke that lingers unsaid in the air. *There are other ways to blow off energy than in the pool.* "I've got a massive adrenaline rush and no bad guys to take down."

"Can I stay here?" I ask, knowing the answer to that question.

"We should be safe here for tonight, but I can't risk it. I promised I'd get you through this safely, and I will. Especially since this entire situation is my fault." Gill whispers this last part under his breath. *I want that secret,* I think, hoping I won't have to pry it out of him. "Come sit in a chair by the pool? You don't even have to get in. I'll swim a few laps and then we'll order room service."

I cross my legs at the knee and lean back, supporting my body weight with my arms. I'm wearing a tourist T-shirt with fish on it, dirty panties, and I've got filthy feet from splashing through the puddles in the parking lot while wearing flip-flops. But when Gill looks at me like he's doing right now, I feel like the sexiest woman alive, like my body's waking up from a long, long sleep and it's *ravenous.*

I breathe in deep and lean my head back, closing my eyes for a moment.

"Okay," I say before I let my thoughts run away with me. Honestly, I could use a few more minutes to collect myself before Gill and I have yet another 'talk'. That's all we seem to be doing lately—having serious discussions. I kind of feel like I should just sit him down and we should play Parcheesi or something. "But on the way back to the room, I'm going to stop by the front desk and grab some playing cards from the gift shop. We need to do something normal, Gill."

"Something that doesn't involve jewelry heists, heartbreaking familial revelations, or wild and crazy bareback sex?"

I drop my chin back down and open my eyes, giving him a *look.*

"That's going to stop," I say and Gill smiles.

"Is it?" he asks, moving over to me and leaning down, putting a hand on either side of my hips, not touching but so close I can practically taste it. "It's your choice, of course, but I don't think you want it to stop. I know I don't." When he leans in to kiss me, I turn my head to the side and his lips connect with my cheek.

The feel of his hot mouth so innocently pressed to the side of my face makes me crazy. I get all sick and twisted inside, and a warm flush hits my cheeks like a sudden storm, rolling in from God only knows where.

No!

This is so much worse than a hot, lusty mouthful of tongue. I can see why I'd react to that; Gill's a good looking guy and I'm an adult woman with wants and needs. But this? This is ...

"What do you plan on swimming in?" I ask suddenly, voice breathy and soft. "It's not like you have a bathing suit on hand."

Gill chuckles and turns his head away, brushing his cheek against my own and letting it rest there for a moment before he pulls back and stands up, tucking his hands in his front pockets. His eyes rest on mine and a lazy smile curls his lips.

"Want to drop by the gift shop first? You can get your cards, and I'll grab a pair of swim shorts with the word *Seattle* scribbled on them. I don't think the hotel would appreciate it if I swam in the nude."

I snort and push myself into a sitting position.

"Depends on who you ask. The girl at the front desk probably wouldn't mind so much."

"And what about you?" he asks me as I stand up and smooth my hands down the front of my fish shirt. It's so ugly, it's almost growing on me. Maybe I'll keep it to sleep in?

"What about me?" I ask coyly, raising my eyebrows at him. Gill laughs again and watches as I move over to the table by the window to grab a bottled water from the tray of edible amenities. "If you're asking if I'd like to see you nude, I think we both know the answer to that question."

"Then it's a yes?" he asks, and even though he keeps his distance, I feel like he's right behind me, breathing against my neck, sliding his arms around my waist. I hate that I want him to. *I wish I could call Leilani.* My fingers tighten on the water bottle until it crinkles.

I turn around suddenly and lean my thighs against the side of the table.

"Just pray to whatever gods above that the gift shop

also sells underwear," I tell him with a tight smile, trying to keep the mood light. If Gill and I managed to devolve into rutting animals in an SUV in a parking lot, then what might happen to us while sharing a room with actual *beds*?

"Clean panties," he says, a distinctly masculine smile twisting his lips. "If I get them for you, then you'll come to the pool with me?"

I imagine that it might be slightly dangerous to see Gill bare chested and dripping, but I can see the tightness in his shoulders, the rapid rise and fall of his chest. He's pent up and needs to burn some energy; I get it.

"It's a deal," I say, wondering what kind of trouble I might be getting myself into.

x x x

I lean back in the white plastic lounge chair, a folded pool towel behind my head as a pillow and a book under my palms, resting on my bare thighs. I managed to snag some new underwear (with the Space Needle on them, no less), as well as some black pj shorts that I decided to wear down to the pool. Gill managed to grab some hunter green swim shorts with *Emerald City* scrawled across the ass. Like he needs more attention drawn to that particular asset. I'm not counting or anything, but no less than three women did serious double takes on our way down here.

My eyes follow Gill as he splits the water open with his powerful arms, hands diving into the sparkling blue of the pool while he swims laps. His dark hair is even more beautiful with the water as a backdrop, keeping my

215

attention well after I should've looked away.

"Shit," I whisper under my breath, forcing myself to crack open my book and read the first line. I have to read it four times before it makes sense. My mind's too scattered, too full of thoughts, of questions, of Gilleon Marchal. The whisper and splash of his swimming draws my eyes up again, right to those perfectly sculpted muscles in his back, to the speed and power with which he moves his body. Gilleon reaches the end yet again, flips and kicks off the side, twisting his form under the water with a fluidity that I can only envy. He's always been comfortable in his body, in charge of it, in a way that most people just aren't; it's mesmerizing.

I lean my head back and close my eyes, wondering vaguely what Mathis might be up to back in Paris. The poor guy. He was only trying to defend me and I left him there like he meant nothing, too caught up in my own world to wonder what was going to happen to his when I left. Gill promised me that he had one of his guys take Mathis back to his apartment and leave him on the bed. But what did Mathis do when he woke up? Did he go straight to the authorities? And then what happened when they told him that Karl Rousseau, the owner of the shop, denied ever having a break-in?

Ugh.

I've been surviving by pushing all of the details from my mind, drifting along with the flow and hoping it'll all work out. It's a coping mechanism, sure, but it only makes me more determined to find out what this was all for. I need Gill to look me in the eye and lay it all out there. It's the only way I'm going to be able to keep going, to move past whatever sort of emotional shock I'm still in, and get back to normal.

I open my eyes again and glance over my shoulder at the wall of windows behind me, at the splatter of wet, cold rain that pings off the glass, the spread of evergreen trees that line the parking lot, giving the area an almost parklike feel. It's so dark out right now that they look like living shadows, twisting and turning and dancing in the wind.

When I turn back to the pool, I see the last guy here, some skinny blonde, climb out and grab his towel, disappearing from the room and leaving me alone with Gill.

I suck in a deep breath, tasting chlorine on the back of my tongue, and try to breathe out slow. Tonight, we're going to play cards and watch a movie, figure out how to sleep so close but not touch, and then get back to business tomorrow. I need to take a more active role in all of this; I realize that now.

"I can do anything I put my mind to," I whisper, flipping through the pages of my book and letting the paper brush my fingers. "I will use this experience to become a better person." I stare at the door, waiting to see if anyone else is going to come in, but it seems pretty dead in here tonight. Besides, it's almost time for the pool to close. I'm probably safe if I want to keep talking to myself. "I will not allow myself to be seduced by Gilleon, simply because he's attractive." I swallow hard. "I'm also going to try to stop lying to myself. From now on, I'm going to be nothing but truthful."

Unfortunately, sometimes the truth hurts.

X X X

I'm swimming laps—or at least I'm trying to. I'm not very good at it, but I need something to do, somewhere to go. Even with a brand-new baby, I don't have a sense of purpose, don't feel like I have a reason to get up in the morning. I'm starting to hate myself for it, and that's not healthy at all. When Cliff suggested I find a class or something to sign up for, I ended up here.

I like it best at night, when moonlight leaks in the skylights above. I know the night manager, so when it's a particularly slow evening, she lets me turn off the lights and swim in darkness. I'm also supposed to wear a swim cap, but I can't stand them, so she lets me get away sans cap, too.

I wonder in the back of my mind what Cliff's doing with the baby. Is he holding her? Singing to her? Feeding her? Why am I not there helping? When am I going to get myself together?

It's been a year since Gilleon left. A whole fucking year. And I haven't heard a word from him. He's called Cliff a time or two, just to let him know that he's safe, but he won't talk to me, even if I beg. I can see the pity in my stepfather's eyes, and it's starting to get to me. Am I pathetic? Does everyone think that about me?

I duck my head under the water to wash away the tears and stay there.

I'm so tired of feeling sorry for myself, of feeling like my life's been derailed and there's nothing I can do to get the train back on the tracks. I let Gill's and my apartment go, moved back in with Cliff, even let him be the parent to my baby. I have no job right now; I have nothing.

But it also means I have nothing to lose.

I open my eyes under the water and watch my golden hair float around my face, feeling a little dizzy from my lack of breath.

I have to stop letting all of the bad things that have happened to me maintain control over my life. I used to know how to do that, when Gill was around. I could push away thoughts of my father's death, my sister's abandonment, my mother's murder. But then when he left, I forgot how. Or maybe I never really knew? Maybe I just used him as a crutch?

I won't let one incident dictate my entire life.

The thought bursts through my brain at the same moment my desperate need for air takes over, and I crash through the surface of the water with a massive breath. I tread water for a moment, gathering air in my lungs, tilting my head back to stare up through the glass at the stars.

"I'm going to be strong," I tell myself, thinking of my mom sitting in front of her mirror everyday and smiling, telling herself all of the things she needed to hear most. If you can't support yourself, how can you expect anyone else to know how to do it? My mom knew best how to take life by the horns, how to make the best out of a bad situation. You are so beautiful, Elena, *she'd say, not in a vain or self-patronizing sort of a way, not with any*

narcissistic undertones or the bite of a superiority complex, but just to make herself feel good. *After all, people have a tendency to follow self-fulfilling prophecies. My mom just made sure hers were good ones.* You can do anything you set your mind to. *Once upon a time, I'd tried to emulate her, tried to sit in front of the mirror I'd inherited and do the very same thing. Gill's leaving ... I won't let him take this away from me, too.*

"*I will make a life for myself,*" I say, voice echoing strangely on the water, words for only me to hear. "*Tomorrow looks like a good day for a good day.*"

I smile. For the first time in a long time, I smile. The expression hurts my face, and it doesn't feel entirely genuine, but it's there, and that's what counts.

I swim to the edge of the pool and haul myself up and out, standing shakily on the wet pavement and moving over to grab my towel. I don't expect to make a sudden turnaround—nothing in life is that easy—but I've managed to talk myself in the right direction. That's something, isn't it?

I wrap my towel around me and slip my flip-flops on, making my way towards the door when I realize I forgot my cell phone on the lounge chair; I bring it with me in case something happens with Solène and Cliff needs to get a hold of me. I might not be the world's greatest mom, but I'm trying my best. I turn around, intending to go back for it, and manage to slip in a puddle of water on the floor.

I fall hard and fast, smacking my head on the side of

220

the pool as I tumble into the deep end, completely confused and disoriented, pain blanketing my thoughts and shooting white stars across my eyes. I go limp for a minute, on the verge of passing out, but snap to like I've been slapped. I can't die here. *How sad would that be?*

I kick my legs and find that the towel is soaked and heavy and clinging like greedy fingers to my skin. It's a struggle to untangle myself from it and try to focus myself upwards. I push forward, reaching for the surface as my vision blackens and flickers at the edges, reaching for the air above. Instead, my fingers brush up against pavement and I realize that I'm going the wrong way.

No! *My mind rails against the lack of oxygen and I start to thrash, my body panicking even though my thoughts have just gone eerily calm. In the back of my mind, I recognize a dark shadow and a splash above me, but I decide that I don't care, that I'm too tired. Right now, all I want to do is sleep. When I get up, I'll find a way out of this pool.*

Something warm and strong wraps around me, something familiar, dragging me through the water and into the air like I'm floating. Somehow, someway, I end up on my back on the pavement, breath still a far gone dream as I try to blink away the pain and droplets of water clinging to my lashes.

Warmth presses in on my lips, a tingling sensation that feels too good to be dragging water from my lungs. I sit up slightly, the hot dance of fingertips on my arm, and cough until my chest hurts, until my stomach muscles are aching from clenching so hard, and then I fall back to the cement.

It takes several moments of slow breathing for me to orient myself, and when I finally do, I realize what just happened. I almost died. *And somebody had to save me.*

I sit up suddenly and look around, the ghostly tingle of familiar fingers still on my arms, my lips.

It's stupid. And impossible. And pathetic for me to even think it, but ...

"Gilleon?" I ask quietly, voice echoing around the empty room. Somewhere in the hallway, I think I hear one of the locker room doors slam, but by the time I get up and peek inside the ladies' room, I can't find anyone. Dizzy and unsure on my feet, I wait outside the men's until I get too fed up and barge inside anyway.

There's nobody there either.

There's nobody here at all, least of all Gilleon.

I dry off and change clothes, heading outside and starting down the sidewalk back to Cliff's apartment.

I can't seem to shake the feeling that someone watches me the entire way home.

X X X

I sweep some hair off my forehead and blink away the memory. I've got enough to worry about in the here and now that random trips down memory lane are probably best left off my schedule, but still ...

I wait as Gill climbs out of the pool, his dark green shorts slung low on his hips, his powerful pecs glistening with water, and his nipples rock hard. I can't seem to look away.

"Hey," he says, raven dark hair dripping onto his

forehead. "How's your book?"

"I haven't even looked at it yet," I admit, drinking in his body like I'm parched, like I'm trapped in the desert and Gilleon's my oasis. He notices it, too, and his eyes shimmer with amusement as he lifts his powerful arms up to towel dry that dark hair of his, leaving it damp and tousled and oh so sexy. "Gilleon," I start, wondering if I'm about to make a terrible mistake in asking the question that's tingling my lips, "can I ask you something?" I set my book on the plastic side table next to the chair and sit up, swinging my legs over and onto the pavement so that I'm facing Gill, so that I'm perfectly at eye level with the waistband of his wet swim trunks and the small dark patch of hair that trails beneath it, leading down to better places.

With effort, I force my gaze up the long line of his body so that I can look into his eyes.

"Of course," he says, his voice a rough whisper, like he can sense what's on my mind. "You can ask me anything." Gill's lips twitch in amusement. "But I might not be able to answer all of it."

I take a deep breath, drawing the sharp bite of chlorine into my lungs. It's that smell, I think, that triggered the memory. They say scent's the most powerful reminder there is. I can totally believe that—Gill's spicy sweet scent still gets under my skin like nothing else.

I keep my eyes trained on his, even if they'd rather wander elsewhere. Fool me once, shame on you. Fool me twice, shame on me. What happens if I get fooled a third time? Where does the blame lie then?

"About six months after Solène was born, I started swimming at one of the public pools late at night, on a favor from the manager." I wet my suddenly dry lips. *Mon Dieu, this is harder than I thought it would be.* It should be a simple question, an easy ask and an even easier *no* for Gilleon because there's no way in hell he could've been there, right? But it's not. This is one of the hardest questions I've ever asked in my life.

I notice right away the sudden tension in Gill's powerful shoulders, the way his blue eyes darken and his breathing turns rapid.

There's no way. There's just no way.

"I tripped and fell in the pool," I say, unable to stop the words even though I think I already have my answer. "And somebody saved me, gave me mouth-to-mouth. Gill ... was that you?"

The silence that follows my question is more than enough to confirm my suspicions.

I feel my eyes go wide and my fingers curl around the edge of the lounge chair.

"Gilleon," I say, feeling my own breathing picking up speed. "How could you? How could you have been so close and still have said nothing to me? I was aching, Gill. I was bleeding, and it wasn't just from hitting my head on the cement."

"I'm sorry, Regi," Gill growls, anger riding up and over him. Not at me, I don't think, but it's there. At who, at what, that's what I need to know. I watch as he rakes his fingers through his wet hair and lets the towel fall around his shoulders. "I couldn't be with you. I shouldn't even be with you now, but I couldn't take it anymore. Being separated from you was killing me. It was fucking *killing* me, Regina." He fists a hand over his heart and closes his eyes, taking a step back like he needs to find some space for himself, a moment of alone time to process this. I don't let him dodge the questions, reaching out and curling my fingers around the waistband of his shorts.

The contact between us ignites in an instant, my fingertips grazing the smooth, hard planes of his belly as I swallow hard against the surge of emotion that rises up in me.

"Why run away only to come back? I don't understand, Gill, and I want to. I *need* to."

"I love you, Regi," he says with a sigh and a shake of his head. "I love you, and love is selfish."

He breathes out, a rough, harsh sound that makes my fingers curl tighter around his waistband. Down below, an aching begins, hot and fierce, and I can't seem to get it under control. Gill either for that matter—the bulge in his shorts is painfully obvious.

He stares down at me for a long moment and then tries to pull away again. I won't let him. Against my better judgment, I reach up with my right hand and grab his waistband. Without even thinking about what I'm doing, I tug his shorts down, letting the hard, rigid length of him spring free. He sucks in a harsh breath, but doesn't fight me as I run my hands up his hips to his belly, my eyes dropping to his cock instead of his face. Believe it or not, it's easier to look at.

225

I cast a quick glance at the door to the pool area, but I don't see anyone. I know this is wrong, that it's highly inappropriate, that I'm probably making a really poor life decision, but I can't help it. I wrap my fingers around the long, thick length of him and lean forward, flicking my eyes up to Gill's face one last time before I put his cock in my mouth.

He holds his breath for a moment, like he can't quite believe this is happening. To be quite honest, I'm sort of in the same boat here, so I hold my breath, too, curling my fingers into a fist around his shaft and squeezing while I dip my head low. My lips meet my hand before I pull back, the left coming up to cup his balls. Like our previous two sexual encounters, this is just a quick flash, a bandage to cover the wounds we're both suffering from. I don't revel in it or try to drag it out, it just is what it is.

I'm taking the initiative here, taking hold of Gill— quite literally—and there's no excuse this time. There's no pleasure in this for me other than the fact that I'm getting off on getting him off. It's like a compulsion at this point, an unstoppable force. As much as I want to blame my body for this one, pretend this is all just some animalistic rut, I can't. I can't keep lying to myself.

I want Gill. Bad.

I pull back with a gasp, sucking in the air I just refused myself, and find my eyes drawn up to his face again. He's staring down at me, openmouthed, almost slack-jawed, his eyes hooded and dark, fists curled tight at his sides. I can see every muscle in his body quivering with need right now, with a violent rush of adrenaline and

226

desire that's taking every ounce of his self-control to hold back.

Gilleon licks his lips like he's about to say something, but I cut the words off by taking him back in my mouth, gliding along his hard flesh with my tongue until he fists a hand in my hair. He tangles his fingers in honey blonde, but he doesn't hurt me, doesn't even bring a lick of pain to my scalp. I can *feel* the power there in those inked up fingers of his, the possibility of pain. He could hurt me bad right now if he wanted. Hell, he could kill me. But he won't.

I love the feeling of him holding back like that, but I can't help but wonder what it would feel like if he didn't, if I got to see the full force of him, *feel* the full force of him.

I lean back again and tilt my head to the left, licking down the side of his shaft and listening to his breath as it hitches then stops before turning into a harsh pant. The tip of my tongue traces across his balls as I pump my fist, listening to the sounds he's making as I try to judge the level of his pleasure. A groan breaks past his lips, almost like he doesn't have the willpower to hold it back anymore. Sliding my tongue back up, I take him in my mouth again and move until I feel his entire body go rigid, muscles standing at sharp attention under his warm, wet flesh. He tastes like chlorine, like a long ago memory that I'm only now just starting to understand. I move faster, squeeze harder, and listen in satisfaction as a growl escapes his throat before he comes inside my mouth.

Leaning back, I swallow the salty sweet taste of him, reach down and pick up my book before rising to my feet and starting for the door.

Gill adjusts his shorts and follows after, the sound of his wet feet loud on the concrete.

CHAPTER
Sixteen

"We're not gonna talk about this?" Gill asks as I lean back into the pillows and shuffle the brand-new deck of cards I grabbed from the lobby gift shop. I keep my gaze on them and not on Gill. I can't look at him right now, and the only way I seem able to keep going is to *not* mention the fact that we keep ending up in ... questionable situations.

"About the blow job?" I ask, hoping that if I mention it first, it won't be as embarrassing. I don't look up, but I can hear the tight smile in his voice.

"I'd love to talk about that, actually, but I was referring to the rest of it, to the swimming pool and you falling in, to me being there. Don't you want to know why?"

I keep shuffling, bending the stiff cards with my ferocity. All I can see right now are the glossy images of spades and clubs, diamonds and ... hearts. Fucking hearts. If there was a manual override switch for the brain to push back the tender feelings of that particular organ, I'd be using it right now. I need to get my head together, my thoughts in order. I think the most important thing is to find some distance from Gilleon. Since that's not an option right now, we're going to try a different tactic. Me and him, we're going to watch a movie, eat our shitty room service food, and play Go Fish.

"Gill, I don't just want to know why; I *need* to know why. But truthfully, I'm a little pissed off right now. You were there, right there, right *fucking* there, and you didn't even let me come to enough to see your face."

I stop shuffling and look up at him, trying to judge his reaction.

Gill looks right back at me and purses his lips, dark hair still wet but thankfully covered head to toe in clothing. I don't think I could take even an inch of bare chest at this moment.

"There's so much," he says, but I'm already shaking my head.

"One thing at a time," I tell him. "Answer me, please. I deserve that, at least, don't I?"

Gill stands there for a long moment and then reaches down to grab his shoulder holster, tucking the gun we snuck to the pool back into it. He made me carry the damn thing in the Saint Laurent. I'm keeping the purse as payment for all of this shit.

"When I first left, I was trapped, Regi. I couldn't have come to see you, no matter how I felt about the matter. After about a year, he let loose on the reigns enough that I was able to sneak away now and again. That night at the pool, that was the first night I got to see you since the day I left."

"Who's *he*?" I ask, still looking at him as he moves between the beds and sets the guns on the nightstand between the two.

"Karl Rousseau," he tells me without hesitation. "After that first year, I kept a close eye on you. I couldn't be with you or even talk to you, but I watched."

"Do you know how creepy that is?" I ask, my voice raising as I toss the cards onto the white bedspread and watch them splay out into a sea of scattered symbols. "You *watched* me? So you stalked me then? You're a *stalker*?" I can't keep the edge of anger and confusion out of my voice. "I don't get it, Gill. I'm sorry, but I just don't. Stalking is for people too disillusioned to realize they'll never get what they want most. You had me, Gill. You *had* me—hook, line, and sinker. I was yours. So why run away and then come back just to watch?"

Gill lets me finish my rant as I sigh and lean forward, putting my face in my hands.

"It's all I could do, Regina, the best I had to offer. I wasn't *allowed* to be with you; Karl wouldn't let me." I'm shaking my head again because I have no clue what's going on here. Allowed? Nobody ever allowed or disallowed Gilleon Marchal to do anything. *Ever.* "I

231

watched because I had to make sure he'd keep his word. I needed to know you were safe."

"Why wouldn't I have been?" I ask, lifting up my face to look over at him. He's not looking at me anymore, pretending to be interested in the room service menu. "Gill?"

"Are you hungry?" he asks me, voice soft but hard-edged, like this conversation is taking ten times more out of him than he ever thought it would. "I want to order before the kitchen closes."

My turn to purse my lips.

"Why go work for Karl Rousseau if he was going to keep us apart? I thought what we had meant more to you than that."

"It meant everything to me," he says, and a chill travels up my spine. I pray that he doesn't lift his blue eyes off of that menu. "So I did what I had to to keep you safe."

"From who?" I demand, hating the roundabout road of questioning we're hurtling down.

"Karl."

I just stare at the top of his head before looking away and examining the photographs hanging on the wall opposite me. In typical Seattle fashion, they're all artsy shots of the city, signed in the corner with a silver scrawl that says *local photographer* to me. Underneath each picture, there's a small plaque with the name of the piece, the artist, and a price. I almost want to buy one for my new place. Only I don't have my money yet.

"Let me get this straight," I say, taking a deep breath

and trying to wrap my head around all of this. "You went to work for ... Karl, to keep me safe from ... Karl, so we could one day rob ... Karl."

"That's about the gist of it," he says, and I can feel his blue eyes boring into me. I don't look his way.

"So who do you work for now?" I ask as Gill reaches over and drags the black hotel phone towards him.

"Max."

"Max?" I ask, but I can see that Gill is desperate for a break from this conversation.

"If you don't pick something, I'm just going to order you a burger and call it a day."

I sigh and reach my hand out for the menu, still not looking at him. Gill passes it over, our fingers brushing in the process and making my breath catch. I slap the menu on my lap and stare down at the words, waiting for them to stop spinning in front of my face.

"Just ... order me whatever you're getting. Oh, and a slice of chocolate cake. *Je ne pense pas pouvoir m'en sortir sans chocolat.*" *I don't think I'll be able to get through this without chocolate.*

"*Bien sûr.*" *Of course.* "That sounds like a good idea. I could go for some chocolate, too."

"What? Did you lose your expressionless mask back at Pike Place?" I cringe at the words falling from my mouth and realize that I've let *mon visage laid* creep back over my features again. I smooth away the scowl and take a deep breath. "*Désolée.* Sorry. I just ... You showed up in Cliff's kitchen without a single shred of emotion and now you're all over the place. I'm having trouble understanding you, your motives, your emotions."

"Let me make that all clear right now," Gill says, one hand on the phone, the other curled tightly around his knee, fingertips digging into the denim of his jeans. "I have one goal, one motive. Regina, I want you back."

I groan and swing my legs over the edge of the bed, standing up and moving towards the window and the darkness swimming outside of it. I'm sure it's raining again, but it's hard to tell if the moisture on the glass is just from earlier.

"You can't be serious," I say, and the whisper of bare feet on carpet is the only indication I have that Gill's moving toward me. I have just enough time to spin around before he slams his palms on either side of my head, flat against the glass of the sliding doors.

I suck in a sudden breath, the heat from his body radiating off of him in waves—part of it lust, some of it anger, a good portion of it something else. Love. Maybe. I don't know. I look up at Gilleon, right into his blue eyes and feel his breath teasing my face as he struggles to control himself.

"I'm dead serious," he says, leaning down and taking my bottom lip between his teeth. I groan as Gill's knee slides forward and dips between my legs, rubbing up against my throbbing, aching heat.

Shit.

"Stop it," I snap, putting my palms on his chest. Only I can't push him away because his body feels too good, too warm, too familiar. "Didn't I tell you to leave me alone? I don't want to get back together with you,

Gilleon. You left me alone with a baby in my belly and a ring on my finger, so fuck you. Fuck off. *Casse-toi.*"

"I wish I could," he tells me, his mouth still way too close to mine for comfort. "I tried once or twice, really tried. I knew you'd be better off without me, but I can't help it. I have a lot of fight in me, Regina, a lot of strength. But you know what I've figured out? You're the only thing worth fighting for."

I duck under Gill's arms and head for the bathroom, hating how open and vulnerable I feel in these stupid pj shorts and tank top. I want my jumpsuit back, my earrings, my heels. I want to go down to the lounge and flirt with a cute bartender, anything to get my mind away from Gill and out of this headspace.

He catches me on my way in, curling his fingers gently around my bicep. He doesn't make me stop with force—although he could if he wanted—but instead gets me to freeze by his touch alone.

"I know that what I did was unforgivable, and I'm not asking you to forgive or forget, but I also know what I want, and I won't stop until I get it. Regina, you're mine, and I'm yours. That's how it's always been, no matter how much distance I put between us. I need you, Regi."

I want nothing more than for Gill to pull me back, slide his fingers up my inner thigh and under my loose pajama shorts, but I control myself. Finally.

"I'm going down to the lounge. You can join me if you want, but obviously, this whole evening isn't working out well for either of us. I need to get out of this room."

Gill lets go of me suddenly and steps back. I turn to

find him with his palms up and out in surrender, dark hair falling into those bright eyes of his.

"If I promise to behave, will you stay?" He tries to smile, some of that old humor leaking into his expression. "Just burgers, cards, and an overpriced in room movie."

I narrow my eyes at him.

"You'll let me call Solène and Cliff?" Gill shakes his head and his smile turns apologetic.

"They're safe, I promise, but we're not if we give away our location."

I sigh. I hate that he's the expert here.

I reach back and run my fingers through my blonde hair, letting the loose strands flutter around my face.

"Okay. Okay, Gill. I'll stay, but please, no more confessions. I've heard what you have to say, no need to repeat it. I get it." I swallow, but my throat's gone suddenly dry. Damn it. "We can talk, but let's start with mindless conversation. If things get too serious again, I'm leaping off the goddamn balcony."

x/ x/ x/

"So tell me when you got the fox?" I ask, tossing over my kings and wrinkling up my nose as I count Gill's cards. That asshole is too good at reading people—he's got five sets of cards lying in groups of four on the nightstand between us. Me, I've got two. Gilleon is absolutely winning this game of Go Fish.

"Do you have any eights?" he asks me, and I shake my head, listening to the soft murmur of the rom-com we've got playing in the background. Probably not the best choice of movie, but it was that, a raunchy comedy with the word *sex* in the title, or porn. So ... pretty much stuck between a rock and a hard place. I hate that that phrase makes me think of Gill, of being trapped between his rock solid body and the hard mattress beneath me.

"Go fish," I tell him and watch as he draws a glossy card and adds it to his hand.

"I got this," he says, pointing at his left arm with his handful of cards and smiling, "about two years after I left. Getting ink was one of the few things that made me feel alive again. I liked the pain, the whole artistic process of it." I study the wicked fox tattoo with its double tails and the dark gray shadows that make up its eyes. The piece is big, wrapping around the raven and the skull that decorate Gilleon's bicep. The more I look at his sleeve, the more I like it.

"Got any fives?" I ask and he grunts, passing over a single card. I grin and slap the four of them down on the table. "Any queens?"

"Just one," he whispers and goose bumps break out across my arms. I take the damn card without meeting his eyes and add it to my hand, ignoring the innuendo in his words. "Tell me about Mathis," Gill asks randomly, continuing our trend of quid pro quo. I feel like Clarice Starling in *The Silence of the Lambs,* only worse because Gill's ten times scarier to me than Hannibal Lecter. Gill has love in his eyes and that's the most dangerous thing there is.

"He was nice, cute, available." I study my cards and let my eyes drift over to Gilleon. He's watching me, of course, studying my face for clues. "You're sure he's alright?" I ask, feeling guilty again for what happened. Gill's no lightweight; that punch he threw must've hurt.

"He's fine. You can even call him if you want. Like I said, we don't have to worry about the authorities, and Karl already knows you're with me." Gill grumbles this last bit and then grits his teeth. I'm not sure if the expression's for Karl or for Mathis.

"Sevens?" I ask and Gill shakes his head.

"Go fish."

I draw a card and get what I'm asking for, flashing it to him with a smile.

"Tell me why Karl Rousseau hasn't flipped his lid over a hundred million in diamonds," I say, praying that Gilleon will finally give in and forget about being so close-lipped. "I mean, that's a lot of money, Gill. I don't know anything about jewelry heists, but that's got to be up there on the top ten list of hauls, right?"

"It is," he admits with a shrug of his powerful shoulders. "One for the history books. Well, if anyone knew about it that is. But nobody will ever find out. Karl and Max, they'll make sure of that."

"But *why?* Gill." I sit up a little and drop my cards into my lap. "I understand why you're always so stingy with information, but this, I feel like I should get to know why." Gill sighs and sets his cards aside, reaching for the pint of beer that's sitting next to the phone. I grab mine, too, and take a sip. It's a little bitter for me, but alcohol is as alcohol does.

"I thought this evening was supposed to be about mindless conversation?"

I narrow my eyes, fingers wrapped around the frosty glass in my hands.

"Compared to you and me, this *is* mindless conversation." I take another sip of my drink and set it aside. On the bed next to me, a half-eaten burger and a pile of cold fries sits on a silver tray. I pick one up and dip it in ketchup, slather it in the stuff. There's not a lot of ketchup in Paris, and I *missed* it. "So. Are you going to answer the question?"

"I'd rather talk about you," Gill says, deflecting my words, the same way he's done since the moment he walked back into my life those few months back, his sapphire dark eyes closed and shuttered, hiding his emotions away from the world. I'd thought that the boy I'd loved, the one who'd picked the lock to my bedroom door that very first day and curled up on my bed, was gone. But ... I look up into Gilleon's eyes, such a richly brilliant blue that I feel like I'm falling straight through the sky when I stare into them.

"Answer my question first and I'll tell you whatever you want to know," I say, sliding the fry between my lips, watching as Gilleon's pupils dilate and he mimics me by running his tongue across his lower lip. He shakes his head and turns away, towards his own empty plates. I got one burger and barely managed to eat half while he ordered *three* and finished them all. Thing is, there's not an ounce of fat on this guy; it's all hard, sculpted muscle. Guess he just needs a lot of energy to run that beautiful body on.

"Karl doesn't need or want government agencies

getting involved in his business."

"Because he employs people like you?" I ask, leaning down and dragging the small silver tray that holds my chocolate cake towards me. "To steal things for him?" I hazard a glance at Gill and see his lips twitch in amusement.

"You were always one smart cookie," he says without even a hint of sarcasm. "Besides, Karl has resources that some governments can only dream of. He believes that he'll get back what we stole. I think he's excited to finally put a bullet in my head, too."

A chill tickles my spine as I lift the lid off the cake and pull it onto my lap.

"Why does he want you dead?" I ask casually, hoping Gill's already in the groove and will just answer me straight. He's too smart for that.

"You said if I answered your first question, I could ask whatever I want. Well, I *want,* Regina."

I scrape the end off the cake—some fancy triple chocolate something or other—and slide it between my lips. Gill watches me the entire time, tracing my mouth with his eyes, swallowing hard when I pull the fork back out. I knew that blow job was a bad idea, but ...

"Have you ever been in love?" he asks as I blink away my surprise and turn slowly to stare at him. "I mean with anyone other than me," he adds with a smirk that doesn't quite reach his eyes. I could lie right now, play with him a little, throw him offtrack. But I don't. Why bother? I just promised myself I'd be truthful. Not a lot of good ever comes from lying.

240

"No." I take another bite of cake and then set my fork down. "But that's not a very mindless sort of a question, Gill. Ask me what my favorite food is, my favorite song, ask me what your daughter and I do for fun." I see the anger slide across his face for a moment before he pushes it back.

"If I still know you as well as I think I do, then your favorite food is and always will be cheesecake. And your favorite song ... A lot can happen in ten years, but I can't believe you'd let anything kick Queen out of your top spot. *Don't Stop Me Now,* that's still your groove, isn't it?" He grins, a wickedly impish little grin, one that shaves these last ten years right off of his face. If it wasn't for the rough edge of stubble coming in on his chin, I'd still think he was seventeen.

"I ..." All the things he just said are true, so how can I really respond to that?

"And my daughter," he says, testing the words like they're foreign to him. Hey, they're even foreign to me, so I get it. "I want to know everything about her, Regina. I know it's a little late, but I still want to be a dad if I can."

"Cliff is her dad, Gilleon."

"Ah, yes, *Cliff,*" Gill growls, his voice taking on a rough edge. "Don't you mean *Papa*?"

"What's that supposed to mean?" I ask, my own defenses sliding into place as anger laces my voice. "Are you angry with him? With me? Because if you are, then you'd best just say something now."

"I'm not angry with you," Gill says, but he stands up

and grabs his plates, tossing them onto the room service tray with a clink of china. His tense muscles are telling a different story than his words. "I just think my father should've said something to me is all. I can get why you didn't. Why you couldn't."

"I *asked* Cliff not to tell you, Gill. You said yourself that knowing wouldn't have changed things, so why does it matter?"

I sit up straight and set the cake on the nightstand. Since Gill found out about Solène, we've been avoiding the issue—mostly by fucking. I don't think that's a great long-term solution.

"It shouldn't," he says, but even though he's not looking at me, I can tell he's gritting his teeth. "But it does. I see how close you are with my dad, with Solène, and I can't help but wonder how things would've turned out if ..." Gill pauses and turns to look at me, running a hand down his face. He's still holding secrets, clinging to them, and I can see why now. He's *afraid* to tell me. Doesn't bode well for me, does it? "Anyway, it doesn't matter. I'm here now, I know now, and I want to be a dad to our daughter."

"Well, that's something you'll have to earn the right to. I'm still working towards my right," I say, crossing my legs at the knee and noticing as Gill's eyes travel up from my ankle to the swell of my calf, and towards the creamy expanse of thigh that's exposed under the bunched up legs of my shorts. "Once you get us our money, we'll find a place, and we'll start living a normal life again. If you're able to make some concessions in your work and stick around for a while, you can get to know us all again and we'll see how things go from there."

Gill watches me for a long moment and then nods, like he's thought better about saying whatever words are hovering around his lips.

"I'm gonna take a shower," he tells me, and I try really hard not to think about him soaping up that strong, hard body of his. "Will you be up when I get out?" I shake my head, realizing that this is a golden opportunity for me to crawl under the covers and try to fall asleep. If I wait for him to lay down next to me, I'll have to listen to the rhythm of his breathing and remember the many, many nights that we drifted off to sleep in one another's arms.

I shake my head.

"*Je vais dormir.*" *I'm going to sleep.*

Gill smiles tightly at me, pausing at the door to the bathroom.

"*Fais de beaux rêves,*" he says. *Sweet dreams.* "*Ma belle petite fleur.*"

I watch as Gill disappears into the golden light of the bathroom and shuts the door behind him.

X X X

Three o'clock in the morning.

That's what time it is when Gill wakes me from sleep, wrapping a hand around my mouth and pulling me tight against his body. I know that only because my eyes have sprung wide open and I find myself staring right at the green letters of the alarm clock on the nightstand. Fear whispers through me, its cold fingers tracing up my spine and dulling any excitement I might've had at being pressed up so tight to Gill.

"Don't make a sound," he whispers, his voice low and rough, laced through with violence. I go completely still as he releases me, sliding his hand away from my lips and rolling from the bed without making any noise at all. *How long has he been lying there?* I wonder as I stay right where am I, one leg outside the blankets, one pillow tucked between my knees, and another clutched in my arms. I've slept this way every single night since Gill left —whether I had a boyfriend or not. Apparently nobody was good enough to replace the solid feel of him in my arms.

I want so badly to ask what's going on, but I don't. I don't even turn over. If Gill wanted me to do anything but lie here, he'd have said something. So I wait there in the dark, my heart pounding, my mind racing, and I listen to the click of a lock, the slight whisper of the hotel room door sliding across the carpet.

Seconds tick past, but they feel like hours. My whole body starts to itch, my muscles cramping, suddenly desperate to get out of this position now that I know I *can't* move. This psychological torture lasts for all of about two minutes—I know that because the only thing I can do right now is stare at this damn clock.

And then I hear the first of two gunshots, whipping myself up and around to catch sight of a man collapsing to the floor in a heap. I manage to actually *see* the second shot take place as Gill emerges from the shadows like a panther, melting into the slight glow of light from

244

the cracked bathroom door.

His face is so cold, almost inhuman. I clamp a hand over my mouth to hold back a scream as he oh so calmly levels his pistol at a second man's head and pulls the trigger. Just. Like. That.

I jump, my back slamming against the headboard as Gill's blue gaze tracks the body's descent to the floor. The sound of the gun going off is loud, yes, but not the earsplitting sonic boom that I'm used to from days spent on the range, earplugs stuffed nice and snug on either side of my head. The noise I just heard was more like a really loud *click.* I'm not an idiot—I know the suppressor on the end of his gun isn't the sole reason for the decrease in noise; they don't work like they do in the movies, where silencers turn pistols into laser guns, sending a *pew pew* noise out towards the audience. Subsonic ammo, then?

I realize that my mind is spinning with useless facts, trying to cover up the truth of the moment with shock. Who gives two fucks about subsonic ammo and pistols and the fact that Gill's tattooed fingers are still wrapped around the butt of a Walther PPQ .22? Who cares that he's standing there in the shadows between the bathroom wall and my bed, lowering his gun with muscles taut, face expressionless? I notice all sorts of random things in that moment, like how the blood from the two men is splattered on the wall behind them in a red blotch like a firework blooming in the night sky. I don't see any bullet holes in the wall or anything, but maybe it's just too dark to notice? I know subsonic ammo moves much slower than supersonic ammo. Maybe there just aren't any?

I turn my head slowly, *painstakingly* slowly, towards Gilleon.

He just *killed* somebody. Two somebodies.

Holy. Shit.

I drop my hand and take in a gasping breath that hurts my chest and makes me shudder. The sound causes Gill to jump, like he forgot I was there for a moment. I watch as he lowers the gun and turns to look at me. He must sense some of what I'm feeling because he doesn't move any closer, giving me a second to gather myself together.

Gilleon just murdered two men.

Knowing that someone's capable of something and seeing it firsthand, those are two very different things. In the back of my mind, past all of the whirling thoughts and the shock, I realize that these are probably very bad men, maybe one of them is even the same guy who tried to kill me all those weeks ago. I get it. I really do, but …

"Are you okay, Regina?" Gill asks, moving over to the edge of the bed and kneeling down to eye level with me. A few feet away, warm corpses dot the beige carpeting. I swallow hard and nod, refusing to descend into any sort of freak-out. When Gilleon came back, invited me into this, he gave me a warning, told me that something like this might happen. And I realize that ten years in this sort of lifestyle has to have led to some serious situations, but Jesus H. Christ, I've never been around anything like this before. "Just wait here and I'll take care of it," he says, voice calm, eyes like icebergs floating in a black sea, bright around the pupil but darker at the edges.

He stands up and switches the gun out for a cell, stepping over the bodies and tucking himself in the brightness of the bathroom, so I can't quite hear whatever it is that he's saying.

I look back up at the blood on the wall again. Nope. Definitely no bullet holes. I remember reading something about how .22s are often used to assassinate people because the round gets stuck inside their skull and bounces around their brain.

I lean back and close my eyes, sucking in a big breath that turns out to be a mistake. The air smells like gunpowder and copper, metallic and tangy. I almost throw up, but push the urge back, opening my eyes and reaching out for my half-full pint of beer on the nightstand. I throw it back, sucking down the amber liquid like it's water.

When I slam it back down on the table, I can see Gill standing near the door to our room looking back at me. Half of his face is covered in shadow, the other half limned in light. It's a perfect analogy, but a sad one. Here he stands, the love of my life, a man who I'm still fairly certain is my soul mate—if one can believe in such things—and he's on the precipice of darkness, ready to topple over the edge. I've always seen him fight back against that, against the roughness inside of him, against whatever happened between the time Cliff and his mom got divorced to when he came to live with us. I know it was bad because he'd tell me his tamest stories with a frown on his face and his fists clenched at his sides. But I've never heard the worst of it.

Maybe I don't want to know. If it's taken over him so thoroughly, then maybe it really is better that he left?

No.

No. That's just me trying to rationalize what I saw. If Gill's half dark, then he's also half light. What if I gave him a push in the right direction? Even scarier, what if I *don't*? What will happen then? Will that shadow take over his face and consume him from the inside out?

"Aveline will be here in a few minutes to pick you up," he says, his tone even and undisturbed. I stare right back at him, at the slight stubble on his jaw, the firm set of his lips. The jovial, smiling Gill, the bit of teenager that I keep seeing pop up in him, is buried deep right now. So I just nod and sit still. If Aveline's coming, then I'll wait right here until she gets to the hotel. "She'll take you home." Gill glances down at the two bodies on the floor. "This should send Karl a strong enough message that he shouldn't bother us there. Not tonight anyway, not with Max's guys on patrol."

I just nod again because this isn't my world; *Gill* isn't a part of my world anymore, and I can never, ever forget that.

CHAPTER
Seventeen

"*Bonjour,* Regina," Solène says brightly, skipping into the kitchen where I'm sitting with a cup of coffee clutched between my palms. She pauses in a square of sunshine leaking in from the window above the sink, and twirls. Her pink and purple striped skirt spins in a dizzying circle around her, revealing a pair of white leggings stamped in red roses underneath. With a pair of black Doc Martens on her feet and a white sweater with a ghost on it, she's the walking epitome of *fashion* at its finest, far too trendy for me to pick up on, but that's the beauty of the industry, right? "I sewed the skirt myself," she says, and then points to her top, "and Aveline found this *fantôme* and said she thought of me. I think it's positively perfect with these leggings." She lifts up a leg and pats it fondly, dropping her boot to the floor with a thump.

The sound reminds me of Gilleon and a chill travels down my spine. I clutch the cup tighter in my hands and try not to think about him. My thoughts have become almost maniacal lately, a spinning, twisting mess where I waffle between two extremes: wanting him out of my life forever and ... wanting him back in it.

It might've been nice if he hadn't decided to disappear for three days. I don't know how to work my way through all of this without actually seeing him, talking to him. *Shit.* Seeing him shoot those men should've been the straw that broke the camel's back, the obvious end to any feelings I might've still carried for the man. But it wasn't. When I saw that deadly balance inside of him, all I wanted to do was fix it, shove him as hard as I could towards the light. *I won't be one of those women who try to fix men,* I think to myself, staring down into my coffee before looking back up at my daughter. *She deserves better than that.*

"I think you'll be showing at Paris Fashion Week before you turn twenty-one," I say with a slight smile. Unconsciously, I reach up to touch the diamond pendant at my neck. *I wish you were here, Mom. Things would be so much easier if you were.*

"Good morning," Cliff says, moving into the kitchen and heading straight for the coffeemaker. I've been avoiding him since that night at the hotel, and he knows it. I take a deep breath and toss back the rest of the coffee in my cup. I know a talk is coming on—I can *feel* it. "Solène, *mon étoile,* could you excuse Regi and me for a few moments to talk?"

Solène wrinkles up her face for a moment and then nods.

"I don't much enjoy gossip anyhow," she says with a sniff, leaving the room in a whoosh of skirts and the clomping of boots. There's a brief exchange between her and Aveline before I hear the pounding of feet on steps and the slamming of a distant door.

My stomach twists up tight and I find myself standing up for another cup of coffee, anything so that my shaking hands have something to do.

"Don't you look lovely this morning," Cliff says, pausing to give me a kiss on either cheek. I smile through a face of perfectly applied makeup—a dark chocolate liner with a touch of brown shadow, a nude lip, a gentle kiss of blush. My hair's up in a messy chignon, and I'm completely and utterly overdressed for yet another day spent trapped indoors. My open-front halter top shows way too much cleavage and the high waisted slacks I'm wearing are definitely too chic for an afternoon watching Netflix, but ... I need the uniform right now, more than I ever have before. I need to feel polished and put-together. If I keep pretending that I am, the feeling's bound to wear off on me at some point, right? *I look beautiful today,* I tell myself trying to stay confident and in control. Every little sound, every footstep and opening door, it all makes me jump, gives me a serious case of butterflies and goose bumps because I think it's Gill, come home at last.

Only for three days, it hasn't been.

"*Merci*, Papa," I say setting my cup on the counter next to his. He lifts his own mug to his lips with a very neutral expression hovering on his face. I try to remember that I'm not sixteen, but Cliff's perception of me is so important that sometimes I get worked up over nothing. And this, this is not nothing. "What did you want to talk about?" I ask, trying to get the jump on the conversation before he does. *Control*.

"What happened in that hotel was not your fault," he tells me and I cringe slightly. Someone must've filled him in—probably Aveline.

"I know," I say, because I do. I didn't make those men come after us, break into our room, and I didn't shoot them either.

"But it's also okay to let yourself be affected by what you saw." I take a sip of my coffee and slam my cup back down on the counter, a little harder than I intend to. I lift my eyes up and glance left, out the window that looks onto the hedge of trees that line Gill's property.

"Thank you, Cliff, but I'm fine. Really. I knew that signing up to rob a hundred million in jewels could come with consequences." I try to make a joke out of it, throw a smile onto my face, but Cliff sees right through me. His expression darkens and he moves away to sit at the table.

"Gilleon's a dangerous man, Regina," he says, and even now it still weirds me out to hear him talk about his own son like that. "And whether he wants to admit it or not, his time with his mother changed him. This last decade of his life, it changed him even more." Cliff spins in his seat to look at me as I turn around. "Now, you're an adult and I can't tell you what to do, but listen to an old geezer's advice." I roll my eyes a little because Cliff's been referring to himself as an old man for the last fifteen or so years. "My son is charming, handsome, mysterious." I laugh but Cliff raises his graying brows at me. "Don't make light of this, Regi."

"Papa, I'm thirty-one years old," I remind him, but he just shakes his head and points a finger at me.

"Don't throw your age at me. I'm sixty-five years old, so I've got decades on you. Listen, all I'm trying to say is, once this is over, let Gilleon go. Cut him off and say goodbye. It's the best thing for you, for me, for Solène."

"He's her father, Cliff," I say, exasperated, wishing suddenly that I was back in Paris, that I'd looked past those secrets in Gill's eyes, that quiet plea for help, and that I'd walked away. Because I'm just now realizing that no matter what he's hiding from me, whatever real life purpose this heist was supposed to serve for him, the real reason I went along with it all is because I saw it then just like I did a few nights ago at the hotel: Gill is slipping away and he wants to be saved.

And he wants me to do it.

"Yes," Cliff says with a sigh, "he is, but he's also a coward, and that makes him a very scary person to be around."

"Glad to see you've got so much faith in me, Dad," Gill says from the entrance to the kitchen. I jump and slosh hot coffee all over my hands, hissing at the burn as

I shove the mug on the counter and rush to the sink for cold water.

"I'm just trying to talk some sense into Regina, Gilleon," Cliff says as I wash my hands and dry them on a paper towel. Only then do I turn around and look at him, hating the way my heart skips and jumps inside my chest. There's some fear there, yes, but there's also desire, and that horrible little L-word called *love,* that immortal beast that never dies.

I stare into his blue eyes and he stares right back into my brown ones.

"Somehow she's got it into her head that this could still work."

"What?" I snap, breaking my concentration with Gilleon to stare at the side of his father's head. "I never said that, Cliff."

"No, but I can see it in your face. You can't save him, Regina. He's beyond that now."

"Goddamn it, Cliff," Gill growls, curling his hands into fists. He looks dangerous right now, like his claws are sheathed but only with the utmost effort. A pale blue shirt and shoulder holster, gray army fatigues and a leg holster, and a thick ass pair of steel-toed work boots. Gill's armed and ready to kill right now, just like he was in the hotel. Hot desire, cold fear, all of it swirls around inside of me until I feel like I'm choking. "Are you really gonna sit here and talk shit about me after all you've done?"

"You mean like raise your daughter in your absence?" Cliff says, easy as pie, like the words are nothing to him.

I can feel Gill's anger from here, a hot heat that charges the very molecules in the air around us. It's not *me* he blames for Solène and the decisions that were made, not himself, but his dad.

"You don't know the half of what I've been through," Gill snarls, his face twisting into harsh lines of pain, his blue eyes darkening. Black hair falls across his forehead as he rakes his fingers through it. He's got that perfect five o'clock shadow that looks effortless, but takes a ton of work to keep looking nice. Even though I know that, that he groomed himself for some reason—probably me— it just looks like he's rough around the edges, wild. "You don't write off your family for reasons you don't understand, *Cliff.*"

"You know I love you, Gilleon, just as much as I love Solène and Regina, but as angry as you are with me, you must at least be able to grasp where I'm coming from here."

"I left, I get it," Gill says, his voice rising with each word. "I fucking left, and I fucked everything up."

"Gilleon," Cliff says, his voice a warning. Aveline peeks her head around the corner and raises her red brows at us. "Calm down, son."

"Calm down?" Gill asks, his face cracking into a million pieces. "My father's sitting in my kitchen looking at me like I'm the scum of the earth while the love of my life stares at me like I'm a fucking monster. My daughter thinks I'm her goddamn brother, and everything I ever wanted is so far outside my grasp, I might as well be reaching for the moon."

I swallow hard and shake my head. Seeing him break apart like this, drop the expressionless mask of ice, it's terrifying. I don't want Gilleon to come apart at the seams. Despite everything, I want to sew him back together again.

"I don't think you're a monster, Gill," I say, but the words don't entirely ring with truth. I've thought that about him before, I have. "But if you won't tell us why you left, then how can we truly understand why you want to come back?"

Gill turns around and walks away without bothering to answer me, his boots hard against the wood floors as he takes the steps two at a time. I set my coffee down and go after him, even though I can hear Cliff behind me.

"Leave him be, Regi," he says, but I can't. Not right now. I chase Gill up the stairs, my heels loud as I come up against his door and find it unlocked. An invitation that I shouldn't take.

"Gilleon?" I ask, stepping into the room and finding him right there waiting for me.

I pause, my breathing frantic, my heart pounding in my chest. I lean back and use the weight of my body to close the door behind me, flicking the lock with my right hand.

"I'm sorry, Gill," I say, even though I'm not precisely sure why I'm saying it.

"For what? Taking me at face value? No, I get it. I'm a lowlife, the worst kind, a man who abandons his soon-to-be wife and unborn child. A man who kills other men in cold blood and doesn't bat an eyelash. I know the kind

256

of man I am, Regi."

Gill stares right back at me, his breathing slowing, his voice surprisingly calm and reasonable, but I can see the tension in his muscles, the way his shirt strains across the tightness in his chest.

"But I can't stand it, seeing that information reflected in your face, in my dad's face. I *know* I'm a bad man, but seeing you both come to that realization, it hurts."

"I don't think you're a bad person, Gill," I say as he takes a step forward, effectively pinning me against the door with his presence. He's not touching me, but I couldn't move if I wanted to. I lick my suddenly dry lips and notice Gill's eyes following the movement. His gaze continues downward, to the circle of cleavage revealed by my shirt. When he lifts his hand and traces his finger along the edge of my breast, I find it very hard to breathe, my breath catching sharp in my chest.

"Regi," he says, and his voice is everything I ever wanted it to be—gentle, affectionate, loving. It's strange, seeing him dressed to the nines to kill, guns everywhere, a knife hilt showing at the top of his boot, and then hearing that soft sound scrape past his lips. "Regi, if I could never tell you another secret, never say a single other word about it, about why I left or why I came back, but I told you that it was all with good reason, would you believe me?"

I wait to answer, my breathing growing heavy in tandem with his, our foreheads close, eyes locked. Gill slides his hand inside my shirt, right underneath the cup of the ridiculous U-plunge bra I had to wear to get into this silly shirt. It has a hole cut right out of the middle of my chest, giving me side boob action and a back covered only in white mesh.

I feel so exposed right now.

I groan as Gill's strong hand caresses my breast, his grip a little tighter than it probably should be. But I don't pull away. I don't *want* to pull away, and that's the problem.

"Gilleon," I say, reaching up and curling my fingers around his wrist, tugging on his arm until he releases me and takes his hand back. His eyes darken and the skin on his forehead gets tight, but he doesn't say anything, waiting for me to respond. I can't think straight with his rough fingertips grazing my nipple. "If you don't want to tell me why you left, you don't have to. I'm not going to force you to do anything you don't want to do. It won't mean *anything* to me if I have to pry an answer out of you." I take a deep breath and reach up to adjust my shirt, the memory of Gill's hand still tingling across my skin. I can't help but notice the bulge in his pants, the tightness of the fabric as it pulls across his arousal. Between my legs, I feel an answering heat, a throbbing that refuses to let up, even when I pull my gaze back up to Gill's face.

"Leaving me," I start and then have to take a big breath to steel myself. "There was no reason good enough, Gill. None. I ... I'd love to hear why, so maybe I can understand, but to me, it won't change anything. I can't ever forgive you for that, Gilleon. I can never trust you again."

He closes his eyes tight and then opens them back up,

running his tongue over his lower lip and dragging his hand down his face. I watch in horror as he shuts down completely, defenses sliding back into place as he turns away and takes a few steps towards his half-open closet doors.

"Gilleon, please," I say, but I'm not even sure what I'm asking with that plea. "Don't close up on me. We can work things out, so you can have a relationship with Solène. And your dad, I'm sure he'd love to spend more time with you. Despite everything he said downstairs, I know he'd like that."

"And what about you, Regi?" Gill asks, sliding his shoulder holster off and laying it down on his desk. The powerful movements of his shoulders, his biceps, the slide of black and gray tattoos over his skin, it's all mesmerizing to me. "What would you like to happen?" He turns around to look at me, his stoic facial expression chilling me to the bone.

"I ..." I reach up and touch the pendant hanging around my neck.

A knock at the door gives us both pause.

"Can you please open up?"

It's Solène.

Gill turns away, lifting his booted foot up onto the chair and reaching down to undo the leg holster that's wrapped around his thigh.

I take several deep breaths to gather myself and open the door a crack.

"May I come in?" Solène asks, as polite as ever, far too mature for her age. I glance over my shoulder at Gill as he lays the holster aside and crosses his arms over his muscular chest. His brows are pinched now, and he just looks sad.

I step back and open the door, allowing Solène to come in, her fingers curled together behind her as she slides across the floor like an ice-skater, skidding along in her black Docs.

"I wish you'd stop fighting," she says, looking first at me and then at Gill. I open my mouth to apologize, hoping like hell she didn't hear any of the things we said downstairs. I don't want her to have to find out about Gill and me like that. How traumatizing would that be? But, like usual, I'm three steps behind this kid. "Um, if it's about me then I already know, okay?"

"Know what, honey?" Gill asks, his voice softening considerably.

"I found a picture once," she says and then makes a face, lifting up the front of her shirt and sticking her hands underneath. "It was Regina with a baby inside her. I asked Papa about it, and he said it wasn't his truth to tell, so I figured it out myself."

I feel the blood drain from my face and before I even realize what I'm doing, I'm sitting on the edge of Gill's bed with my eyes wide open and my lips parted in surprise.

"Anyway, Papa's old, way older than all my friend's parents. Plus, he's Regi's dad so there's no way they'd make a baby together." She wrinkles her face like she has some idea of what that entails. Holy crap. Did Cliff give her the *talk*? What age is that supposed to happen at anyway? "And there are lots of pictures in Papa's closet of you two hugging and kissing and stuff." Solène shrugs. "So I guessed I must be Regina's baby. Besides," she looks up at Gill and points to her face, "we look alike, you and me. You'd have to be blind not to see it."

Solène smiles at Gill and me, turns on her heel, and leaves.

X X X

"I had no idea she'd made the connection," Cliff says as I pace back and forth in the living room, hating that Gill's still here, standing on the other side of the couch staring right at me. *Just go away and leave me in peace,* I think at him, but he doesn't move. I don't even know if he's blinking. "Yes, she found the picture, but I didn't think it was anything to be concerned about." He chuckles, like this whole situation is hilarious. "Knowing how intelligent she is, I should've guessed." He shakes his head and takes a sip of the white wine clutched in his right hand.

"When was this?" I ask, wanting to know how long Solène's known but too afraid to ask her myself. Can you believe that? I'm too nervous to talk to my own daughter about all of this. It's too much. The heist, the shootings, Gilleon, this. I can't take it anymore.

"A couple months before this whole thing started," Cliff says with a grumble, glancing up and to the left, like he can see his son standing behind him. "But if she's not upset about the whole thing, why impress that sort of emotion on her? Everyone handles things in their own way."

261

We all pause at the sound of Solène's door. Her footsteps move down the stairs and she pauses, hanging her head over the banister with a sad puppy dog look on her face.

"Am I in trouble?" she asks, and I can't help it. A laugh explodes from my throat before I can stop it. I clamp a hand over my lips and she smiles. "Can I call you *Maman* now?" I nod but keep my hand right where it is. I'm not sure what expression I'll have when I pull it away. Solène comes down a few more steps and then looks at Gilleon. I feel my heart stop in my chest. "I already call Papa, *Papa* so I've decided that you can be *Père*. Will that work for you?"

"It'll work for me," Gill says softly, his voice rough and unbalanced.

"I realize that this will be a transitionary period for us all," she continues as I drop my hand and curl over with laughter, the sound bursting from my throat, half in relief and half in shock. I can't help it. It comes and it just won't stop.

"*Tu es vraiment quelqu'un d'incroyable, mon petit chou,*" I say. *You're an amazing person, my little cabbage.* Yes, cabbage. It's a French thing. Think of it like sweetheart or something.

"*Qu'est-ce qui est si drôle, Maman?*" Solène asks, wrinkling up her forehead. *What's so funny, Mom?* I shake my head, but I can't stop the sound, dropping into the overstuffed armchair to my left. I'm sure everyone thinks I'm crazy right about now, but that's okay. I think we all feel a little crazy sometimes, and if you can't laugh yourself out of a weird, awkward situation like this, then what's left?

"I'm sorry, I just ..." I trail off and lift my face up to look at Solène as she comes down to stand next to Gill. He's smiling sadly at me, but that expression shifts when Solène reaches down and takes his hand in hers. My heart catches sharply and I suck in a sudden breath. "I'm sorry, baby. I'm sorry for not telling you, for lying about it, for ... just for everything." Cliff sets his wine down on the coffee table, reaching over to put his hand on top of mine.

I appreciate the support, but I don't need it, not really. I'm actually okay with all of this, really okay. My biggest secret is out and it's no big deal. Well, I'm not naïve—I'm sure we'll have some hiccups down the road—but for today, this is good. This is great even.

"Hey," Gill says, kneeling down and brushing some dark hair from Solène's forehead, hair that's the same shade as his own. His fingers are so gentle as he touches her, and his eyes ... God, those eyes. I've always been a fan of those baby blues. "I know this is all a little weird, and that I haven't been around much, but from now, I'm going to be here, okay? I loved you as my little sister, and I'll love you as my daughter."

Solène smiles and slides her arms around Gill's neck, hugging him tight.

This is the same man that shot and killed two people just days ago.

Maybe something's wrong with me because ... I can't seem to find it in myself to hate him for it.

CHAPTER
Eighteen

"Tell me everything."

I have Aveline cornered, trapped at the edge of the deck, her arms crossed on the wet wood, a cigarette dangling from her mouth. She's wearing a pair of baggy acid wash jeans and a black tank, red hair tumbling down her back in loose, wavy curls. When she turns to look at me, her green eyes are sharp and on alert.

"About?" Aveline asks, sliding her cigarette from her mouth with two fingers. I move over to stand next to her, mimicking her position on the railing.

"Gill wants me to go to dinner with him." I pause and my lips twitch. "Again. This time he swears that we won't be tailed. Is that because of ..." I don't finish my sentence. Don't have to. Aveline knows what I'm talking about.

"Maybe," she says, tapping her cigarette over the edge of the railing. Ashes drift in the cool air, floating like snowflakes down to the bright green grass below. "Karl didn't expect Gill to, uh, take care of things in as public a place as a hotel. Big risk. Difficult cleanup." I shudder at the thought of what that might entail.

"So those men weren't trying to ...?" I have no idea how much I should say aloud, how much is safe.

"Kill you?" Aveline supplies and I smile tightly, my diamond pendant swinging loosely in front of me. "Not at that particular moment in time, no. I think at this point, Karl's still hoping that Gill will leave the Max bandwagon and come back to him. Your brother's worth a hell of a lot more money than a bag of stupid shiny rocks will ever be. He's a fucking cash cow."

"That good, huh?" I ask with a sigh. The sound gets caught on the wind and whips up into the trees, their evergreen branches dancing with the rhythm of autumn, the promise of winter. "Is it okay to talk about this stuff outside?" Aveline glances sidelong at me and smirks, standing up and sticking her cigarette back between her red lips. She cups her hands around her mouth and shouts loud enough to make me jump.

"Gilleon Marchal is a master thief!" she screams as I stare wide-eyed and openmouthed at her. Aveline shrugs. "This is too big, Karl's net too wide, for any of these suburban yuppies to be able to do anything about it."

"Huh," I glance around anyway, trying to see if Gill's nosy neighbor is looking out her window at us. Instead I find that someone's fixed the gap in the hedge trees by rearranging the branches. Thank God. "So Gill, uh, robs a lot of … jewelry stores?" I ask, knowing how stupid that question sounds, how surreal.

"He works jobs, yeah, but mostly he plans them out. And not just jewelry stores—museums, the occasional bank. Jewelry stores are the easiest though because security is usually lack as fuck. They turn off the cameras at night, leave the merch right there in the display cases, right behind easy-to-break glass. No gates on the front, no security guards, dim lighting. Shit, it usually takes about three minutes to rob one of these places blind. Gill and me, we can work a job by ourselves and come out with bank."

Aveline takes a drag on her cigarette and shakes her head.

"Your brother though," she says and then pauses, glancing over her shoulder at the side of the house where Gill and I screwed like horny teenagers, "sorry—stepbrother—he's good, almost too good. He can hit places that nobody would ever dream of aiming for."

"So what was so special about this last job? That's what I'm having trouble understanding. I mean, the haul was huge, but that doesn't seem to be a motivating factor for either you or Gill. Aveline, he won't tell me, so I'm asking you, woman to woman." I give her a look and she smiles, red lips twisting into a slight smirk.

"If I tell you his secrets, he'll skin me alive. Look, I get the whole girl power thing and honestly, I'd rather be your friend than his, but I won't piss Gilleon off." I purse my lips and glance back at the yard. It's a good size, a perfect size really, for a family. My heart constricts a little as I imagine living here with Gill, with Solène. We really could've had a beautiful life.

We still could.

I lean over, putting my forehead on my forearms. I can't believe I'm even considering this. Considering him. Fucking Gilleon.

"All I can tell you is that this job, we couldn't have done it without you. You were the only person with the code to that safe. To get in there and out as fast as we needed to, we needed *you*." I lift my head up, brows pinched. I think about the store manager—a guy named Bernard Rossi—and I try to think when he gave me the code to the safe. Only ... he didn't. He asked me to make up my own code. I just assumed that everyone had numbers of their own, to keep track of everything.

"Why have me set the code?" I ask, completely and utterly perplexed. It doesn't make any sense, none of it does.

"Because," Aveline says on the end of another drag, "to keep Gill in line, Karl used you. You were his safety net, his security, his ball and chain." She gives me a sympathy grin and reaches out to pat me companionably on the back. "That's why Karl hired you, you know. He knew his shit was safe with you right there in plain sight, that Gilleon would never do anything to risk you. If Max hadn't stepped in with an offer of protection, you and your family, you'd be dead right now."

"Gill."

He's sitting at his desk, a gun in his hand, some rounds sitting on the cluttered surface next to him. He doesn't even look up when I come in. In fact, since that day with Solène, he's only spoken to me in short, clipped sentences, most of the time when we have an audience. Other than his invitation to dinner, I haven't been able to get anything out of him. It's driving me nuts, just like it did when he first came back. I hate seeing him pretend not to care. It's so much worse than knowing he still does, hearing about it, listening to him tell me everything I ever wanted to hear. If he hadn't waited ten years to say it, I probably would've taken him back. Five years ago, I would've wept at the offer. But now, I've grown past that, grown up.

Gill finishes loading the magazine and inserts it into his gun, setting the whole thing aside as I shut the door behind me.

God.

Being in an enclosed space like this makes my brain muggy, my thoughts scrambled. When I lean back and rest against his door, I get hit with the memory of his hand sliding inside my blouse.

"Are we going to talk about this?"

"Which *this*?" he asks, his voice calm and reasonable, his expression neutral.

"What I said really hurt you, didn't it?" I ask, refusing to shy away from the subject. Why should I? I'm tired of this affecting my life, affecting Solène's life, Cliff's. Gill and me, we need to deal with everything, just get it all out in the open and walk away from it. I used to think that meant walking away from him after this was all over, but now that Solène knows he's her father, I can't do that, not if Gilleon's serious about having a relationship with her. "About no reason being good enough?"

"It's the truth though, isn't it?" he asks on the end of a long sigh, running his fingers through his hair. The tattoos on Gill's arm ripple like shadows in the dim light as he stands up and puts his hands on his hips. He's wearing a black T-shirt today that pulls tight across his chest, and a pair of green camo cargo pants—casually badass and sexy as hell, as usual. "Why should I be hurt? What you said was true, and you're right." My heart skips a beat as Gill takes a step towards me and pauses, searching my face for something.

"That's it? Just *you're right,* and that's all? Why don't you tell me, Gill. I can see the secrets in your eyes, and they're killing you." I move away from the door and sit on the edge of his bed, the smell of Gilleon enveloping me, like he's somehow marked his room with that spicy male scent of his. Goose bumps crawl up my arms and I have to take a breath to calm myself. I pat the mattress next to me and put a smile on my face. "Look, we've been letting our emotions get the better of us, but that's obviously not working out so well."

Gill's mouth twitches into a small smile.

"I've been okay with the way it's been working out," he says, voice darkening into a sensual purr that makes me seriously question my desire to come in here. Between one heartbeat and the next, the amusement in his face fades, almost as quickly as it came, leaving Gill frowning down at me while some sort of internal struggle goes on behind his eyes.

"How can telling me really hurt the situation, Gilleon?"

"I don't want you to hate me, Regina," he says, the words cutting deep, striking a chord in me.

"I don't hate you, Gill," I say with a sigh, but he's already shaking his head, turning away and looking down at the floor as he tries to gather himself together.

"Not now, but you will. If I tell you, you will."

I purse my lips and stand up straight, crossing my arms over my chest.

"Why don't you give me the benefit of the doubt, Gill? Try me, see what happens." I watch Gill's back, the purposeful rise and fall of his chest, like he's doing his best to contain his emotions. "Two days ago, our daughter called us Mom and Dad for the first time," I say, and that catches his attention. He turns around, his heavy boots loud on the floor beneath his feet. "Three days before that, I watched you do something unspeakable, something that should have me running for the hills. But I'm not, Gill. I'm right here. I'm still *right here.*" I drop my arms as he moves close to me, lifting his hands up and sliding his fingers down the long sleeves of my white cashmere sweater. I swallow hard as Gill's right hand plays with the black lace-up ribbon detail on my shoulder.

"Maybe you should be running, Regina? Maybe you should get as far away from me as you possibly can?

Take Solène and go. Hell, take that old man with you, too. Just go and forget everything about me." He slides his hands down my upper arms to my elbows, rubbing his thumbs against the soft fabric and making me catch my breath. If there's one thing Gilleon's an expert at— besides robbing jewelry stores—it's being sensual. Sensual. I can't get enough of him.

"Why come back into my life like this and then tell me to go?"

"Because if you don't, I won't be able to control myself," he whispers, leaning down and brushing his lips against mine. The kiss only lasts for half a second before Gill's pulling away and I'm reaching out—*again*—and grabbing onto his arm. The last time I reached for him, I sucked his dick. This time ...

"Maybe that's your problem, Gill? Control. Stop trying to control everything. Let go. Live a little." My nails slide across his bare skin, across the hard bulge of his bicep, and I watch in satisfaction as goose bumps follow the lines of my fingertips. I drop my hand, fully aware that Gill's standing between the bed and the door, blocking me in with my thighs pressed back against his mattress.

I curl my hands into fists, determined not to let this situation get out of control.

"You asked me to dinner again, so let's go, let's talk, let's figure this all out."

He's just staring at me now, staring with that sapphire blue gaze of his, eyes half-hooded and lips gently parted. Gill looks anything but gentle right now though. He

271

caresses the stubble on his jaw with one hand and then pauses, taking in a deep breath and then reaching down and curling his fingers under the hem of his T-shirt.

"I'd fight an army for the privilege to take you out, Regi." Gill gives me a rough smile. "But I'm not going out like this. Let me shower and shave first." And then he rips his shirt up and over his head, tossing it onto the bed next to me.

Gill's body is built like a god's, like some artist's impossible goal of perfection, chiseled over years from a block of unyielding stone. Only I know that if I touch him, his skin will be warm, hot even, that the softness of his lips will make up for the roughness of the stubble on his face. I try not to stare at the rounded swell of muscles in his tattooed arm, at the way the ink of his tattoos climbs up and over his shoulder, the face of a panther staring back at me from his right pec.

I feel lightheaded and sweaty, like an addict staring down their drug of choice. It's not fair that he can do this to me.

"That's a dirty move, Gilleon," I say, pointing at him. "Real dirty."

He watches me, just like the jungle cat inked on his body, as I move carefully around him and reach for the doorknob, sweat beading on my forehead and lower back.

"I'll meet you downstairs at six?" I ask.

"I'll be there, Regi." Gill smiles and nods briefly before reaching down to unbutton his pants. I don't stick around long enough to see *that* show.

✗ ✗ ✗

"If I'd known we'd be moving to Paris, I would've started taking French in junior high, before German." I pause and take a sip of my coffee, looking at my stepdad over the rim of my mug. "Well, maybe instead of Spanish. My German teacher was actually kind of cute." Cliff laughs and shakes his head, his salt and pepper hair catching the light from the chandelier hanging above us.

"Well, that Rosetta Stone program we got was the best thing that ever happened to me. Even after living in Toulouse with Gilleon's mom, I had yet to pick up more than a few words of French." He chuckles again and sets his coffee down, trading it out for one of the colorful macaroons that are sitting pretty in the center of the table. "It's not easy to learn via immersion when everyone around you speaks English."

"And interrupts your French like it's the most painful thing they've ever heard in their life," I say with a laugh, copying Cliff and going for a goodie. "I could barely get a 'bonjour' out before there were raised brows and cringes all around." I smile at the memory and take a bite of my food, closing my eyes in bliss. Pierre Hermé makes the best freaking macaroons in the city. I make a mental note to order a box of them for my sister, Anika; her birthday's coming up.

"Your mother spoke the most beautiful French," Cliff says with a sigh, his eyes getting faraway like they always do when he reminiscences about Elena. They weren't together long, but he claims that she was his soul mate, that he'll never date again. I hope that's not true— I want my stepdad to be happy—but the sentiment is

273

sweet. Holding onto lost loves ... it's not worth it.

I swallow down my bite of macaroon and pick up my coffee again. No way am I letting my mind go down that particular route. It's too beautiful this morning, too sunny, the streets too bustling. I won't think about Gilleon right now.

"On pourra aller au parc tout à l'heure? Je sens que j'ai besoin de sortir aujourd'hui. Je déteste être enfermée dans cet appartement," *Solène says, appearing in the entrance to the kitchen with her dark hair in ringlets, a white and yellow dress flouncing around as she twists from side to side and rolls her eyes dramatically.* Can we go to the park later? I feel like I need to get out today. I hate being cooped up in this apartment.

"Oui, we can go out together, just me and you. It'll be a girls' day," I say, responding in English so Solène can get some practice in. She takes English in school, too, but it never hurts to hear more than one language at home.

"Oh, Regina, you're so lovely," *she tells me in a tone that's far too mature for her age. I should stop letting her and Cliff watch all those old movies together. Solène bounces into the kitchen, kisses me on the cheek, and steals a macaroon. I watch her skip away, my heart twisting at how much like Gilleon she is—fair skinned, dark haired, blue-eyed, full of wry humor. I wish he could've known her growing up. I've given up on that dream though. Hell, I gave up on that one a long, long time ago. I've resigned myself to the idea that my daughter might never known I'm her mother and not just her way older sister.*

Cliff reaches out and pats my hand before withdrawing it with a sad smile. I give him a tight one back.

"I'm proud of you, Regina. You've come so far in the last ten years. For a while there, I was afraid I'd lose you." I brush away the sad feelings inside, push them back, and let my smile get a little more real, a little brighter. I try to stay positive at all times—it's the only way to truly live.

"Thanks, Papa," I say, looking down into my coffee.

"Enough of that," Cliff says, waving his hand dismissively as I glance up. "What we were talking about again?"

"How your French is still clipped and barbaric, even after all these years." My stepdad laughs as I grin at him. "Don't worry—another ten years in Paris and I think you'll be able to converse with the locals without them cringing in disgust."

"Dad."

Cliff and I both startle, chairs sliding across the hardwood floors. I manage to spill coffee all over my own lap. It drips down my legs, staining my white Herve Leger pencil skirt and splattering my new black suede booties.

But I don't notice any of that—not my ruined clothes or the stinging burns on my fingers from the hot liquid. All I can see right now is him.

Gilleon Marchal.

My stepbrother, long lost love, and the father of my

daughter—all wrapped up into one tall, sexy package. A package I haven't seen in over a decade. Over. A. Decade.

I choke on my own saliva, stumbling to the sink and leaning over as I try to breathe in through my nose.

"Gilleon?" Cliff sounds almost as shocked as I feel, and he's seen his son a handful of times over the last few years. Plus, they chat on the phone every now and then. For me, though, this is like seeing a ghost. "How did you get in here? Isn't the front door ..."

"I picked the lock," Gill says, the slightest hint of amusement in his voice and the quirk of his lips. It fades as quick as it came, leaving that gorgeous face of his a blank slate.

I'm so dizzy that I can barely stand, but I make myself face him, pushing up from the sink and trying to maintain my balance in the four inch heels on my feet.

"Regina," he says, his voice a rough whisper. There's no emotion there though, just a simple greeting, a hello he'd give to any stranger. I stare right back, my own voice caught in my throat, struggling to get out, to do something drastic. I want to scream at him, throw something, but at the same time ... I want to run into his arms, feel those strong muscles wrap around my body and hold me close.

He's gotten so ... big, *I think as I stare at my former lover, at his wide shoulders, his taut abs, his towering height.* Guess he filled out a little after he left. *I swallow hard and realize that our daughter is screaming some pretty horrendous curse words and flailing around*

276

a can of pepper spray. Shit, she must've snagged that from my purse.

"Solène!" *I shout, my voice covering Cliff's as he tries to get his granddaughter under control. Gill turns slowly to look at her, at his own child, and nothing flickers in his gaze, no recognition, no acknowledgement of the life he left behind. Of course, he never knew I was pregnant, but look at her. Just look at her. She looks exactly like him.* "Honey, that's your ... brother," *I say, my voice coming out in a sharp whisper. My vision flickers and blurs, and I sit down heavy in my chair again, trying to come to terms with what I'm seeing.*

Gilleon Marchal, here, in the flesh.

I've dreamed about this moment for years, only now ... it seems the dream's come true too late. All I feel when I look at Gill is anger, a truly passionate rage that I have to swallow three times to get past.

"It's just your brother." *My voice comes out in a whisper, drawing Gill's gaze away from Solène and back to me. The sapphire blue of his eyes triggers a mudslide of memories that churn my stomach as I look up at him.*

"Oh dear," *Solène whispers, staring down at the pepper spray and then placing it in Cliff's outstretched hand.* "Gilleon, of course." *She glides across the floor and smiles up, up, up at Gill's tall frame as he fills the archway between the foyer and the kitchen.* "How lovely to see you again!" *I watch as my daughter throws her arms around Gill's imposing form and squeezes tight. His mouth twitches into a small smile as he pats her head, his eyes still on my face.* "It's been what, four *years?" she continues, drawing some of the awkwardness out of the air with her infectious smile.*

I still can't seem to find my legs, can't seem to stand up with Gill so close. Flickers of memory—his hand wrapped around mine, my body wrapped around his, our lips meeting in a rush of passion—assail me again and I turn away. I've moved on. I have. But this? This is just the sort of thing that could set me back.

"What are you doing here, son?" Cliff asks, his voice not entirely free of anger. I know he's worried about me, about what Gill's sudden presence might mean. He's so intimidating now with that blank stare, those big muscles, an entire sleeve of black and gray tattoos. And when Solène hugged him? I didn't miss the flash of guns beneath his black jacket.

"I need to talk to you," he says, calm, rational, completely free of emotion. "You and Regina." Where's that passion I knew so well? That heat? The little electric bite in his voice when he said my name?

I stand up suddenly because I'm not going to sit here and quiver in his presence. I can't. I won't. My fingers curl into fists as I meet his gaze head on, waiting for something, some spark of the love that used to reign king between us. But there's nothing. Nothing. Nothing.

I feel sick.

"Can we speak in private?" he asks, gesturing lamely at his still beaming daughter. Cliff nods and whispers something to Solène in French that I can't quite hear before leading her away towards the back hallway and the bedrooms. I watch them go, pulling my gaze away

278

from Gill's so I can catch my breath. Even if he can look at me and feel nothing, I feel everything: fear, hope, anger, love. "It's good to see you again," he says blandly, coming closer, his boots loud on the hardwood floors. My eyes snap down to them, to the black leather, and then travel up the dark denim on his legs, past his tight black T-shirt and jacket, right up to that achingly familiar face. His nose is still straight and perfect, his lips still full and inviting, but there's something missing there, something that I got so used to seeing that I didn't think twice about it. Passion. Gill used to be passionate about me; he's not anymore.

I stiffen as he moves forward and drapes an emotionless hug over my shoulders, giving me a weak squeeze that's all space and formality, not closeness and love. I don't even get the hug a normal stepsister would get. Just this. This nothingness.

I swallow hard as he steps back and I look up into his face.

I don't know why Gilleon is here or why, but I can tell right off the bat that this isn't the reunion I've always dreamed of.

Gill doesn't love me anymore.

I try not to be sad about it, to stand there strong and empty, but inside, my heart breaks into pieces all over again. Until this moment, I never truly realized how much I missed the love in his eyes.

And he will never, ever look at me with that same passion again.

XXX

I barely make it three steps out of that room before Gill's moving after me, grabbing me by the arm and yanking me back into his bedroom.

The door slams shut behind me as Gilleon pushes me against it with his half-naked body, one arm wrapped around my waist, his other elbow leaning against the wood to the right of my head. We're both panting, staring into one another's eyes like we're not sure how we ever managed to look away in the first place.

In his gaze, I see it again, that something that I never thought would come back, that I feared was dead forever.

Love. Passion. Desperation.

I want to pull away, open this door and walk out.

But I can't.

It's irresponsible, and it's stupid, and I know it's probably a big mistake, but I find my fingers traveling up the sides of Gill's face, over the slight stubble on his cheeks, until I curl them in that thick, dark hair of his.

"I can't do this again, Gilleon," I whisper, feeling a slight brush of tears, tears that I've fought off since the moment he first walked back into my life, his face blank and empty, but his heart full. That terrifying moment in the kitchen when I was certain he didn't love me anymore, it was all a fucking performance. But he can't fool himself anymore.

And neither can I.

I can't keep lying to myself about Gilleon.

I love him with a passion so bright it blinds, so hot it burns, so wild that it can't be tamed, no matter how hard I try or how long I fight, how mature I think I am or how much distance I put between us. Despite what he did to me, to our daughter, to the life we should've had ...

"No, Regina," he says, his voice a shattered sea of glass, cutting into me with the rough tenderness in his words. "There's no *again,* not ever. I couldn't walk away from you if my life depended on it." He swallows hard and closes his eyes. "Not even if yours did." He turns his head away slightly and pulls back, releasing me and leaving my skin hot and aching for him. "I told you," he says again, "love is selfish."

I reach up and find warm tears trailing down my cheeks, the emotions that I've been fighting back for so long just come flooding up and out to the point that my knees go weak and I find myself sliding down the door. Gill catches me before I hit the floor and hauls me up and into his arms like I don't weigh a thing, setting me on the edge of the bed and stepping back. I think we both need some space right now—even if my body's telling me a different story. I want him to fuck me again, fill me up, capture my mouth with his.

But my heart is rocked with a revelation, and I need a breather.

"I still love you," I say, and the words drop from my lips in a near sob. No. I don't want to be like this; I'm strong.

But then ... maybe I'm trying to measure strength by the wrong rules? Maybe strength isn't about how well you push the emotions back, maybe it's in how you embrace them? They don't have to rule your life, but they're always there and they need to be acknowledged.

That's what I'm doing now. Acknowledging them. And if I thought my heart couldn't hurt anymore than it already did ... I was wrong. I feel like I'm being torn into pieces, blood oozing from old wounds as I try to come to terms with everything.

Gill still loves me—never stopped loving me if he's to be believed. And I do. I believe him.

And me ... I know I never stopped loving him. In fact, that whole *absence makes the heart grow fonder* bit, I think that's true. I feel so full of emotion that I can barely breathe past the tightness in my chest.

"I love you," I say, my voice cracking as I put my head in my hands. "I shouldn't, but I do. I do."

Gill says nothing, but I can feel him looking right at me, his gaze cutting straight through my soul.

"I love you, too, Regina. More than anything. That's why I left before, because I was afraid for you. Karl, he promised me he'd do the same thing to you that he did to your mother."

My gaze snaps up suddenly, my hands falling into my lap.

"What?" I ask, brushing away the tears as I stare wide-eyed at a shirtless Gilleon, his jeans undone, muscles tight, but expression sober. "What the hell does that mean?"

"It means," he says, running a hand down his face, his voice a rough whisper, "that I can't keep secrets from you anymore, Regi. I can't keep ducking around the truth." Gill's breath hitches and he looks me straight in the face, scaring the hell out of me with his expression.

"Karl had your mother killed, Regi. Because of me. Elena, she's dead because of *me.*"

CHAPTER
Nineteen

My heart pounds in my chest, rattling my bones, speeding up my pulse until all I can hear is the sound of my own blood thumping inside my head. Those words spoken by anyone else would mean nothing, a ridiculous statement that I wouldn't give a second thought to.

But Gill ... Gill wouldn't joke about this. Or exaggerate. Or lie. Not about *this*.

I stare into his blue eyes, so focused on mine that I wonder if he's even breathing; I know I'm not. The silence stretches uncomfortably between us as I wait for an explanation and he waits for a reaction.

"I don't understand," I whisper finally, my chest tight, the tears drying into salty lines on my cheeks. Gilleon turns away suddenly, raking his fingers through his hair and shaking his head like he's regretting his sudden confession. But no. When he turns to look at me, there's enough fear and hope in his eyes that I can tell: he needs to speak the truth as much as I need to hear it. But he's afraid he's going to lose me in the process ... and he's praying to God that he doesn't. "What are you talking about? My mom ... she was in the wrong place at the wrong time." I stand up, but my legs feel weak, too weak to hold me, so I sit back down again, the mattress dipping beneath me. "Gilleon, you better explain yourself before I have a goddamn heart attack."

"Regina," he says, his voice breaking a little on the last syllable, trailing into a rough growl that brings goose bumps up on my arms. "I'm sorry, baby. I'm so fucking sorry, *mon cœur*." *My heart.*

"You seem to be saying sorry a lot lately, Gilleon, but before I can forgive you, I have to know what exactly it is that you're apologizing for." I suck in a deep breath and close my eyes, trying to control my pulse, trying to still my frantic nerves. *What the hell is going on here?* I can't take a single second more of not knowing.

He nods, but he doesn't look at me, turning so that his back is facing me, the tail of the panther curving with the movement of his muscles as he bends down to grab a shirt. I guess we're both aware of how much harder this will all be if he doesn't put some clothes on. Gill shrugs the shirt over his head, mussing up his black hair.

I stare at him as he turns back to face me, and I wonder: if his words are true, will I hate him for it?

But no. No.

I watched him kill two men right in front of me, and I

285

can't summon the feelings of disgust or shock or outrage that most people would feel. Gilleon Marchal, he's my weakness and my strength, has been since the day he picked the lock on my bedroom door. I have a feeling that not even death will change that, so what about this revelation of his?

I reach up and realize that I'm crying again, tears leaking down my cheeks as I stare at the wetness on my fingertips in surprise. *I think I'm in shock already, and I still don't have the full story.* What's going to happen to me when I do?

"Karl Rousseau had your mother killed to teach me a lesson, Regina." He pauses and his voice drops into a deep rumble more akin to a growl than actual words. Gill's angry, but not at me. "My mother, too, Regi," he whispers, trying to keep the sound from ascending into a yell. "He had my mother murdered, too."

I stare at him in stunned silence. Until this moment, I didn't even know she was dead. I let that knowledge brush away some of my fear, focusing on Gill's mom instead of my own. It's just ... easier that way. Without even realizing I'm doing it, my fingers curl around my mother's diamond pendant. Gill doesn't miss the gesture.

"I ..." I try to think up some way to respond to the sadness in his eyes, the regret, but there's nothing. I swallow hard and close my eyes. "I'm sorry to hear that." My words come out in a whisper, but I hope he can tell how sincere they are. I mean, he's Gilleon, of course he can. I open my eyes back up and meet his gaze.

Gill smiles tightly at me.

"It was twelve years ago," he says with a slight shrug, like it doesn't matter. But I know it does. Family's as important to Gill as it is to me, or at least I always thought it was. It was one of the things that drew me to him. When he left, I figured it'd all been a lie. But maybe not? Maybe, just maybe ...

Fuck.

I just want all of this shit out in the open, so I can stare it straight in the face and figure out what to do about it. I just admitted my feelings to him; isn't that enough for one day?

"Gill," I begin, wishing I could just lean back and drop into the mess of blankets on his bed, curl them around my body and close my eyes, forget this day ever happened. I start again. "Gill, I'm sorry about your mom, but I ... I don't understand how any of that relates to mine. You were with me the day that she died, Gill— in *Paris* no less. How could you have been responsible for what happened to her in Seattle?"

As the seconds tick past, my mind whirs with possibilities, trying to convince my heart that Gill's over-exaggerating or overestimating his influence on the situation. But I know that's not true. Gilleon doesn't make mistakes like that.

Karl had your mother killed, Regi. Because of me. Elena, she's dead because of me.

Gill reaches up and rubs at his shoulder, where the bullet grazed his flesh. The wound's mostly healed now, pink and ragged at the edges but closed up. That's how my heart feels—or how it felt before now. The wounds

287

were there, yes, and they still hurt sometimes, but they weren't open and oozing, waiting for infection to take over. I'm terrified that this conversation is going to rip them wide open.

"When I lived with my mother," Gill begins when I don't say anything else, running his hand down his face again. I know he doesn't like to talk about that part of his life, all of the horrible things he endured while trying to keep his mom from plunging into the deep end. He pauses and takes a deep breath, the muscles and tendons in his hands standing out against his tight knuckles as he curls them into fists. "Fuck," he growls, looking down at the floor and putting his hands on his hips as he tries to pull himself together. Me, I feel like I'm in a dream right now. Okay, nightmare. But I feel like I'm asleep, floating through a fantasy world that'll burst into bubbles at first light. So, since I can't do anything about my own hurting, I decide to focus on Gill's.

Without thinking twice about it, I stand up and move across the room, sliding my arms around Gill's strong midsection and resting my head against his chest. He sucks in a deep breath before returning the favor, holding me tight, fingers fisting in the back of my white sweater.

"I remember," I tell him, my breath coming in short, quick bursts as I push back another set of tears. At this point, I don't even really know what exactly it is that I'm crying about: Gill, my mom, his mom, maybe even … me? I haven't cried for me in a long, long time. "I remember when I was nineteen," I say, closing my eyes against the warmth radiating from Gill's chest, "you'd just turned twenty, and we were supposed to go to dinner for your birthday. Me, you, and Cliff. I remember you calling your mom because you were surprised she hadn't called you on your birthday. You went into your room, and you didn't come out. You told Cliff and me that you weren't feeling well."

"I called my mom's number and some guy answered," he says, filling in the blanks for me. "He said she'd been shot during some drug deal gone bad." He takes another breath and scoots me back just enough to look into my eyes. "I didn't tell you because we were so happy then: me, you, and dad. And you'd just started to really smile again." Gill reaches up and brushes a stray tear away with his thumb, making my breath hitch.

I imagine him smiling through the pain, struggling with that loss alone, and I feel a wave of sadness break over me.

"Thank you for sharing with me," I tell him, and I mean it, too. The things he's telling me now, these are things that Gill never shared before. It gives me hope, too much hope, that this could really work between us again. *Shit.* I step back out of his arms, crossing my own over my chest and staring down at his bare feet on the hardwood floor. "But I assume this all ties together in the worst of ways?"

One of my tears hits the floor and splatters on Gill's toes. I'm transfixed by it, can't even bring myself to look away.

"It gets worse," he admits, and I nod because hell, I'm invested now, all in. I gave up the life I'd built, the only

289

life my daughter had ever known, that my stepdad loved, and I dragged them all into this with me because I still love Gilleon. I could live a thousand years and still love him with a fierceness that hurts. Whether we end up back together or not, I'm a part of all this, so I have to see it through. "It gets so much worse, Regina."

And it does.

Because all of this, this pain and this tragedy, it all leads to the day that Gilleon left. And even though I miss my mom, miss her so fucking much that I can't breathe sometimes, I missed Gilleon more. More. *Most.*

The idea that my mother is dead because of ... Gilleon. I don't see how all this fits together yet, but I'm scared, a cold chill traveling from my heart right down to my toes.

"I need a minute, okay?" I say, realizing that I can only take so much, can only process so much at once, and he nods again, not trusting himself to speak. In the back of my mind, I know why I'm doing this, why I'm asking for a break: I don't want whatever this is to come between us, to push us apart, to make me lose Gilleon again. *I'm afraid.*

I glance up, and we look into one another's eyes for a moment, the feelings I admitted earlier floating in the air between us. We need to talk about those, sure, but first, I have to hear what Gill has to say about all of this. After more than a decade, I'll finally know why he left.

But, I can't help but wonder, *is it too little, too late?*

x x x

I take the cell phone Gill gave me into my bathroom and

perch on the edge of the refinished claw-foot tub, rubbing my thumb across the screen to unlock it. The picture he left me is still there, the words *I'm Sorry, Can You Ever Forgive Me?* floating in front of my blurry gaze.

"How the hell did I ever get myself into this mess?" I murmur, my fingers twitching as I consider dialing up Anika or Leilani. But no. They don't need me dragging shit into their life, putting them in danger just because I feel like I need a friend to talk to. It's not fair, and their lives are worth way more than that. Instead, I sigh and turn the screen off, tossing the phone onto the vanity and dropping my head into my hands.

Elena, she's dead because of me.

I try to wrap my head around Gill's words, around the secret that burst from his lips like a bird with wings. That, and the truth of my own heart finally revealing itself. *I love him, and I want him back.* I feel like it's a disaster waiting to happen, a trap waiting to be sprung, an inevitable future heartbreak, but I can't stop the feelings. They're there and that's that.

I sit up and rub the tears from my face, rising to my feet and staring at my reflection in the mirror. Honey blonde hair curls gently around my shoulders while pale brown eyes stare back at me, the expression on my face so foreign yet so familiar. I lift up a finger and trace the heart-shape of my face, the gentleness of my parted lips. *Love.* It shimmers in my gaze, layered over heartache and fear and grief.

I close my eyes and turn around, leaning back against the sink as I lift my chin up and let my hair hang down my back as I think things through. After that kind of conversation, most people would just assume that dinner plans were out the window. Not Gill. He'll be downstairs at six waiting for me. I stand up and open my eyes, checking the phone for the time. *Five-fifteen.*

Okay.

I can do this.

No matter what Gill says to me, I can handle it.

I pull my sweater over my head and drape it over the closed toilet seat, sitting down to pull my heels off. I'll get through this. I will. I'll get through it and I'll do it looking fabulous because my clothes are my armor, my beauty a shield, my makeup a mask. And right now, I could use all the help I can get.

I turn on the water for the shower and finish stripping down in the ensuing steam, letting the warmth caress my naked skin. I can only imagine the filmy mist is Gilleon, curling his body around mine, holding me close, touching me everywhere. Just the idea makes my body throb, my heart pound, my breath catch.

I climb into the shower, letting the hot water wash away Gill's confessions until I can't think of anything but the pressure of the spray on my skin. I wash my hair, condition it, scrub my body, and I manage to keep all of the feelings and the thoughts at bay until I climb out and wrap a towel around myself.

The first thing I do is put the diamond pendant back on, letting it rest against my heated skin as I lay my palm over it and close my eyes.

"Regi."

Gill's voice startles me so badly that I jump, spinning to face him in a whirl, the towel sliding off my body and hitting the floor with a wet thump.

"Jesus, Gilleon!" I yell, my heart beating frantically as I bend down and snatch the pink fabric back, letting it dangle in front of all my most important bits. "Don't sneak up on me like that!"

Gill's sitting on the edge of my bed, elbows on his knees, hands in fists, chin resting against his knuckles. He glances over at me with a small smile, a real one this time, not even a hint of bitterness. Guess my reaction is funny enough that we can pretend the rest of the day didn't happen—for at least a few minutes anyway. Personally, I could use a break from all of that intensity; you won't find me complaining about a change of subject.

"What are you doing in here?" I ask him, not bothering to inquire why my locked bedroom door did nothing to keep him out. I think Gilleon impulsively picks locks for fun, just to prove that he can. I turn away, sacrificing a small view of my ass so that I can get the towel in order, tucking the end in over my breasts before I spin back to face him.

Gill's blue eyes are half-hooded and dark, drinking in my near-naked form before he turns away like he's ashamed of himself.

"Don't think that just because we had one emotional moment together that you're welcome in my bedroom whenever you damn well feel like it." I take a deep breath and force myself to stop talking. I'm using anger as a shield right now, and I hate that.

293

"I don't think that," Gill says in a near whisper. I watch as he clears his throat, composes himself and turns back to me, rising from the bed until he's standing there looking down at me with a fierce tenderness burning in his eyes. "I was worried about you, Regi. It's almost six-thirty, and I can understand if you don't want to go to dinner, but—"

"Six-thirty?" I ask, retreating back into the bathroom and grabbing my phone. *Holy crap.* It really is as late as he says. Which means ... I was in the shower for that long? Our conversation must've affected me more than I realized. "Oh my God."

"Regi," Gill says, drawing my attention back to the doorway. He's leaning against the doorframe, his massive form filling the entire space. I notice that he's shaved his face again, leaving a stark contrast between the conversation we just shared and now. *Dark and light.* I watch him tilt towards the latter and wonder if I have the strength to catch him. "Are you sure you're alright?"

"I'm fine, Gilleon," I say, making myself smile. "If it's okay, I'd still like to go out tonight. I think I could use a night away, you know?" *And if we're going to have this conversation, I want it to happen in public. Everything gets toned down in public. I don't think I can survive another moment like the one we just shared.*

I take a deep breath and turn away, reaching up to rub the fog off the mirror. As soon as I do, I see that Gill's standing right behind me.

"Shit, Gill," I gasp out as one of his strong arms encircles my waist and pulls me close. "Stop doing that."

I reach down to pry him off, but I find that I can't do it. Instead, my fingers curl around his wrist and my eyes close of their own accord. It feels too good to do this, to fall back into old habits. And it's easy, so easy. When Gill touches me, I can almost imagine that it's still that day, the day that my life stopped. I imagine for a moment what would've happened if he'd been there waiting for me, if I'd handed over the bag of baby goodies and smiled shyly at him. *So different ... everything would've been so different.*

I open my eyes up and move away. He lets me go, waiting as I turn around and look up into those bright blue eyes of his.

"I said I loved you," I tell him, the words making me feel queasy. It's not easy to look somebody like Gilleon in the face and admit the most private thing in your heart. "I didn't say that we were a couple again. I didn't say that I'd take you back."

"But you want to?" he asks me, taking a step closer, his boots squeaking on the wet floor. I back up, not because I'm afraid of Gilleon, but because I'm afraid of what I'll do if he touches me again.

"I haven't heard the whole story, Gill," I admit, because that's a huge part of all this.

"But if you do, if you can find it in your heart to forgive me, I'll spend every second of the rest of my life making it up to you."

Shit.

"You can't just barge in here and say things like that," I mumble, running my hands down my damp cheeks,

knowing as I do that they're tinged with a hint of pink—
and I can't blame any of that color on the warmth still
clinging to the bathroom. "I'm not a teenager anymore,
Gill. I need more than blushes and butterflies."

"I give you butterflies?" he asks with a small smirk,
running his knuckles down my bare arm, knocking stray
droplets of water from my skin with the motion. I shiver,
can't help it. Gill's touch is ... well, it's always made me
feel like this. I spent the second year after he left trying
to prove that it wasn't true. At the time, I'd only ever
slept with one man, only ever kissed one man, so how did
I know? But, as I soon discovered, nobody could make
me feel like this, touch me like this, love me like this. It
was a heartbreaking conclusion to have to come to; the
one man I wanted would never be mine again.

Only ... he could. Right now, the only person
standing between us is *me*. Part of me wants to throw up
my hands and say forget the past while the other part ...
can I ever really forgive and forget? Those scars will
always be there, but can I live with them *and* with Gill at
the same time?

"You know you do," I tell him, unashamed. I take
another step back, trying to put some space between us
and end up bumping into the countertop. Gill follows me
in, leaning down and brushing some wet strands of hair
from my forehead.

"Listen to the rest of the story, Regi, and give me a
chance. That's all I'm asking. When you know
everything, all of the reasons why and how, then think
about it. If you decide you don't want me, then I'll let

you go."

I snort and shake my head, trying not to let his nearness affect me. He's dressed in boots and jeans, and here I am in just a towel, warm and damp and wet from the shower. I feel a certain vulnerability standing before Gilleon like this, but I like it. I like it even though I shouldn't, even though I know he's dangerous, that he's teetering on the edge. I think I could save him, I do. Under normal circumstances, I'd be rolling my eyes: women who seek damaged men in order to fix them, usually not a story that ends well.

But Gill isn't just any man. He's my man, and he always has been. Since the moment we met, when I was sixteen and he was seventeen, I knew. For half my life, I've loved him.

"I can't see you giving up so easily," I say as he runs his finger across my naked collarbone and I shiver again, goose bumps racing down my arms.

"Maybe you're right," he says with a bemused smile, getting awfully close to the tucked edge of the towel. "But I'll at least try to leave you alone."

"That's not creepy at all," I say, trying to imagine him keeping an eye on me all these years. When I wept for him, he was there. When I ached, and I hurt, and I wanted to give up on everything, he was *right fucking there.* I know I couldn't have watched him from afar and never reached out. How and why he did it I'll never understand. Unless, of course, I let him finish his story and I listen, really listen, and keep an open mind, an open heart.

I take a deep breath as he reaches for the edge of the towel, pulling it open and letting it drop to the floor at my feet. I wrap my arms around my bare chest and close my eyes for a moment.

"I'll listen, Gill," I tell him because I'd always planned to. "And I'll think about it, really think about it."

"So there's a chance?" he asks me, and I nod.

"There's a chance."

My voice comes out in a whisper as his arms slide down my sides and take hold of my hips, his mouth dipping to mine in a soft brush of lips that sends those pesky butterflies flapping around inside my belly.

"Say it again for me, Regina," he whispers as he moves his mouth to my ear and nibbles on the lobe. I should be telling him to get out, to stop touching me, but I can't. I just can't. No matter what happens, I need this right now. I *need* it.

"Say what?" I ask, my fingers sliding under his shirt, greedily taking in the hard planes of his abs. If I'm in right now, I'm all in. Then, even if I decide to walk away, I can have this night for the rest of my life.

"That you love me," he growls, his fingers tightening on my arms for a moment before he relaxes and breathes deep, leaning in so that our bodies press close—his warm, dry, clothed and mine, wet, shivering, naked. The contrast excites me enough that I feel like I should fight against it, the feelings so intense that I'm scared by the fact that they could backfire on me. But no. No, I'm saving those thoughts for later. Right now is only for ... this.

"I still love you, Gilleon. And I never stopped. That's why it hurt so much, all these years." I reach up and run my fingers along his smooth cheek, turning his face to mine so our lips can touch, so we can kiss long and deep and sensual, slow. We've been fucking lately, but we haven't been doing this, loving each other like this.

"God, I missed you, Regi," he says, pulling back just long enough to speak the words before he reaches down and scoops me up into his arms. I don't stop kissing him as he carries me, running my mouth up the side of his jaw to his ear and enjoying the shiver I get in response. "I missed you so fucking much."

Gill lays me down on the bed and stands up, pulling his shirt over his head and reaching down to remove his belt before climbing in between my legs, looking down at me with an arm on either side of my head. I can't help myself, finally giving into the wonder I felt after seeing him again for the first time. I touch his face, trace his lips, run my fingers up into his hair.

When Gilleon leans down to kiss me, I wrap my arms around his neck and drag him down so that our bodies are pressed close, naked chest to naked chest, the firm bulge of his erection brushing against me through his jeans. We don't rush things though, not this time, letting our hands roam, our mouths taste, our breathing even out until the pulsing pound of our heartbeats feels like it's in sync.

Gill pulls back, moving his mouth to my breast, running his tongue in a circle around my nipple before reaching up to knead and caress the tender flesh. His fingers scald my skin as they travel down and trace my ribs, making me realize that I'm holding my breath again. I let it out in a rush as he continues kissing down, across my belly and towards the patch of honey blonde hair between my legs.

I spread my knees as Gill runs his fingers up the insides of my thighs, drawing me open before he dips his mouth down and breathes hot against me, making me arch my back and bite my lower lip so hard it bleeds. No more words pass between us. We're beyond them now.

I moan, turning my head into the pillows to keep my voice down. Stars flicker across the insides of my eyelids as I bite the fabric and gasp at the sudden pressure of Gill's fingers gripping my hips tight. I realize why a moment later when he moves his lips over my clit, kissing me gently and testing the waters before increasing the pressure.

I'm so wet right now, so desperate to feel him inside of me again, but I don't push it. I wait, letting him circle my clit in slow, lazy whorls, drawing his mouth down to my opening and teasing me for a split second before working his way back up. By the time Gill's fingers slide inside of me, I'm lost, floating on a sea of pleasure, but sinking fast. I tighten around him, clamping down hard and feel him groan against my body, breath fluttering against the inside of my thigh.

My girlfriends back in Paris used to say that they thought oral sex was a step up from vaginal intercourse, an act of intimacy that wasn't acceptable during a one-night stand. Coming from the States where people act like oral isn't even sex at all (a sentiment I never echoed, by the way), I didn't really get it. I mean, it's sex, obviously, but is it really more intimate? In this moment with Gilleon, I see where they're coming from. I feel so open, so exposed, and I know he's there and he can see *everything,* and not just the physical bits. Gill's pleasuring me, watching me writhe and moan, but he isn't wrapped up in his own body, in the slide of his cock between my legs; all he's doing right now is watching. Looking. He's looking right at me.

I drag a pillow over my face to hide a scream as Gill's knuckles slam into me, his tattooed fingers disappearing between my legs as he continues working his tongue around my clit. Always patient, never rushed, Gill listens to the rhythm of my body, the pulsing ebbs of pleasure that radiate through me, and he holds steady until I'm gasping into the pillow, fireworks flickering and flashing behind my eyelids.

Without missing a beat, Gill sits up and unbuckles his pants, dragging the pillow away from my face and tossing it to the floor before he enters me in a slow, smooth motion, riding right through the blooming pleasure of my orgasm. His blue eyes look right into mine as he slides deep, rocking our hips together until I can feel him hit the end of me. Gilleon's just long enough to tease, not long enough to hurt.

I gasp and grab the sides of his face, pulling him in for a kiss, flickers of an old life riding through me like the last waves of pleasure from my orgasm. Our first time— and the many, many others that followed it—drift in and out of my mind as I wrap my legs around my first love and wonder how the hell I ever even considered saying no. Of course, it's hard to think when a fucking Adonis is gliding above you, muscles defined and taut, hard beneath my fingers, laced with sweat.

I pull Gill's head down to me, and he growls, biting his lip hard as I lick the sweat from the corded muscles of his throat, nibbling and tasting that spicy masculine sweetness, breathing in the bergamot scented perfection of him. In that moment, in that fucking moment, he is *mine.*

You're my constant, Regi.

Gill's words ring in my head as I trail my hands over his muscular shoulders and down to his chest. Without having to say a single word, Gilleon knows what I want, rolling onto his back and letting me straddle him. All of that strength, all of that power, I want it beneath me, and I want to own it.

We lock gazes again as I position Gill's cock at my opening and slide down his shaft until our sweaty pelvises meet, my fingers splayed on his chest, his hands gripping my hips again. I start to move, slow at first, and then faster, grinding us together, my clit rubbing on his hot, hard body. The only sounds I can hear are our panting breaths and the slick slide of flesh in flesh, my wetness betraying my desire, the brightness in Gill's gaze betraying his.

Gill's hands tighten, squeezing hard enough that his grip almost hurts, but I know that's still just a tiny fraction of the power inside of him, that if he wanted to flip me over and fuck me, he could. But he wouldn't; he won't. I know that he can tell I need this, that I need to possess him, convince myself that he really could be mine again, that we could actually be together.

I shove some stray strands of blonde behind my shoulder as Gill moves his right hand over to my belly and up, palming my breast, cooling some of that sharp ache with his fingers as he runs his thumb over my hardened nipple. His touch is gentle at first, and growing rougher as the pleasure builds tight and tense between us.

It's my turn to watch Gill's face as he comes inside of me, his back arching, lifting me up off the bed like I'm weightless, flying, floating above him. Those stubborn blue eyes won't leave mine though, not even as his body spasms with pleasure. I bend down and bite his lip roughly, hard enough to draw the slight metallic tang of blood, refusing to slow the rhythm of my hips.

Our lovemaking takes a strange turn, from an emotional roller coaster to something … much more primal. Gill makes a face then, like a snarl, and pushes me off and over onto my back. I hit the pillows with a gasp, arching my spine as Gill kicks his boots off and tosses his pants to the floor, climbing between my legs and sliding his palm up my belly. I writhe under his touch, watching through half-hooded eyes as sweat drips down his chest, glistens on his tattooed right arm, on the gunshot scar on his shoulder.

"So beautiful," I say, the words slipping past my lips before I can stop them. Gill rakes a hand through his dark hair and shakes his head.

"I could say the same thing about you," he whispers,

voice rough and dark as he slides our sweaty bodies together, fisting his fingers in my hair and kissing me hard, as hard as I just kissed him. I can still taste the blood dancing between our tongues, at war with the bright citrusy taste of him. My hips arch up and slide against Gill, finding him just as hard and ready for me as he was before. *Fuck.*

What we just did, that was us trying to find a way to get close again. What we're doing right now … is making up for lost time. It's fierce and hard and full of anger and sadness and fear. I want it, need it, but I also want it to be over. Then I can move on, really truly move on—whether I'm with Gilleon or not.

"Hard and fast, Gill," I breathe as he pulls back and I turn over, stretching like a cat, using some of my own feline grace to entice Gilleon to thrust into me, his hands pulling my hips back, slamming his pelvis into my ass. The bed creaks, the headboard hits the wall, and goddamn it, I know there are people in this house who will know *exactly* what that means, but I don't care.

I moan, struggling to keep myself up on all fours, held up more by Gilleon's strength than my own. I'm melting, wasting away into dirty, filthy, guilty pleasure. When I feel him tensing up, getting ready to come again, I let myself go completely, collapsing beneath him as Gill releases his pleasure inside of me, thrusting long enough that I clench down around him and come hard, fast, and messy.

With my cheek pressed into the pillows, I'm asleep before I get a chance to overanalyze what just happened.

CHAPTER

Twenty

I wake up sometime later—much later if the clock on my nightstand has anything to say about it. I reach out clumsily and spin its face away with a groan, my right arm flopping unceremoniously on the bed.

The bed I shared with Gilleon last night.

I sit up suddenly, covers rustling against my naked body as I fist my fingers in the fabric and glance over at the empty space beside me. I could be offended that Gill's gone already, but I'm not. I bet he's around here somewhere, and if he's not, then he just left. Even though I was out cold last night, I could feel Gill beside me, his body wrapped around mine. If I'm honest with myself, it's the best sleep I've had in years—in over a decade actually.

I rub the heel of my hand against my bleary eyes and stifle a yawn. It's five in the morning which means ... after Gill and I had sex, I must've passed out into an emotionally exhausted coma, sleeping right through our proposed dinner date. Oh well. I don't mind, and I'm guessing he doesn't either. I lift my arms up into a stretch, letting the blankets settle around my waist and exposing my bare breasts to the cool air of the bedroom, nipples already hardening into points.

"*Merde,*" I curse, shaking my head and swinging my legs over the edge of the bed. When I go to stand up, my knees almost buckle, and I have to sit back down again for a moment. I am *sore* downstairs, my heart still all gooey and messed up inside from everything that just happened. When I think about the lovemaking, about gazing into one another's eyes, I flush from head to toe. When I think about the fucking that happened after ... it gets worse. I groan and drop my face into my palms for a moment.

The guy tells me that my mother's death is his fault somehow and I jump into bed with him? Tell him I'll consider giving him a second chance after he abandoned me? I must be crazy.

I drop my hands and raise my head, staring through the darkness at the empty wall in front of me. I must be crazy ... but I don't feel crazy. Somehow, this seems like the right thing to do, the right move to make. And it's not just the sex—although that's a bonus. Good sex isn't everything; it doesn't make the heart feel full, doesn't challenge the mind, doesn't listen carefully to secrets in the dark. But Gill ... he can be all of that for me and more. Trust me, I know, because he's been all those things before. Gilleon's not just a good lover; he's a good partner, too.

A good partner who once made a terrible, terrible mistake.

I shake my head, take in a deep breath. I don't want to think about Gill leaving, not right now, not after what just happened between us.

I stand up and head to the bathroom first, debating the merits of my stolen hotel robe versus a proper outfit. The robe says *yeah, I'm cool with this whole thing,* gives off a comfortable sense of domestic bliss that I'm just not ready to admit to yet. A dress practically screams *trying too hard to look like I don't give a crap.* Hmm. I give myself a moment to think by fussing with my hair. Since it's already a hot mess, I twist it up into a chignon and call it good, slipping my body under the hot spray of the shower for a second, just to cleanup. And there's *a lot* to cleanup after—Gill and I had a good fucking time last night.

When I climb out of the shower and spy Gill's discarded shirt on the floor near my bed, the compulsion is almost impossible to resist. I have so many memories of slipping into his clothes, letting the extra fabric billow against my naked thighs as I moved into the kitchen to make a cup of coffee or snuck over to his side of the bed to give him a kiss. Gill's spicy scent would rise around me, tease my already tender body with the promise of more.

Hell no.

Okay, *that* shirt is an absolute no go.

I decide to wear the jeans Gill bought for me, the ones I used when we were sneaking around Pike Place incognito, and my white Ella Moss tank, the one that reminds me of my mother. Clean panties and a bra are musts, but I decide to skip the shoes, even if a pair of Louboutin red sole sandals seem to be calling my name from the corner of the closet ...

I give myself a quick once-over in the bathroom mirror, my swollen lips and reddened cheeks impossible to miss. *Damn you, Gill.* I shake myself out, take a deep breath and head into the hallway, letting my bedroom door snick softly shut behind me.

I can't wait to see him. The thought bubbles up inside of me, stripping the years away, making me feel like a teenager again as I head for the stairs. I pause for a moment and run my hands down the front of the lacy top, wondering what our interaction's going to be like this morning. Will he be as happy to see me as I am to see him? I'm damn near positive that the answer to that question is a radiant, effervescent *yes.* Gill's words come floating back to me: *Let me make that all clear right now. I have one goal, one motive. Regina, I want you back.*

I brush some loose strands of hair back and glance at Cliff's and Solène's doors. Both closed, no light shining from underneath. Good. I need to see Gill, talk to Gill, before either of them sees me with him. I need to know exactly what I'm working with here. Well, besides butterflies. Those pesky bastards are back and making my stomach twist with each brush of their metaphorical little wings.

I start down the stairs before I let myself get too worked up about this. *It's just Gill—and probably Aveline.* That oughta be fun. If she didn't hear us fucking earlier, I'll be awfully surprised. I move down the steps slowly and then pause at the first landing, one hand on the railing, my gaze focused on the stained glass window in front of me. I can hear them both from here, talking in the kitchen, their voices nothing more than murmurs in the quiet dark of the house.

I take a deep breath and pull my eyes away from the rose pattern in the glass, turning and taking the last few stairs loudly enough that I'm sure they know I'm coming by the time I set foot in that kitchen.

I pause in the doorway, curling my fingers around the decorative molding.

I hate to admit it, but my heart is *pounding*.

"Up early?" I ask casually as Aveline turns towards me, her red hair draped over one shoulder in a braid. She smirks at me as my eyes flick over to Gill's back, his shirt stretched tight across his taut muscles. *Oh God, I can still remember how those felt beneath my fingers.* I drop my hands to my sides and move through the archway and over to the coffeemaker without waiting for him to acknowledge me. Even though I want him to—more than I'd care to admit.

"Up late more like," Aveline responds, sitting down at the kitchen table and shuffling through some papers. She snorts like the whole thing's amusing to her and tugs her laptop closer with her left hand. "There was some sort of strange mix-up where this guy was supposed to take over watch last night ..." Aveline trails off as I glance over at Gill's back again, my heart stuttering as he turns away from his laptop, perched on the edge of the counter. His eyes find mine and steal my breath away, a small smile curling his lips. I have to lean against the counter to fight my body's visceral reaction. "Never missed a shift in his life, never even showed up a moment late, and now ..."

"I said I was sorry," Gill replies, voice cool and calm, gaze still glued to mine. We stare at each other for a long moment, communicating wordlessly about what happened last night, about what still needs to happen. I have to know; I have to know *everything*. But ... "I got caught up in something."

"Yeah, I heard. Hell, we all did. You know, in all this time, I've never seen Cliff look anything but mildly amused. Last night, well, all I can say is ..." Aveline shuts her laptop and stands up, glancing over her shoulder at me. "Good luck with *that* conversation. I'm off to grab some shut-eye. See you on Friday?" Gill nods and Aveline salutes me once, computer tucked under one arm, before disappearing down the hall and out the front door.

After a moment, Gill follows after her and locks it, sliding the chain and dead bolt back into place. I linger in the hallway behind him, a cup of coffee warming up my hands as I listen to the torrential rains outside the window. It's still dark out there, the night still thick as ink. With the cloud cover like it is, I bet it stays gloomy and gray all day today.

"Good morning," Gill says finally, acknowledging me fully now that Aveline's gone. "Did you sleep well?" I don't miss the twinkle in his eye, the slight twitch of his lips as he gives me a once-over that makes me shiver. There's approval in his gaze ... and longing. I pretend not to notice, lifting my coffee to my lips and sipping it slowly before responding. I decide to be truthful again, even though it'd be a hell of a lot easier to lie.

"Perfectly. Best sleep I've had in years." Gill nods like he's not surprised.

"Me, too," he responds, moving towards me and pausing less than a foot away. "I'm not content unless you're there. I just realized that I haven't actually felt rested in ten years." I swallow hard and look away for a second before glancing back up at Gilleon's face.

There's warmth there, the passion that I missed so badly, that I never thought I'd see again. I can read love in his eyes, in the curve of his full lips, in the careful, considerate way he keeps his distance, waiting for me to close it. Gilleon is mine for the taking, waiting there like an apple dangling from a low branch. All I have to do is reach up and pluck it.

"I ..." I'm having a hard time figuring out what to say, my emotions as jumbled as the spools of thread in Solène's room, all of those colors twisted and mixed and tangled. Some part of me that's been locked up for years, held prisoner by my melancholy and my longing, it's free

311

now and I don't know what to do with it. "We still need to talk," I blurt, and Gill nods. "Too bad we missed dinner last night. I had a great dress picked out." Gill sucks in some breath between his teeth and stands stone-still, the darkness of the hallway like a blanket wrapping the two of us up tight together.

"I'm sorry I missed it," he says, humor lacing his voice. I know he's happy right now; it doesn't take an expert to see that. *I* make him happy. Me. I do. I'm Gill's happiness, his ticket back into the light. "But don't fret too much. I was thinking we could go out on Friday?"

"Friday?" I ask, raising both brows. Today is Tuesday; Friday feels like forever away. "Why not tonight?" I try to sound casual as I ask. Pretty sure there's some eagerness creeping in there, too. Oh well. I *want* to go on a proper date with Gill, so sue me.

"I wish I could, *mon cœur.*" My heart flutters a little at that. It'd be so easy to fall back in with Gill, pick up where we left off. Not sure how I feel about that. "But … we're having some problems with Karl. I have to leave for a few days to deal with it."

Goose bumps crawl across my skin but I nod, swallowing back some anxiety at the thought of Gill leaving, knowing how silly that is. If I'm already worried about him disappearing again, how can we ever make this work? And why do I want it to so badly?

I open my mouth to ask what kind of problems when Gill reaches up and curls his fingers around my upper arms, his thumbs teasing my bare skin into a heated

312

frenzy in an instant. My breath catches; my lips part.

As if that's the invitation he's been waiting for, Gilleon leans in, brushing his mouth against mine, tasting me, drinking me in like it's been years since we last kissed instead of hours.

"I see you kids have made up." Cliff's voice startles us both, and I almost spill my coffee all over Gilleon's shirt, fumbling with the mug as we step back from one another and glance up at the stairs. I can't see my stepfather's face, but he doesn't sound particularly happy about it. "Or rather, I *heard* that you made up." I flush from head to toe again, letting my eyes flutter closed for a second to get control of myself.

"Good morning to you, too, Dad," Gill says, reaching up and squeezing my arm once more before moving past me, back into the brightness of the kitchen and the heady allure of fresh caffeine. As if already anticipating an argument, Gill shuts his computer harder than he probably should and turns back to me, forcing his lips into a smile, just to show it's not me he's frustrated with.

"Papa," I say as Cliff comes down the last few steps and breezes past me, fully dressed, lips only slightly pursed. *God, please let this go well.* I take a deep breath to gather myself and move after him, leaning against the archway and putting my coffee to my lips. "Please don't be upset."

Cliff's busying himself with a cup of coffee, plopping a spoonful of sugar into his mug with a vengeance. Throughout it all, he's shaking his head like he's disappointed. That's a hard thing to take in, see, because he's been disappointed in Gilleon for a long, long time. I know this look is mostly for me, and it hurts.

"My son," Cliff says, cutting to the chase and pointing at the man in question, "is a thief, Regina. He's a criminal. And he's a man who doesn't have his priorities straight. Yes, I know he's a good-looking man, and I know you've missed him all these years, but think of your daughter."

"I *am* thinking of her," I say, trying not to get righteously indignant. Cliff stepped up for Solène when nobody else would, took care of her when both Gill and I couldn't, and he loves us all with a beautiful strength and fierceness that I could never scoff at, but ... "Gilleon's her father. If the two of them want to purse a relationship, that's their choice to make, not ours."

"He's a sperm donor," Cliff says frankly, causing Gill's fingers to curl tightly around his biceps as he leans against the counter, arms crossed over his chest, and scowls.

"You don't know why I've done what I've done, Dad," he snarls, and I can hear some resentment in those words, some blame focused on Cliff that I've never heard before. "So hold your judgments and don't act like you never left, never walked away from your child."

Cliff's face tightens, and I sense a conversation a long time coming.

"You wanted to stay with your mother, Gilleon, and if I'd made you leave, you would've hated me for it. If I'd known how bad she'd gotten, I would've taken you sooner, but you lied and tricked your way into staying as long as you could. You can't blame me for that, and you can't blame either of us for your actions."

Gill runs a hand down his face and shakes his head. I can see him quivering with barely suppressed rage, and my first instinct is to set my coffee down, move over to him, and wrap my arms around his waist. *Holy shit, what is happening to me?* I almost do it, too, but right now, Cliff is looking at me like he's never seen me before, and I hate that.

"We're testing the waters right now, Papa," I tell him, wondering in the back of my mind how hard I'm willing to fight for this. The answer scares the shit out of me. *Hard.* I'm willing to fight hard, to alienate one of the most important people in my life, and I haven't even heard the rest of Gill's story.

With a shocking chill, I realize I don't care. I don't care why or how or what because I love Gill more than anything, more than anyone, always have. *Shit.*

"Regina," Cliff begins, taking a step towards me, his salt and pepper hair an easy reminder that even if it feels like no time has passed since Gill left, plenty of it has. That's all he wants: me to remember that, to be careful. *Proceed with caution.* And I will. "I just don't want you to get hurt," he says, looking at me with all the care and compassion that my father used to give. I know without a doubt that Cliff couldn't love me anymore if I were his own. I look away, at the wood floors and the long reaching length of Gill's shadow where it touches my bare feet. That, too, is a reminder, a reminder that I don't just want Gill, but that he needs me. I can't watch the light inside of him fade away to nothing.

"I was there," Cliff continues when nobody else speaks. "I was there when you cried, when you couldn't get out of bed in the morning. He," my stepdad says, voice rough with anger, "wasn't there. He didn't see what I saw, didn't get to watch the fall and the even greater rise. You overcame the pain of heartbreak, Regina. That's not an easy thing to do." Cliff reaches out and touches the side of my cheek. I look up at him with a smile and then flick my eyes to Gill's.

He's staring out the window, arms still crossed over his chest. He looks like a statue right now, like he's stopped breathing altogether.

"I'm not trying to judge you, Regina," Cliff amends with a sigh, taking a seat at the table. "You know I love you, honey." I nod, wondering in the back of my mind if Cliff knows anything about my mother's death—and his son's supposed part in all of it. What would his reaction be then?

"I know, Papa, and I love you, too." Gill looks back at me then, and I see something in his beautiful blue eyes that damn near seals the deal for me: fear. He wants this, wants his family back. Is his sin really so unforgivable? There are worse things, much worse things. And the world is already cruel enough, isn't it? Shouldn't family be the one place we always know we can turn to for redemption? "When Gill gets back, we can talk about this." I take a deep breath. "About how we might want to think about making this living arrangement ... a little more permanent?" My statement comes out as a question, but at least it's out there.

Hope flickers in Gill's eyes before he pushes it back, putting on that expressionless mask of his. I don't mind so much this time, seeing it for what it is: a shield. He's just trying to protect himself, and that's okay.

"Gets back?" Cliff asks, reaching out for the paper that Aveline left lying in the center of the table. "And where is it that you're going, son of mine?" Neither of us misses the bite still present in his words or the look on his face: *this conversation is not yet over.*

"To deal with the mess I've made of my life," Gill grumbles quietly, eyes still locked on mine. "But I won't be gone long, I promise. I won't ever leave like that again."

I swallow hard and look away, desperately wishing I could throw myself into Gill's arms. But Papa's looking right at me again, and I need time to think. I reach up and find that I'm still wearing my mother's necklace. Must've slept in it last night.

Silence stretches uncomfortably between the three of us; I *hate* silences.

"I'm gonna take a quick shower," I say, looking to each of them in turn, keeping a neutral smile on my face. My thoughts are whirring so loud that I can barely discern what they're trying to say, the decisions they're saying I have to make. "When I get out, maybe I can make some pancakes?"

Gill smiles softly.

"I'd love that, Regina," he whispers, taking a slow step towards me, "but I'll already be gone by the time you get

317

out. A colleague of mine will be here until Aveline gets back tonight." I must make some sort of face because Gill adds, "he's good at what we do." And I believe him. In this, I completely and utterly trust Gill's judgment.

In other arenas ...

I nod, and then there's this awkward moment where neither of us knows whether we should hug or kiss or ...

"I'll miss you, Gill," I say, taking a step forward and brushing a gentle kiss across his mouth. "Be careful out there, okay?" He gives my hip a little squeeze and lets go, nodding as I step away and head up the back stairs, taking my coffee with me.

Getting back together with Gilleon seems like an inevitability for me.

I'm not sure whether I should be ecstatic—or terrified.

The first time Gill betrayed me, he broke my heart; I wouldn't last a second time.

CHAPTER
Twenty-One

The rest of my week is uneventful; I'm not sure if that's because it pales in comparison to what happened between Gill and me, or because Cliff's been carefully avoiding spending any alone time together. The only remarkable things that've happened since Tuesday are the sappy texts I've been getting from Gilleon—*I'm spending every single second dreaming of your smile*—and the introduction of some guy named Ewan who barely talks and whose expressionless mask is twice as hard as Gilleon's. I can only wonder what happened to make him that way. At the very least, he seems a capable bodyguard.

As for the texts ... I don't really know how to respond to them; they're so reminiscent of the notes he used to leave around the house when we were together that I find myself drifting off into wistful remembrances every time I get one. It's gotten so bad that I even switched out my usual horror movie watching last night for a *romantic comedy*. It was as terrible as I'd expected it to be.

I'm curled up in my usual spot on the couch, a Netflix movie—back to horror again—flickering in the background, when I get my first actual phone call on my new cell. I'm in the process of reading yet another text from Gill—*home soon, ma belle petite fleur*—when a familiar number pops up on the screen. I should probably recognize it, but my stomach's still in knots over *last* night's text, and I'm not thinking clearly. Right now, I'm actually awaiting a pretty exciting delivery: Gill had most of our items shipped from France. Since the authorities aren't involved, there's no reason to pretend that Cliff, Solène, or I am ... well, *dead*. That was the whole point of the operation: leave no trace, leave no trail. The scariest part about all of that is—as Gill relayed to me in his text—that's the usual MO for his new boss' teams. Gilleon claims that he'd never hurt an innocent, and I'm inclined to believe him, but still ... I can't help but remember those two men in the hotel room.

"Hello?" I ask, slightly confused, my mind wrapped up in Gill and Karl and all of the secrets I don't yet know, that I have to know, but that I'm not sure I want to.

"Regina!" It's Leilani, my childhood best friend, the very first person I ever admitted my crush on Gill to, the girl with an entire sleeve of *Star Wars* tattoos. We're pretty much polar opposites on the interest scale, but our mannerisms and personality are similar enough that this friendship works well. Even long distance, we manage to stay close. "Oh my God, oh thank God." I can hear the raw relief in her voice, the pain that I must've caused by disappearing into thin air.

I swallow hard, remembering Gill's warning about putting her and Anika in danger.

"Gill called me this morning and I just about had a heart attack."

"He *called* you?" I ask, completely and utterly baffled.

"He did, gave me your number and everything. Regi, if you're really in Seattle right now, then you're going to meet me for coffee, so I can wring your neck. How could you?" she asks, her voice warbling with unshed tears. I blink some of my own away, the full realization of what I was willing to give up hitting me hard. My friends, my sister, my boyfriend, my fucking freedom. All for Gill. Since the first second I saw him, I should've known. I. Should. Have. Known.

"I'm in Seattle," I say, knowing that if Gill told her where I was that it's okay to admit to it. Hell, it's not like Karl's been having problems finding us anyway.

"Shit," Leilani whispers, her voice muffled. "When I hadn't heard from you in weeks, I thought you'd been kidnapped or something. Don't ever do that again."

"I'm sorry," I say, leaning back into the cushions, relief flooding through me at the sound of a familiar voice, my voice of reason from a very, very young age. "You wouldn't believe the shit that's going on over here."

"Yeah, uh, Gilleon for starters. Why on earth are you

at Gilleon's house? What are you doing with him, Regi?" I lick my suddenly dry lips and try to come up with a response. Leilani knows everything about Gilleon, our whole story, including Solène. "No, no, no, don't answer me right now. I'm getting coffee and some of those salted caramel things you like from Fran's."

"I think Gill'd gut me if I gave away his address," I say, concerned more with the idea of Leilani coming here to meet me and putting herself on Karl's radar. I can hear her exhale over the phone, can imagine her running her fingers through her chocolate dark hair, a red flush coming over her olive rich skin. "Soon though, soon. You, uh, know how his *work* can get." Leilani also knows pretty much everything I know about Gill's business ventures—well, as much as I knew before this heist.

"Okay, okay, sure, but ..." I can hear her struggling to find the words to talk to me, to make sure I'm alright without outright asking. "If you need me, I'm still where I've always been, the little green house in North Beacon Hill." A smile stretches my lips as I press pause on my movie.

"I remember from the pictures you sent me. Still working on that whole *Food Not Lawns* thing?" A soft chuckle passes through the line, tinged with a bit of relief that I'm not ending the conversation yet. Just because we can't meet up in person doesn't mean we can't chat. Hell, I haven't seen Leilani in person in a long, long time. At least there's Skype, right? Although a lagging video chat isn't nearly as good as the real thing ...

"Not officially, no, but you'll recognize the place from the dead corn stalks wilting in the front yard. We had *legumes* this year, too. You know, beans. Oh, God, and the pumpkins? I still have some homemade pumpkin bread. I'd love to give you some." A pause. "Are you in trouble, Regi?" she asks finally.

I bite my lower lip and try to decide how best to answer that question.

"It's ... complicated."

"Gill complicated or ... just complicated, complicated?"

My turn to pause.

"Both."

Leilani sighs again, and I can just imagine her shaking her head, glancing over at her boyfriend/soul mate, Ellard, the only person I know who loves online roleplaying games as much as she does. In fact, they actually *met* playing an online video game. Go figure.

"Well, if you need to, you can always come and stay here—Solène and Cliff, too. You're all welcome always." I notice she doesn't mention Gill's name in there. Of course she doesn't. This is her subtle way of voicing her disapproval over whatever she thinks might be happening here between me and my ex. Too bad that whatever she's thinking can't possibly be worse than the real thing.

"I know, and thank you." I pause and fiddle with the blanket in my lap, pulling at the fibers with my nail. "Have you talked to Anika lately?" My breath catches in my chest as I wait for a response.

"Yes, I have. And as soon as Gill called me, I called

her because I was afraid you wouldn't. She was worried sick, too, Regi."

"I know." I glance over at Aveline who's stopped typing on her computer and is now staring right at me, green eyes sharp and lips twisted to the side in bemusement. The woman doesn't even try to *pretend* that she doesn't eavesdrop. Since Gill's not around, I guess I'll be asking her if it's safe to call my sister. "I'll see if I can get ahold of her after I'm done talking to you. If not ..."

"I'll call her tomorrow just in case," she says, without needing an explanation. Sometimes that's all you really need in a best friend, somebody that doesn't judge, that doesn't ask; I appreciate that about our friendship. Leilani didn't even balk when I told her I was in love with the stepbrother I barely knew, and she cried a river the day I said we were moving to France.

"Thank you," I say, and I mean it. I hope she can tell.

"Now go call your sister," she demands and then pauses as a voice sounds in the background. "Ellard says hi, too, and he can't wait for you to come over, so he can cook you something out of our garden and we binge on another *Supernatural* rerun."

I grin.

"I'm already looking forward to it. Oh, and call me tomorrow, too, if you don't hear from me sooner."

"Will do! Stay safe. Night, Regi."

I end the call before my tongue starts wagging, and I beg her to stay, just so she can hear me moan about Gilleon. But I won't—especially not with Aveline raising her eyebrows at me.

"What?" I ask, setting the phone down in my lap and turning to look at her. Aveline just shrugs and gets back to whatever it is she was working on. "Would Gill really call my friend and give her this number?" I think I'm being paranoid here, but I figure it doesn't hurt to ask.

"I think he thinks you need council or something," Aveline says with yet another shrug. "Although the man must be overconfident as shit if he thinks your girlfriend's going to convince you to stay with him. Never known a person not to want the impossible best for her friends."

"Impossible best?" I ask, pushing aside the blanket and standing up. I need to take this outside if I'm going to call Anika; I'll want the privacy in case we get into an argument. Since our conversations often end up that way, I'd rather be safe than sorry.

"So good it doesn't exist," Aveline responds, attention completely focused on the glowing screen in front of her. "But then, maybe they just want for us what we're afraid to want?" A chill travels down my spine even though I know I'm taking Aveline's words the wrong way. *Afraid to want.* I'm afraid to want Gilleon. Hell, maybe I am taking it the right way. Leilani wants me to be happy, to never have my heart broken again, to move on and let the pain go. But what she can't possibly know, what only I know, is that the pain is only there when he's not. His presence is like a soothing balm, wiping away the past. And I hate that. I do. I wish I could stay mad at him, give him what he deserves by telling him to fuck off, but

325

I can't do that because I'd only be hurting myself.

"Ugh." I run my fingers over my hair and down my ponytail. "I'll be out back," I say and Aveline nods.

The weather outside is dreadful, rainy and gray and blustery as hell, but at least it gives me a chance to wear the Burberry Brit cashmere cape that's been sitting in my closet since the day I went shopping with Aveline. I slip into it and slide out the back door, fully aware that there are people in and around the edges of the yard. I have no idea how many, but I just about had a heart attack the other day when I spotted a woman in the hedges.

Gill's buffed up security, and I have no idea what to think about that.

I decide a distracting conversation with Anika is better than worrying about this Karl Rousseau guy and his missing diamonds.

I stare down at the phone, knowing that Gill wouldn't have had Leilani call me if he didn't think it was safe. I realize then that at least some of my hesitation in calling Anika was selfish, was more than just my fearing she'd get dragged into all of this. My sister's ... well, she's judgmental. And harsh. And she asks way too many questions. Kind of like the opposite of Leilani.

I dial her up and wait.

She picks up on the third ring.

"Anika Corbair."

"It's Regi," I say before I let the solemn seriousness in her voice put me off. Anika's always been ... stern. And stubborn, too stubborn for her own good. It was that stubbornness that drove her away from me and mom, from Cliff and Gill before she'd even met them. Honestly, if I hadn't forced a connection between us back then, there's little doubt in my mind that we'd be complete strangers now.

I can practically hear her purse her lips at me.

"Where have you been, Regina? Leilani was considering getting on a plane to Paris." *Leilani was. Leilani, and not you.* My older sister's seeming lack of care doesn't bother me though; it used to, but not anymore. Anika cares in her own way, but family doesn't mean the same thing to her as it does to me.

"If I could explain, I would," I tell her and imagine an eye roll in response. Unlike Leilani, Anika isn't privy to many of my secrets. I mean, she knew about Gill and me, but she never knew I was pregnant, doesn't even know she has a niece. Back then, telling my other girlfriends before Gill didn't seem like a big deal, like I was letting them in on a surprise party planned for him. But Anika? All she knows is that Gill and I broke up, not that he left, not that he's a thief. Nothing. "I'm sorry for disappearing, but things are complicated over here." I take a deep breath and try to make myself smile. Maybe she'll be able to hear it through the phone? "The good news is ... I'm in the States now. Seattle, actually."

My sister doesn't seem to give two shits that I'm in our old hometown.

"Gram's not doing well, Regina. I'm busy moving her into my place." Anika pauses, and I can actually hear her tapping her manicured nails on something. "Plan a visit here soon; this could be her last Christmas."

I cringe at my sister's bluntness and wonder if I should ask to speak to my grandma? But no. My mom's mom hasn't spoken to me since we moved to France, considering that a betrayal of the worst kind. Two weeks before she died, I listened to my mom call and cry on the phone to Anika, but Gram never called her back. I try not to, but I think I'm still carrying around a lot of anger towards her.

I put a hand up to my forehead. I can't let any of that old pain get to me, not now. I'm already dealing with dredged up hurt, dug up secrets. I force myself to take a deep breath.

"I'll see what I can do," I tell her, glad that at least we're not arguing, that she's not bringing up the day she ran away to California, moved right onto the Yurok Reservation with my grandma. It's one of her favorite subjects after all—trying to convince me that *I* made a mistake in not coming with her, that our mother was the bad guy for falling in love again. I feel sorry for her that she never got a chance to really know Cliff or Gill.

Gill.

I swallow hard, my most current and pressing problem making me sweat despite the cool weather.

"I'll call you back when I have a spare moment," she says and then hangs up on me before I get a chance to say goodbye. I take a deep breath and let it out slow, closing my eyes against the wind.

"Anika, right?" Warm fingers graze my wrist and I jump, spinning to find Gill standing on the deck next to me, once again appearing seemingly out of thin air. "You only ever get that look when you're talking to your sister."

Gill lets his hand drop and takes a step back, a real sight for sore eyes in his black wool coat, eyes blue and bright and on fire. I can't help but notice that that's new, that flame there. I put it there. Me. *Oh God.* I take a small step back and smile, blowing air out and up to push some stray strands of hair away from my forehead.

"When you said *home soon,* you really meant it, huh?" I ask, shoving my phone into my pocket to give my shaking hands something to do. My pulse is pounding and my throat is dry, sweat beading on my lower back as I try to figure out what to say, how to act. It's been three days since I've seen the guy, not three weeks; it feels like three years.

Gill smiles at me, like he can sense what I'm feeling, like maybe he's feeling a lot of the very same things. I watch the wind pick up strands of his dark hair, drag it across his forehead. I want to reach up and brush it back. Without even realizing it, I take a step forward.

Gill's smile turns into a grin.

"Are you just popping in or are you back for a little while?" I ask, feigning disinterest. I couldn't be anymore interested if I tried; he knows that.

"I'm back to stay," he tells me, the double meaning in his words not lost on either of us. "The only way I'm missing our dinner date tonight is if you'd rather spend it in your bedroom again."

"Gill."

"Or my bedroom," he adds, moving forward and

wrapping his arms around my waist, pulling my close. I
don't resist—why bother? I think we both know we're
beyond that now. No more running or hiding or being
angry, none of that. Everything we both think and feel,
it's got to be out in the open now.

Because of me. Elena, she's dead because of me.

I swallow hard and push the thought back. Tonight,
I'll hear what Gill has to say. For now ...

"You called Leilani?" I ask as Gill reaches up and
touches his warm palm to my cheek. My fingers tingle
with the desperate desire to reach out and touch him, too,
while other parts of me ... well, let's just be polite and
say they tingle, too.

"I thought you could use a friend," Gill says and then
pauses, blue eyes sliding to the side like he's just been
caught doing something wrong. "And since she's in the
area ... I thought it might help you think of this place as
home." I purse my lips, pretend to be irritated with him.
Only I'm not. Not at all.

"You didn't think she'd try to talk me out of getting
back together with you?" I ask, raising an eyebrow. Gill
glances back to me and lifts both of his.

"Already? I thought she'd at least wait a week or so."
He pauses and narrows his eyes slightly. "Why do you
think I refrained from calling Anika?" I give him a look.

"Come on now, as much as Anika dislikes you, there's
nobody in the world that hates you as much as Leilani."
Gill laughs, leaning his head back for a moment and
breathing in the cool crisp air of winter. Autumn is well
on its way out, frost already nipping at its heels. The

330

new year's right around the corner, a perfect time to make a fresh start ...

"God, I missed you," Gill says, looking back into my eyes, caressing the side of my face. I don't say it aloud, but I missed him, too. *Terribly.* And he was only gone for three days. Could I really ever say goodbye again? Watch him walk out and know we could've given this a second chance?

I lean up on my tiptoes and press my lips to Gilleon's, sliding my tongue into his mouth and taking control of the kiss. My arms come up and wrap around his neck as his hands find my hips, fitting there like they were made for it, like we were made to be together like this.

"I thought you'd be back late," I tell him honestly, wondering how we're going to kill the few hours between now and our date. I could think of a few ways ... "But I'm glad you're here now."

"I wanted to be here for the delivery," he says and I glance up at Gill's face, at his still smooth cheeks and his half-smile. "Are you sure you still want everything delivered here? I could have it taken to a storage unit?" Gill's voice is calm, but his hands clench tight, fingers digging into my hips, as he waits for an answer. By all rights, I *should* ask for the majority of our stuff to go into storage until Cliff, Solène, and I decide if we're staying for sure, but ...

"It's fine." I force a smile and try not to let myself think too long or too deeply about this decision. I haven't officially decided to take Gill back ... but I'm strongly considering it. "I miss my clothes." Gill grins and leans forward like he's considering kissing me again, but he stops short, letting go of me and taking a small step back. We're in a weird place, me and him.

"I'm sorry about your furniture," he says and I shrug. All those old pieces that belonged to my mom, I sold those to friends. There was always the very real possibility that I'd never get *anything* from my apartment back, and I wasn't willing to take the chance; Katriane and Jacqueline will take good care of it all. Hell, I could probably call them and—once they got over screaming at me for disappearing, and for moving—I could probably buy it all back from them and get them to ship it for me. Expensive, sure, but I should be able to afford it now. If it weren't for the whole 'trying to kill me and Gill' thing, I'd almost be glad that Karl was after us and not the authorities. Not having to go quiet and stay quiet with my friends and family ... kind of priceless.

And I was willing to give it all up for Gilleon.

I cough into my hand and shake my head.

"Don't be sorry, Gill," I say, turning to go back inside when he reaches out and takes my wrist.

"Dinner," he says and then grins at me. "Six o' clock, for real this time?" The sparkle in his eyes tells me he really doesn't mind if I decide to change my mind and stay in—as long as he's invited, of course.

"You better not flake on me," I tell him as he lets go, fingertips scorching across my skin. "Because I have a scalloped lace midi dress sitting sad and lonely in my closet." I pause as Gill's grin softens into a loving smile, so at odds on his strong, rough face. All of that strength, that muscle, that power, it's all mine. Or it could be. If I'd just let myself have it.

I take another deep breath.

"Thanks for calling Leilani," I say and then pause, wetting my lips, fully aware that Gill's eyes are following the movement. "She's not in any danger though, is she? I mean, I didn't tell her where I was or anything, but just phone calls should be okay? For Anika, too?"

"I'd never let anything happen to your friend or your sister," he tells me and then reaches out to swipe some hair from my face. My breath catches at his wild beauty, at the strong, wide silhouette of him against the darkening stormy sky. "I think Karl and Max are going to reach an agreement soon. It's almost over, baby, almost over. I promise."

I return Gill's smile, take a step back, and go inside.

If I stand out here with him any longer, I might lose my nerve and throw in the towel, even before hearing what he has to say about my mother's death.

At this point, it feels like the only thing I'm really fighting against is Gill's future and my own happiness.

CHAPTER

Twenty-Two

"Knock, knock," Cliff says from behind me, pushing in the partially cracked bedroom door and giving me an almost sad sort of smile. My stepfather's emotions are written all over his face, scribbled there in black ink. *You're making a mistake.* I look right back at him and force a smile of my own. "Gilleon says you're going out tonight?"

"Yup. Dinner—again. Hopefully we don't get chased by bad guys this time." The words come out like a question as I grab my dress for tonight and withdraw it from the closet. Cliff watches me for a moment before running his fingers through his salt and pepper hair, the gesture so very like Gilleon that for a moment, I see Cliff as he probably looked thirty years ago.

"I guess you'll be discussing ... things?" I lay the

dress on the bed and glance over my shoulder at him, one eyebrow raised.

"Yes, Papa, *things*. Lots and lots of things." I return to the closet and pick up a different shoe in each hand, glancing over at the dress for reference.

"The slingbacks," he says, pointing at the black shoe in my right hand. "Those Oscar de la Renta knockoffs are trying too hard." I grit my teeth and turn towards Cliff, gesturing with the embellished pump in question.

"You know I don't wear knockoffs," I tell him, my sneer as fake as the insult he just hurled at me. Cliff and me, we know our designer shoes. "Besides, don't you think these have a Cinderella vibe?" I twist the crystal pump so the light hits it just right.

"*Ma belle fille,*" he says, coming into the room and closing the door behind him. "Cinderella was a helpless girl; you're anything but. You have so much more to look forward to than simply marrying a handsome prince." A real smile slides across my face, can't help it.

"I know." And I do. And Gilleon is anything *but* a fairytale prince. In all honesty, he might even qualify as a villain. Still, the heart wants what it wants, right? "You know I've always wanted to be in fashion, right?" I swallow hard and look back down at the shoe. "Maybe I should give it a shot?" I glance up at Cliff and grin. "Think *Project Runway* would take me?"

"Regina," Cliff says, moving over to the bed and running his fingers across the lace of the dress. "Don't make fun of yourself. If you want to be in fashion, then go for it. I've always told you to pursue your dreams." A dark look chases across his face when he looks back at me. "But since Gilleon left ..."

"You can't blame Gill for my lack of initiative," I tell him with a shrug. And he can't. But it's something to think about. I toss the designer shoe back in the closet and pick up the matching partner to the one in my hand. "It's just a lot easier to put yourself out there when you've got someone in your corner." I sigh and stand up, moving over to the bed to lay the shoes next to the dress. Cliff was right; these slingbacks are so much better than those pumps.

Cliff reaches out and squeezes my shoulder.

"You always have me," he says. "Me and Solène. We're always right here cheering for you."

"Speaking of Solène," I say, sitting down on the edge of the bed and looking up at my stepfather. "No matter what, you're still her Papa, right?" He nods and scoots the dress over to sit down on the opposite edge. "Gill and I ... I'm not exactly sure how we're going to work through this whole thing, but we're not just going to jump in and start playing family. Being a parent ... it's not a right, but a privilege."

Cliff slaps his knee and points at me.

"And that's why I love you, kid. Your mama raised you right." Cliff chuckles and puts his hand up over his mouth, rubbing at the gray stubble on his chin. He glances over at me, blue eyes darkening as memories overtake him, memories of the short-lived love he'd shared with Elena. I think Cliff knows as well as I do that once it hits you, really and truly hits you, you can't run from love. Not a day later, not a decade. "That's why I can't understand this thing with Gilleon," he whispers. "You're always so practical."

"Are you saying I'm being stupid?" I ask, looking at the wall in front of me, at the painting my friend Katriane did for me, the one I left behind. First thing I did when the truck got here with our stuff was dig out some art for my walls. I focus on the whorls and bumps of the oil painting, the bright blue eyes of the black cat crouched within it. Kat painted this one for me and Gill before he left, off the story I like to tell of the old Siamese cat and its litter of feral kittens. Right there, that sleek predatory grace, that focused expression, that intent, it's all Gilleon.

"No, of course not. I ..." Cliff takes a big breath and stands up, moving towards the door. "I don't think you're stupid, and I know you're in love." He looks back at me. "It's not that I don't love Gilleon or the idea of you two being together with Solène. Honestly, it's always been a dream of mine that he'd come back." Cliff puts his hands on his hips and stares down at his brown loafers. "I just don't want you to get your heart broken again is all."

"I know," I say, my fingers unconsciously reaching for my mother's pendant again. "Trust me, I'm not keen on the idea either."

X X X

I dress up for dinner this time—and by dress up, I mean *all* the way up.

My hair is perfect, long and loose and waving gently at my shoulders, strands of honey blonde to complement the teal-blue of my dress, the scalloped lace, the open back. The opacity of the dress ends mid-thigh and the rest is all sheer lace in teal and black, leaving my legs mostly bare, drawing attention to the black slingback pumps on my feet. I line my eyes with black, feather the darkness into some silver-gray hues across my lids. My mouth feels full and luscious in bright red, glossed over so that it shines in the light. With my diamond pendant, my earrings, and a black Nancy Gonzalez clutch, I feel ready to tackle this evening.

This time, I can't deny that it's a date.

"Just breathe," I mutter, pushing open my bedroom door and stepping out with my shoulders back, my clutch held loosely in one hand. Gill's not waiting for me, but Solène is. She smiles shyly at me and tucks some dark hair behind her ear.

"You look positively chic, *Maman*," she says, and the sound of my new title sends a thrill through me. I smile at her as she crosses her arms over her chest and leans back, examining me from head to toe. "You know how to dress a woman's figure," she says in that soft French accent of hers. "I can see you going places, you know."

"Maybe," I say, moving around the bannister and pausing in front of her. "But I know for sure that you are."

"Ah," Solène says, snapping her fingers like she's just thought of something. "Wait one moment for me, will you?" She turns in a flutter of pink skirts and disappears into her room, re-emerging with a black notebook that I haven't seen in years. "I meant to bring this along when we first left, but I couldn't find it anywhere. Thank goodness *mon Père* had the sense to ship it over." She hands the book to me and shakes it.

I reach out slowly, my fingers curling around the spine.

"Where did you get this?" I ask, opening the book and letting the pages flutter as I stare down at my sketches. Dresses, jackets, and jumpsuits stare back up at me.

"Everybody needs a dream, *Maman*," Solène says, tucking her small hands into the pockets of her dress. "Let this be yours." I feel my lips twitching as I glance up at my nine-almost-ten year old daughter. She's by far the wiser of the two of us.

"The Seattle fashion scene isn't quite like the one in Paris," I say, tapping at a black jumpsuit with my fingernail. I haven't thought about designing in a long, long time. It's not an easy industry to break into and chasing a far off dream like that takes strength and dedication, two things that I've been lacking for quite some time. But with this money from the heist ... I could actually devote my time and energy to this.

"It's not about the destination, but the journey. If you'd already arrived where you were meant to be, then how would you ever enjoy the ride to get there?" Solène reaches out a hand for the drawing book back. "I've been using these for inspiration, so if you don't mind ..."

"Oh, of course," I say, leaning down, my diamond earring swinging with the motion. My daughter and I exchange a pair of cheek kisses before I stand back up. "*Ciao, ma belle fille,*" I say with a little wave before starting down the stairs.

"*Au revoir, ma magnifique et talentueuse Maman,*" she says, leaning over the railing and looking down at me with a grin. "And good luck."

"Good luck with what?" Gill asks from the bottom of the stairs, his brows raised and his eyes taking in my entire body from head to toe. A thrill flushes through me, heats my blood and makes my pulse thunder. I know I look good, and I know Gill's fully aware of it. I think he's also aware of my own stare that starts at his face, at his dark hair and blue eyes, and travels over the suit he's wearing. The top two buttons of his shirt are undone and he's not wearing a tie, but he's still dressed up—sexy but casual. What the suit can't hide is the ripple of muscles in Gill's back and shoulders, the strength of that blue-eyed gaze or any of the passion that's resting behind it.

I step down off the last stair and look him straight in the face. In four inch heels, he's only a tad taller than me, so it makes eye contact easy.

"With you," I tell him, not bothering to hide the questions in my eyes. Solène might not know exactly what's going on here, but she can sense my emotions. Smart cookie, that one, all the best parts of Gill and me. "She's wishing me luck with you."

"You're going to need it," Cliff shouts out from the kitchen as I raise my brows and Gill smiles wryly.

"No bad guys tonight?" I ask and he shakes his head, dark hair shiny and gleaming, fresh from a wash.

"I'd like to say no, but who knows? Did you come prepared this time?" The smirk on his face makes me grit my teeth. *Yes,* I have some baby wipes, a tampon, even a pair of clean panties in my clutch, but he doesn't need to know that. It might be overkill, but you never know with Gilleon.

"I have extra Chapstick and my phone charger if that's what you're asking." I smile and lift my clutch up, giving it a little shake. "Thank God for extra large clutches, eh?"

"Praise the Fashion Gods," Gill says, reaching up to pull my coat off the rack. He raises an eyebrow in question, but I don't bat an eye as I let him help me into it. If I'm going to try this, then I'm going all out. *But I'll decide that for sure after I get my answers,* I think, knowing deep in my heart that they don't really matter. This, right here, it's all a formality. "Regina Corbair," Gill says, holding out an arm for me. I take it and let him lead us outside, down the wet steps and across the driveway to tonight's car.

It's an SUV again.

My turn to raise my eyebrows as Gill grins at me and shrugs, opening the door and standing back.

"I figured it'd be nice to have the space," he purrs, leaning in and looking down at me with half-hooded eyes. "Just in case."

"Yeah, right," I say, but my body's already responding to his words, my thighs clenching together in anticipation. Gill closes my door and moves over to his side, climbing in and starting the ignition. "Where's dinner tonight?" I ask, silently praying Italian is still on the menu.

"Same place I planned for last time." Gill pauses as

we pull out of the driveway, swallowing hard before speaking again. "Just because something doesn't work out the first time doesn't mean it isn't worth another try." My breath catches and I glance out the window, afraid to look at him when he's talking like that, voice low and deep and husky, slamming me hard with a double meaning that makes my throat tight.

"Are we waiting until after the appetizers come to talk about ... what we need to talk about?"

"I'm ready when you're ready," he says, but he doesn't sound very sure of himself. It's not an emotion I'm used to seeing in Gill. Gilleon Marchal is always perfect, always prepared. The man of today is different from the sweet, romantic, humorous boy he used to be. Or at least that's what I thought when I first saw him again in Cliff's kitchen, but ... the asshole's starting to show cracks. I can't even talk myself out of remembering the clear passion burning in his gaze when we made love. Eh. As if that wasn't enough of a sign. I've only ever had sex with other men, never made love. Never that.

I glance out the window for a few minutes, my eyes following the rush of rain, the flutter of autumn's last leaves, a beckoning call to winter. Some of Gill's neighbors already have Christmas lights up on their houses, little blurbs of white and red and green that flitter past as we drive. I feel my heart clench tight as I imagine decorating Gilleon's Colonial with lights, of turning the nearly empty sitting room downstairs into a workshop, of inviting Gill into the master bedroom with me ...

I take a deep breath.

I'm getting a little ahead of myself here.

"Got any Christmas plans?" I ask Gill, and he glances over at me suddenly, expression sharp, like this is something he's never thought of before. Not likely though. Gill thinks about *everything*.

"I haven't had Christmas plans ..." he begins, but we both know how that sentence is going to end, so he doesn't say it. *In ten years.*

"I think we should do what my mother always did: get the biggest tree we can fit in the house and decorate it with salt dough ornaments and popcorn strands. Then I'll dress up in the nicest gown I've got and dance the waltz with Cliff."

"Or you could dance it with me," Gill says, voice smooth and low. I reach up a hand and wipe the fog from the window, clearing my view to the outside. I can't look at Gill, not yet. Inside, I'm preparing, steeling myself for whatever he might say to me tonight.

"I didn't know you could dance," I say, remembering clumsy twirls in the living room of our parents' Paris apartment.

"I learned," Gill says and then pauses. "For you. There's never been anyone I've ever wanted to dance with but you."

"Stop it," I say, turning suddenly in my seat, the leather creaking as I spin to face him. Gill glances over and our eyes meet. "I'm ready," I say.

x x x

I sit across the table from this guy, Gill, Cliff's son, and give my mom a narrow-eyed look that doesn't even come close to penetrating her bubble of joy. She's unfolding a white linen napkin and laying it across her lap, ever the picture of elegance, even at our own dining room table.

"Have I told you that I adore a man who cooks?" she asks, Dad's diamond pendant sparkling at her throat. I feel my fists clench in anger at my sides. How can she wear a necklace that my dad bought her and gaze at Cliff with such longing all at the same time? I want to be mad, to stay mad, but my sister's already put up enough of a fight for both of us.

A foot pokes me under the table, drawing my eyes to Gill and his wry grin, sitting directly across from me. He's cute enough, I guess, with his raven dark hair and his bright baby blues, but I'm still mad that he picked my lock and invaded my bedroom. I mean, who does that? Picks the lock to the bedroom of a girl he's never met?

"I think you might've mentioned it a time or two," Cliff replies, laughing and serving her a steaming plate covered in food I can barely pronounce. He's a gourmand, this guy, my prospective new stepfather, and a pretty damn good chef. I mean, he's a cool person and all, but really? I guess I just miss Dad.

My mom notices me glaring, both at Gill and Cliff, and reaches out, curling her fingers around my hand and drawing my attention to her.

"It'll be alright, Regi," she says, her hair as golden as mine, her skin as pale, not at all like my sister's straight black locks and tanned skin. She looks more Native American than both of us—I kind of think that's one reason my Grandma likes her better. Despite the fact that Gram's only a quarter Yurok—mostly she's French and English—she acts like Mom and me are freak genetic anomalies. Not my fault she married a white guy. Heck, despite Lana's insistence that I follow my sister down to California and abandon Mom, I bet she's happy, glad to be rid of both her daughter and me.

"Nothing feels alright," I whisper back, fully aware that that boy's still staring at me. In fact, it feels like he hasn't stopped staring at me since he got here. "There's gonna be a stranger sleeping in my house tonight." I glare at Gill and his smile only gets wider.

"A stranger is just a friend you haven't met yet," Mom says as I roll my eyes at her.

"Or a serial killer that hasn't decided on a knife or a gun," I respond sarcastically, and my mother laughs, the sound ringing like church bells in our cozy little dining room. Outside, the Seattle rain pounds down hard, pinging off the windows and turning our lawn into a mud bath.

"Don't be so cynical, Regina," she says, winking and watching as Cliff sets a plate of food down in front of me. I mumble my thanks and reach for a fork to dig in. "Cynicism is cyanide for dreams."

"Aren't we full of quotes tonight," Cliff says, leaning down to kiss my mom on the lips. I watch them, half-disgusted and half-fascinated. Clearly there's love there, even I can tell that. They kiss like the world around them is falling away, fading into nothing, like all that matters is the feel of her mouth, his lips. Their kiss only lasts *about half a second, but it feels like forever.*

I look back at Gill and find his grin fading into a wistful smile, like he's as eager to taste that forbidden fruit as I am. And I don't mean kissing, just kissing. Anyone can put their mouth up against someone else's. What I want, what I secretly dream of, is a love worth dying for but a love that never dies. Somehow, someway, I can see that same sentiment reflected in Gill's eyes.

I blush and turn away.

"Have you ever heard this one?" Cliff continues, sitting down on the opposite side of the table next to his teenage son. "Never miss a glance at a second chance romance?"

"You made that one up, didn't you?" Mom asks, tossing some hair over her shoulder, far too elegant and beautiful for a Seattle suburb. In her burnished gold gown, she looks like royalty, destined for great things. I hope this new job of hers can deliver.

"Maybe," Cliff says with a soft smile, his hair as dark as his son's, black and gleaming. "But that doesn't make it any less true, right?" When he looks up at her, she flushes, taking in his handsome good looks with a soft smile.

"True," she says in a small whisper, and the room goes quiet for a few seconds, nothing but the sound of forks clinking against Mom's best China.

"Elena," Gill says, breaking the bubble, drawing the attention over to him. He leans back in his chair and tucks his hands into the front pocket of his hoodie. He's talking to my mom now, but he's looking right at me.

"Thanks for taking me in."

My mom looks over at him with an almost startled expression on her face.

"Taking you in? Oh, honey, don't look at this as me doing you a favor." She smiles her best smile at him, a look that always draws the attention in a room towards her. "Me and you, we're family now, and this is what family does. We take care of each other."

Gill's blue eyes flicker over to my mother's brown ones and he smiles shyly.

"I'll try not to cause you any trouble," he says, looking back at me, right into my eyes. "No trouble at all."

x x x

"Are you sure?" Gill asks as I blink back stars and memories of a different place, a different time.

"Positive," I say, meeting his gaze when he looks over at me, searching my expression for a moment before he glances back towards the windshield. "And Gill?" My voice wavers with the words, but I know I have to say them now or he'll never really be able to know how serious I am, how much I mean what I'm about to say. "No matter what you tell me tonight, it won't change the decision I'm going to make." I swallow hard and close my eyes, letting my emotions come together, letting the truth roll over and through me. When I open them, I know I'm really ready. I sit up straight and turn in my seat, knowing I should probably wait until Gill's stopped driving to tell him this.

Somehow, someway, he seems to feel that something

big is coming and pulls over, just parks us on the side of a suburban street sparkling with fresh rain and white Christmas lights.

This time, when he turns to look at me, the full force of his gaze is like a heat wave, rocking me back and forcing me to sit up straight or wilt beneath the passion in it; I choose to face it head-on.

"Take a walk with me?" I ask, echoing Gill's words from that day at the hotel. He looks at me for a long while and nods, opening his door and stepping out into the rain. I follow suit in my four inch heels, knowing they're going to be almost as trashed as my poor feet after this. Oh well. Compared to the pulsing ache in my heart, this is nothing.

"I've got an umbrella," Gill says, but I grab his wrist before he can move to get it. I know it's raining, and I know I'm going to get soaked, but I can't wait anymore. I have to say this and I have to say it *now*.

"Walk with me." I reach down and squeeze Gill's hand, the hot warmth of it searing through me. It almost feels like the rain should be sizzling when it hits us, turning to steam and drifting off to join the distant stars. I grit my teeth and shake my head, trying to keep myself calm, logical, thoughtful. Because, really, I've put a lot of thought into this—but I've also got a lot of heart invested. And some of it's broken, and some of it's still bleeding, but it's all still there and I'm starting to wonder if it might not be so bad to try to put it back together with Gill's help.

We start off down the sidewalk, rain pattering softly

on green lawns, sloped roofs, dragging my carefully styled hair into my eyes. The drops sneak inside my coat, no matter how hard I try to keep them out, sliding down the back of my neck, beneath the lace of my dress.

"We never seem to be able to get to our destination, do we?" Gill asks with a small smile. I can tell he's nervous. The tight set of his shoulders, the tenseness in his fingers, the strength with which he squeezes my hand. He wants this. Bad. Probably more than I do. And I want it, too. I'm still struggling with the idea, but it's there and it won't go away. I almost quote Solène's words back at him.

It's not about the destination, but the journey. If you'd already arrived where you were meant to be, then how would you ever enjoy the ride to get there.

Instead, I wait, letting the words curl up inside of me, stepping over puddles in an attempt to save my shoes from the worst of it.

"I don't know what you're going to tell me," I say, running my tongue across my lower lip, tasting sweet Seattle rain, "but it doesn't matter." Gill tries to stop walking, but I drag him along with me, shivering against the cool breeze scraping past my lower legs.

"Regina," he says, his voice a rough plea that I ignore. His words don't matter right now; I've made my choice.

"Gilleon, listen to me," I say, pausing and turning, forcing him to look at me, the stray strands of a distant porch light limning his dark head in light, turning his face to shadow but highlighting the full curve of his lower lip. Somehow, I've manged to stop us beneath the branches of a massive tree, providing at least a little bit of cover from the increasing fury of the sky. The rain slams down in sheets, leaking between the leaves and splattering on my nose. "I've known this since the first moment I saw you, when you looked at me with a blank face and a closed heart." Even though Gilleon's in shadow, I can visibly see him tense further, a primal sort of fear infusing the rigid movements of his body as he runs a hand through his damp hair, droplets sprinkling across my face.

This is going to shock the shit out of him, isn't it? I think with a small amount of triumph.

My heartbeat picks up speed; my breath catches in my chest.

"Gill, I still love you," I say, prefacing my statement with those ever important words. I think it's virtually impossible to say *I love you* too much. For whatever reason, that scares the crap out of him and he takes a step forward, caressing my jaw with wet fingers.

Big breath here, the feel of my heart racing in my chest, pulse pounding in my head. I lift up a hand and push aside the black wool of my coat to touch the pendant.

"Gilleon ..." There's a million ways to say this, an infinite number of phrases that could work to convey what I need to tell him, but I can think of only one. "I forgive you."

Gill swallows hard, throat moving as he turns his head to the side and runs his hand over his mouth, knocking stray droplets of rain water to the pavement.

I'm shaking right now, but I don't know why. The cold maybe? The wet? No, I don't really think it's either of those things. I let out a breath and it comes out in a rush, fogging in the autumn air. I feel ... lighter somehow. I'd told myself I wasn't holding a grudge, that it didn't matter anymore, that I'd grown past it, but that wasn't entirely true. This, it was *this* moment I'd been waiting for, a second in time ten years in the making.

"I feel like now, I have two real choices, two good ones. I've said what I need to say, made my peace with what happened between us." I tuck my hands in the pockets of my coat and wiggle my fingers against the smooth silk lining. "I could walk away from you right now, take the money from the heist and be content with the fact that I really do forgive you, Gilleon. I'm not mad anymore; I'm not upset. I think that I could actually be happy by myself or, in the future, with another man."

Gill sucks in a harsh breath and turns back to look at me.

"But I don't want another man, Gilleon," I say, my voice strong and clear and loud enough that the shattering break of rain doesn't matter, the cars driving by don't matter, the distant murmur of voices don't matter. Gill can hear me, loud and clear, I know he can. "Gill, the only man I want is you."

CHAPTER

Twenty-Three

Shock passes over Gill's face for a split second before he's stepping forward and sliding his arms under my coat, wrapping them around my waist. His fingers manage to find the bare skin of my back, fingertips warm but wet, his prints searing my flesh with whorls and ridges.

A laugh bubbles up and out of his throat, a murmur of surprise that he quickly suppresses as he pulls me against him.

"Are you ..." he begins and then shakes his head, splattering me with water again. I blink away the droplets on my eyelashes and let the smile I'm feeling in my heart show on my face. "I want to ask if you're serious because it's hard to see someone offer the one thing you've always wanted and not question if it's real, but ... I feel like it'd be insulting if I did." Gill takes a deep breath as he presses our bodies close, the firm planes of his chest and stomach the perfect partner to the softer, rounder curves of mine.

"Not what you were expecting?" I ask, unconsciously pitching my voice to a whisper. It just sort of feels like the right moment for quiet reflection, gentle passion, the perfect look from a pair of bright blue eyes. It was a look I was afraid I'd never see again, and the sight of it is nothing short of miraculous to me.

"Not what I was expecting, but everything I was hoping for," he says and then pauses, pulling his gaze away. "Although I'm worried that you'll change your mind when you finally hear what I have to say." I shake my head, wet hair plastered against my forehead, my cheeks, the back of my neck. My legs are cold and I'm uncomfortable as hell; it's the happiest I've ever been.

"I know that what you're going to tell me could change my world, break my heart, tear me into pieces, but what it won't do is affect how I feel about you, Gilleon." I lean into Gill, resting cheek to cheek with him, his breath warm on the side of my neck. "The only reason I agreed to the heist was because I could tell you needed me. My friends, my apartment, my life in Paris, I was willing to give it all up to help you, even if you didn't love me anymore. I realize that now, that I'd do anything for you Gill. If that includes forgiveness for something horrible, for something you did to my mother, then so be it. But I know you. I know you *think* that it was all your fault, that you somehow caused her death, but I know you're better than that. You'd never hurt my mom, not on purpose. If something happened, it was out of your control." I try to take a step back, but he won't let me go, holding me closer, tighter, harder.

"Are you sure you're real?" he whispers against my cheek, his lips as soft as his body is hard. "Because for years I tried to convince myself that you were some sort of dream, that nothing in this life could really be as good as I remembered you." I smile, pulling back just enough that I can look into Gill's beautiful eyes.

When he kisses me, I open my mouth, letting the hot heat of his tongue warm me up from head to toe. The sensation of his wet lips on mine is thrilling, a distant reminder of our first kiss back together outside of the restaurant. But this time, I'm not going to pull away, run away. This time, I'm here to stay.

Gill's hands roam down, over the teal lace of my dress, until he reaches my ass, cupping my flesh in tight fingers, kneading until I moan into his mouth and raise my own hands to his chest. I pull buttons apart until I can feel skin, teasing that smooth, hard flesh with my fingertips. Since my fabulous little slingbacks put Gill and me at just about the same height, I can feel his erection pressing in all the right places, wiggling my body against him until I get a reaction.

"Fuck," he murmurs as I bite his lip, giving him a short second to breathe. "We should probably take this back to the SUV."

"Probably," I whisper as he turns us around, my heels splashing in a puddle. I don't even care at this point. Right now, I don't feel at all like I'm thirty-one, but like

I'm sixteen again, kissing Gill for the very first time. His scent, mixed with the smell of rain and wet leaves, is intoxicating. And the taste of him ... oh God, the *taste*. Gilleon's got all five of my senses enveloped, wrapped up in that dichotomous perfection of his, that strange mix between light and dark.

I reach my hands up to Gill's cheeks, pressing my palms against either side of his face.

"Somehow, no matter what else happened, I knew tonight was going to include a quickie," I whisper as my back presses up against something hard—the trunk of the tree that's currently providing us shelter and hiding us away from the rest of the world. *Thank God.* With the dark and the rain, I don't think anyone can see us here.

At least, I hope they can't because this is happening.

I brush some dark, wet strands of Gill's hair off his forehead and study his expression. He looks right back at me, moving his tattooed right hand to my face, trailing his fingertips over my cheek and across my lips. There's a look of wonder there, a flicker of light that is all me and nothing else. I'm not trying to be arrogant here or overplay my own importance, but it is what it is.

For better or worse, I want this.

For better or worse, Gilleon Marchal is mine.

I gasp as Gill pushes up the lace skirt of my dress, a smile curling the edge of his lip. On the street behind him, a car rumbles by, lights flickering in the rush of rainwater. The danger of getting caught, it's all mixing up with the danger of Gill, the unknown, the infinite possibilities that a new start will give us. It could be good, great even, but there's always a risk—just like there is right now. I shouldn't take it … but I'm going to anyway. Why is it that the things that make you feel most alive in the world are the very same things that can bring you to your knees?

"Are you sure about this?" Gill asks as I drop my hands to the button on his slacks. I'm not sure if he's asking about the sex or about getting back together. Either way …

"Yes." Easy question, easy answer. "Now let's do this before the neighbors call the cops."

Gill grins; I'm sure he of all people doesn't give two shits about the cops.

His lips drop to mine, hot tongue darting into my mouth, tasting me as I free his dick from his pants, sliding my hand down the long, hard length of him. His wet fingers slide away from my bunched up skirt, down the sensitive flesh of my bare thighs, drawing my right leg up. *Thank God I wore tall heels today.* Certainly makes things a lot easier in this department.

I release my hold on him, switching my fingers to the back of his neck, curling them together in a tight grip. Without skipping a beat, he pushes my panties to the side and drives into me, filling me up until we're pelvis to pelvis, gasping and squinting at each other in a deluge of rainwater. The skies crack open and come down hard, raindrops sticking his dark hair to his forehead, blinding me with heavy wet strands of blonde.

I raise my lips to Gill's again, tasting the wet and the autumn cold and his body's natural warmth. We move together, grinding our bodies tightly against one another, probably committing some sort of felony (or at the very least a misdemeanor). But I don't care, not right now. Right now, all I give a shit about is Gilleon.

In that moment, in the freezing rain, my breath frosting against his lips, I feel more alive, more awake than I have since the moment we first met. Our chests tight together, I can feel his heartbeat pounding against mine, like the sweet sonata of a new beginning.

x x x

My lips are tingling so bad, I can't resist touching them, scraping my fingertips against the tender flesh. Even though I know they aren't, my hands feel rough, like sandpaper. Gill glances over at me from his position behind the wheel and smiles knowingly.

"I was just thinking," I say, grabbing my purse and withdrawing a tube of lipstick, "that it seems like a good time to reapply."

"Sure it is," he says with a warm chuckle. He's a mess; I'm a mess. We're both sopping wet, hair tangled and dripping, my makeup melting down my face. But at least I have my fresh pair of panties ... Gill, at least, had the good sense not to laugh when I switched them out and shoved the wet ones in the glove compartment. Hopefully one of us remembers to clean those out before he turns the rental in. Wouldn't that be embarrassing ...

"I'm glad we're still going to dinner," he says and I nod.

"Me, too." I slide my hands down my dress, the fabric clinging to my body and emphasizing the gentle swell of my breasts and hips. Gill notices and swallows hard, like he's already ready for round two. I can't blame him, I guess, since I was there about two seconds after we finished.

"We really need to start having sex in beds more," I say, reaching back to pick a leaf out of my hair. I'll be lucky if my designer dress doesn't have any holes in the lace. At least it was all worth it—so, so worth it.

"Speaking of," Gill begins, clearing his throat and tossing me a grin, "are you going to let me move into the master bedroom?" I open my mouth to protest, but ... if I'm going to do this, then I might as well go all the way.

"Yes," I say, and then pause. "You get to tell Papa about it though."

"Done," Gill says and then his voice drops low. "So ... that whole speech ... you weren't just caught up in the moment? You'll stay? We'll give this the go it was always meant to have?"

"If you leave me again, you're not getting another chance," I say, and I'm dead serious about that part. "But yes, I'm here and I'm doing this." I reach over and curl my fingers over Gill's hand, meeting his bright blue eyes so he can feel the truth behind my words. "Like I said, no matter what you tell me tonight, it's okay. My forgiveness isn't conditional, and it's not something I can ever take away. It's there, it's yours, and that's that."

"Did I ever mention how much I love you?" Gill says absently, pretending like his words aren't that big of a deal. We both know they are.

I turn back towards the windshield, my eyes on the

wet and the dark, the sounds of my heartbeat mixing with the pound of raindrops on the roof. I don't take my hand away from Gill's and he doesn't move either, letting the comfort of skin to skin contact ease us both into a companionable silence.

When we hit the parking garage at Pike Place Market, I know I'm ready to hear whatever it is that Gill needs to say.

※ ※ ※

Gill takes me to our destination, a restaurant located on Post Alley between Virginia and Stewart, his arm hooked in mine, his body warmth radiating through the fabric of both our coats. I even let him hold the door open for me, stepping inside and finding my gaze drawn up, up, up to the rough wood planks on the ceiling and the chandeliers hanging at regular intervals. The windowless brick facade and the industrial steel door hide the true beauty of this place from prying eyes.

"Fancy," I say as Gill checks our coats at the door and a waiter guides us to a waiting table in the back. "Good thing, too, because I'm from Paris—we're experts at being wined and dined." I give Gill a smile that he returns, almost sheepishly. Only ... I wouldn't consider anything about Gilleon to be 'sheepish'. Wolfish, more like.

"Voted best place in Seattle for a first date," Gill says after we're both seated and staring at one another across a table too tiny to be accidental. This place is designed to breed closeness, to beg romance. I reach out and poke the velvet soft petal of a red rose in the small glass jar that decorates our tabletop, my senses heightened and my breath still coming in small gasps. I'm nervous as *hell,* won't lie about that. It isn't everyday that you declare your intent to ... date isn't the right word ... partner with? To partner with someone? God, I know I just confessed my love to Gilleon, but this is all still new and weird for me. Time to do what we do best—talk shit out.

"Ahh," I say, trying to keep the mood light, "this qualifies as a first date?" Gill grins at me, handsome as hell with his mismatched buttons and mussed up hair. I consider telling him he should fix his shirt, but no ... I always liked Gill's imperfections. Loved them, actually. Besides, I think I was the one that buttoned him up in the first place. Hard to remember considering the hot, heavy quickie that transpired only twenty short minutes before.

"If my only other choice is to consider that time Cliff took us both to the mall as our first date, then yes, this is our new official first date." His words are playful, his grin lopsided, but I can see the tension in his forehead, in the strong set of his shoulders. Gill's nervous. But that's okay—I'm nervous, too.

"I recall you buying me a hot dog and a soda, some chips and a really dry chocolate chip cookie for dessert." I smile, drawing my eyes away from Gill just long enough to accept a glass of water from the waiter. "I think we held hands, too, if I remember correctly."

"You do," Gill says, his voice soft, his long legs brushing mine beneath the table. His slacks are still wet, the fabric cool against my bare skin. And the memory of his body inside of mine is still so fresh. Ugh. Not to mention the things I just said, that I admitted to. *Gill,*

360

the only man I want is you.

Yikes.

Guess the romantic comedy I watched the other night really wore off on me.

"I want to tell you everything," he says, leaning back and taking in a deep breath. Even now, even in the midst of all this, Gill is still Gill; his eyes still sweep the restaurant, and under his suit jacket, I know there's still a gun. He makes it seem casual, but I know he's on the lookout for trouble. Better not be any tonight or I'm liable to grab that gun and shoot someone myself. I swallow hard and push that thought from my mind. A romantic dinner isn't the best place to bring up memories of people being shot—or the fact that the guy sitting across from you is the one that did it.

"So tell me," I prompt, leaning back and crossing my legs at the knee. I haven't even *looked* at the menu yet. I hope our waiter's used to less frantic dining experiences because we're taking our time tonight. If we were in Paris, I wouldn't have to think twice about it. Here in the States ... well, we'll just order drinks and desserts to keep him busy. "I can take it."

I smile, even though the subject isn't really something to smile about at all. But I want to set Gill at ease—*need* to set him at ease. We both can't go into this with emotions high and feelings bubbling up; good couples take turns being vulnerable.

I cross my arms over my chest and then spot the wine list lying next to my menu. I reach out and pick it up, scanning the names until I find one I know I'll like.

When the waiter comes back, I'm ordering a whole bottle of it. Maybe two.

Gill glances away for a moment before looking back at me, the quiet murmur of the other restaurant patrons a perfect backdrop for this conversation. I can't freak out in here, can't yell or sob or pace. Putting myself into this environment forces me to keep calm, to listen, and to process anything and everything Gill says in the most rational way possible.

But shit ... it's hard to be rational with those baby blues locked onto my face like that. So intense, so focused. It takes a physical effort to hold his gaze.

"I hate that a mistake from so long ago is haunting me today," Gill says on the end of a breath, shoulders straight, black hair drying under the warm lights from the chandeliers. "But I love that you're sitting here with me now, willing to forgive those mistakes ... and all of their unintended consequences." Gill pauses again, eyes taking in my face, tracing my lips. Unconsciously, I find my tongue traveling over them. Gill blinks several times and then shakes his head like he's trying to stay on track here. "Even if you change your mind after you hear what I have to say, I still owe you a thanks." He smiles at me. "So thank you, Regina. For listening to me, for trying."

"For *doing*," I say, reaching out and laying my fingers atop his, doing my best to ignore the jump in his pulse, the way his eyes flick to my hand and back to my face. "Because I won't change my mind, no matter what." I lean forward, damp strands of hair falling across my forehead and brushing against my cheeks. "Let it out; let

362

it fucking go."

Gill adjusts himself, leaving his left hand in my grip but glancing casually over his right shoulder, like he's just checking for our waiter or something. In all reality, he's probably trying to decide how much he should say here, how much detail he should give, or how loudly he should give it.

He turns back to me.

"Too bad this story doesn't begin with *once upon a time*," Gill says, voice tight.

I keep smiling.

"They never do." I shrug my shoulders like this is nothin', like I talk about my dead mom every Sunday over lunch with the girls. Inside, my stomach twists into a knot. "Just ... start wherever you feel comfortable." I make my smile a little wider and lean back. "And maybe if we're lucky, it'll all end with a happily ever after?"

"Fuck, I hope so," Gill murmurs and then shakes his head like he either can't or won't allow myself to think too hard about that. "I guess ... my mom. This all started because of her." Gill stares at me for a moment longer and then drops his eyes back to the tabletop, like he'd rather not look directly at me right now. Guilty. That's what it is: he looks guilty.

"My mom," Gill begins again, and already I can feel his fingers curling into a fist beneath my hand, "you know how bad she was before I came to live with you and Elena. The drugs, the abusive boyfriends, the religious babble." Gill runs his tattooed hand over his face. "The only thing I ever wanted to do was keep her safe."

Gill stops talking suddenly, like he can sense something I don't. It ends up just being our waiter, pausing to take our drink orders. At least I'll have a glass of wine in my hand when I hear this story. Knowing Gilleon and what he went through with this mother, I can tell this story's going to break my heart. Even now, today, all these years later and he hurts for her. His depth of emotion's admirable.

"I killed a boy," he says quietly, the words barely escaping his lips before they're drowned in the sea of voices and the clank of glassware, the rush of cool air as a new couple enters the restaurant and checks their coats. "A teenager, I guess," he adds, eyes glazing over a bit as he stares down into his water glass, lost in a memory. The dialogue pauses again as our wine appears and I stop to taste it, nodding in approval before our waiter pours Gill a glass and disappears again. He doesn't ask if we're ready to order, like he can tell we need more time.

"How?" I ask, refusing to be judgmental, to think too hard about what he's saying to me. Not yet, at least. I need the whole story before I can even consider going there. I run the tip of my finger around the rim of my wineglass, the burgundy liquid red as blood in the dim, atmospheric lighting. "Why?"

"We were living in a van for a while," Gill says and I feel myself tense. I definitely haven't heard this particular story before. "Traveling from church to church while my mom searched for some sort of salvation. From what, I don't know. All I knew then was that there was a man threatening my mother's life and that I'd do anything to save her. From him and from herself."

Gilleon taps his fingers on the table and then drags his hand back into his lap. He's always hated talking about his mom. I can see why. All of that anger, that fear and pain and confusion, that loneliness he felt back then, it all comes rushing to the surface, as hard to deal with now as it was back then. I don't think he's ever really gotten over it.

"It's not your fault, Gill," I tell him, because sometimes, even when somebody knows something, it's okay to tell them, just to reinforce the feeling. His mother, her decline, her demons, whatever they were, were not Gilleon's fault and he should never have been burdened with them.

I get one of those tight smiles, the ones he throws out to calm a situation, make it seem more casual than it really is; this is probably the most important conversation we've ever had or will ever have. I take a deep breath.

"I know," he says, voice dropping, memories lacing his every word. "But it doesn't make it any better, doesn't erase what I did then or all the things I've done since then." When he looks up at me again, I know we're talking about the hotel and those two men. I'm not sure if the switch in conversation is intentional or ... no. Nothing Gill does is ever unintentional.

"Don't change the subject, please," I tell him, taking another breath. The air smells like pasta, like wine, like garlic. The scents soothe me. "When I said I forgive you, I meant even that. You did what you had to do to protect your family. Some people might judge, but you won't find me among them." I drum my fingernails on the tabletop. "This ... boy or teenager or whatever he was, what happened?"

"I was thirteen at the time, so maybe he was eighteen or nineteen, I don't know. All I knew was that he was several years older than me and that he was sleeping with my mother. Sometimes in the back of the van while I tried to sleep in the front seat, sometimes in a hotel while I waited outside." Gill's jaw tightens and his pulse flickers with old rage. "He was supplying her with drugs and she was ..." Gill doesn't finish his sentence, and I don't ask him to. "I don't know what happened between them. I heard a scream and I picked the lock on the hotel room door, found my mom with blood running down the side of her face and a gun not two feet from her skull. I didn't think too hard about it, honestly, and I didn't lose much sleep either." We keep our eyes focused on one another, and I make sure I tell him with my gaze that it's okay, to keep going. "I hit him with his own baseball bat, one he left in the van. I didn't mean to kill him." *But you didn't know your own strength yet, did you?*

I look at Gill and his wide shoulders, his muscled frame obvious even beneath the black fabric of his suit jacket. It's not hard for me to believe that he could kill someone with a bat—especially not when I once saw him break a man's arm with his bare hands. At age seventeen. Go figure.

I play with my mother's necklace for a moment, thinking this over. I have the bare facts now: Gill killed a drug dealer to protect his mother, my mother was shot, then his, and then he left. I see the four events. Now all I need is for him to tie them together. I cross and uncross my legs, trying to get comfortable. Inside my chest, my heart pounds and my breath hitches. *Gill left and he didn't come back.* After a decade, I'll finally know why.

I yank the white napkin into my lap, unroll it and put the silverware back on the tabletop. Gill watches me with a bemused half-smile.

"This is designer," I say with a smile of my own. "Very expensive. Would not do to get red sauce on the lace, right?" *I can get through this. We can get through this. After tonight, everything's going to be different.*

"I love you, Regina," he says again, making my pounding heart flutter. We both pause again, like runners taking a break between sprints. When the waiter comes back over again, I order garlic bread, fried raviolis (not exactly traditional but damn good), and something I can't pronounce. Might have the Spanish, German, and French down, but I've never taken up Italian.

"I love you, too, Gilleon." I lean forward, putting my elbows on the table and dragging my wineglass towards me. Next to the rose, there's a white tea light flickering in a silver holder. I look at the flames and then glance back at Gill. "This kid, who was he?"

"Karl Rousseau's son."

I can feel the blood drain from my face, that sickening lurch as it all cascades down to my feet and makes me dizzy.

"What was this guy's son doing living in a van and selling drugs?"

"He had a fallout with his dad, and Karl threatened to disown him, did for a while, too. I think that's why it took so long for him to find me."

Fuck.

I can see where this is going, and I don't like it.

"Karl?"

Gill nods and lifts his wine to his lips for the first time, draining the entire glass in one go.

"When they found out he was dead, naturally they wanted to find out who killed him, something the police had never been able to do. It took them longer than it should, with all their resources, their money, their connections." Gill grins at me, but there's no joy in it, just a sense of honesty, an admittance. "I'm good at what I do, even before I knew I'd be doing it for a living. By the time Karl found me, he wanted me. I told him no."

My turn to pick up my wineglass and drain it. Before the waiter can come over and refill our glasses for us, Gill does it, taking his almost to the rim. I watch him drink half of this before he continues.

"Your mom ... they thought she was my mom at first." Gill closes his eyes, takes several careful breaths through his nose. *Karl had your mother killed, Regi. Because of me. Elena, she's dead because of me.*

I can feel my skin prickle and the fine hairs on the back of my neck stand up. My lips part; my eyelids flutter.

Retribution. Vengeance. That's what it all came down to? That's why my mother died?

"Well, I think that's bullshit because Karl doesn't make

mistakes like that. Maybe he knew that at that point, I loved your mother as much as I loved my own." Gill sucks in a breath like he's in pain, like he's about to admit something terrible. "Maybe more. She was all the things I ever wished my mom would be." I can feel tears threatening, glossy drops clinging to my waterproof mascara, just waiting to fall. I want to walk away right now, put my hands over my ears, take a break. But I can't. I'm sitting here in this restaurant, full of all these people. As I intended, I have few choices that make sense. Go to the bathroom, disappear outside into the rain, or ... stay put.

I keep my seat.

"He even warned me that if I didn't come to him, he'd do it again, that he'd find my real mother and put a bullet in her. At the time, I told myself I was calling bullshit on his threat. In reality, I was being selfish." Gill closes his eyes again, and when he opens them, they look brighter somehow, like a clear blue summer sky. "I didn't want to leave you, Regi. But I also knew I couldn't bring you into that life, that Karl would never let me live happily ever after with you. So I left to work for him, just two days before the anniversary of his son's death, two days before he promised that you were next. And then Dad. Every two years he would kill someone I loved because it'd taken him two years since he started looking to find me."

CHAPTER
Twenty-Four

I exhale in a rush, my pulse pounding so hard that for a moment, I'm overwhelmed by dizziness. Gilleon tenses and his own breathing slows, making me wonder if he's actually stopped altogether. I don't know what he thinks I'm going to do. Run, maybe? Curse his name? Throw something at him? I'll be honest: the first thought never crosses my mind. The other two ... well, I briefly consider them—but only briefly.

Am I still mad that Gill left? Hell yeah, I am. Does his reason for leaving make it hurt any less? No. But it all makes at least some small semblance of sense. In his own way, Gill thought that leaving me was akin to saving me, that he had no other choice. The revelation isn't about to wipe away the sins of the past, but it does bring me a reasonable amount comfort to know why. I hadn't thought it mattered; it does.

I fight back tears, clutching the stem of my wineglass and holding in the surge of emotion I feel as the waiter lays out our appetizers. The poor guy looks stressed enough as it is, has way too many tables to take care of on his own, and the last thing he needs is some stranger weeping over a plate of deep fried raviolis.

"*Merci*," I say, raising my glass in salute. The waiter gives me a weird look, but at least he smiles.

"Regina?" Gill asks, his voice carefully neutral. He's waiting for something from me, some sort of confirmation that I heard and understood what he said. *Elena, she's dead because of* me. In the strictest sense of the English language, Gill's right. If he hadn't killed Karl's son to protect his mother, my mother might still be alive today—might being the key word. But she could just as easily have died in a car accident or from falling off a ladder or, like my father, from some hidden monster like cancer. Life is absolutely chock full of *what-ifs*. All we can really do is exist in each moment and make the best decision we know how.

Right now, that decision for me remains the same: I'll stay with Gill.

"I don't consider what happened your fault, Gilleon. Your mom's, maybe, or Karl's son's, or most especially Karl himself. But not yours." I pull my gaze from my wineglass and look up at him, past the garlic bread and the raviolis, the tea light and the rose. Gill's blue eyes are full to bursting, like somewhere in there he has as many tears waiting to spill as I do, but neither of us sheds them. Tonight isn't a night for tears. "But you leaving like that ... you should've told me. Everything. I should have known *everything*. As a couple, as a team, as a partnership, it wasn't *your* responsibility to decide what to do." I take a deep breath. "It was *ours*."

Gill nods and scoots in closer, like he wants to get up and come to me. But again, the public nature of our surroundings makes things easier, simpler, smoother. If he took me in his arms right now, I might actually start crying and that won't help. Instead, I let Gill reach across the small table and wrap his big hand over mine, the tattoos on his fingers stark in the dim lighting, but beautiful nonetheless.

"You're right, Regina, and I'm sorry. If I could do it all over again, I'd make different choices."

"Like asking me to rob Karl's store with you? To run? To start a whole new life? Gill, I saw through you right from the start." I lean in towards him, my pulse pounding in my throat, my heart thumping hard and heavy in my chest. "Again, you should've told me what and why and how right from the get-go. You came to me with an agenda, with—and correct me if I'm misinterpreting this—the sole purpose of getting back together, but yet you acted like you couldn't care less about me."

The way his muscles tense, hand curling tighter around mine, I know he isn't going to argue: I'm right and he knows it.

"You risked my life, and your father's, and your *daughter's*," I pause for a moment to take a breath, "just so you might have the opportunity of having a life with me." My lips twitch a little. It's so tragically romantic that I almost smile. Almost. "But you didn't tell me the truth. If you had ..." I close my eyes for a moment and breathe deep. *If you had, we might've ended up here a whole hell of a lot sooner.* But what's past is past. I can't let it affect me anymore. I *won't* let it affect *us*. "You know what?" I open them back up and look Gilleon straight in the face. "It doesn't matter. The point is, you should've told me the truth."

"I'm sorry," he says, voice low, his gaze searching my expression. When Gill tries to pull his hand away, I won't let him, tangling our fingers together and watching as his breath hitches and his eyes grow hooded. "Regi ..."

I wave my hand like it's not important. It is; it so is. I've waited over a decade to hear *why*, to understand how —when I never could've even dreamed of being separated from him—Gill could walk away and never come back. Now I know. It's strange, like a hole I've been carrying around forever is suddenly full, and I don't quite know what to do with it.

"I'm still with you, Gill." This time, I do smile. It hurts, just a little, but there it is. He smiles back at me, but only for an instant. There's still a lot to talk about, and he's still worried. I am, too, but for different reasons. This thing between us, it'll work. I know it will. All of the, uh, criminal activity we're having to deal with ... that's another story. "Now, tell me everything." I point my finger at him and sit back, keeping our hands clasped together. "And I mean everything. If we're going to do this, I need to understand what's happening with you." I lift my wine to my lips and let the taste linger on my tongue for a moment. "According to Aveline, you traded the tyranny of one criminal mastermind for the protection of another, is that right?"

"It is." Gill's voice is husky and rough, deep and low. I can see dark shadows creeping across his face, but that's okay. I'm here now and we can get through this together. "Although nothing's going the way it should. Max ... Aveline ... me ... we all underestimated how much Karl cares about my future." Gill clenches his jaw tight, but keeps those perfect eyes focused on me. I have to resist the urge to lean across the table and kiss his forehead.

"Where have you been all week?" I ask him, giving him the chance to come clean so we can start this out the right way, work towards a future together. Because the only person I've ever seen myself with is this man sitting across from me—master thief status and all. If our fight's not over yet, then it's not over, but I want to know about it.

"With Max," Gill answers without hesitation, pouring himself yet another glass of wine. Bottle's empty now. Somewhere near the front of the room, some live music starts up, all haunting strings and aching bows. "Trying to figure this all out. Karl offered Max a deal—the diamonds for me, free and clear, no bad blood between them. Max thought we could try the other way around—give the diamonds back and forget about me." A small shake of his head. "Max knows I can make back that

374

money and then some given enough time." Gill runs his left hand down his face. The stress from the last few weeks is starting to get to him, to tighten the muscles in his face and shoulders. "No deal."

I raise my eyebrows at that.

"He'd rather have you? Over a hundred million in jewels?" I keep my voice low and lean forward, trying to smile, to make light of a situation that's nothing but dark. "I might think you're worth that much, but wow. Your boss, too?"

Gill tries to smile back, but the situation, and the stories, have taken their toll on him.

"Max promised our protection." Gill sighs and shakes his head. "And Max and Karl have too much history to ever really make nice with one another, so I'm not worried about Max selling me out. I just ... I was supposed to be able to retire after this, to settle down ... with you." Now he smiles, at least a little.

"I knew it," I whisper, sliding my hand away from his and spooning some raviolis onto one of the small plates our waiter left. I set it in front of Gilleon, hoping it'll force him to eat something. He looks like he could use a pick-me-up. "You've had this all planned for a while now."

Gill nods and takes up his fork, but he doesn't eat.

"Unfortunately, as long as Karl is threatening Max, I have to keep working, to prove I'm worth the effort."

"You pulled a job this week?" I ask, my eyes going wide thinking about Gill ... well, doing what Gill does best. I mean, it's not like it's a surprise to me, but the thought of him taking risk after risk after risk ... he's gotten lucky this long. What happens if his luck runs out?

"I did," he says, but he doesn't elaborate, not here. "Too close to home to talk about right now," he adds before I can question him about it. "But if you want to know, I'll tell you. Shit, Regina, I'll tell you anything." Gill's blue eyes darken as we stare at each other for a long moment. "I can keep working, no problem, but what happens if Max decides I'm not worth it? I need to get Karl off my case." He glances away, towards the bar, eyes sweeping the people seated on leather stools, working the counter. There's nothing there; it's just part of his process. Gill turns back to me as I spear a ravioli and bring it to my lips. "I want to be done with all of this," he says, looking right at me. "Now."

I put the food into my mouth, hardly tasting it, my mind spinning in a million directions as I wonder what I've just gotten myself into. I know it's worth it, to be with Gilleon again, but for whatever reason, I'd convinced myself that it was all over, that we'd solved our problems, that life would flourish and blossom into a garden of possibility. And maybe it still can ... but I have to figure out how to help Gill.

Now.

Especially now.

X X X

"Well, that was nice," I say as Gilleon moves over to my side of the SUV and opens the door, a slow smile spreading across his face. There's some bitterness there, some fear for the future, but there's also a tentative joy. I take Gill's hand and climb down, reaching my other up to brush across his cheek. "More than nice. A proper first date, really, Gum Wall and all. It might not be the Eiffel Tower, but it still counts as sightseeing, right?"

"*Oui,*" Gill says, pulling me into his arms. I can see a million questions resting behind his eyes, but I won't let him ask them. Nope. We covered what we needed to cover and now, the rest of the night is *our* night. "Regina ..."

"No." I put a finger against his lips and then trade it out for my mouth, kissing Gill long and hard and deep, his hands roaming over my back and down towards sweeter places. Without even realizing I'm doing it, I find myself taking a step back, my body bumping against the cooling metal of the SUV.

Our make out session only lasts for a brief instant, both of us going stone-still when a car idles slowly by. Gill's grip on my body tightens, but when we both glance over, it ends up just being his neighbor, glaring out her window at the two of us like she's just caught us vandalizing her house.

I wave and then turn my attention back to Gilleon. I can see the weight of his relief in one glance. How scary is that? A car driving slowly by is just as likely to be an actual threat as it is to be a neighbor.

"Can't even make out in our own front yard," I tsk, trying to lighten the mood. Fortunately, it works and Gill smiles. "What is this world coming to?"

"Don't mind her." Gilleon steps away and slides his

right arm around my waist, leading me toward the front steps. When he leans over and brushes my hair away from my ear, hot breath searing against my flesh, I can feel goose bumps climbing up my arms. "She's just upset because I turned her down for a date once." I gasp as he pulls away and grins, looking for an instant exactly like teenage Gill, all of that playful mischief burning in his eyes. My heart stutters and I bump my shoulder into his.

"Because you were waiting for me?"

Gill pauses thoughtfully and crinkles his brows.

"No, not really. Mostly because she tried to file a complaint with the city about the length of my lawn." A laugh bursts from my throat, echoing into the night air, chasing away the demons, the worries, the fears. For a moment there, I feel like everything really will be okay.

"Asshole," I mumble, but I'm only half serious.

After the necessary ugliness of our conversation, dinner got better, good even. I actually felt like I was on a date and even now, with thoughts of Karl and diamonds and guns sitting heavy in the back of my mind, I'm actually ... happy. Maybe I shouldn't be, but I can't help it.

Gill unlocks the front door and gestures for me to go ahead of him, casually scanning the street before he closes it behind us.

"Hey," I say, giving Aveline a little wave that she returns without even looking up from her computer screen. My heels click across the floor as I make my way to the kitchen, finding Solène and Cliff up to their elbows in flour and sugar. My mind clears just a little bit more and I suddenly see things as they could be, as they *will* be if Gill and I can get past this one last obstacle. It's a bit of a doozy, but I have hope.

"*Bonsoir, Maman,*" Solène glances over her shoulder and grins at us. "*Père.*"

"*Bonsoir,*" I say with a smile, dropping Gill's hand and moving over to kiss either of my daughter's cheeks. Her smile is just as infectious, just as friendly and gracious, as it was when she thought I was her sister. So far, it doesn't feel like anything between us has changed. Maybe, in my own way, I was being a mother all along? I suppose it doesn't matter. I meant what I told Cliff: being a parent is a privilege and I'm still going to do my best to earn it. "What are you two up to?"

"Making lemon bars," Solène states proudly, pressing the shortbread dough into the bottom of the pan. "Extra tart for Papa and his discerning taste buds." Cliff laughs and shakes his head, sliding Gill and me a glance that says so many things without words. There's hope there, frustration, fear, disappointment, love—just this crazy mixture of feeling that's going to take a while to sort out. But that's okay. I'm in no rush.

"How was dinner?" he asks, giving me a kiss to either cheek. Gill and Cliff pause for a moment staring at one another before Cliff pats him roughly on one shoulder, turning back to Solène and her dessert prep.

"Good," I say, glancing at Gill, at those blue eyes that always have and seemingly always will take my breath away. "We worked out a lot of things." I keep my description vague. These problems that Gill and I are having, these demons from our past, none of them are Cliff's or Solène's issues to deal with. Cliff deserves a peaceful retirement and my daughter deserves a happy childhood.

I take a deep breath and set my purse down on the table, shrugging out of my coat and handing it to Gilleon. He takes it gingerly, our eyes catching, my breath hitching in my chest.

A groan from Solène draws my attention back to her workstation and a pair of raised black brows.

"You two are simply *impossible,*" she snorts, emphasizing the last word in French. "Like two lovebirds long separated, finally freed from their cages."

"And what movie did you two watch tonight?" I ask as Cliff grins and opens up a new bag of sugar.

"Breakfast at Tiffany's," he says, watching Gill watch Solène. I follow my stepfather's gaze and see Gilleon caught at the edge of the kitchen, his coat still on his shoulders, mine draped over his arm. He's watching our daughter intently, sadness and longing mixing with just the smallest sprinkle of hope.

"Of course," I say with a small smile, moving next to Gill and taking my jacket back. "Because that's the logical choice for a nine year old's movie night." I wink at Cliff and he grins right back at me. Gill's still staring at the two of them, at this odd example of domestic bliss taking place in his kitchen. Better get used to it because Cliff's obsessed with passing his foodie knowledge down to Solène. "Hey," I say, snapping him out of it, drawing his attention back to me. I feel a hot flush as those sensuous lips curve into a smile. "Give me your coat." I nod my head in Solène's direction as she washes her hands in the sink, balancing on a small stool that puts her close to Cliff's height. "Go mix some sugar and lemon juice. Doesn't sound like much, but it's actually kind of fun."

Gill watches me this time, his gaze taking in every inch of my face, before he finally slips off his coat and suit jacket, removing his gun holsters and laying them on the table.

"Thanks," he murmurs, eyes half-hooded and still focused on me.

I reach over and grab his arm, the hard bulge of his muscle beneath my fingers forcing me to swallow twice to regain my composure before I can let go. Without another word, I disappear down the hallway and deposit our coats on the rack, catching Aveline's eyes from her place at the dining room table. She gives me a wicked half-grin that I ignore as I sneak back and watch from a distance, watch as the love of my life cautiously approaches our daughter and gets swept into the family like he was always there. She's gracious like that, Solène is.

A smile curves my lips as I watch Gill try to measure out a cup of sugar. Those big hands, those tattoos, all of that strength ... it's beautiful to watch him work in a different light.

Fucking Karl.

We'll figure this shit out, me and him, because we're a family—albeit one that took a brief hiatus. But that doesn't matter now, never really did matter. I've loved Gilleon for ten years without a hiccup, despite my best efforts not to, so if I'm going to welcome him back, I'm going to do it with open arms.

Family.

We're a family now and I'll do *anything* for family.

X X X

Dear God.

I'm blushing like a teenager on prom night, my hands clutching my bare upper arms, my black lace nightgown shifting in the gentle rush of air from the heating vent above my head. Quickies are one thing ... even making love after a serious emotional discussion is easier than this, this casual *normalcy*.

Fuck.

Gill's sitting on the edge of my bed—shirtless, mind you—and smiling. Not grinning or smirking, just smiling. Despite our conversation, despite the ugliness in our past, this man, this guy who's six foot four and God only knows how many pounds of muscle, he stood next to his daughter and he baked and he spilled powdered sugar on the floor and he sat next to her on the couch while she showed him all of her designs and drawings. My lips twitch. *And some of mine.* Solène even came up with a plan for our 'studio' downstairs—complete with artful renditions of us pinning gowns together on a dress form.

It's a dream I don't mind sharing with her. In this house. With this man.

I've made my decision and even though Cliff keeps giving me a slight stink-eye, I'm sticking to it. This is it, the thing I've been waiting for forever.

I swallow hard as Gilleon glances over at me, his dark hair shining under the white moonlight from outside our window.

"Are you sure you want me in here?" he asks, his voice light and playful, the shadows on his face just a product of the light, not even a trace of that inner darkness showing right now. "Because if you want to keep sleeping in separate beds ..."

"Don't tease or you might just get your wish," I tell him, knowing that my next conversations with Anika, Leilani, and the whole gaggle of girlfriends I left behind in France are going to be regarding ... this. I'm already so not looking forward to any of them. I quirk an eyebrow. "You should be nicer to me. Do you know how much shit my girlfriends are going to put me through when I tell them we're getting back together? Then it won't be Karl you'll have to worry about coming after your ass, but Katriane and her five inch stiletto heels, sharp as blades."

Gill grins at me and stands up, his flannel pj pants slung low on his hips, teasing me with rock hard abs and the bright shining eyes of the panther tattoo on his right pec. He even looks badass with the fading remnant of that gunshot wound to his other shoulder. Tough as nails Gilleon Marchal. *Holy shit, he's sleeping in my bedroom tonight. Tomorrow night. All of our future nights.*

I reach up and run my fingers through my hair.

This is going to work. It's going to work and it's going to be beautiful.

383

The self-talk calms me down enough that I take a few steps forward, bare feet padding across the hardwood floors.

"Can I ask you a question?" Gill says, tilting his head to the side and regarding me as I pause, a stray shaft of silver moonlight falling across my breasts, drawing his gaze down before it slides back up.

"You can ask, but it doesn't mean I have to answer it," I say, mimicking him as I cross my arms over my chest and lean back. I smell his scent, that spicy bergamot oil breeze that clings to his warm skin like cologne. I want to lick it off. But I pretend I don't give a crap.

"Whatever happened to the ring I gave you?" Gill swallows and his jaw clenches tight with old anger, not at me but at Karl. Or Karl's son. Maybe even his own mother.

I glance up and over Gill's shoulder, out the window and down to the dark chasm where the lake should be. The way the moonlight's falling tonight, I can't even see it. Doesn't mean it's not there though.

"Why?" I ask, glancing at Gill's face again. "Because if you ask me to marry you right now, it's a no." He raises his dark brows at me and I smile. "But you can certainly date me and consider asking again in, oh, I don't know, two years or so?"

"So that's how it's going to be?" he asks, reaching forward and sliding his warm hands around my waist. I gasp at the touch, my thoughts flitting in my skull like butterflies. *Goddamn things are back again.* My lips part as Gill leans in and breathes hot against my mouth.

"That's how it's going to be," I whisper back, reaching up to tangle my fingers in his dark hair. My skin feels like it's on fire, pulsing flames dancing across every square inch as I struggle to find my breath, to remember why I was nervous again. Standing here, doing this, everything feels right. For the first time in a long, long time.

"But you still didn't answer my question," he says, loosening his grip on me and taking a step back. "If it's too painful," he starts, but I raise a hand and stop him, moving over to my purse and reaching inside to unzip an inner pocket. Tossed in with a handful of change and some earrings that Anika sent me for my last birthday is Gill's engagement ring, the infinity twist that still shines as brightly today as it did back then. I haven't taken very good care of it, no, but I also debated tossing it out the window several times. The fact that it's still with me is an accomplishment to say the least.

I turn back to Gilleon and wait for him to come to me, reaching out my hand and dropping the ring into his palm, curling his fingers around it.

"When the time comes," I begin, looking up at him with honey brown eyes, taking in his bright blue ones with a confident smile on my face, "and the time will come someday, then use this. Nothing else would feel right."

Gill nods, reaching up to run his thumb over my lower lip, sliding his fingers down to cup the nape of my neck. Without responding in words, he leans in, pressing a scalding hot kiss to my mouth at the same moment he slips the ring into his pocket.

Our tongues tangle together as he pulls me closer, diving deeper, tasting me like I'm tasting him. Just like the night of our very first kiss, the one we shared as innocent teenagers all those years ago, Gill tastes like lemons. This time, instead of sherbet, it's lemon bars, and instead of a park, we're standing in this beautiful old house, but the love's still the same, the passion.

Time slows for me again, reverses, takes me back and wipes away the pain, the suffering, the loneliness, until all I can feel and taste and hear is Gill and his warmth, his strength, his love.

All I can taste is *us*.

CHAPTER
Twenty-Five

"Mornin' sunshine," Aveline drawls as I yawn my way down the back staircase in my stolen hotel robe and a pair of white cashmere-blend slippers. All of these in-depth emotional revelations are taking their toll on me. I'm usually a morning person, but today, eh, I kind of feel like poking the sunrise in its golden eye. That, and Gill is gone. I make myself smile and greet Aveline before I ask about him.

"*Bonjour,*" I mumble, snatching a mug from the cabinet and removing the coffeepot. Somehow, even after last night's baking storm, there are no dirty dishes in the sink. I doubt Aveline's the domestic type, and I know Cliff and Solène far prefer cooking to cleaning, so ... the only person in this house on top of things enough to wash dishes is Gilleon. I stare at the rumbling silver face of the dishwasher and then glance back at Aveline. "A master thief who does dishes?" I ask.

Aveline shrugs, her back to me, red hair braided and hanging between her shoulder blades.

"He even rinses them before he loads it up. Pretty weird, huh? The world is just full of idiosyncrasies." Aveline runs her fingers over the keys on her laptop, clicking away at the speed of light before she turns to face me with a slight grin curling her lips, braid flopping over her shoulder. "But why don't you ask the question you *really* want to ask about Gill?"

I raise both my brows and bring my coffee cup to my lips.

"Okay, fine, I'll play along: where did he disappear to this morning?"

. "Dunno," Aveline replies, winking at me and turning back to her computer. "I just wanted to hear you ask." I roll my eyes and move out of the kitchen and down the hallway, pausing next to the staircase and letting my eyes drift left, into the nearly empty sitting area. Just past that, through the currently closed pocket door is a blank canvas with a whole wall of windows and no discernible purpose. My best guess is that it used to be the original dining room and someone walled it up to add all those extra cabinets in the kitchen. Normally that kind of thing would bother me, but here ... I like how it's tucked away but not excluded.

It'd make a great studio.

Before I realize I'm moving, my slippered feet are

whispering across the floor and I'm pushing back the pocket door to find gleaming hardwood floors and sunshine streaming through the wall of windows on my right.

"It's yours, if you want it."

I jump, sloshing coffee onto the floor near my feet, and turn to glare at Gill.

He leans casually against the wall in the sitting room, but the intensity in his gaze betrays his easy stance.

"I thought you'd disappeared on me," I say just as casually, trying to hide the relief in my voice. I *have* to trust Gilleon to make this work. Trust. That's going to be a tough one.

Gill notices and his expression softens a bit as he slides his fingertips into the front pockets of his jeans. There's no missing the pair of pistols hanging on either side of that muscular body. As warm, as cozy, as wonderful as this house feels, there's still danger afoot.

"I had a meeting with Max." Gill stands up straight and tilts his head to the side ever so slightly. "You're beautiful in the morning, you know that?" I reach up and touch the tousled mess that my hair's become. Normally I make a point to clean up before I let anyone see me in the morning, but ... I'm not living alone anymore. If my luck holds out, I won't be living alone ever again. Time to let my hair down, so to speak.

"Not a fan of the lipstick?" I ask, reaching up to trace my lips with my free hand. Gill smiles and takes a step forward.

"Definitely a fan of the lipstick," he says, running his

knuckles down my cheek. "And the dresses." His lips twitch. "Most definitely the heels. But I like this, too. I *missed* this, all this messy, sleepy perfection." Gill drops his hand as I raise an eyebrow. Inside, my heart might be pounding a million miles a minute, but I don't have to let the expression show on my face. I might be Regi, but there's still some Regina Corbair in there.

"Nice change of subject," I say, stepping around him and heading towards the kitchen to grab a paper towel for that coffee splash on the floor; Gill follows closely behind me. "It almost worked. What was your meeting with Max about?"

Gill's lips purse and he exchanges a look with Aveline before heading to the coffeemaker.

"Not good then, I take it?" I ask as I grab a roll of paper towels and tuck them under my arm.

"How would you feel if Aveline and I went out for one last job and left Ewan here with you?" Gill's trying to make the request sound casual when it's anything but. Even the tight curve of his ass under that dark blue denim isn't enough to distract from me from that statement.

"You mean you want to go after Karl? To kill him?" Both Gill and Aveline raise their brows and look over at me. I set my coffee cup down on the counter and raise my hands in surrender. "Look, if I'm being too frank, let me know, but I just want to get things straight here. Is this what you're asking?"

"You nailed it, Princess," Aveline says, slugging down the rest of her coffee and tossing the mug into the sink with a small wince from Gilleon. *Everything's going to be okay,* I tell myself, closing my eyes and taking a deep breath. When I open them, they're both still staring at me. I consider asking why Aveline would be willing to help Gill out with such a risky job, but ... I've kind of gotten the sense that Gilleon isn't the only one trying to wiggle out from under Karl Rousseau's thumb.

"Then what exactly is the plan here?" I ask, refusing to back down. I don't care how top secret this shit is. Gill promised me last night that he'd tell me everything; I'm putting our new relationship to the test right here and now.

Gill exchanges another look with Aveline, but all she does is shrug.

"The only way to fix this," Gill says, and his voice holds this old, stale sadness that I wish I could whisk away in an instant. He focuses his blue eyes on mine and I have to force myself to take a deep breath. "Is to get rid of Karl."

"Won't he have, like, a million bodyguards or something?" I hope I don't sound too ignorant, but really, who *wants* to truly understand how crime syndicates actually work? Not this chick right here. Some things are better left to the professionals. This being one of them. "I don't need all the details." I take another deep breath and run my hands down the front of my robe. See, if I were dressed, I'd be able to handle this situation better. I feel ... vulnerable in my pajamas.

"Karl will have lots of hired guns, yes, but ..." Gill glances at Aveline. "Not all of them care whether he lives or dies. Truthfully, some of them would actually *prefer* him dead. An expired crime boss leaves a vacuum of power that some people might be interested in filling." Gill takes a step forward and looks down at me, so tall, so handsome, his face a dangerous slice of dark and light. He *needs* this shit to go away. It's hard to get better when you're constantly straddling the line. "We have a contact, a possible way in the back door."

"And if this contact fucks up or fails?"

Gill's face answers my question more thoroughly than words ever could.

Fuck.

He lifts his hands up and wraps his fingers around my upper arms, rubbing the fabric in slow circles with his thumbs. My heart's racing again, but not for the same reason as it did before. I'm scared now.

I'm *terrified.*

I knew robbing a jewelry store could—more than likely *would*—lead to trouble. But this?

"I could keep working jobs for Max. In fact, that's what the boss called me in for today: another job." Gill swallows hard and shakes his head, taking a small step back, his boots loud on the kitchen floor. "But after last night ..." Gill trails off and drops his hands to my hips. "After waking up next to you this morning, it didn't feel the same. It didn't feel right. I can do it, but I don't want to, not anymore."

Gill leans over and presses his forehead to mine. Without realizing it, I drop the paper towels and watch as they roll across the floor and hit the fridge.

"One last job, and we can have that happy ending we

always deserved."

"But if something goes wrong, you die, am I right, Gill?"

No response, just the tightening of his fingers on my hips.

"One last job," he says again. "One last job and it's all over."

✗ ✗ ✗

One big risk—or lots of small ones.

That's essentially what Gilleon's asking me: which one do we take? Because his fate—and in turn, my own—was sealed the moment that Karl's son threatened Gilleon's mom. I adjust my diamond earrings, my mother's pendant, run my hands down the front of my black flounce-hem dress. It's covered from chest to knees in white daisies, a decidedly cheerful ensemble choice for today. I picked it on purpose.

"Regi?"

Gill's standing behind me, just out of view of the mirror I'm gazing into. How he keeps managing to sneak up on me is anybody's guess—maybe my reflexes are just not up to speed—but I'm hoping and praying that I'll get better at it. That, or I'll eventually die from a stress induced heart attack.

Gilleon closes the door behind him and moves over to me as I turn around, smiling at my dress, my makeup, my *heels*. Cheerful blue Manolo Blahnik pumps, in keeping with the theme. The heels on these babies are a good four inches, putting me up at Gill's height. I like that, being able to look straight into his eyes. Something to

393

keep in mind for shopping.

"How's that plan of yours coming along?" I ask, my pulse picking up speed. Just *talking* about the whole damn thing makes me crazy.

"Fuck that," Gill says, pulling me to him, gazing at my lips. "I don't even want to talk about it."

His mouth finds mine, his kiss warm and desperate, like he's trying to memorize the taste of me. I don't like that. If Gill's already stressing the possibility of failure when we haven't even decided for sure what we're going to do, that's a bad sign, right?

"Gilleon." I push him back with a firm hand on his chest, trying not to ogle the tight muscles in his chest too much. *He's all mine again, just like he was once, just like he always should've been.* "Did something happen down there?"

I don't like the way Gill pauses, like he's weighing how to phrase things.

"If we want to try this, we have to go in tonight."

The words are like a slap to the face.

I step back, but Gill doesn't let go of me, following a step forward so that we're toe to toe.

"You *just* told me about this idea this morning. We *just* worked things out between us last night. Gill, this doesn't work for me. You and Aveline, you talked about this whole thing like it was something you'd do in the future. A month from now, a few weeks, at the very least." I'm already shaking my head and trying to extricate myself from Gill's arms.

The asshole only tightens his grip and drags me closer,

his fingertips pressing tightly into my hips.

"I have to do this."

"No."

Gill furrows his brow as he finally lets go of me, watching as I step back and cross my arms over my chest.

"I'm sorry, but no. My mind is made up." I glance away, catching a view of myself in the full length mirror. The clothes really do help—I look put-together, self-assured—and they hide the fact that my hands are already shaking.

"You knew there were risks—the same risks, worse ones—when you signed up before. You were willing to risk that, to risk *everything,* because you knew I needed help." Gill takes a deep breath and runs his fingers through that raven dark hair of his. "This isn't any different, Regi."

"You could die, Gill. That's a pretty big risk right here."

He shrugs off the fear, the pain, the possibility and tries to put on a smile. I see right through it. This is risky, way riskier than robbing Karl was to begin with. But I guess this is an outcome of all that, isn't it? A consequence that Gilleon suspected might be coming. And yet he still jumped in.

For me.

Always for me.

I stop staring at his reflection and look back at him, at his face, at those bright eyes staring right into and through me. *I already lost you once, Gill. Don't put me through that again.*

"It's worth the risk, Regi, for us to be free." He takes a deep breath and steps toward me again, close but not touching. "But if you say *no,* then I won't go. I'll work jobs for Max, and I'll try to figure out another way to get through this."

"I'm saying *no,* Gill," I tell him, keeping my arms crossed as he reaches up and brushes some hair behind my ear. *"Tu n'y vas pas, un point c'est tout."* I let my eyes flicker shut for a moment and try to control my racing pulse. *You're not going. It's that simple.* "Stop trying to convince me."

"If I don't go," he says, pushing on with that steel-toed determination that's always been a part of who he is, "then Karl will keep sending people after me." My mind flickers to that gruesome scene at the hotel. "And Max might decide I'm more trouble than I'm worth." Gill licks his lips nervously. "Max won't sell me out to Karl, but maybe my associates will just ... stop having my back. It'd be that easy to lose, Regina, and we're so close to winning." Gill lowers his voice to a murmur. "So close."

"Gilleon, stop," I say, because for whatever reason my eyes are brimming with tears even though I've already told him no. *Merde.* This motherfucker is making me cry and we've officially been back together for a day.

I blink back the tears just as Gill lifts his thumb and brushes some liquid away with his fingertip.

"I know you're a badass and all, and you've probably taken way worse risks than this in the last ten years, but ... it seems silly to wager it all now, doesn't it?"

Gill chuckles at my comment, but the sound holds this

sense of finality to it. One way or another, this whole situation is coming to a head, isn't it? I reach up and touch my mother's pendant. At least I know for sure now: all of this, it was for more than just diamonds.

"I won't disagree with the badass comment," Gill says with a small smile, "but I won't lie either. This would definitely be the biggest risk I've ever taken because this time, I've got you. And Regi, that's all I've ever wanted."

x x x

I run my fingertip around the rim of my wineglass and watch the clock on the wall tick towards midnight. If I'd let Gilleon go, he'd have left already and I'd be wondering if he was dead or alive, not sitting across from him at the kitchen table with a glass of white wine in front of me.

His expression is shuttered, his mind focused inward, no doubt worried about Aveline. After I made myself clear that there was no way in hell I was agreeing to this, Gill told Aveline, and she left the house with fire burning in her eyes. What's on the line for her, I don't know. All I can do is make the best decisions for us—Gill, me, Cliff, Solène.

As I stare at the clock, I know I've made the right choice.

I drop my gaze and look across the table at Gill, waiting for him to emerge from his own thoughts as I sip my wine.

"What's Ave's story?" I ask, because this silence is killing me. I feel like I have to fill it.

Gill glances up, blinking to clear his mind, and smiles

397

at me. I was worried that putting my foot down like this might push him away, but no, he's being true to his word, reaching over and laying his hand atop mine.

"She's been tangled up with Karl for as long—*longer* —than I have, fighting for something she doesn't like to talk about." Gill lifts his own wine to his lips and takes a long drink. "She and I, we're in the same boat with Max. This heist was as much about her as it was me."

"Did I fuck everything up tonight for her?" I ask, hoping to God that's not the case. I'd hate for my own happiness to come at the expense of somebody else's. Gill, bless his heart, gives me a tight smile and shakes his head. "You better not be lying to me," I tell him, pointing a finger at that perfect, muscular chest of his.

"Another opportunity will come up," Gill tells me with confidence. I wonder if that statement's as much for him as it is for me. "We'll figure this all out."

I nod, but I'm not entirely convinced, lifting my drink to my lips and staring at the pale smudge of lipstick on the glass. I went with a nude lip today, some blue-gray shadow and bright highlights on the cheeks. It's a spring look, really, but I needed something to brighten up the dark winter day outside. Maybe some Christmas lights would help? And a tree? Now that I've made up my mind to stay, I need to make this place feel like home.

"Thank you," I tell Gill, drawing his gaze back to mine. "For listening to me. Part of me was convinced that it didn't matter what I said, that you'd go anyway."

"It's the least I could do," he tells me, voice dropping, eyes half-lidded and focused on my face. When he scoots his chair forward and pulls mine out to face him, I feel a small smile creep over my mouth. "After everything I put you through, I definitely owe you."

I raise a brow as Gill leans in and cups the back of my head, brushing a scorching kiss to my lips.

"Are you offering to make things up to me with your body? Because if so, I'm in."

Gill's grin is bright enough to chase away the shadows of the past, to put a smile on my face and send my heart racing. *Oh God, this was so worth it.* I run my tongue over my lips and watch as Gilleon follows the motion with his eyes. I think I'm short a few self-talks today, so I throw some in for us for good measure. *We're going to be so happy together. We're going to have a good life, a great one.*

I'm about to give in and let Gill try *really, really* hard to make things up to me when he pauses, his entire body going stiff as he raises his head up and looks toward the front of the house. All I can hear is rain, rain, and more rain, but I'm not about to question Gilleon's razor sharp instincts. It might just be our neighbor again, but it also might ... I shake the thought away and sit quietly.

I don't speak, don't even move. Whatever it is that's piqued Gill's interest, I'll either hear about it after he decides there is no threat or ...

"Go upstairs," he tells me, his eyes darkening as our gazes meet. "Get Cliff and Solène, lock the door to her room and use the attic access to get upstairs. There's a padlock on the inside." Gill rises to his feet, drawing his gaze away from me and towards the front door. "And take your phone," he adds, his voice dropping to a rough whisper. "Call Aveline, and if she doesn't answer, then call Ewan. I programmed his number into your phone." Gilleon takes a big breath and blinks those dark blue eyes at me, the color more akin to a midnight sky than anything else right now. "If I don't come get you in ten minutes or less, call the police."

I blink back at him in shock for a second before setting my wineglass down on the table. Like I did that time in the SUV, I follow his instructions, trusting that in this, at least, he knows what he's talking about.

Pistols still in place in his shoulder holster, Gill stands up and moves around me towards the front door, muscles tense and hard beneath the fabric of his shirt. He moves like a jungle cat, all grace and agility. I stand, too— much less agilely, I might add—turning to watch him for a second before I start up the back staircase.

Just a false alarm, I tell myself. *That's all this is.* Wishful thinking on my part, I'm sure, but I can't help but pray that I'm right.

As my fingers curl around the railing, I hear it: a knock at the door.

Crap.

I guess when you live in Gill's world, a knock at midnight is never a good sign.

I start up the stairs, pausing when I hear the front door open, Aveline's voice drifting to me along with a gust of cold air. If she'd sounded even the least bit normal, I'd have backtracked down the stairs and poured myself another glass of wine, started some water boiling on the

400

stove and cooked up some pasta.

Nothing that normal's going to happen here tonight.

I retreat a few steps, just enough to glance around the corner.

My heart stops dead in my chest.

Holy. Shit.

I watch in disbelief as Gill slams and locks the door behind Aveline, his gaze narrowed in on her bloodied body as she leans heavy against the wall near the staircase, smearing a hazy red shadow across everything.

"You did it anyway, didn't you?" he asks, and my heart stutters back to life, pounding with a sudden rush of adrenaline. I know I should head up the stairs, grab my stepfather and my daughter and hide, but I can't stop watching as Aveline slides to the floor with a groan, her right hand curled around her waist, staunching the flow of blood. And oh my God, the *blood*. It's everywhere: in her hair, on her clothes, streaking down the wall behind her. There's so much of it that it's hard to make sense of the mess her face has become. Somebody really laid into Aveline tonight, took some teeth, left some bruises, turned her eyes into swollen lumps of blue-purple flesh.

When she doesn't answer Gill's question, groaning instead, blood spilling over her lower lip, he bends down and takes her by the shoulder. "How much time do we have before they get here?"

My stomach roils, and I clamp a hand over my mouth.

"Should I call an ambulance?" I mumble past my nausea, snapping Gill's attention back to me. His eyes are wide and the skin on his face is tight and strained.

"Upstairs," he growls, his face twisting into a snarl—not *at* me but in fear for me. I try not to take offense. "Go, now, *please*." It's that last word that gets me, spurring me up the stairs as fast as my heels can go.

I hit Cliff's door first, opening it quickly but not dramatically. There's no need to freak anybody out. For all I know, we might be safe tonight. Whatever happened, it could've ended with Aveline. This could just be Gill and his usual careful meticulousness, just him taking extra care with his family. Or not. It's that last part that really freaks me out.

"Papa." I reach out and grab his shoulder, shaking him awake in an instant. Cliff's always been a light sleeper; he used to make it really hard for Gill and me to sneak into each other's rooms way back when. "I need you to get up and come with me." I force a smile that I'm sure my stepfather can't see. "Gilleon's orders."

"Is everything okay?" he asks as I move away and head towards Solène's room, opening the door with care. The last thing I want to do right now is scare the crap out of my daughter. I don't bother to answer Cliff as he shuffles in behind me, tucking a blue robe around his pjs as I lean down and swipe some dark hair from Solène's face.

"*C'est l'heure de se réveiller, ma jolie petite fille,*" I whisper, gesturing at Cliff to close the door behind him. *Time to wake up, my pretty little daughter.*

"*Maman?*" she asks on the tail end of a yawn, sitting up and shaking out a headful of disheveled curls. Her pink pajamas are covered in wrinkled ruffles and

402

splattered with bows. Pretty sure she made them herself. *"Qu'est-ce qui ne va pas?" What's wrong?*

I shake my head and shrug my shoulders, like this whole thing is no big deal. At least it's dark enough in here that the sweat beading on my forehead won't show. *Shit.*

"Everything's fine," I say, standing up and taking a few steps back as I search the ceiling for the attic door. I can *feel* Cliff's gaze on me, as powerful and intense as his son's. "You know how they make you do fire drills in school?" I ask as I find the pull and reach up, curling my fingers around the string.

"Oui." Solène yawns again. "But they're never in the middle of the night like this." I yank hard and the catch comes loose, exposing a wooden ladder that I tug down to the floor, trying to be as quiet and gentle as possible. If there is something happening downstairs, I'd rather not alert whoever might be down there to our presence.

"Cliff, would you be so kind as to lock the door?" I stand up and move over to the French doors that lead out onto the balcony, checking to make sure they, too, are locked up tight. The windows are next.

"Maman?" Solène asks again, standing up and giving the ladder a wary look. Cool air drifts down from the open space, reminding me to grab a blanket and a stack of Solène's drawing books so she'll have something to do. I toss a pillow to Cliff, ignoring his pointed stare. He knows better than to push though; we both do.

"Come on, honey. Let's get upstairs and then we'll talk about it." I keep smiling. Inside, I might be screaming. But just a little bit.

I help Solène up the rungs first and then gesture for Cliff to go next.

"Is Gilleon okay?" Cliff asks as I hand him my cell phone. *I hope so,* I think, and then my heart starts to flutter with panic. *He better be.* I still can't get the image of Aveline's bloody body and swollen face out of my head. Instead of answering Cliff's question, I swallow hard and repeat Gill's instructions—minus the Aveline part. Obviously, she's already here.

A chill trickles down my spine, cold as ice.

"Call Ewan. His number's in my contacts. And if Gill isn't up here in ten minutes or less, call the police."

"You're not coming?" he asks, his graying brows raised in disbelief. With the moonlight streaming in through the window, his hair looks almost completely white. *This is my fault. I should never have put them through this. I should've gone with Gill and left Cliff and Solène behind.* Gill's right though, I suppose—love *is* selfish.

"Papa, I'll be right behind you; I just need to grab something," I say, urging him up and glancing at the door for emphasis. "*Go.* Solène needs you."

Cliff makes a noise of frustration but follows my instructions, reaching down to take the blanket and the books. All the while, he's shaking his head at me.

"Don't do anything reckless, Regina," he adds, peering down at me with narrowed eyes. If he could, I bet Papa would wrestle me up this ladder. But he can't. We both know that.

When I bend down and grab the bottom rung of the ladder, we all hear it: the doorbell ringing.

Good sign or bad?

"Regina?" I glance at the bedroom door again. This whole situation ... it could be nothing. But it could be everything. For the same reasons I told Gill not to leave tonight, not to go to Karl, I make the decision *not* to go up the ladder. I can't lose him. And I can't leave him, not when I have no idea what's going on.

I lift the ladder up, forcing Cliff to move or get hit with it.

"There should be a padlock up there. Use it. Lock the door. Don't open it for anyone but Gill."

"*Regina,*" Cliff growls, but it's too late. I've made up my mind. I give him one last look and a small smile before I shove the ladder the rest of the way up, letting the hinges do their magic as it slides into place.

"I love you guys," I whisper up with a small wave, pushing the hatch back up before I can see either of their faces and change my mind.

I pause there in the dark room, listening for sounds above me, but I don't hear anything. Must be well insulated.

I take a deep breath.

Good.

I can do this. We *can do this.*

You are fucking crazy, Regina Corbair.

I bend down and take off my shoes, clutching them in my left hand as I tiptoe to the door and press my ear against it. Again, nothing. Stupid solid wood craftsmanship. With yet another breath, I flick the lock and ease the door open. Voices filter up to me, too many for just Gill and Aveline. I don't know who's down there, but I'll be damned if they get the jump on me.

Leilani is going to freak when I tell her about this ... and Gill is going to kill me.

I swallow past the thumping of my own pulse and wipe my sweating palms on the cheerful daisy dress. I'm not a master thief or a black belt or an expert marksman, just a woman in love, but that's enough to push me forward, through my own fear and anxiety. I doubt anyone expects anything from the chick in the Dolce & Gabbana dress, but that's why this idea of mine might, *might,* actually pay off.

For Gill, it's worth the try.

I open the door just wide enough to slip out and think about closing it behind me. But no. No. The rest of the doors on this floor are cracked open. If I close this one and lock it, it'll just make it more obvious that we've got something to hide in here.

I creep over to the stairwell and pause, listening carefully.

Voices, low and dangerous, drift up to me, but I can't make out a single word. My heart's beating too loud, and the sounds are masked by a low moaning that can only be coming from Aveline. *Mon Dieu, this shit is serious, isn't it?*

Hardly taking a breath, I move into Gill's room next and fish some keys out of the top drawer on his dresser. In another drawer—a locked one this time—on his desk, there's a small arsenal: a revolver, a pair of hunting knives, and a few semiautomatics. This is only one of a dozen or more caches like this around the house, protected well enough that Solène shouldn't accidentally stumble across them but easy enough to get to if you know where to look.

The sight of all that firepower stops me cold for a moment, makes my heart stutter a little. *What if I don't load it right? What if I forget to disengage the safety? What if I actually manage to shoot someone?*

Focus, Regi. Focus.

I blink away my fears and take a deep breath, dropping my heels on the bed behind me. *Okay, revolver first. Revolvers are easy.* I dig around for ammo and set the box carefully on the desk, hefting the revolver in my palm and flicking my eyes to the bedroom door. In the back of my mind, I'm keeping an ear out for the telltale creak of the bottom stair. *Heh. Maybe I'm a little more perceptive than I thought?* I load the gun with shaking hands and lay it on the desk next to the ammo. I'm only just wrapping my fingers around one of the other guns when I hear it: the sound of someone coming up the steps. No, no, not *someone,* but *two* somebodies.

As quietly as I can, I shove the rest of the weapons back in the drawer before grabbing the revolver and a knife, closing it enough that the lock clicks back into place. I snatch the keys in my other hand and drop down to my knees at the edge of Gill's bed.

Clever, crafty Gilleon has his mattress set on a wood frame surrounded by drawers—a typical design for a platform bed. What's not typical is the false drawer on the right side, the one that's really a small door. I yank it open and shove my weapons in first, sliding on my belly after them. It's a tight fit—an *extremely* tight fit—but my slender frame definitely has some advantages over Gill's muscular build.

I just barely manage to crawl in there and yank the door closed behind me before one set of footsteps moves into Gill's room. Huddled there on my stomach, surrounded by shallow drawers and drowning in darkness, fear sparks bright and hot inside of me, but I don't make a sound. I clamp a hand over my own mouth, my elbow jutting into the back of a drawer as I force myself to take slow, shallow breaths through my nose.

I could be overreacting. Maybe the person walking around Gill's room is a friend of his, an associate. Or hell, maybe it's even Gilleon himself? Still, I don't make any noise, don't call out, don't even twitch a muscle.

This person, whoever they are, checks the bathroom, the closet, walks the perimeter of the bed and even pulls out one of the drawers on the end. I watch, frozen in terror, my body cramping up from the tight quarters as the wood glides out smoothly, exposing some sweatpants and old T-shirts. Light spills in behind the drawer, highlighting the wood floor next to my right elbow. *Shit.* I tuck my arm against my body as tightly as I can, avoiding the splash of color next to me. Seconds pass, long as hours, as I hold my breath and wait for the drawer to push back in.

After a while, the footsteps fade away, but the drawer

stays out. At first I'm worried that I've been spotted, that the false drawer at the end is going to be wrenched open and I'll be dragged out screaming, but the steps head into the hallway and towards Solène's bedroom. Instead of feeling relieved, a new wave of adrenaline spikes through me, crashing against my anxiety and masking my fear for the time being.

I reach my left hand out, searching for the weapons I tossed in here and close my fingers around the revolver, dragging it towards me before I search for the knife. *Crap!* I slice my fingers on the sharp blade and hold back a hiss of pain, sliding the knife forward with several silent curses. Using the small splash of light from the open drawer, I check my fingertips and find a nice little slice along my middle and ring fingers. Oh well. Better to have the blade than not.

Taking my weapons with me, I scoot back and ease open the false drawer, listening as I go to the receding footsteps of one of the two people that came up the stairs. When the other follows from the direction of my room a few moments later, I climb out from under the bed, sweeping my hair over one shoulder as I pause and look around the room, trying to find something to put the knife into. I know Gill has loads of holsters and sheaths and straps and whatever-the-fucks around here somewhere.

I don't have the luxury of searching around for long, so I end up grabbing a hoodie off the end of Gill's bed and slipping it over my dress. The knife goes in the front pocket—not the safest place in the world, I know, but where else am I going to put it? It's in that moment that I

409

start wishing I'd paid more attention to Gill's random lessons, that I'd taken more of an interest and asked important questions. Christ, I spent more time alternating between loving and hating him, mulling over our past.

I hope we're still going to have a future after this.

I take another breath and sweep my free hand over my hair, the revolver clutched in the opposite. *Double-action means I don't have to pull the hammer back, right?* Another deep breath. At least I ended up with the revolver and not the semiautomatic; there's a lot more that can go wrong with those. Revolver's about as simple as it gets, that much I do remember.

Right hand around the grip, finger on the outside of the trigger guard. I force myself to breathe slowly as I adjust my hold on the gun, curling my left hand around my right, pressing my thumbs together. It's been a hell of a long time since Cliff took Gill and me to the shooting range, but I'll be damned if I let my lack of preparation screw this family over. *Damn it, Gill, why didn't you teach me?* But I know why. Gill doesn't want me involved in any of this and maybe, just maybe, Gilleon Marchal is capable of mistakes, capable of being *human* —just like the rest of us.

I shoulder the door to the bedroom open, unwilling to relax my grip on the gun. *If* I need to fire off a round, my only advantage is surprise. I *have* to take the first shot because it'll be all I'll get.

Breathe, breathe, breathe.

I move towards the main staircase and listen carefully.

If I had to hazard a guess, the voices are coming from the direction of the kitchen, so the back stairs are out of the question. At the same time, do I take a chance at the front? What if there's someone guarding the door? God. My mind is spinning with movie references, with images of mob bosses with canes and thick glasses surrounded by goons in dark suits. For all I know, the people here are in Max's employ, just like Gill. If I run around shooting people, and I find out they were innocent—well, at least that they were on *our* side—then I'll never live it down. Hell, that might even be the thing that ultimately fucks everything up.

Shit.

I pause at the top of the steps, conflicted and confused. This isn't my thing. I like espresso and warm baguette, shopping in *Le Marais,* designer shoes. I don't do heists or guns or knives.

A small drop of blood drips down the front of my hand and falls to the floor in front of my bare feet.

My knees go weak.

My hands start to shake.

And then I hear the first shot.

411

CHAPTER
Twenty-Six

It's like a crack of thunder, ricocheting up the staircase and straight into my brain—nothing at all like the nearly silent click of Gill's gun at the hotel. My head screams in protest and my ears start to ring, loosening my grip on the revolver.

What the fuck am I doing? I know why Gill didn't teach me to shoot. Because I can't do it. This isn't me. It isn't. I can't.

I take a step back, away from the stairs when another shot goes off, scrambling my brain and making me grit my teeth. *Gilleon.* Gilleon is down there somewhere, and I'm standing here shaking like I'm helpless.

But I'm far from it, aren't I? I survived for ten years without Gill, birthed his kid, robbed a jewelry store. Me.

I can do this.

Never thought I'd be using self-talk to convince myself to join a shoot-out, but ... well, there it is.

Another breath.

My fingers curl tighter around the grip and I ready myself to head down the stairs.

Just as I'm about to take the first step, I hear boots slamming against the wood and, out of some long forgotten instinct, scoot to the side, back towards Solène's room. I wedge my body half behind the partially open door and peek out. From my current view, I can see straight across the second floor, past the decorative arch and the small sitting area to the back staircase.

Gill appears, blood draining over his temple and his right eye, a gun locked in his hands and a grim set to his lips. His eyes flicker to the main staircase and back down—chased from both sides.

I watch in fascinated horror as he lifts his weapon and fires off a pair of shots down the steps at the same moment two heads appear, jogging up the main staircase, right in front of me. Neither of the people that appear are wearing suits or sunglasses nor they do look like goons.

I lift my arms out in front of me, elbows relaxed, pulse pounding in my skull, competing against the violent ringing in my ears.

I almost hesitate because ... these people look so normal. And maybe they're like Gill? Trapped in a web not of their own making? Just a man and a woman, one with short dark hair, the other with a slicked back sandy ponytail. Just two people.

But then they point their weapons at Gill. At my first

love. At my new love. My *only* love.

Shit.

I want to squeeze my eyes closed and fire blindly, hide myself away from all of this. But I can't. And I won't. I said before that I wouldn't hesitate to pull the trigger if someone was threatening my family.

I meant it.

I aim at the man first, at the wide expanse of his back, sliding my finger inside the trigger guard.

One, two, three.

Deep breath.

I fire, knocking him forward against the railing of the stairs as the recoil hits me in the web of my hand and I take a small step back. Unconsciously, my eyes flick up and find Gilleon's, watch them go wide as he notices me standing there in the shadows. We stare at each other for a split second, but that's long enough for the woman to turn towards me, her long ponytail swinging as she brings her own gun up and looks for the second shooter in the room.

I'm sure she's had hundreds of hours of practice with her gun, struggled through dozens of situations just like this, but she doesn't expect me to be there, really doesn't expect me to bring the muzzle of the revolver up and aim it at her shoulder. I'm not entirely certain *how* I manage to get the shot off. Maybe it's the daisy dress or the blonde hair or the little girl's room silhouetted in shadow and moonlight behind me.

I'm sorry.

The thought pops into my brain at the same instant I

pull back on that trigger a second time and hit the woman in her right shoulder. She gets a shot off, too, but the momentum of the bullet entering her body throws it off just enough that the drywall explodes to the left of me, just outside Solène's bedroom.

I feel like I've gone deaf, like I'm standing in the bell tower of a church listening to the ringing of God. My mouth goes dry; my grip loosens; I lower my arms.

Gill's moving towards me now, backing away from the second staircase as he reloads his gun, dropping a magazine to the floor and sliding one out of his pocket. He drags his gaze away for the briefest of seconds, lowering the pistol on my two assailants. I open my mouth to tell him to stop, but it's too late. He takes aim and makes the fatal shots I could never bring myself to fire.

The revolver drops from my hands and hits the floor like a scene in a silent movie. I can't even remotely hear the sound of it hitting the wood, not through the massive headache burning in my brain, the constant ringing in my ears.

Gilleon turns toward me, sucking in a massive breath that expands his chest in slow motion. His blue eyes are dark, so dark I can hardly make out his pupils, and the whites of his eyes ... they're stark with fear. *Feral.*

"Regina." I can see Gill's mouth moving to form the word, but the actual sound remains distant, like an echo underwater. The blood on his face drips down, reminding me of the cuts on my fingers. I lift my hand up and examine the red droplets at the same time I marvel at my luck. I managed not to blow my thumb off, not to get shot. Nothing short of a miracle.

A miracle that two people are lying dead in front of me?

No, no, a miracle that *we're* not lying dead in front of them.

I blink stupidly and try to shake away the shock, putting my hands over my ears.

Gilleon's there in an instant, wrapping his fingers around my wrists and gently pulling my arms down.

"Regi," he says, voice cracking. I can barely hear him, but the worry in his voice is clear. "*Mon cœur.*" *My heart.* I glance up at Gill, unable to suppress a shiver at the feel of his fingertips pressing into my skin. That sort of thing shouldn't matter at a time like this, so why does it suddenly seem to matter so damn much?

"*Je vais bien,*" I say—*I'm fine*—even though I'm not a hundred percent sure that's true. A quick glance down at my bare feet, at the drops of red on my toes and the drywall dust sticking to my skin like powdered sugar, is enough to make my head spin. "Cops," I say, because that's suddenly all I can think about. I have no idea how long it's been since I left Cliff and Solène, but if they haven't already called the police, then one of the neighbors most certainly will. "Cops," I repeat, but I can hardly hear the sound leaving my lips. *All that goddamn ringing.*

A second later, Ewan, the expressionless guy that spent a few days as our acting bodyguard, appears at the top of the steps, moving over the bodies like they're piles of old laundry instead of cooling corpses. I pull my arm from Gill's grip, clamp a hand over my mouth, and close my eyes. *I didn't kill them, but I did shoot them.* And hell, it doesn't make it any easier to know that my *lover* shot them dead.

I open my eyes as Gill murmurs something to Ewan and then returns his attention to me, laying the fingers of his tattooed hand against my cheek. His skin is warm and comforting against my face, even if his black T-shirt is wet with blood. I lean into the touch and meet that sharp, penetrating gaze of his.

"Solène?" he asks me as I flick my eyes to his mouth and read his lips. "Dad?"

"In the attic," I whisper and Gilleon nods, his expression softening as he takes a step closer to me, sliding his fingers under my chin and tilting my face up to his. "Regina ..." he begins again, but I shake my head, the pounding in my brain very quickly becoming a migraine. Right now, I think I'm in shock. Seems to be my go-to method for dealing with scary shit.

"I'm okay," I promise, looking into Gill's face. There's so much there—guilt, love, fear, anger. "I am, really. I just ... need a minute." I take a deep breath and start to ask about the police again when Gilleon leans down and closes his mouth around mine, diving deep, tasting me. *He could've died just now. If I'd hesitated, he'd have been shot.*

My hands lift up of their own accord and curl in Gill's T-shirt, blood smearing across my fingertips as it drips down the side of his face and onto my curled fists. I raise myself up onto my toes to deepen the kiss, relief and fear ricocheting through me like that bullet would've done if I'd been hit with it. *I could've died, too. I almost did.*

Gill pulls back, gazing down at me with such a tender expression on his face that for a moment, my eyes blur with tears. I blink them away and my ears pop, making me grit my teeth as the ringing seemingly rises in pitch. My hearing returns just enough for me to hear Ewan say something about Aveline.

Oh God.

"Is she okay?" I ask Gill, my heart racing for a million different reasons. He nods at me, but the grim look on his face tells me that it's bad. Or that this isn't over. Maybe both.

"She will be," he says, a strange note in his voice as he watches Ewan check the pulses on the bodies in both stairwells. "And Regina," he begins again. I try to cut him off, but he says it anyway. "Thank you." A small, sad smile. "I think you might've just saved my life."

Gill leans close and presses another kiss against my mouth. With a last lingering look and a brush of fingers against the nape of my neck, he moves by me and into Solène's room. I can tell he wants to say something else about my involvement in all of this, but ... I guess I really did save his life. Well, maybe. Knowing Gill, he'd have probably finagled his way out of the whole situation. Still, he knows better than to think he can chastise me, even if my being involved scares the ever living crap out of him.

"Don't worry about the police," Gill adds, finally

answering my question as I follow behind him, his voice already wrapped up in his thoughts again, plotting, planning, calculating. That's Gilleon. "Max has an in with the police chief. They'll write this off as illegal target practice in the backyard."

"He ... holy shit." I run my fingers through my hair and studiously avoid looking at the stairwell. Like at the hotel, I imagine that these bodies, too, will disappear. I don't want to know about it. I don't. One quick flick of the eyes and I see splatters of blood that I hope to Christ I'll be able to *un-see*.

I shiver and focus on Gilleon's broad back instead, on the muscles that always feel so good beneath my fingertips. After our date, I knew I wanted to live with Gill, love Gill, but now? Holy crap. I want to marry him and have fucking babies. Okay, maybe one baby. Maybe. Anyway, I want a dog and a cat and a studio downstairs. I want to sleep next to Gill every night and let him smile at my mussy hair every morning. If I'd have lost him, *really* lost him this time ... I can't even think about it.

I take another deep breath to calm down as Gill calls up to Cliff and waits for him to unlock the attic door. When Gilleon does open it, he just barely cracks it and speaks quietly with Cliff. I can't hear what they're saying, but I'm grateful when Gill pushes the hatch back in place. The last thing I'd ever want is for Solène to witness the gruesome aftermath in the stairwell.

"I have to go, Regina," Gill says suddenly, turning to look at me and laying a hand on my shoulder. He leans in close enough that I can feel his breath on my lips. "I need to see this through."

"What happened down there?" I ask as Gilleon presses his forehead against mine. "What happened to Aveline?" Gill's lips purse, but he doesn't pull away. Instead, he closes his eyes and breathes deep. The air smell likes blood and gunpowder now though. I think we could both use a break outside.

In the distance, I hear sirens and my body stiffens.

"Ewan will take care of it, don't worry."

Gill stands up straight and reaches out for my hands, frowning at the blood on the backs of my knuckles. After a moment, he makes the connection and reaches up to touch his own head. I raise an eyebrow, hoping I don't have to pry an explanation out of him.

"Aveline used our contact and went in without me." Gill's pursed lips turn into a frown and his blue eyes shift away from my face and over to the staircase. "It didn't go well."

I lift my hand up, unable to keep my fingers away from his dark hair.

"I should've let you go," I say.

It's not a question.

Gilleon looks back at me and shakes his head.

"We'll never know what might've happened if I'd gone. Maybe I'd be lying down there bleeding? Maybe I'd be dead?"

"Maybe Karl would be," I whisper, dropping my hand to my side. "Now what?"

"He sent eight people here to deal with me." Gill smiles, but it's a grim expression on his blood splattered face. "When they don't come back, there'll be hell to pay." He sighs and the stiff smile disappears as his tattooed hand runs over his face. "I should never have dragged you into this. Regina," Gill turns back to me, eyes flickering with anger, "you should never have had to step in like that. I think I owe you another apology." He tries to make a joke out of that last bit, but it falls flat in the copper tinged air. *In the scent of blood.*

"Love is selfish, Gilleon. You said it yourself. But it's also self*less*." I take another breath, but the smells are starting to get to me and all it does is make my stomach roil. Still, I don't drop my gaze from Gill's. "You were willing to leave me to keep me safe, to suffocate in isolation. Well, I'm willing to die for you." I hold up a hand before he can protest. I realize it's still shaking and drop my fingers to my mother's pendant. *Mom, I'm sorry. Sorry you got dragged into this, that you paid the ultimate price. But I still love him. I do. I really, really do.* "What do we do now?"

"*We* don't do anything. *You* head up into the attic with Dad and Solène while I deal with this. Once the house is cleaned up, I'll have someone take you guys to a hotel."

"No." I cross my arms over my chest and then glance down at the floor until I locate my revolver. "This is my house now, Gill. This is my life. And you ... you're mine. It's *us* now, or it's nothing at all. You promised to give me that." I move over and pick up the gun, cradling it in my fingers like it's made of glass. When I turn back to him, I hope he can see how fucking serious I am. "So I'll ask you again: *qu'est-ce qu'on fait maintenant?*"

What do we do now?

x x x

The answer to my question is surprising, to say the least. I'd been expecting ... well, I don't really know what I was expecting, but it wasn't this. Who would ever expect to wear a designer dress to take out a bad guy? To be more specific, a designer dress with *body armor* underneath it. Makeup, heels, diamonds in my ears and around my neck. It's a nice look, I'll be the first to admit—I mean, I'm wearing a navy striped Marchesa Notte gown, so what's not to love?—but it's definitely a little uncomfortable with the vest shoved up underneath it.

I know I'm not fooling anybody—there is most definitely a bulky bulletproof vest under my outfit—but Gill insisted on it. I'm even wearing the knife I found earlier strapped against my lower back—scout style I guess it's called. It's better than having it stuffed in the front pocket of Gilleon's hoodie, that's for sure. Now, the chances that I'll ever have to use it ... or that I'd even be successful in using it? Pretty slim.

I glance over at Gilleon, sitting bathed in the ambient light from the front porch. The lines of his face are tight and his jaw is clenched hard, teeth gritted together as he stares at the steering wheel and works through whatever it is he needs to go over before we leave.

Me, I still have no idea what's going on or why I'm dressed to the nines—quite literally. Underneath the flowing organza of my skirt, there's a nine millimeter strapped to my upper thigh.

I turn my face and look out the window, breath

frosting against the cool glass. Surprisingly enough, the street is quiet now, and the police cars are gone. As promised, a phone call to the boss and a few quick words with the cops was enough to send them on their way. Gill's nosy neighbor was outside, standing at the end of her driveway, glaring at us. But after she—and the rest of the busybodies—on the street noticed the cops leaving, they went back inside and shut their lights off, one by one.

It feels like we're all alone out here.

That's not even remotely the case.

I can see Gill's ... coworkers? Hell, I don't know what to call them. They're loading up a van, using the back door and the gate to avoid carrying their very large, very illegal parcels outside. I avert my gaze, knowing that eight—*eight*—people are dead tonight. As sad as that is, as wasteful as this all seems, I don't feel as sick as I should about it. They came after me, after my family. If Gill wasn't such a badass, it'd be me in the back of a van and not them.

I swallow hard and lean my head back against the leather seat of the SUV. I think it's the same one we fucked in, but I'm not sure. Could just be a different rental. I wonder if my panties are still in the glove compartment?

"I shouldn't have put you through this," Gill says, voice rough and low. He's practically growling.

I glance back at him, at his handsome face covered in shadow. Tonight, only half of that is metaphorical. The rest ... if we can get through this, it'll be over. That's it.

We'll get our cut of the heist money, as promised, and Gill can retire.

If.

If. If. If.

I hate that word.

"Is Max really trustworthy?" I ask. Having never met the guy, I haven't the slightest clue.

Gill's mouth twitches.

"Not really. But, like I said, Karl and Max have a history." He holds up his hands. "Again, I don't know much about it, but ..." He sighs and that grin that was slowly forming, it fades away in an instant. "We all have our secrets, I guess."

"At least ours are out in the open." I turn to face him fully. I know why Gill left me, know the truth about my mother's death, and he knows about our daughter. "So let's keep it that way." I reach up and run my fingers through my hair. It's freshly washed, blown out and tousled. For what reason Gill asked me to do that, I can't even hazard a guess. "Karl ... he can't be that easy to kill, right? I mean, if you could just walk in there guns blazin' and take him out, you would've done that a long time ago, wouldn't you?"

Gill turns to face me, reaching out and touching his thumb to my lower lip. His chest expands with a tired sigh. The very same chest that just so happens to be covered in a black suit jacket; I'm not the only who's dressed up ... or the only one wearing body armor under my clothes.

"Of course. Anything to get back to you, Regina."

Gilleon glances away for a moment and then turns his gaze back on me. "But Max ... is willing to go out on a limb after tonight. This ... what happened to Aveline, it's too much."

I raise an eyebrow.

"Why would Max give a shit about Aveline?"

Gill licks his lips nervously and takes another deep breath.

"Regina," he begins as I push his hand away from my mouth. It's hard to think when he's touching me like that.

"What?" I ask, fear trickling down my spine. "I know that voice. You're keeping another secret from me."

"Some stories aren't mine to tell," Gill says, raising both brows, like he's trying to get me to understand without speaking the words aloud. "Especially not when their owner is on her way to the hospital." Something clicks into place in my brain.

"Aveline. You really *do* know her secret, don't you?"

Gill sighs again and runs his hand over his face.

"If I tell you this, I tell you in complete confidence." Gill leans in close to me and whispers hot against my ear. "If Max—or Aveline—ever found out I told you this, I'd have a lot more than just death threats from Karl to worry about." He leans back again and glances casually out the window. I know better though, know that he's checking to make sure the coast is clear before he tells me whatever it is he needs to say. "I want to be truthful with you, like you asked." Gill sighs and stares down at his lap for a moment, looking so much like the teenage version of himself that I have to tighten my fingers around the edge of the seat to keep myself from leaning over and pressing a gentle peck against his mouth.

"Max called a meeting tonight, to hand me over."

I blink away my surprise as Gill glances up at me. He must've arranged all this while I was getting changed. Bye-bye daisy dress, hello evening wear ... plus bulletproof vest. I think it's Aveline's, but I didn't bother to ask. For all I know, Gill might have one in his closet for Cliff and Solène, too. Fortunately for us both, they're still sitting pretty in the attic.

"Why would Karl agree to a meeting with Max?" Gill smiles tightly at me.

"Because they were married once."

I blink stupidly back at Gill and risk a glance out the front window. Max's guys are finished loading the van, closing the white doors on the pile of bodies in the back. I shiver and turn my attention back to Gill, leaning close and lowering my voice to a whisper.

"They were *married?*" I definitely don't want to imagine how *that* divorce went. "*Mon Dieu.*" I shake my head and sit back up. "Okay, that's certainly a shock. The two rival crime bosses were hitched." Gill's still smiling, but it's a humorless expression. "What does that have to do with Aveline?"

"Aveline's their daughter."

Holy shit. Was not expecting that one.

"Aveline's been caught up in Karl and Max*ine*'s war for a long time now. Tonight, he took things too far for Max's liking."

"So I'm assuming ... Maxine is ...?" I begin and Gill

chuckles softly.

"Yes, Maxine is a woman."

"I had to check." I hold up my hands in surrender. "There's no reason a guy *couldn't* be called Maxine." Gill's smile gets a little wider, warming my heart from the bottom up. The way tonight's going, I don't expect it to last, but it's a nice sight to see. "You never told me Max was a woman," I add, trying to recall any memories I might have of the various mentions of Gill's boss' name. I guess he never said she *wasn't* one. Not that it really matters. Hell, there isn't room for sexism even in criminal enterprises I guess. Go Maxine.

"You never asked," Gill says, that small smile still curling his lips. It fades just as quickly when he gets a signal from one of his guys at the front door of the house.

"The man you ..." I really don't want to say that particular verb aloud. "Karl's son ... Max's son?" I ask tentatively, but Gill's shaking his head.

"No, they were half siblings." He sighs and looks up, watching as the van starts backing down the driveway, pulling alongside us and then disappearing into the dark in a blur of red taillights. "Point being, Max never wanted to take things this far. Tonight, though, she changed her mind. I guess seeing her daughter in that state was enough to push a few maternal buttons." Gill's mouth twitches. "Though I'm sure it's not much. Max isn't exactly ... the motherly type." He takes a deep breath. "So. I go in tonight; I end this."

My turn to purse my lips.

"Where do I fit into all this?" There's got to be a

reason that I'm dressed up. Gill never does anything without a purpose.

"Karl wants me to bring you along." Gill looks deep into my eyes, searching for something there. Whatever he finds, it must satisfy him because he takes a deep breath and continues. "Like collateral, something to keep me from doing exactly what it is that I'm going to do." My turn to take a breath. If I said I wasn't scared, I'd be lying. I can hardly even believe I'm sitting here like this, a bulletproof vest under my dress, a knife at my back, a gun on my thigh. I feel ridiculous. I can hardly use any of this stuff. But I have to try tonight. For Gill. For me. For *us*. "I don't want to use you like this, Regina," he adds, but I'm already shaking my head.

"I'm in."

I take another breath and look Gill straight in the face. No, of course he doesn't want me there, doesn't want to take even the smallest risk with me. But I know Gill. And I know myself. I *have* to be a part of this, and I'm confident that Gilleon knows his stuff. If he didn't think we had a good chance to get out of this alive, he wouldn't have even taken the suggestion.

"Max has promised me your safety, but ..." I nod. Situations like this are hard to control. Anything could happen. Anything. "There's a plan in place, but I need you to promise to listen to me, no matter what. When we're in there, you're not my ..." Gill pauses and smiles softly at me. "You're not the love of my life, you're my assistant. You take my orders." I raise both brows and sit back, giving Gill a look. "Regina."

I roll my eyes and raise my hands in surrender.

"Okay, I got it, boss." I don't like following orders, but in this, I trust Gill completely and implicitly. This is his thing, his area of expertise, not mine. Besides, I told him not to go in tonight and he listened to me. It's my turn now.

I lean across the car, curling my fingers against the nape of his neck as he reaches out and wraps the fingers of his tattooed hand around my waist.

"I love you, Gilleon Marchal," I tell him, because I can never say it enough.

"I love you, too, Regina." He kisses me then with a dangerous passion that curls my toes and brings goose bumps up on my arms.

Tonight, we're risking our lives for a future, the future together we never had, but that we deserve.

Tonight.

It's all over tonight.

CHAPTER
Twenty-Seven

The car ride to ... wherever it is that we're going is filled with a tense sort of silence, the kind that begs to be broken, but that I can't for the life of me figure out *how* to break.

"Gill?" I ask after a few moments, my heart racing, my hands clammy in my lap. I *want* to help, need to really, but that doesn't make it easy. I'm not exactly trained for this, but if Karl wants bait, I can be bait. I can be the chance that Gilleon needs to get the shot in. Because that's all it'll take—one shot. Once Karl is down, if there is a firefight, Gill's promised that Max's people will take care of things.

"Yeah?" he asks, blinking a few times to clear his head before he glances over me, knuckles white on the steering wheel.

"Everything's going to be okay." Gill smiles tightly at me, but I can tell from his tense facial expression that he doesn't believe it. "And not because it has to be, because nothing really *has* to happen. But because we'll make it happen." I stare out the front window at the darkness and the rain, reaching up to wipe some condensation from the glass. Outside, the I-90 floating bridge rumbles past, the water from Lake Washington black as pitch beneath it.

A quick glance back at Gill shows him with brows furrowed and expression dark. *Shit.* I run a hand over my face.

"So, where exactly are we going?" I try to make myself smile, but my lips refuse to budge, images of Aveline's bloody body and the mess in the stairwell stroking goose bumps up on my arms. "I mean, where do big time crime lords like to host their get togethers?"

At least I get Gill's mouth to twitch. But he doesn't smile. Guess that's out of the question for either of us right now.

"Medina," he says, looking over at me for a split second. "Evergreen Point Road."

I raise my eyebrows.

"Ritzy."

"It's one of Max's safe houses," Gill says with a shrug. And then he really does smile. "She has *much* nicer places elsewhere." I roll my eyes and make myself smile back. This is better. This is good. I feel a bit of the stress melting away. I'm sure it'll all come rushing back when we get to wherever we're going, but at least this is better than mind wrecking silence.

431

"Uh, of course. You forget where I'm from." I reach up and pretend to fluff my already perfect hair. "I'm from *Paris,*" I say, emphasizing the French pronunciation. "While I'm sure the place is nice, it's still in Seattle. How much is this one worth? A mere three million USD?"

"Close—two point eight." I snap my fingers.

"Damn. So close. Well, it's awfully nice of the boss to meet us in such a shit hole."

Gill's smile gets a little wider but then fades just as quick when his phone buzzes. A glance down at the screen and then his eyes flick to the windshield with an intensity that'd be frightening to me if I wasn't in his good graces.

"Karl's just arrived," Gill says, taking a deep breath. He slides his phone back in his pocket, that strange, tense silence falling like snow around us. "And we're eighteen minutes out. *Fuck.*" I glance over and watch as Gill runs his tongue across his lower lip. "Regina," he begins, but I cut him off.

"No. I'm doing this, Gill." I drop my hands to my lap, unconsciously fishing in the fabric until I feel the gun beneath all of that striped organza. My hands tremble as I take another breath.

"All I was going to say was ... no matter what happens, I'll keep you safe."

I nod my head, but I don't like the tone in his voice. Maybe I'm reading too much into it, but I see two things in that darkened expression of his: *you'll make it out of this okay* and ... *I don't think that I will.*

432

Max*ine*'s safe house is really a fancy ass McMansion with a circle drive, perfectly manicured bushes, and a set of double glass entry doors that glow with the false promise of hospitality. In the driveway, there are two black SUVs similar to the one we're driving, an unremarkable silver sedan, and a big, shiny red pickup truck. I wonder if that one belongs to Max? Like mother like daughter, maybe?

Gilleon pulls all the way around the driveway, angling to put us at the exit. Unfortunately, there's a man standing there, leaning casually against a tree. He doesn't even bother to look our way, but I have feeling that if we tried to leave right now, he'd shoot us. At least, he'd try to.

"Wait for me to come around and open your door," Gill says, his voice strained and angry. Honestly, I'm surprised I even made it this far. I half-expected him to drop me off at Leilani's on the way, handcuff me to her fence or something. But then he'd have to know that I'd never forgive him. Getting over him leaving, that's going to take time. I can't take a single lie or betrayal right now.

Gilleon climbs out, a sight to see in his dark wash jeans, suit jacket and white button-down. He's washed the dried blood off his temple, but I can see a bruise forming next to his right eye. We're both lucky those are the only injuries he suffered tonight. *Eight people.* Jesus, Gilleon really is a fucking badass.

As instructed, I wait for Gill to walk over—as slow and casual as could be—and let me out. He takes my hand and closes the door behind me, fingers tight around mine.

"Karl knows that starting shit with Max tonight is a really bad idea, so if you do what he says, you'll be alright. *Don't* try to be a hero." I open my mouth to protest, but Gill squeezes my hand harder. "Don't say a word, not even to answer a question. Not to anyone." Gill pulls me forward, linking our arms as a woman with short dark hair and a shy smile opens the door for us. Her eyes flick to where Gill's guns are hanging beneath his suit jacket, like she can tell they're there without even seeing them. Surprisingly, she doesn't say anything. I wonder if she's a part of all this or some innocent bystander? Somebody's got to take care of all Max's houses when she's not around, right?

"Gilly!" A voice calls as soon as we step inside. There's a sitting room to our right, filled with austere white and silver furniture, a terrible complement to the polished concrete floors beneath us. I try to follow Gill's lead and smile, but ... this is all too weird for words. Aren't we supposed to have some tight-laced confrontation in an abandoned warehouse? This place—as ugly as the décor is—looks like somebody's home. There are white pillar candles burning on the mantle, a fire blazing behind the ornate silver and glass screen, and soft music trickling from some hidden speakers. Is that ... Alizée playing in the background? Did not expect to hear French pop music when I walked inside. "How are you?" Maxine asks, standing up from the couch with a smile curving her red lips. "Champagne? Karl and I are already on our second glasses."

I study the woman in her wide leg pants, the color of newly bloomed poppies. She's got to be around Cliff's age, at least, based on the graying color of her copper hair, but she carries herself with a timeless grace that's magnetic. I can practically feel her gravity pulling me into orbit. I blink back the urge and focus instead on the strapless beaded top she's wearing, exposing a line of perfectly flat belly beneath it. Over her shoulders, she's got on a shawl-collar vest that hangs nearly to the floor. *Chic et moderne, non?*

When I try to look past her clothes, searching for some resemblance to Aveline, all I get is the red hair and the green eyes. The man on the opposite couch on the other hand ...

"Gilleon," Karl Rousseau says, rising to his feet with a smile to match his ex-wife's. You'd think we were at a dinner party or something. I prop my right hand on my hip, trying to mimic casual the way I've seen Gilleon do. I probably look ridiculous, but at least now I get why he does it. Gives him something to do with his hands in a tense situation. "How nice of you to join us."

Karl looks right at me, his face the perfect match to Aveline's—sharp, smart, tinged with mischief. If I didn't know better, I'd think he was an alright guy. He certainly looks the part. His hair is dark, no sign of gray anywhere to be seen, but his face is lined and worn, and his suit probably costs more than my apartment in Paris.

This ... is the guy we have to kill?

My head is spinning.

I'd so much rather be at Leilani's house watching *Supernatural* and eating organic soybean paste. Ugh.

"It's good to see you both," Gill begins, looking between them and smiling as if it was the most natural expression in the world for him. "And so nice to see you in the same room." Before I can protest, Gill's pulling his guns from the holsters at his side and tossing them onto the coffee table. His knives go next—one from the small of his back, one inside his boot, one on the *underside* of the other boot. He turns to me next and holds out a hand. Without even having to ask, I know what he wants. *Holy crap.* What was the point of getting all dressed up like this if he wants me to hand it all over?

I do it anyway, trusting that Gill knows best. I start with the knife, reluctant to lift up my dress and pull the revolver out in front of these people.

"So beautiful, this Regina," Maxine says, coming over to me and taking my knife from Gill's hand. She hefts the weight in her fingers and then smiles, turning and setting it down on the table along with her champagne flute. "I've heard so much about you, I feel like we know each other." When Maxine turns back around, she steps closer to me and puts her hands on my waist. I open my mouth to protest, but the look on Gill's face tells me to be quiet.

I'm forced to stand there as Maxine pats me down like a TSA employee with OCD, touching the insides of my thighs and putting her hands places I'd only really like Gilleon to touch. I grit my teeth, glaring at Gill as I stand there, arms up and out, as Max checks me for weapons and then steps back with a smile. I know she

436

felt the revolver because her hands went right over it, but she didn't take it from me. I'm confused as hell, but since neither Gill nor Maxine is mentioning it, I decide not to say anything. That's what Gill asked of me, isn't it? I'll stay quiet and observe then.

"Come, sit," she says, as if she didn't just have her hands all over my body. I follow her instructions, sitting in the chair across from where Gill still stands, waiting as Karl moves over to him and the two take a whole moment staring into one another's eyes. In the back of my mind, I get that this guy, this seemingly charismatic gentleman, is the reason my mother is dead, that I was attacked in my home tonight, that Gilleon left me, but it's hard for me to put it all together. In spite of the weapon check, this evening is just too normal.

I sit down and accept a fresh glass of champagne, keeping my lips sealed and my eyes open. As Karl pats down my lover, I glance around and blink in surprise when the woman with the shy smile comes into the room and scoops our weapons into a wooden box, taking it away with the click of a lid.

The alcohol fizzles and bubbles between my tight fingers, but I don't take a drink, not unless Gill wants me to. We meet eyes across the coffee table as he takes a seat in the matching chair opposite me, a contraption made of steel pipes and covered with a thin beige cushion that does almost nothing to protect my ass from the metal underneath it. I can't read his expression, so I sit stone-still and let my eyes wander around the room.

"I'm so glad we could come together this evening,"

Karl says, his voice as smooth as silk, distinguished, trustworthy. *Jesus.* "Let's call a toast." He lifts his drink and gestures his chin in Gilleon's direction. Without a second of hesitation, Gill leans forward and takes his own glass, standing up and lifting it out to clink against Karl's. "To a peaceful negotiation."

"I'll second that," Max says with a velvety laugh. I follow along and stand with them all, lifting my own glass to theirs. When it hits Karl's, a chill travels down my spine and I feel my stomach twisting into knots. "Now, should we wait for appetizers or get down to business? I asked Kayla to make up something French." She tosses a wink in my direction. "An *hors d'oeuvre,* they call it over there, am I right?"

It takes a considerable amount of effort not to bare my teeth. I can feel *mon visage laid* moving to take over my expression. I try not to sneer at her, at Karl, at the whole mess they've made of my life, Gill's life, *our* life.

"We're not here to eat," Gill says, breaking the false niceties for the first time since we walked in the door.

"Oh, don't be like that, Gilly," Max says, leaning back into the cushions, her arched brows raised nearly to her hairline.

"I'm sorry, but I've still got the taste of blood on my lips from earlier."

Surprisingly enough, Karl laughs at that, like this is all some big practical joke, like *eight* fucking people didn't die tonight. I wonder briefly where Max's people go with the bodies but decide that's still not a subject I want on my mind, especially not now.

"Gilleon, don't exaggerate," Karl says, sipping his drink, his eyes moving over to me, taking me in like a slide under a microscope. This guy is good, smart, prepared. How Gill thinks we're going to get the jump on him is beyond me. Right now, I feel trapped. When I look to Gill for reassurance, his face is shuttered and empty. "You were well aware that the actions you took would have consequences." Karl pauses and sets his glass down, sitting back and folding his hands over his bent knee. *Consequences.* Like eight dead people at my house.

I suck in a breath.

Big mistake.

Everyone—including Gilleon—turns to look at me.

"What do you think, Regina? Food first? Or business?" Karl looks right at me, his expression innocent and untroubled, like it's not his fault my life took a completely different track than I'd planned. *But that doesn't matter now. None of it does. Gill and me, we're back together again. That's all that matters.* When I don't respond, Karl's mouth turns down in a gentle frown, like a grandfather catching his grandkid drawing on the walls. Disapproving, but not angry. "What's the matter, Mademoiselle Corbair?"

I curl the fingers of my free hand in the blue striped organza of my gown, biting back a hundred retorts that Karl absolutely deserves but that'll probably get me shot. *Fuck you, you creep.* I turn my lips up in a smile.

"Leave the girl be, Karl," Maxine says, leaning forward, her green eyes big and bright, sharp as thorns.

The gold bracelets at her wrists clink as she finishes off her drink and sets it aside. "We all know why we're here. I'd say, let's get this ugliness out of the way so we can enjoy the fig and olive tapenade that Kayla's whipped up." Max smiles, her lashes long and dark, makeup minimal but complementary. Jesus. She looks more like a fashion designer than a mob boss. "Gilleon has very kindly decided to offer you his services in exchange for his family. Isn't that right, Gilly?"

Gill says nothing and my stomach twists yet again, curling into an infinity knot like that ring that Gill better be around to give me in the future.

"Oh thank God," Karl says with a chuckle when Kayla —the dark haired girl from the door—appears, her black pantsuit as well tailored as Karl's. "All of that debate for nothing." He smiles at the platter and reaches out for a thin slice of French bread, taking a small spreading knife and cutting into the artfully piled mound of goat cheese, olive oil and herbs. It smells good, but there's no way in hell I'm touching it. "I hate to chat business on an empty stomach. Maxine?" Karl holds out the slice of bread and waits for Max to take a bite, closing her eyes as she savors the food. Once he deems it safe, Karl digs in, too.

Mon Dieu, these people are insane.

"Me for my family, Karl. That's it. Take it or leave it," Gill growls, his body stiff, muscles tense and ready to pounce. He looks like a jungle cat that's been cornered by hunters. They might have guns to his face, but he's going to take at least one of them out before they get him.

"And my diamonds?"

"Aveline," Max says, her voice rising sharply, a warning in her tone. "You can have your baubles back, but I want you to leave my daughter alone. Do you understand me, Karl? There's a reason I was given full custody."

"The girl's thirty years old, Maxine. How much longer do you want to do this?" Karl finishes his bread and picks up a cracker. I close my eyes against the scene, my dress pulling at my shoulders, squeezing my waist. I feel like I'm suffocating, like I want to rip it off and run away back to Paris.

But I won't.

I won't leave Gilleon.

"You put her in the hospital, Karl. I don't have a lot of boundaries, but that's one of them," Max grinds out, her perfect pretty shattered for just the briefest moment. "Take your diamonds, take Gilleon, and go."

"Well," Karl begins, daintily brushing a stray crumb off his collar, "I'd like to do that, but I feel like at this point, it's more of a hassle than it's worth. Gill, and the diamonds."

There's a moment there where everything seems still; nobody's eating or talking or even breathing.

And then there's a gun in Karl's hand and he's aiming it at me.

In the span of a blink, he's pulled the trigger and Gill's out of his seat, tackled from behind by someone I didn't even know was there. One of Karl's guys? Max's? Not like it matters.

The bullet hits me in the center of my chest, driving

right into my body armor and knocking me backwards into the unforgiving metal of the chair. I try to scream, try to move, but it feels like I've been hit in the heart with a bat, like no matter how hard I try I'll never pull in another lungful of air again.

I glance down at the smoking hole in my dress and manage to actually *see* the second shot hit me about two inches down and to the right. Whatever ammo Karl's using, it's as quiet as Gill's was at the hotel, so the only sound I hear is the sound of my chair hitting the concrete floor as it topples over.

My head snaps back and my vision goes white at the edges.

Somewhere far away, I can hear screaming, a growling bite of rage that can only be Gilleon.

"Oh, stop being dramatic. I only shot her in the vest. Don't worry, when I do kill her, I'll make sure you're ready for it."

I roll away from the chair and end up on the floor, my body on a white and yellow rug, my head precariously close to the metal grate of the fireplace. I can feel the heat against my hair, but I find it hard to give two shits about that.

A groan escapes my lips as I clutch my stomach and dry heave against the floor, my mouth pressed to cold cement. With a gasp, my chest contracts involuntarily and sucks in two massive lungfuls of air that hurt so bad I want to scream. As soon as I get the breath for it, that is.

"Get up." It's Karl, his voice behind me, a hand curling around my hair. Pain sears my scalp as he pulls me away from the floor and tosses me unceremoniously back into the tipped chair. Somebody—one of his people, I guess—pushes it back up as my vision swims and blurs and I sit there, slumped and useless as a doll.

As soon as I'm upright, I see Gilleon on the floor with blood oozing from his thigh, his face tight with pain, teeth gritted as his blue eyes lock on mine. *Gill's been shot?!*

Panic washes through me and in an instant, everything else fades away, and I see him as he looked the day he picked the lock on my bedroom door, a lost boy who needed help. I didn't know it then, but Gill was hurting and he was looking for something, someone, to get him through it. That person, however unknowingly, was me.

And I'd do it again, a thousand times over. Like I said, I'd die for him.

I meant that.

"I don't make deals with men who break their word, Gilleon. You know that." I'm staring at Karl's side, his face in profile, his gun in his hand. Behind me, someone shifts. There are people everywhere here, aren't there? Of course there are. Otherwise Gill would've shot Karl in the head the moment we walked in the door.

I suck in another shuddering breath, the gun under my dress burning my flesh, like the metal's molten and searing my skin. I know it's all in my head, but I can't shake the urge to reach down and brush it away. But no. No. *Maxine left the revolver there for a reason.*

"Karl, listen to me," Gill begins, his voice stretched and tense with pain. I feel the beginnings of panic

443

creeping up in my chest, but I blink them away. Things could be worse: Gill could be dead. He *will* be if I don't do something about it. I want to believe that he's still got a plan—and that this is all part of it—but I can't count on it.

"Maxine," Karl begins, turning to look at his ex. She's sitting there with her legs crossed, her designer shoe bumping rhythmically as she slathers another piece of bread with goat cheese, like Gill's blood isn't splattered across her floor, like the smell of gunpowder isn't burning our nostrils. "I'll take Gilleon—and the girl." He gestures loosely at me, like I'm nothing more than an object to be bartered. "And you can keep Aveline." His lips curl. "And the diamonds. Consider them a belated alimony payment."

The sound of a car pulling up outside gives everyone pause.

"Who the hell is that?" Maxine snaps, sending Kayla scurrying towards the door. A few seconds later, it's swinging wide and Aveline is standing in the doorway, breathing hard, dressed in a fresh set of clothes. Her eyes are practically swollen shut and she's leaning on Ewan for support, but she's here.

I struggle to sit up, the organza of my gown crinkling and drawing Karl's eyes back to me. He disregards me as useless and turns his attention back to his daughter.

"What are doing here?" Maxine asks, sounding genuinely perplexed. I bet it's hard to pull one off on this woman. Behind Aveline, there are two men I've never seen before. Without batting an eye, she turns and puts a bullet in one of their heads.

Gill shoves up from the floor, using the moment of surprise to pull away from the man holding onto his shoulders, swinging around and hitting him so hard in the face that I hear a distinct cracking sound before he turns his attention back to Karl.

I don't have time to think or debate or wonder how my morality might suffer. Gill is *mine,* and he's in trouble, so I'll do what I have to do. I lean over, grunting at the pain and flopping forward like a rag doll, my body screaming in protest at the motion. I dig my fingers under my skirt, shoving the fabric up my thighs with no attention to modesty, exposing my black lace panties and the gleaming silver of the revolver.

Behind me, Karl's man shifts, a gun in his hand, the muzzle pointed not at me but at Gilleon. I see him get a shot off before I manage to raise my own up and point it at his chest. *He might have body armor,* my thoughts scream, so I adjust my grip just in time for him to notice me. We both shift our aim and fire. His bullet hits me in the shoulder, knocking me back from the chair again, sending my body towards the floor with a spray of blood. As I tumble back, I hear another sound, like an overfilled grocery sack slamming into the pavement. *I got him. Maybe. Hopefully.*

I feel like my arm's on fire for a second, but just a second, and then the pain fades away. Still, psychologically speaking, I feel fucked up. Just the *idea* that I've been shot scares the hell out of me and a scream rips from my throat as soon as I make contact with the ground. The initial impact of the shot is the worst part though, wrenching my shoulder back before the cement pushes it forward again.

Even with all of this happening, with the pain, the shots, the blood, there's only one thing on my mind.

Gilleon.

Gilleon.

Gilleon.

Please be okay, Gill.

My vision swirls as I listen to the sounds of gunfire, struggling to sit up, my left arm moving more slowly than I want it to.

I look around for my revolver for a while before I realize I still have it clutched in my right hand.

"Holy shit." I blink stupidly at the gun as my head throbs and my ears ring from the noise. Once again, that strange, white calm of shock rolls over me, taking the place of fear and anxiety and confusion.

I lean forward, gasping at the pain in my stomach, the bruising under my vest hurting worse than the gunshot wound in my shoulder. Right now, I can barely even feel it.

I yank myself up, stumbling a little in my silver Louboutin peep-toes.

Gill's there in an instant, his arm curving around my waist, pulling me against him.

I glance up, trying to take in his facial expression, but all I see is darkness, swirling around him like a cloud.

"You're okay, Gilleon," I say, my voice a little slurry. "We're okay."

His gaze snaps down to me for an instant before he lifts up his Walther PPQ .22, the same gun he used at the hotel. Is it weird that I recognize it? It is, isn't it? I glance down at the revolver in my own hand and wonder absently why I can't name the brand on this baby.

"Regi, honey, you're in shock," Gill says, dragging me backwards, pushing me into a corner around the edge of the decorative archway. "Just sit down, *ma belle petite fleur.* Sit right here and don't move."

But I don't sit. I don't want to sit.

What am I even doing here?

I stare at my gun again and then glance up in time to see a woman appear from the kitchen. It's Kayla. I raise my weapon to shoot at her, but Gill grabs my arm and forces it down.

"No, she's on our side, baby. Our side."

Gill steps away from me and takes aim through the archway, pulling off three shots before he moves back again. Kayla joins him, her shy smile gone and a strange, eerie cold taking its place. Ugh. Would not want to get on her bad side.

I stumble against the wall, smearing blood against it as I push back the curtains and look out the window. The yard here is huge, sprawling grounds dotted with perfectly round bushes and trees dripping wet with rain. It's from the corner of my eye that I see someone running, sprinting through the back like their life depends on it. Hell, maybe it does?

I crack the window and sit down, reaching down to yank off my shoes. Gill looks back at me, but only for an

447

instant. He's more concerned with watching both our front and our back, taking turns with Kayla as they keep their guns up and level with the action.

Me, I just reach up and touch my fingers to the wetness on my arm. Redness smears across my skin as I rub the warm red liquid together. *Shit, Katriane's never going to believe this one. And Leilani is going to kill me when she finds out about this.*

Standing up from my seat isn't easy, not even with the cool moist breeze leaking in the window behind me. What it does do, however, is help to clear my head a little, push back the fog.

"Gill, what do I do?" I ask, unable to keep my voice from wavering. His lips are tight, expression grim as he takes a step back. When he looks at me, I can see how scared he is written into every line of his face. *We might get out of this one,* he tells me without words. *But we won't be so lucky next time.* And there will be a next time, won't there? As long as Karl's around, so is all of this shit.

"Just stay here," he tells me, eyes as dark as the night sky. "Don't move."

"Gilleon." This from Max. I can't see her, but her voice sounds just as calm now as it did when she was drinking champagne. "Leave Regina here and go with Karl, please." Another pause. "That's an order." Gilleon glances over at me and my heart starts to race inside my chest. "Let's end this, Karl. Take him and go. Leave it at that. Neither us can afford an all out war."

Silence descends, thick and heavy, cloaking the room

448

and blocking out everything but the sound of my own pulse.

Gilleon and I stare at each other for a moment, lost in each other's eyes. Behind him, Kayla levels her weapon at the back of Gill's head. I bet if he wanted to, he could turn and disarm her, probably break her arm. But then what? Two more people appear in the archway to the kitchen, weapons at their sides, just as normal, as unassuming as the ones I shot in the stairwell.

"Regina," Gill begins, but I'm already shaking my head.

"No."

"Yes."

Before I can protest, Gill's sweeping me into his arms, searing my lips with his, diving into me, tasting me like it's his last chance, his only chance. Even with the smells of blood and gunpowder overpowering the room, Gill's scent fills my nostrils, that warm, spicy heat that always gets me. I'm melting into him, molding our bodies together, my mind calming at the feel of him pressed tight against me.

"I love you, Regi. I love you so goddamn much." I open my mouth to tell him the same when he steps back, suddenly and without warning; a coldness settles over me. I'm not sure exactly what's happening, but I'm smart enough to know that it's bad. Really bad. "Aveline," Gill begins as he takes another step back and my body starts to tremble.

"I've got her, babe," she slurs, appearing in the doorway as Gilleon moves away from me with a finality

449

that scares the shit out of me. *No. No. No.* They exchange a look of their own, and even with the damage to her face, I can see the same resigned melancholy in Aveline's expression. "I'll take care of her, Gill. You have my word."

Take care of me?

That sounds … an awful lot like Gill's giving up. But he's not, right? He has a plan, doesn't he?

With a nod, Gill steps away from me and I follow, only to find Kayla's fingers wrapped around my upper arm. Surprisingly, she leaves the revolver in my hand. Luckily for me, she's not as smart or as perceptive as my lover; she doesn't think I'm a threat. Or maybe like Maxine, she *wants* something to happen. *She left that revolver there for a reason, right?*

I stare after Gilleon, taking in the angry look on Karl's face, the harsh jerk of his chin. One of the men that's appeared in the foyer steps forward to take Gill by the shoulders and shove him to his knees. He winces but goes down without any resistance, blood staining his jeans, his blue eyes faraway and broken.

"This clears the air between us then?" Max asks, reaching into her pocket and emerging with a cigarette. There's no sign of a gun in her hand, no blood anywhere at all on her person. But on the floor at her feet, Ewan lays sprawled and motionless.

One look is all it takes to tell me that he's dead. Dead. He is as dead as the man lying next to him, the man with the bullet wound through his skull. The man that I killed.

My stomach roils again and my gaze snaps back to

Gill as Karl hefts a revolver of his own in his long, pale fingers.

"It certainly doesn't hurt," Karl says, lifting up his gun. But I saw him before. I *saw* him. This is a man that doesn't hesitate, that doesn't care. There won't be a speech or a long drawn out instance. The second that muzzle levels with Gill's skull, it's over.

Gilleon is gone.

Gilleon is dead.

My elbow snaps up and back, right into Kayla's face, some leftover remnant of the *Fight for the Night* self-defense class that Katriane made me take. Revolver up, finger on the trigger, silver gleaming.

Not even a breath passes between my lips as I squeeze.

Karl won't hesitate; neither will I.

My thumbs press together, my left numb but still able to obey my body's commands.

Never underestimate the blonde in the designer dress.

I squeeze the trigger; the bullet hits Karl right behind the ear.

Blood splatters Gilleon's face like wet paint.

That's the last thing I remember.

CHAPTER
Twenty-Eight

"Are you ..." Leilani pauses for a moment and sits back in Cliff's armchair, the color draining from her face as she looks me over like she's never seen me before. I try to smile, but my face hurts from where Kayla hit me, knocking me out cold. I hear she tried to shoot me, too, but Aveline got her ten times better than she got me. Guess *she* didn't mean to leave that revolver in my hand. Maxine though ... I guess I'll never really know.

"Going to finish that sentence?" I substitute for Leilani, taking small, slow breaths. It still hurts to inhale. I glance up at the sound of footsteps and smile as Cliff hands me an iced tea with a straw and a lemon bar on a tiny plate. *"Merci beaucoup, Papa,"* I say, squeezing his hand as he steps back. He knows I'm thanking him for a whole lot more than dessert.

"Don't push yourself," Cliff warns, giving me a look and then switching it over to Leilani. I might be in my thirties, but the parental warning still makes me feel guilty. Or maybe it's just the memory of Cliff's face when I first woke up, freshly washed sheets tucked up around my chest, the smell of laundry detergent tickling my nose. Gill and me, we scared the shit out of the old man.

Outside, the sun gleams bright, drying up yesterday's rain. I'm almost disappointed, as nice as it is to have a break in the storm. Just a few more days until Christmas, and since there's no way I'm getting a white one, at least a grayish wet one, please?

"Are you ... *fucking crazy?*" Leilani finally gasps, brown eyes moving to the staircase to check for Solène. But nope. She's upstairs unpacking some of our boxes from France, almost as excited as I am that we're staying here.

Almost.

Although nobody's as excited as I am, especially not after what Gill and I went through. If I'd had any doubts about getting back together with him—I didn't, but that's beside the point—they'd be gone now.

"You could've been killed, Regi." Leilani puts her fingers up to her temples and shakes her head, dark brown ponytail flopping back and forth. "Don't tell me anymore or I'll feel obligated to call Anika. She calls me everyday now to check up on you. I think she's too afraid to call you herself."

I glance down at my lap and smile, poking at the

powdered sugar on the top of my dessert.

"I was wondering why she hadn't called me back." I feel my lips twitch with a small smile and then groan, pressing the fingers of my right hand against my face. It hurts too much to lift my left right now. At the very least, the bullet just barely missed a major artery of mine. I could very easily have bled out in Maxine's fancy ass safe house.

Bleh.

I don't want to think about it.

Right now, all I want to think about is Gilleon. He and Aveline are meeting with Maxine today. What about, I don't know yet, but I'm sure he'll tell me. It better be about his retirement though because I think what we just went through is a once in a lifetime situation. Not sure I could survive another.

With Karl dead, there's nobody around to give two shits about our hundred million dollar heist. Maxine can keep the diamonds, we can get our promised cut, and I'll get to start a new life here in Seattle. No, it's not as glamorous as Paris, but it rains a hundred and fifty plus days a year, and the people here buy reusable paper towels that other people here made from recycled hemp plants. What can I say, but that it's home?

"Anika misses you, Regi. Sometime soon, you guys should get together. Go there or bring her here." I nod because I'd already planned on doing just that. The way things are going, I'll probably head down there, visit my grandma ... get a dog off the reservation. I can't wait to tell them both about Solène. Finding out your sister actually has a nine year old daughter ... priceless. Anika may very well kill me for not telling her sooner.

"Do you two need anything else?" Cliff asks from the direction of the kitchen, leaning around the archway to smile tightly at us. I know he's still mad at me although I think he's more pissed about my almost dying than about getting back together with Gill. Go figure. Cliff's as stubborn as his son, so maybe I should consider that a positive? As far as negatives go, I've been avoiding the main staircase and I keep waking up in the middle of the night.

But every time I do, I wake up next to Gilleon.

That makes it all worth it. So, so worth it.

"I can't ... are you sure you're not making any of this up? Did you really shoot some semi-famous crime lord?" I smile at Leilani, but I don't have to answer. She can tell, I know she can. It's written all over my face.

I fought; I struggled; I survived.

I fell back in love with a second chance.

"Oh my *God,*" Leilani murmurs as she sits back with a slump and a sigh. "You are a special sort of crazy, you know that?"

"Now that I've told you everything, can we watch *Supernatural* now? I could use some Sam and Dean in my life." Leilani raises her dark brows at me.

"With Gilleon? I think you have more than enough man cake to deal with."

"Man cake?" I ask, trying to stifle a laugh. Laughing hurts ten times as much as breathing right now. "Did you just make that one up?" She grins at me and shrugs, a breeze from the window teasing her hair around her face.

"He's cute, I can agree to that. Everything else about him, eh." Leilani shrugs her shoulders. "He'll have to prove himself again. Leaving you, that was bullshit, even if it was for the right reasons." We exchange a look, the kind of look you can only get from people who know all your secrets.

Did I say I was sad about leaving Paris? I've got Leilani back. Kind of makes it all worth it.

We both pause as the front door opens and Gilleon appears, his eyes immediately straying to mine as he steps inside and closes it behind him. As soon as I see him, something bursts open inside of me, that font of love and admiration and tenderness that I feel towards him, that I've always felt, that I'm sure I always will. Okay, and maybe there's some relief in there, too. I have to keep reminding myself that he's safe, that we'll be okay.

"The meeting with Max ..." I begin, but Gill's already smiling, nodding his chin at Leilani and moving around the couch towards me. I set aside my tea and lemon bar, abandoning them on the coffee table. With Gill around, who needs sugar?

"It went well," he says and then, acknowledging Leilani, "I take it you two had a good afternoon together?" Leilani rolls her eyes and adjusts her *Legend of Zelda* T-shirt.

"Yeah, well, based on the story she just told me, I can tell Regi needs me in her life. I can be the voice of common sense." Gilleon laughs, his gait just a little off from the wound in his thigh as he comes to sit next to me, sighing in relief as he takes the weight off his leg and sinks into the sofa.

"I can agree with that," Gill says and then looks over at me, love filling his blue eyes. "You be her common sense, and she can be mine."

I roll my eyes, but ... he has a point. Gill needs me in his life. Today, tomorrow, forever.

"Oh God," Leilani groans in anticipation, but what can I do? I'm in love. And love is selfish.

When Gill leans over and presses his mouth to mine, I wrap the fingers of my right hand in his hair and let myself get swept away into a memory.

A memory of *us*.

✗ ✗ ✗

"Hey Gill?" I roll over onto my side, Gill's hoodie wrapped around me, his spicy scent drifting up from inside the folds of the ebony cotton, heady and dangerous and mysterious. We barely know each other, but ... it feels like he's been living with Mom and me for years.

Gilleon turns to look at me, that beautiful dark hair of his falling over his forehead into his eyes. He might be seventeen, but he has a gaze that goes deeper than any of the other kids at my school, like he's been places, done things. It's not a bad look, but I think it makes him weigh what he says, what he does, carefully. He's still goofy sometimes, still has a sense of humor, but there's a darkness there that's he cautious about.

I should ignore it, treat him cordially, like the acquaintance he is, a stepbrother who will never feel like a brother, not when we didn't grow up together.

457

But today, I forgot my jacket; he gave me his sweater. I can't stop sniffing it. Does that make me crazy?

"Yeah?" he asks, grinning at me from his spot on the floor of my bedroom. His arms are covered in bruises from the mother he still loves, the one he had to leave behind. I can't even imagine. "What's up?"

I swallow hard, toying with the strings at the neckline of my borrowed hoodie.

"What do you want to do when you grow up?" I feel a red blush color my cheeks and struggle to correct my statement. What am I, five? "I mean, like, what do you want from life?"

Gill turns to face me, wrapping his arms around his knees, his blue eyes bright as sapphires, his perfect mouth twisted to the side in a smile. Our faces are so close we could kiss. We don't, but ... we could. Just a few more inches ...

"You mean what do I want to do? As a job? Or what do I really want?" I shrug, keeping my honey brown gaze on his. No way I'm looking away first. This is my bedroom, my turf; Gill's the new guy.

"Either one."

He pauses for a moment, thinks, and then his smile gets wider.

"Je veux être avec toi pour toujours, *Regina.*" Gill unclasps his hands from around his legs and sits up on his knees. Our mouths are even closer now ... oh God. My mind struggles to translate, but I'm not far enough into my French class to do much more than say my name and classify school supplies.

"Not fair!" I say, sitting up and putting some distance between us. I don't know how many times I can feel his breath feather against my cheeks and not do something about it. "What did you just say? You know I can't translate that."

Gill follows me forward, standing up and putting an arm on either side of my crossed legs. He leans in, closing the distance I just put between us, headphones hanging over his neck.

"Veux-tu être ma petite amie?" he asks and I laugh, smacking him in the chest. When he grabs my hand and curls his fingers around it, I can hardly keep my breath.

"I don't know what you just said," I whisper, but Gill won't stop smiling.

"Just say yes," he tells me, and I do.

× × ×

It takes me fifteen years to remember—and properly translate that.

I want to be with you forever. Would you like to be my girlfriend?

I smile.

One day, he'll ask me to marry him—again.

I'll say yes—again.

And this time, this time we'll get what we always deserved.

A second chance.

A happily ever after.

Fin

THE END

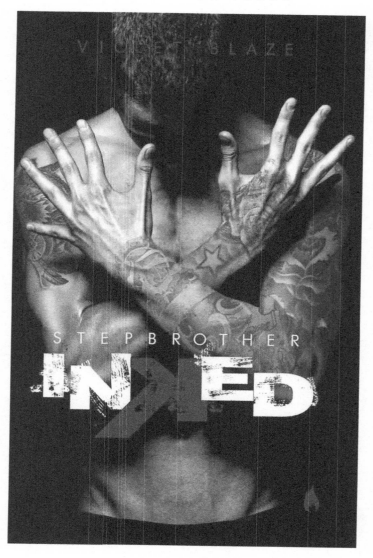

A STAND-ALONE

ORIGINALLY PUBLISHED UNDER THE PEN NAME VIOLET BLAZE

ALPHA
WOLVES
MOTORCYCLE
CLUB

THE COMPLETE SERIES

Trinidad   *California*

USA TODAY BESTSELLING AUTHOR

C.M. STUNICH

The Complete Collection

I WAS BORN RUINED

I Was Born
RUINED

DEATH BY DAYBREAK MC

FIRST IN
A NEW SERIES

INTERNATIONAL BESTSELLING AUTHOR
C.M. STUNICH

Death by Daybreak Motorcycle Club, #1

RICH BOYS OF BURBERRY PREP, YEAR ONE

FILTHY RICH BOYS

ALL BETS ARE ON ...

USA TODAY BESTSELLING AUTHOR
C.M. STUNICH

Rich Boys of Burberry Prep # 1

GROUPIE

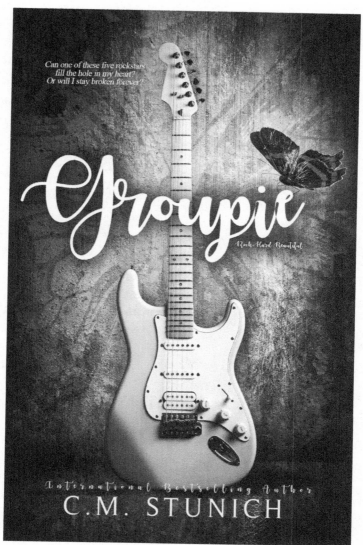

Can one of these five rockstars
fill the hole in my heart?
Or will I stay broken forever?

Groupie

Rock-Hard Beautiful

International Bestselling Author
C.M. STUNICH

Rock-Hard Beautiful, #1

JOIN THE
C.M. STUNICH

Discussion

Group

Want to discuss what you've just read?
Get exclusive teasers or meet special guest authors?
Join CM.'s online book clubs on Facebook!

www.facebook.com/groups/thebookishbatcave

STALKING

Links

JOIN THE C.M. STUNICH NEWSLETTER – Get three free books just for signing up
http://eepurl.com/DEsEf

TWEET ME ON TWITTER, BABE – Come sing the social media song with me
https://twitter.com/CMStunich

SNAPCHAT WITH ME – Get exclusive behind the scenes looks at covers, blurbs, book signings
and more http://www.snapchat.com/add/cmstunich

LISTEN TO MY BOOK PLAYLISTS – Share your fave music with me and I'll give you my
playlists (I'm super active on here!) https://open.spotify.com/user/12101321503

FRIEND ME ON FACEBOOK – Okay, I'm actually at the 5,000 friend limit, but if you click the
"follow" button on my profile page, you'll see way more of my killer posts
https://facebook.com/cmstunich

LIKE ME ON FACEBOOK – Pretty please? I'll love you forever if you do! ;)
https://facebook.com/cmstunichauthor & https://facebook.com/violetblazeauthor

CHECK OUT THE NEW SITE – (under construction) but it looks kick-a$$ so far, right? You
can order signed books here! http://www.cmstunich.com

READ VIOLET BLAZE – Read the books from my hot as hellfire pen name, Violet Blaze
http://www.violetblazebooks.com

SUBSCRIBE TO MY RSS FEED – Press that little orange button in the corner and copy that
RSS feed so you can get all the latest updates http://www.cmstunich.com/blog

AMAZON, BABY – If you click the follow button here, you'll get an email each time I put out a
new book. Pretty sweet, huh? http://amazon.com/author/cmstunich
http://amazon.com/author/violetblaze

PINTEREST – Lots of hot half-naked men. Oh, and half-naked men. Plus, tattooed guys holding
babies (who are half-naked) http://pinterest.com/cmstunich

INSTAGRAM – Cute cat pictures. And half-naked guys. Yep, that again.
http://instagram.com/cmstunich

ABOUT THE AUTHOR

C.M. Stunich is a self-admitted bibliophile with a love for exotic teas and a whole host of characters who live full time inside the strange, swirling vortex of her thoughts. Some folks might call this crazy, but Caitlin Morgan doesn't mind – especially considering she has to write biographies in the third person. Oh, and half the host of characters in her head are searing hot bad boys with dirty mouths and skillful hands (among other things). If being crazy means hanging out with them everyday, C.M. has decided to have herself committed.

She hates tapioca pudding, loves to binge on cheesy horror movies, and is a slave to many cats. When she's not vacuuming fur off of her couch, C.M. can be found with her nose buried in a book or her eyes glued to a computer screen. She's the author of over thirty novels – romance, new adult, fantasy, and young adult included. Please, come and join her inside her crazy. There's a heck of a lot to do there.

Oh, and Caitlin loves to chat (incessantly), so feel free to e-mail her, send her a Facebook message, or put up smoke signals. She's already looking forward to it.

Made in the USA
Las Vegas, NV
28 January 2024

85024920R00288